THE HUMMINGBIRD

THE HUMMINGBIRD

Stephen P. Kiernan

wm

WILLIAM MORROW

An Imprint of HarperCollins*Publishers*

THE HUMMINGBIRD. Copyright © 2015 by Stephen P. Kiernan. All rights reserved. Printed in the United States of America. No part of this book may be used or reproduced in any manner whatsoever without written permission except in the case of brief quotations embodied in critical articles and reviews. For information address HarperCollins Publishers, 195 Broadway, New York, NY 10007.

HarperCollins books may be purchased for educational, business, or sales promotional use. For information please e-mail the Special Markets Department at SPsales@harpercollins.com.

FIRST EDITION

Designed by Lisa Stokes

Library of Congress Cataloging-in-Publication Data has been applied for.

ISBN 978-0-06-236954-3

15 16 17 18 19   OV/RRD   10 9 8 7 6 5 4 3 2 1

In memory of Melissa Millan

THE HUMMINGBIRD

CHAPTER 1

ALL I KNEW at the beginning was that the first two nurses assigned to the Professor had not lasted twelve days, and now it was my turn.

When I drove to Central Office that morning to collect his medical records and case-management plan, I also checked the staffing file to see who had bailed on the old guy so quickly. Or maybe he had bailed on them.

Timmy Clamber was first, and a short stint for him was no great surprise. Sure, Timmy was the most medically skilled person on the agency's home-care team. A lightning-fast diagnostician, he had worked for years as an EMT before deciding that hospice was his calling. But Timmy was also flamboyantly gay, his manner almost aggressively feminine. Some clients loved it: the perfect physique, the bitchy humor. Clackamas County's wealthy women, when their time came, knew to ask for him by name. Once I was standing in the hallway and overheard him promising a client that he would not let anyone into her room at the end until he'd arranged her wig perfectly.

"Darling, I will take it as a personal failure if every person who sees you does not shrivel with envy."

The woman in the bed, a sixty-nine-year-old with the wispy locks of post-chemo regrowth, gazed at Timmy with unconcealed adoration.

Obviously that style would not suit everyone. I opened the file to Timmy's notes, the hasty scribbles of a man who hated paperwork because it took time away from providing care. The patient was Barclay Reed, white male, seventy-eight, primary diagnosis of kidney cancer, with advanced metastatic tumors in liver, right femur, and right lung.

"Ouch," I said aloud. But I glanced around, and no one else had come into the cubicles yet that morning.

From the one wall of Central Office that was all windows, I saw a beautiful Monday in June, glorious sun after three days of drenching rain. Only a woman eager to get out of the house would arrive at the office this early on such a day. Someone who found work a welcome escape from difficulties at home. Someone like me.

The file said eight days, so the Professor's decision to fire Timmy had not been immediate. Maybe it hadn't been a culture clash at all. Whatever the reason, why the office sent Sara Schilling next was a mystery.

It's not that I didn't respect Sara. On the contrary, when my time comes—may it be many decades from now—I hope someone just like her is at my bedside. She was the embodiment of devotion and care. But like all saints, Sara was an innocent. I would have said that such an attitude would be impossible to sustain in our line of work. Seeing mortality confirmed on a daily basis will make a realist of anyone. But Sara had somehow managed to work in hospice for ten years and remain unmarred.

Years back I spent six months on central staff, trying to win a promotion to management by handling the necessary but dull work of resource planning. Every day of it I missed the patients and families, their pains and predicaments. Finally I quit seeking advancement and went back to doing what I loved. But in those office-bound days, Sara came in each morning humming a little tune. She'd switch on her computer, and while it booted up, she would turn to me—even if it was the tenth consecutive day of funereally depressing Oregon downpours—clasp her hands together and declare, "What a beautiful day to be alive."

Sara had a pink cover for her cell phone. She decorated her cubicle with posters of cats hanging from tree limbs. At home the woman had six pet birds, named after each of the Seven Dwarves except Grumpy.

Of course there will be clients who find this sort of personality cloying. Where it matters though, in caregiving situations, Sara was more patient and comforting than I could ever hope to be.

Once I was called in to help with a difficult case, Alan, who had tumors the length of his spine. As they grew, they were cracking his vertebrae. Suffering on that order I would not wish on an enemy.

Managing Alan's pain was challenging for Sara, which is why Central Office asked me to assist. I guess that's my strong suit— reducing pain, I mean—which reveals more about me than I might immediately care to admit.

No surprise, Alan's decline was driving his family into conflict. They were all loud, big people, the women bosomy and round faced, the men bearded and grim. They shouted for conversation, let their cell phones ring and ring before answering, left the TV turned up too high.

But of course the hearts of people like this break just like anyone else's. Their father was nearing his final hour, as we were titrating morphine to see if we could mute the pain without making him unconscious. Meanwhile, we could hear everyone bickering in the living room at full volume. Someone in the kitchen slammed a drawer, and I saw Alan wince.

"I'm tempted to go out there and slap sense into someone," I muttered. Whatever my skills, I was still plenty capable of running out of patience.

Sara smiled at me, her freckled face drawn in at the cheeks. "I know you don't mean that," she said. "But I can see how you would feel frustrated."

Ah, the forbearance of the hospice worker, wonderful and annoying.

Sara went to the doorway, hands clasped just like at her desk in the morning, and cooed, "Excuse me? Excuse me, everyone?" It was like a dove flying into a den of bears; I was ready to see the feathers fly.

But she spoke so softly, everyone had to hush just to hear. "I'd like to invite you all in now. He's ready for visitors. I invite you to honor your father by joining hands around his bed. Perhaps there is a song he likes that you all might gently sing."

I could never get away with being so directive. In a crowd like that, I doubt I would even get everyone's attention. But with Sara it worked. They rose as one and moved in her direction. Temporarily at least, she had ushered them from one stage of grief into the next. Not easy.

By the time I'd packed my gear, they were sardined into Alan's bedroom, holding hands or draping meaty arms over each other's brawny shoulders, and singing "You Are My Sunshine" in surprisingly good voices—to a man so riddled with illness the song probably felt like heaven already.

YET THE PROFESSOR'S FILE SHOWED that Sara had lasted only three days. There was no mention of the cause, nor any complaint. In my opinion that woman could charm a box of rocks for three days, and he had jettisoned her like snapping his fingers.

I flipped through the file to her notes. Sara used a fine-point pen, with tiny lettering right to the margins, so that she occupied no extra space. Barclay Reed, no surviving family, tenured professor at Portland State University, nationally recognized expert on World War II.

That explained Timmy's short stint, anyway. I pictured some gung-ho former Marine taking one gander at his male nurse's dangling earring and "All Love Is Good Love" forearm tattoo, and requesting someone else. Likewise, maybe Sara's sweet nature, while often effective, proved too saccharine for him.

I read deeper in the file and discovered something more: We were his third home-health agency, and there were only three in the region. He had churned through both the others before coming to us. I imagined one discarded caregiver after another. Now he'd come to the end of the line. If Barclay Reed wanted hospice care, we were his last chance.

So why me next? Everyone knew Grace Farnham was the diplomat, the champion of tough cases. A dignified African American woman with divinity school courses on top of her RN, Grace had a southern baritone so oratorical she could read a list of prescriptions and it would sound like gospel. Normally if someone can't find a satisfactory nurse, Grace is the answer to their prayers, not me.

She must have been assigned to someone actively dying, so Central Office would not pull her from the case. Nothing is harder on a family than a caregiver's departure after weeks or months of sharing the challenging work, with a new face arriving to learn the issues and personalities just when no one has the patience left for it. One policy of our agency's service I respected most, even though it sometimes ruined a weekend or birthday or Christmas, was its commitment to avoiding revolving doors.

After all, the medical part is just the beginning. Getting breathing comfortable and pain under control only enables the nonclinical things to take place—offering apologies, granting forgiveness, whispering prayers, expressing love. Once a patient and family have come to trust their hospice worker, they deserve to have that person help them for the whole hard ride.

Therefore, me. In addition to pain relief, I am known for sticking. For staying. For never giving up. It wasn't true only of patients but reflected my whole life. Especially in those days, when anyone within twenty miles knew what kind of marriage I had been dealing with since Michael came home. He wasn't a husband; he was a hand grenade.

People were sympathetic, but they sure stopped inviting us for supper. And I dropped all the healthy habits I'd developed while he was gone: the monthly book group with plenty of wine, the Sunday-evening yoga class, and once in a great while joining my girlfriends for a night of dancing to eighties hits at a club in Portland's southwest corner. Michael's anxiety, in that kind of crowd and noise, would register on the Richter scale.

Not that my husband was violent. But the energy he gave off—that he was suppressing an urge for violence, resisting the temptation—was somehow scarier. If he had taken up boxing, I could have relaxed, oddly enough, knowing he was expressing his grief and rage physically. If he had gone back to working out, so that I heard the clank of metal from the basement as he lifted weights till his muscles failed, and came upstairs calm and grinning from endorphins, I would have known he was on a healing path.

But there was no boxing or lifting. Only pursed lips, a furrowed brow, and a temper about the length of a firecracker's fuse.

In my own defense, I say only that caregiving never felt like sacrifice to me. In fact, it usually made me feel so good that I believed service was its own reward. I am not suggesting there was no limit to what I could endure with Michael. But I believe the measure of a vow does not lie in saying it, or in upholding it when things are easy. The power of a promise is proven in times of difficulty, when keeping that pledge is hard. My husband was giving me ample opportunity to prove the strength of my vows.

The office clock chimed seven, which meant Sara would arrive soon. Happy to chat, dear, but not today. I arranged the papers on my desk, weighting them in place with a name plate my husband had made for me out of bumper chrome when I'd finished school: Deborah L. Birch RN MSW. My handprint stood out on the gleaming metal, so I wiped it with my sleeve.

Then I packed my car with supplies—pain meds, an oxygen tank—and returned for the paperwork. As always, the last thing I did before leaving the office was run my thumb down the back of the hummingbird.

It was my ritual. Years ago, a patient named Ryan carved the bird while he fought end-stage emphysema, always tucking it away when I made house calls. Ryan lived with the anxiety anyone would experience if they can't get enough oxygen, so I cringe to think how much the knife work must have cost him in hours and energy. But on the last day, there it was at his bedside—with a slip of paper that read "For Deb"—a fine carving with a four-inch wingspan, meticulous feathered details, a tiny eye on each side of its skin-smooth head.

Was my patient saying that the Grim Reaper is beautiful? Or was he mocking death, making a last carving about speed and flight? Was the hummingbird a symbol of life's unstoppable force, because the art will outlive the artist? I'll never know what Ryan intended.

But it almost doesn't matter because the carving has a strong and specific meaning to me. It is a solid reminder that every patient, no matter how sick or impoverished, gives lasting gifts to the person entrusted with his care.

If that sounds grandiose, so be it. Because I sweep my thumb down the back of that bird before each new patient, and not for good luck. I do it to remind myself that I receive something meaningful from every person. I gain much more than I give.

ON THE WAY TO THE CAR I checked Barclay Reed's address: Lake Oswego. That was convenient. The lake sits a few miles outside Portland, not far past my house. Our house, that is, mine and Michael's. Oswego is an interesting place. It's clean, man-made because it's a reservoir of some kind, and there are pleasant waterfront restaurants at one end. Pretty and friendly.

But so is the high school cheerleading captain, until you cross her. Lake Oswego is actually a closed place. Every inch of lakeshore has a home on it. They're not mansions, in general, more like small works of architectural art. And there is no fence to keep people out. It's more subtle than that: no boardwalk, no beach, no shady cove with public access. Any open lawn is adorned with a TRESPASSERS WILL BE PROSECUTED sign. Lake Oswego is a perfect little body of water, and perfectly private.

So even though I'd enjoyed a sunset margarita on the restaurant decks, and strolled the farmer's market on summer Saturdays, I had never dipped one toe in that water. The patient's address left no doubt about where his house stood: South Shore Boulevard. With a little luck, Mr. Barclay Reed had a dock. With lots of luck, he liked swimmers.

Since I was ahead of schedule, I indulged in a little detour past Michael's shop. I suspect people still think of auto repair as the oil-stained grease-monkey work it was a generation ago. There's plenty of that, sure. But Michael's operation is totally high tech. The first thing he does when a customer drives in is attach the car to a computer. There are still girlie calendars hanging in the parts department. But instead of vocational school, his mechanics have engineering degrees. Instead of Muzak, there is public radio. The coffee is free, local, and delicious.

This approach has won him high-end customers in droves. Sure enough, as I passed that morning, three gleaming Ferraris stood in a row in the parking lot—green, white, and red like the flag of Italy.

Better still, Michael's truck was parked beside the air pump. Just seeing it there untied a knot in my belly. So he was awake, and on the job. During Michael's tours, his cousin Gary moved down from Seattle to manage the shop, organizing the finances maybe a little too well. He offered to stay on as long as Michael needed. So the returning soldier had not felt much pressure to dive right back into his old line of work.

He seemed more content to sit at the kitchen table, filling page after page with scribbled faces. Thirty-one of them, and he'd done enough drawing that I recognized a few: one with mouse ears, one in shades, one with a scribble at his side. Whoever those faces were, he wasn't telling his wife.

But there was his rig, a tricked-out F-250 he had painted speeding-ticket red. I didn't need to stop in, or say hi. And Michael didn't need to know I was checking on him. I had all the reassurance I needed.

Every day he went to work was a step toward normalcy. Count that as one morning in the plus column. Now it was approaching eight o'clock. I turned up the radio and sped north to Lake Oswego.

WHAT DID IT FEEL LIKE to meet a new client? When I'd first finished my masters at Portland State, it was all anxiety: Am I worthy? Do I know enough? What if I screw up? But that line of thought rarely happened anymore. I now understood that I was completely unworthy, did not know nearly enough, and could be totally depended upon to screw up. What mattered was my intention. This job was not about Deborah Birch being perfect, because it was not about Deborah Birch at all. What a concept. How helpfully humbling.

And of course what I felt before a new client wasn't excitement. Even the most engaging and interesting patients, when they turn to an agency like ours, are entrusting us with their mortality. It's not like we're tour guides. Or if we are, the sights are rarely pretty and the destination is some place completely unknown.

So the feeling before meeting for the first time is solemn, I guess, with a kind of confidence in competence. Almost like a bricklayer: This is hard work and I know how to do it. I'll do the best I can and not stop till the job is done, brick by brick by brick.

The house sat on the lake side of the road, a ranch with cedar siding and white trim. Outside I saw the Beetle belonging to Cheryl, a longtime volunteer. Her husband took three years to die of ALS, nurses from our agency holding her hand every agonizing step. The process left Cheryl nearly bankrupt. Afterward, instead of indulging in bitterness, she became a volunteer and was soon our very best. Barclay Reed was lucky to have her.

The gardens were manicured, tidy almost to a fault. One leaf sat on the walkway, dry and curled; otherwise the place was spotless. I nearly bent to pick up that leaf. I was starting the shift into professional mode.

Before I'd rung the bell, Cheryl opened the front door. A squat woman wearing a red dress with pink polka dots, plus purple cat's-eye glasses, she greeted me with a quick hug.

"How's everything going here this morning?"

She looked at me over the top of her glasses. "Deborah, you are about to have your hands full."

"That's nothing new," I said.

"You'll see. This patient's a prize." She gathered her things into a giant white handbag, pecking my cheek on the way out.

"Is the new one here yet?" a voice yelled from inside the house. "Has the latest victim arrived?"

I glanced after Cheryl, who was climbing into her bug without a flicker of interest backward. "Good morning, Mr. Reed. I'll be right with you."

"I haven't got all day," he bellowed. "I am dying in here, you know."

You sound pretty healthy to me, I thought, then stuffed it away. For many people, appearances of strength are the last thing they want to surrender. I followed the sound of his voice to a half-open door, on which I knocked.

"Dispense with the formalities, would you please?" he barked. "You'll be wiping my bottom soon enough."

And just like that, I had his number. I'd dealt with tyrants before. Often they turned out to be the ones who were most frightened. Fortunately, worry is a treatable condition. I might be able to help him.

I pushed the door open. The room smelled of old newspapers. The man on the bed had burst capillaries on his cheekbones like upside-down tree roots. His shock of white hair stood straight up. He appeared thin but not skeletal, with the distended stomach common to liver involvement.

Cheryl had left him propped up, a rolling tray to one side that held water and a newspaper, with a cluster of remote controls in his lap. Among them there was, I noticed, no telephone.

"A woman," he exclaimed, rolling his eyes. "Yet another woman."

"Good morning, Mr. Reed. My name—"

"Doctor Reed, if you please. Or Professor Reed, ideally. What are your credentials, may I inquire?"

"Oh. Well, I'm a registered nurse with a graduate degree in social work."

"My, my. And your last name?"

"Birch. Deborah Bir—"

"I shall call you Nurse Birch. Did you know that I have already eaten sixteen bananas today? What do you make of that?"

For someone so sick, he certainly had spark. There was a forward set to his jaw, too, a ferocity, that made me like him. He was not going to go gently, and I admired his spirit. "I don't know. Sixteen seems like a lot of bananas. Should I make something of it?"

"Weak evasion, Nurse Birch. But the question," he pointed a bony finger, "the central question is whether or not you believe me."

"Does it matter?"

"Whether or not you believe me? It is the only thing that matters."

"Then I do not believe you."

He folded his hands in his lap. "Your reasoning?"

"A perfectly healthy person would have a hard time eating more than five or six. And someone of your age and intelligence would know better than to upset his stomach needlessly." I smiled at him. "You did not eat sixteen bananas today."

He leveled his gaze at me. "Are you calling me a liar, Nurse Birch, you there with your smug little Cheshire Cat grin?"

"I am calling you a tester, Professor Reed. You are testing me, and I am answering you directly and honestly. So now: How many bananas have you eaten today?"

He peered down at his collection of remotes, stirring them

absently. "I have always detested bananas. I can't abide them. The preferred fruit of baboons, after all."

"Well, if I'm counting correctly then, Professor Reed, the number of bananas you did not eat today is exactly sixteen."

He drew himself up at that, giving me a long appraising glare. "You," he said at last, crossing his arms on his chest. "You may take my blood pressure."

TO SAILORS IN WARTIME there is but one *deity*, and he has a single manifestation: weather.

In July of 1588, the English navy defeated the superior Spanish Armada with the assistance of severe storms off the coast of Ireland. Weather wrecked twenty-four of King Philip II's mighty one-hundred-and-thirty-ship fleet, ending Spain's reign of the oceans and establishing England as a global naval power.

Likewise, Benedict Arnold capitalized on weather in October of 1776 to thwart the British navy on Lake Champlain. Outmanned and outgunned, Arnold sailed through a dense fog and escaped during the night. Eventually he grounded his ships, setting them ablaze to prevent the English forces from capturing even one. It is not difficult to imagine the glow of burning timbers, reflected off the water and refracted by fog, visible for miles—a torch to alert King George III to the colonists' determination to win themselves liberty.

In September of 1942, for the crew aboard the I-25 submarine off the coast of Oregon, weather stood between them and their mission as solidly as a fortress's battlements. Weather tested their stamina. Weather called into question if they would ever make it home.

Home. The dream of all sailors, of all times and races. The crew of the I-25 was no exception. But these were not American seamen, patrolling U.S.

waters in a defensive posture with weekend passes waiting on shore. Home for the crew of the I-25 lay more than 4,800 miles away, in the Land of the Rising Sun.

The sub had orders from Japan's Imperial Naval Command to conduct a surprise assault against the United States, and the weather was not cooperating. But the ship's leader was a patient man. Lieutenant Commander Meiji Tagami, a graduate of the prestigious naval academy in Hiroshima, had captained the submarine since it had gone into service in November of 1941. The attack his orders called for was no Pearl Harbor. Given that the purpose was to incite widespread public distress, one might call it terrorism.

Thus far, however, the mission consisted of waiting. All that Labor Day weekend, the skies hung shrouded with clouds. Wind drove the waves to swells of ten feet or more. Rain poured relentlessly like a melancholy mood. Meanwhile the crew, ninety-four strong—plus one special passenger and his volatile cargo—had a perilous task to perform. It would require surfacing in daylight. It would call for prolonged vulnerability to American defenses. It would depend entirely on that one passenger, and he not even a seaman.

Beneath the waves an ocean is calm, without the churning that characterizes the surface. Thus there remained no point in leaving the undersea; rough waves on top would pound the sub broadside. No sailor could keep a foothold on the decks.

Moreover, the emperor's strategy required clear skies. While some sailors believed His Majesty Hirohito possessed divine powers, so far none had seen his commands flatten the waves. It also did not matter how skilled or courageous that special passenger might be. Without weather as an ally, the mission would fail.

Nonetheless, the essence of the matter is this: In the autumn of 1942, the Japanese navy attacked the mainland of the United States. The plan was to set the forests of the Pacific Northwest on fire.

The U.S. Department of War, in keeping with information-suppression policies later propagandized as "Loose Lips Sink Ships," prevented the populace from learning much about that mission. Today the record is public, but few Americans know what happened.

Yet the events, and their repercussions, warrant examination now because they contain illuminating instruction about the nature of warfare and the challenge of peace. They offer useful instruction to our troubled present time. An age later, they deserve the light of day.

CHAPTER 2

I WISH I COULD SAY I had won him with that first exchange. But then he refused to be bathed. The remotes controlled two televisions, both of which had satellite service and video players attached, but everything he tried to watch that day wound up boring him. He experienced some confusion in the afternoon. And when I tried to help by offering him applesauce, he slapped the bowl across the room.

It happened to spray on a bookshelf. It's my job to be observant, especially on early visits, but I was just annoyed enough with the clean-up task, it wasn't until I finished that I focused on the actual books. The author's name was clearly visible on spine after spine: Barclay Reed, PhD.

I was still kneeling, paper towels in hand, and I bent closer. The publishers were all university presses, so I presumed these were scholarly works. But the titles hooked me even so:

Dying of Thirst: The Role of Oil Supplies in the Japanese Defeat
Lost Words: How Inaccurate Cable Translation Led to Pearl Harbor
Begging to Surrender: Japanese Peace Overtures in Early 1945

Wow. What a mind this man must have. What a body of knowledge. And what a contrary way of thinking.

I straightened with a mouthful of questions, but the Professor had fallen asleep. His head lolled to the side, mouth slightly open, though one hand still clutched a remote. I stood there, watching his chest rise and fall. The moment was a pre-vision, of course, my first glimpse of how I would see him last. How small a thing a human being is, really. How brief.

I hoped he wouldn't fire me like he did the others. He'd won my heart already, the crusty coot.

While he slept, I tiptoed into the kitchen. Now I had a few minutes to collect the man's back story.

The kitchen could have been an operating room, it was so spotless and spare. I prefer soup on the stove and bread in the oven, a rolling pin on the counter with flour stuck to it. A messy kitchen signals a full life.

But this room's sparseness did not feel like impoverishment. Rather, it indicated a fastidious attention to order, not unlike the manicured gardens. I opened the refrigerator: one mustard jar, half a stick of butter. Otherwise the inside was as empty as if the fridge had just arrived from the store.

Some might call it snooping. But part of my job was to understand his wants—and back story was essential, because things can get mighty psychological toward the end. Symbolic. The sicker a patient becomes, the less likely he is to ask for anything directly.

I remember providing care to a farmer with advanced respiratory disease. Neil lived out in the hinterlands, and it was a whale of a commute for me. But I was glad to have his case because his family was determined to honor Neil's desire not to die in a nursing home. They arranged a hospital bed beside the big window in the old farmhouse parlor and took turns caring for him. This family—adults, two sons and a daughter, mom deceased though photos of her hung all through the house—was admirable, very committed, taking time away from work and their own families to help their dad. Every time I drove out there, Neil's pain meds were appropriate, the oxygen tank was handy or in use at low flow, and he appeared comfortable and clean. They barely needed me.

One afternoon during a stretch of beautiful clear weather, he was in bad shape when I arrived. Fidgeting, tossing his head from side to side. The daughter was massaging her father's hand with lotion, which he had loved as recently as the day before. Neil was not responding now, just wagging his head as if he wanted to tell the whole world: No. Whatever it was, no.

The next day was worse. By afternoon everyone's nerves were fraying. The family tried everything: warm compresses, Gregorian chant. After a quiet hour, Neil would start tossing again. They wanted to increase his pain medicine.

I understood the temptation. The lungs are magnificent organs. If you laid all of their crannies out flat, they would be the size of a tennis court. However, the tissue is rich with nerves that sense oxygen deprivation acutely. Even the toughest person, if he can't get a good breath, is going to zoom right up the anxiety scale. A good belt of lorazepam will quiet those nerves right down. But of course the oxygen debt will grow deeper anyway.

In my experience with respiratory disease, head tossing signals agitation, not pain. When I arrived the next morning, another bluebird day, the family was in shreds. They looked exhausted and pale. The elder son said it was like having a baby cry, no matter what you did, for three straight days.

The daughter led me to Neil. He was squirming, unable to speak, but struggling to tell us something. She started to cry. She said, "I think my father's suffering needs to end. I think we need to increase his dose as high as it takes to ease this pain."

That would mean the end. Not that the morphine would kill him. But it would put him so soundly to sleep, he would not wake up to eat or drink, and that is how he would finish.

Sometimes there is no alternative, especially with certain nasty bone cancers. But I saw Neil's body fretting there, and I had a contrary hunch—to lower the meds. It held some risk, of course. I might increase his suffering. But if we cranked up the meds, whatever important thing he wanted to settle would instead go undone for all eternity.

"Let's cut way down for a while," I told her. "If he begins to ache, we can always bring the dose back. But we might get a lucid moment. Maybe we can find out what's eating at him."

The family held a discussion out on the sun-drenched porch. After a while they invited me out to join them.

"Go ahead," the daughter said. "But if he starts hurting, we call the cavalry."

Around noon, Neil awakened a bit and asked for his bed angle to be raised so he could see out the window. At about two, he woke again. I called everyone into the room.

"Now, Neil, I need to ask you something," I said, with the family circling the bed. "We can see that something is not right with you."

He tilted his head on the pillow, eyes fixed on me.

"We are all ready to do our best. What is it that you need?"

Neil raised one arm like an imitation of the Grim Reaper and pointed out the farmhouse window. "That field. Four perfect haying days in a row. That field needs mowing."

The younger son laughed. "Hell, dad, we've been a little busy, you know. Taking care of you, I mean."

"Never mind, damn it." Neil threw back his covers. "I'll do it myself."

And with everyone panicked, helping and fussing, Neil wrestled on his overalls and boots, then shuffled to the barn as slow as a snail. The oxygen tank's wheels squeaked as he pulled it across the barnyard. His sons hoisted him into the tractor seat. They strapped the tank up behind him. They made him promise he would keep the rig in low gear. And by golly, Neil mowed that field all by himself.

I watched from the porch with a mix of worry and admiration. Row by row, the grass behind the cutter bar lay down as if it were resting.

Later, when we helped him back into bed, Neil was sunburned and dehydrated and mosquito bitten and content. At my last check, he slept quietly. I drove home that night feeling better than I had in weeks.

When the call came at five the next morning, I knew what news Neil's daughter would be delivering.

"You all did a great job," I told her. "You let him finish what he needed to finish, and on his own terms. What a loving gift."

I'm just a hospice worker, a temporary visitor to a patient's inner circle. But I believe words like those carry enormous weight. They can leaven the grief of a family that has just done the truly hardest job.

THE PROFESSOR HAD NO FAMILY, I remembered that from Central Office's notes. But that did not mean he was without a past. I wandered into the living room, scanning for clues.

The first noticeable thing, of course, was the glimmering lake. One wall consisted of sliding glass doors. But I examined the room before venturing outside. A wheelchair sat folded into itself in one corner. Furniture in muted colors, not looking especially inviting. Another bookshelf, the titles in Japanese characters. A gong in one corner that was bronze with a black rim, maybe four feet across. Hanging in a little cloth pocket on the dark wood frame was a mallet with a head the size of my fist.

I pushed the gong with one fingertip, swinging it ever so slightly. But my skin left a mark on the polished metal. I wiped it with my shirt, and as I lifted the fabric, the gong made a little sour sound. I stepped away, and the room was silent.

There was a dining table, four chairs pushed snug as if to keep them out of the way of something. On the wall hung rows of black-and-white photographs. There were hooks in blank places where other photos had been, but someone had taken them down. I examined the remainders: Young Barclay in a tux, accepting some kind of award. Tall Barclay, towering amid a group of Japanese men. Sharp Barclay, standing at a podium, one finger raised, mouth open as if he was about to bite something.

One more, at the far end, showed Barclay in Bermuda shorts, but in a formal shirt, hands on his hips and wearing an imperious expression. Facing him in a doorway stood a little Asian girl in the same pose: hands on hips, but with a sweet smile. Since the patient's papers said he had no family, I wondered who she might be.

I slid back one of the glass doors and stepped out onto the deck. From across the lake I could hear children laughing; school must have let out for the day. The water was gorgeous, glinting and bright. On the Professor's deck I counted two lounge chairs, both thoroughly cobwebbed, and a grill with its cloth cover drawn down tight. I dipped my fingers into the lake. Cool. Still too early in the year to swim. As an older couple canoed closer along the shore, I turned back.

I was latching the sliding door when he called out. "Nurse Birch? Nurse Birch?"

I hurried into his room. "Are you all right?"

He appeared completely awake. "That is a preposterous question to ask a hospice patient. Pose a better one."

Always on offense, this one. "Well, do you speak Japanese? I noticed some of your books."

The Professor held up ten fingers, wiggling one at a time. "*Ichi, ni, san, shi, go, roku, shichi, hachi, kyu, ju.*" He wagged his right hand. "*Migi,*" and his left, "*hidari.* As you can see, I am practically fluent. Now it's my turn: Did you strike my gong?"

I drew up. "Excuse me?"

"It's a simple question. Please give a simple answer."

I put my hands on my hips. "No. I did not strike your gong."

He sniffed, his face pinched. Then he selected a remote and switched one of the televisions on. I couldn't see the screen, but it sounded like news with a British accent. He waved one hand dismissively. "You may go."

I returned to the living room with my tail between my legs. Why had I told a half truth? I hadn't done anything wrong. What was I afraid of?

I picked up one of the books with characters on the spine, opening it at random. Symbols ran up and down the page, but to me it was nonsense.

I was still there when the evening volunteer came. I heard her car drive up: Melissa, a college student whose grandmother had died of respiratory disease in our inpatient facility. A beautiful death it was, full of completion and calm. During the final weeks, Melissa slept on a cot we set up in her grandmother's room. I checked on them once during an overnight shift. They were awake, and Melissa was painting her grandmother's nails and her own with identical polish, hand beside hand.

A year later, when Melissa showed up for our six-week volunteer training session, we welcomed her with hugs. Now she was more than competent; she was expert. She was also a triathlete, and when I opened the door for her, I saw yet again the kind of body, lean and strong, that I knew I would never have.

Melissa bubbled away about her amazing bike ride that afternoon while stowing her high-nutrition dinner in the fridge and rubbing her hands together as if she were about to start a race.

"Have you been with this patient before?" I asked her. "I'm new to him."

"It was a fiesta." Smiling, she put up her dukes like a boxer. "I took him two rounds out of three."

"Let me just say my good-byes then."

The moment I reached the Professor's door, he coughed hard into his fist.

"Your evening support is here," I said.

He muted the TV. "You mean your relief. Perhaps I should replace my front walk with a conveyor belt."

"You remember Melissa, right?"

"We are acquainted. She prefers to live a life of the body. I prefer the life of the mind." He sighed. "And as for you . . ."

"Yes, Professor Reed?"

"You may come again tomorrow. After that, we'll see."

"I tend to live life one day at a time."

"It is an uncertain world, indeed." He turned the TV sound back on.

I spoke over the noise. "You don't want any more of me than you have to take, is that it?"

"Nurse Birch, I suspect I will be seeing you again sooner than any reasonable person would desire."

He stared at the TV. But damn if that codger didn't give himself away with the barest hint of a smile.

Well. Not a bad beginning. As I headed to the car, I hoped that the Professor would have a good night. I imagined he had fifty or sixty nights left. It was unlikely that he would live to see Labor Day.

If he inconvenienced me, therefore, or annoyed me, or grew too demanding, the calendar was all I needed to regain perspective. When Labor Day arrived, I would be free to go for a long walk. I might have a few friends over. I might get out of town for the weekend with my husband.

My husband. That reminded me to switch my phone back on. My practice is to have it handy always, in case there's a medical emergency, but turned off so there's no interruption in my work. Powering up that day, it gave a long series of notification beeps: nine calls from Michael, all clustered in midafternoon, but he had left no messages or texts.

I called him immediately. Six rings and no answer. My mind began writing all kinds of stories about what might have happened.

I listened closely to his recording though I was hearing it for the thousandth time. Silly, I know, but I had come to cherish that ten seconds of him speaking because he had recorded it two years ago, before the war changed his voice as it changed everything else. At the beep, I discovered I had nothing to say.

I hung up, tossed the phone onto the passenger seat, and pressed the accelerator hard. Meanwhile, I breathed a quiet prayer that my husband had not killed anyone. Or himself.

THE JAPANESE ADMIRALTY'S INVENTIVENESS—to mount an assault on North America while naval conflict was concentrated across the Pacific Ocean—showed more than military wit. It reflected a cultural context with ancient origins.

In the twelfth century, four feudal clans vied for dynastic control of an island chain in the South Pacific. The dominant group was the Taira, a family of samurai warriors and their descendants with a lineage three hundred years old. In 1179, a Taira patriarch declared an infant of that clan to be the new emperor of the islands. This usurpation sparked years of war.

On February 7, 1184, Yoshitsune Minamoto attacked the Tairas' fortress from an unexpected direction and at an unexpected time. This castle was supposedly impregnable, yet the Minamoto clan emerged victorious. The Taira leaders were driven to the sea. *Shouri.* Victory.

On April 24 of the following year, the Minamoto clan attacked the Taira in the Straits of Shimonoseki. Again the assault was a surprise. Though the Minamoto did not know the waters well, their naval forces outnumbered the Taira three to one. Meanwhile, through espionage, the invaders had learned which vessel carried the emperor, now six years old. After a clash of archers, the battle became hand-to-hand combat, ship beside ship for nearly a full day. Eventually Yoshitsune brought his Minamoto warriors toward the emperor's craft.

Rather than become prisoners or slaves and allow the symbols of their royal might to be captured, Taira leaders killed themselves. After throwing his royal sword and mirror into the water, the young emperor also committed suicide.

Shouri again. The regional struggle for supremacy was ended, the Minamotos' dominion established in perpetuity. Yoshitsune's brother became the joined clans' first shogun. The feudal chain of islands became Japan.

In the Land of the Rising Sun, this story is as familiar as Paul Revere is to Americans. Even now seafood from the Strait of Shimonoseki is considered sacred because it may contain the spirits of slain Taira.

The battle's outcome was more than political. It furthermore established a cultural ethos, a sensibility that sees surprise attacks not as underhanded or deceptive, but as clever and courageous. The idea permeates Japanese society to this day.

Two sumo wrestlers, wearing only the mawashi loincloth, circle one another: grim, rotund, almost comical. Suddenly one of them sees an opportunity, grabs his opponent, and throws him out of the competitive ring. *Shouri.*

Many martial arts embrace this philosophy. Judo depends on sudden throws and shifts in balance. In the fencing art of kendo, there is a technical term—mamono—for the surprise thrust followed by rapid withdrawal.

The concept appears in spiritual practice as well. Zen monastic instruction often includes the teacher delivering a surprise whack across the novitiate's shoulders, using a length of wood to awaken the meditation.

Even in the gentle realm of poetry, one of Japan's oldest forms is haiku— which contains imagery of nature, plus a metaphor for the human condition or the speaker's deepest emotions, all in seventeen syllables. (By contrast, the sonnet of Western literature contains one hundred and forty.)

These twelfth-century morals survived to modern times. In 1904, Heihachiro Togo attacked the Russian Pacific Squadron without having first declared war. While the Russian commanding officer was at a party, Japanese torpedoes destroyed two battleships and many cruisers. By the 1940s, Togo was admiral of the Japanese fleet. *Shouri.*

Pearl Harbor multiplied this cultural notion by a million millions. As the culmination of eight hundred years of Japanese thought, it would be the sudden blow to surpass all others.

But just as sumo wrestlers train for years, the seeds for the attack on Oahu may have been planted decades earlier. In 1925, a British naval reporter named Hector Bywater wrote a novel, *The Great Pacific War*. His thriller imagined a Japanese attack on the American forces in Pearl Harbor, Luzon, Guam, and the Philippines. The book was a sensation. The Japanese navy translated it for top officers and added it to the curriculum at the Naval War College.

In September of 1925 the novel appeared prominently in the *New York Times Book Review*. Isoroku Yamamoto, a Japanese naval attaché stationed in Washington, was known as intellectually insatiable. Did he see that review or read that book?

One is tempted to speculate. Sixteen years later, Yamamoto was an admiral, vice minister of the navy, colleague of Admiral Togo, and an architect of the Pearl Harbor attack.

Spies early that year confirmed that U.S. naval power in the region was concentrated in one place. The day of the week with the most ships in port was invariably Sunday. The harbor's narrow mouth allowed only one large vessel through at a time, making the sanctuary also a trap.

Above all, U.S. attention at Pearl Harbor concentrated to the south, toward a Japanese base on the Marshall Islands. Thus any surprise assault must come from the opposite direction. The Americans would play the role of the Taira.

At 7:48 A.M. on Sunday, December 7, 1941, Japanese Zeroes reached the tip of Oahu. The story has been told before in gruesome detail, but even a brief summary contains multitudes of tragedy.

On that day, 353 Japanese bombers, fighters, and torpedo planes took off from six aircraft carriers, aided by five submarines and five miniature subs. The assault sank four U.S. battleships, three destroyers, three cruisers and five other ships, and destroyed 188 aircraft. Bombing, fires, and drowning killed 2,402 Americans and wounded 1,282 more. It was a slaughter.

Shouri once again. The Minamoto methods lived. There had been no declaration of war. The attackers came from the north.

CHAPTER 3

I WAS A GRADUATE STUDENT AT PORTLAND STATE, one semester away from attaining my final credential, when the transmission in my ancient Subaru gave out. The local dealer said over the phone that the repair would run nearly two thousand dollars. He might as well have said a million, the sum was so far out of reach. Buying a car was out of the question too, new or used. I was living on a teaching assistantship, about eight hundred dollars a month, which was nearly as little back then as it is now. I couldn't borrow my way to a new transmission, either, because I hadn't found a post-graduation job yet. I couldn't stick the repair on a credit card, because my student loan payments would kick in about two minutes after the university handed me my diploma, job or not. I mean, in those days I couldn't even afford a cell phone; I used an empty university office to avoid the cost of the call.

After hanging up I went to the grad students' mailroom, where I found friends and colleagues eager to grouse with me about the inconvenience of being carless, and the general impoverishment of academic life, when Connie West poked her head out of the adjacent office.

"I know what you can do, Deborah," Connie called. Although she was an infamous busybody, with a black belt in gossip, Connie was also den mother to the grad students, manager of our schedules and practicums and sometimes personal lives. "I know just the place."

"Is it cheap?"

"It is trustworthy."

I laughed. "Sorry, can't afford that."

She stepped out into the hallway. "You know my Silas has that ancient BMW, right? Older than Methuselah. He went to this guy Michael Birch, paid huge for a transmission repair, and broke down the next day anyway."

Connie snapped and popped her gum, her usual method of pausing in a story. She held a nail file, inspecting her fingers without using it. "Silas had the car fixed someplace else, then wrote the Birch guy a total nastygram. What a rip-off, you don't know jack, that sort of thing. A week later he gets an envelope, only there's no note inside. Just a check, for the exact amount of the repair at the second place, signed Michael Birch." She pointed at me with the nail file. "This guy must have called the second place and found out what the tab was, and then he covered it."

She finessed one of her thumbnails with the file. "Now Silas won't take his car anywhere else. He didn't cash the check either, despite my input."

"And the moral of the story is?"

She snapped her gum. "This Birch guy has a conscience. He won't take advantage of you knowing nothing about cars."

"But he messed up the transmission."

"He might cut you a deal, too. But you will have to be charming." Connie sashayed back to her office, calling over her shoulder on the way. "Wear a skirt."

With the car stuck permanently in third gear, I strained the clutch and clanked all the way to Birch's Automotive Arts. What a classic Portland name for a business. And yes, I admit it: With the begrudging attitude familiar to those who are habitually broke, I wore a skirt. But not a short one. I still had my dignity. When I arrived, the guy barely noticed me, or my legs. His head was poked too far in under the hood of an ancient Mercedes, its diesel engine rattling and producing a stinky plume.

"Who did you say sent you?"

"Connie West. Over at Portland State."

Pulling his head out from under the hood, he sized up my twelve-year-old car before turning to take a look at me. "I have no idea who that is."

I stuck around while he finished tuning the Benz. He took two phone calls and spent what seemed to me an hour in discussion when the Mercedes owner came to fetch his car. Twice I heard Michael say his conscience would not let him make an expensive repair without the guy realizing that it might not last. Finally he put my rusty rig on the lift and poked around from beneath.

"When did you last change your transmission fluid?" he asked.

I hated that my answer exposed me as a female automobile know-nothing, but my excuse was that I know health care instead. I coughed into my fist. "How often are we supposed to do that, exactly?"

He said nothing, just kept working with his arms raised.

How could I help but notice him? Forget the oil-stained jeans. He was wide chested, big armed, focused. I ventured a conversation. He owned the car business, which had been open nearly two years and already employed six people. He also served one weekend a month and two weeks a year as a National Guardsman—which was paying off his college loans because he invested every spare nickel in equipping the repair shop. And he was a lousy mini-golf player, which I learned the following Saturday on our first date. And a respectable kisser, I discovered later that night. And a few weeks later, a powerful, generous, patient, breathtaking lover. Michael.

WITH BOTH OF MY PARENTS BURIED YEARS BEFORE—a long yarn in itself—my sister Robin flew out for the wedding. We held a small celebration by the water in Hood River, a gorgeous outdoorsy jock town sixty miles up the Columbia River gorge. Mountains rose steeply on both sides of the water, the near bank Oregon and the far one Washington.

People zoomed by on the bike path, some of them cheering when they saw my white dress. It fluffed in the wind like a flamenco dancer's fan. Michael wore a top hat, which looked sharp, but he had to hold it down with one hand because of the constant upriver breeze. My grad-school pals and Michael's friends from the Guard and his shop flirted madly, and I suspect they may have accomplished a tryst or two.

We stood in a little park and declared ourselves, forever and ever and ever, while behind us the gorge's crazy kite surfers sped and soared, zooming across the river or floating above it like all of our dreams of the future, high and fearless and free. All I could conceive of was possibility.

That proved literally true too. When I did not get pregnant after four years of ardent efforts, we went to an endocrinologist. Given my lifelong irregular periods, I felt sure the problem was me. But it turned out that Michael's swimmers could not go the distance. How strange that a man so strong and healthy should have that secret incapacity.

Because of how my mother had died—in an ICU, surrounded by machinery, the whole experience a big reason I had gone into hospice—I was unwilling to bring medical technology to our reproductive aid.

As I told Michael my decision, fully prepared for him to insist we try new measures and never give up, I wept as if I were teaching the sky to rain.

"Then it's just us," Michael said instead, his big arms circling me. "I'm going to have to make enough noise and laundry and joy for a whole family."

He laid me down on the bed, by golly, and he showed it.

THAT WAS BEFORE THE WAR, OF COURSE. Before the longest conflict in U.S. history. Almost everyone has an opinion about whether or not it was a good idea to go there, to spend billions of dollars and thousands of lives with the goal of driving out tyrants and killing the trainers of terrorists. No matter what people believe, they are certain of it.

Not me. I mean: There were no weapons of mass destruction, yes, OK. But at this point, so what? I say leave the debate to politicos and their parrots. All I care about is the plain fact of Michael's condition once he returned.

First deployment: I expected working in the motor pool would be calm. But Michael saw too many Humvees dragged back for demolition, outsides scorched, insides splattered red. He brought home sorrow. A new vocabulary too, expertly obscene. Also a need for lovemaking so ardent and urgent—in the car, on the kitchen counter, one summer night even in the backyard, with the neighbors' TV plainly audible—that was when we began calling each other lover.

The meaning was not entirely benign. Sometimes sex substituted for dealing with things. If we disagreed, or miscommunicated, or were bored, we went to bed for answers. We used the physical to blot out the mental. Evasive maneuvers, I later called it.

Second deployment: anxiety in crowds, jumping at loud noises. Also moments of startling generosity, as if his conscience were trying to atone. The wife of an employee named Russell was arrested for embezzling from the city parks department, and even though she said the money was for her dying mother, the media pilloried her. Michael called Russell in, the man clearly expecting to be fired. Instead, Michael told him that everyone needs help in hard times and gave him a thousand dollars.

Guard duties changed during that home period too: One soldier, selected from each unit, would attend sniper school. Because of his keen vision Michael had always been a good shot, and I wasn't surprised when the orders came. The shock was the manner of his training, more indoctrination than education. Yes he learned techniques, and mastered new weapons. But one night they made him eat meal upon meal, then sent him out early the next morning on an assignment they said would test his commitment to duty. They left him there, prone on a hillside with his scope trained on a grove of trees, until he shit himself. It was supposed to build solidarity, but Michael soured on the military from then on.

Third deployment: The man who'd stood sharply in uniform the past two times would not let me accompany him to the departure muster. I pined by the back door while he took a taxi to report for duty. In Iraq two days later, the expert mechanic found himself under the command of a younger man with less training, from another branch of the armed forces, who used him exclusively as a sniper. Michael followed orders, winning recognition for kills and kudos for accuracy. But he returned home in a permanent mood of nitroglycerine, always just one bump away from exploding.

That's why the politics are irrelevant. No one will repay what Michael lost, no one will be punished. Even so, I count my husband among the lucky ones. He did not give his life for his country. He did not sacrifice a limb. But he completely lost his innocence. His libido. His ability to control his temper.

I WAS HALFWAY HOME when my phone rang, and the caller's number was blocked. I snatched the phone up anyway. It was a detective. Michael was not hurt, but he was in trouble. The cop said he would inform me fully at the station. I changed routes, carrying the sodden weight of dread.

The feeling deepened when I pulled into the station's parking lot and saw Michael's red truck hoisted behind a towing rig. Opened airbags hung from the dashboard like half-rotten grapes. Inching forward, I saw that the truck's front left corner was caved in. I'd ridden in that beast enough times, over enough hard Oregon back country, to know that damage like that did not occur easily. It required something massive.

"Oh, Michael," I said. "Please, God, let him be OK."

The police station smelled like hot metal. Once I'd identified myself, the desk sergeant pointed his pen at a side door. Another uniformed officer held it open, and a moment later I found myself in a windowless room with three mustached men. One wall had a mirror, but I knew what that meant.

Two of the men sat at the table with me and said their names, which I did not catch. The third one, who wore a black business suit, did not introduce himself. He leaned against the wall with his hands in his pockets.

The table was gray, the floor was an ugly speckled linoleum, and the walls and ceiling were painted a kind of institutional white that is actually less than white. I searched for a wastebasket, in case I needed to throw up. A metal can stood in the corner, brimming with discarded coffee cups.

The man in uniform cleared his throat and stroked his bushy mustache downward. "Your husband committed vehicular assault today, Mrs. Birch. Everyone is unharmed physically, thank goodness. But, um, we still have a situation to deal with."

"Is Michael all right? Where is he?"

"We'll take you to him in just a moment." The policeman tapped his pen on the table. "Apparently what happened—"

"It was road rage," the other man at the table interrupted. He was older, his mustache as white as ice. He was wearing a turquoise Seahawks t-shirt. "He got pissed at me for some reason, I have no idea why, and he rammed me."

"He what?"

"With his truck. Then he backed up and rammed me again."

"Under normal circumstances, your husband would face numerous charges." With the pen tip, the policeman counted them off on his fingers. "Vehicular assault, destruction of property, disturbing the peace, moving violations, um, disorderly conduct, resisting arrest—"

"But I saw the parking stickers on his bumper," the older man broke in again. "Camp White, Camp Withycombe. So I knew he was a veteran."

Everyone paused at that point. They were staring at me.

I nodded. "He served three deployments."

"As a sniper," the older man said. Perhaps he was testing whether Michael had told him the truth.

"He's a mechanic," I replied. "Normally he runs a motor pool. But his last deployment was primarily a sharpshooting assignment."

"How many kills did he have?"

I sat back in my chair. Did they really want to know? Did they want to hear about the nightmares? Should I describe for them how he had not touched me intimately, not once, in the five months since he'd returned?

Maybe I should recite to them the suicide statistics from this war? Or inform them that there had been an error, that the real Michael Birch was left behind in the sand somewhere, and would they please go find him and bring him back to me?

The men at the table were leaning forward, waiting. The one in the black suit was inspecting his shoes. I imagined that on the other side of the mirror, someone else was listening more closely now too.

It felt as if I'd been assigned a role: You are the wife of a returning soldier, now we want to watch you act like one. Their desire felt almost pornographic. I crossed my arms. "I'd like to see my husband now, please."

Both men at the table let out a long breath.

"Because I'm a veteran as well," the older man said. "Classic grunt of the Mekong Delta. U.S. Army, Vietnam, sixty-nine to seventy-two."

"Me too," the police officer added. "Desert Storm, Army National Guard, Kuwait-based engineering logistics support group, nineteen ninety-one."

"Well, thank you both for your service." I could not guess where the conversation was going. My mouth was a Sahara. "And?"

"We want to give your husband a break," the policeman said. "Anyone who watches the news knows that the, um, the re-entry experience has been tough for this latest group of soldiers, all over the country." He glanced at the others before continuing. "We have all agreed on this. We're not going to charge him with anything today."

"I'm not planning to sue either," the older man added. "He doesn't need me making his life any harder."

"Though his insurance company will still be held responsible for the accident," the policeman said. "Obviously, if he winds up back here for some reason, any reason, there are no third chances. We are going to impound his vehicle for ninety days, too, while he gets his anger under control. I assume he is receiving post-combat counseling?"

I felt that tug again, their curiosity pulling at me. But on the other end of the rope was Michael, who sat somewhere else in this building, in some other gray room. I wanted to protect his privacy, but I also hoped to keep him out of trouble. "He is."

They glanced up to the man by the door. His mustache was thin and groomed. His face did not change expression, but they seemed to take his silence for consent.

"I wrote your husband a citation for following too closely. Hundred and sixty dollars and two points on his license," the officer said, sliding papers across the desk. "What it really means is that he'll be on the hook for both vehicles' deductibles. I've attached an incident report for the insurers. Also a sheet on where to claim his truck later. Your husband was uninjured, but he may want to keep an eye on that shoulder. It took quite a bump."

"Thank you." I gathered the papers and folded them in half, as if that would help somehow, or reduce Michael's shame. "Is that everything?"

"Let's hope so," the older man said. "Let's hope this is the end of it."

The officer stood. "We'll take you to him now."

I rose from the chair, my legs sticking to it a little. Finally I faced the man in the black suit. "What is your part in all of this? What do you do?"

He put one hand on the doorknob and met my stare. "Worry."

Then he opened the door and strode away down the corridor.

COMPARED WITH EVERYONE ELSE in the holding cell, Michael looked like a giant. The cop made me wait in the hall, but I could still see the others: Wiry kids dressed in black, muzzled old guys wearing multiple raincoats, and there was my husband, athletic and healthy. Except for two pierced and tattooed goths huddled in a corner, everyone else sat apart from the others. Michael stood when he saw me, and I could tell he was furious, just bristling with it.

I did not want to think of him as sexy in that moment, but I couldn't help it. He looked like the strong, smart, passionate man I desired damn near every day. That was one more thing I had learned to suppress in this—what had the cop called it?—this re-entry experience.

"Sweetheart, are you all—"

"Please." He raised his hands in the hallway as if I were holding him at gunpoint. "Not one word till we are out of this place."

The officer led us to the front door. "You all take care now," he said. I glanced back and he was still watching us. He even made a modest wave. It contained zero flirtation, I could tell, but instead conveyed concern. I waited till Michael had climbed into the car before returning the gesture.

"I was just coming back from lunch." Michael began speaking before I was fully in the car. "There were no spots along Merchant's Row, and I wanted a coffee. You know they have that nice open place, no hidden corners to make me anxious about crossfire. I went around twice. Nothing. But there was this one car, a classic American SUV, semi-tricked out."

He sounded manic, thousands of miles from the steady man I'd met those years ago. I placed the keys on the dashboard. "OK."

"It was sideways, taking up three spots. The guy had parallel parked in a place where you are supposed to park nose-in. And one of the places he was blocking was a handicap spot."

"Not good," I said.

"Times five, Deb. Not good. So I looked in, feeling suspicious, and he didn't have one of those cards, you know, the wheelchair hanging from his mirror? So I put on my flashers, and stood by his rig, and waited."

"I don't like the sound of this, Michael."

"I'm all peaceful at this point, Deb. Peace-ful. And out he comes, an older guy, big Burl Ives mustache, and he's on his phone. 'Excuse me,' I say, but he just nods hello and keeps talking. 'Hey, man,' I say, but he brushes by. So I jump ahead and stand in front of his door. I've got a good six inches on the guy, so he finally catches on and asks his caller to hold on a second. 'You're in a handicapped spot,' I tell him. First he looks me up and down, then he says, 'I am?' all innocent, like he didn't know. 'That's terrible. I apologize. I'm just getting out of the way right now.'"

"Of course he knew."

"That's right, Deb. The sign is right there. But as I walk over to point it out, he drives off. Just zooms away."

I held the wheel with both hands. "You couldn't let him go."

"Where is his conscience, right? What if I was a disabled person, and he had taken my spot? What if he had blocked one of my wounded buddies? So yes, I followed him, honking and all. Two hundred yards down the road he jammed through a yellow light, to ditch me, I guess, but two guys in a crosswalk had to jump back."

I lowered my forehead to the steering wheel. "And then?"

"I'm sure they told you."

"Not in any detail."

"I waited till the light changed, and I caught up, and then I rammed him. The selfish shit."

"Ouch."

"Rear corner, so lots of parts will need replacing. I bet the frame's bent too."

The triumph in Michael's voice implied that he felt no remorse. Justice had been done. But I checked him with one eye and it was all bravado, all bluff. He was strangely pale, his jaw drawn backward in fear. Not like I'd seen during his night terrors, when we still shared a bed. But a tremor of self-doubt, of wondering whether he had actually been in the wrong. The man had too strong a conscience not to reflect on his actions.

He stroked his short hair back with one hand. "Then for good measure, I rammed him again."

I lifted my head to face him. "Michael, I—"

"Don't start in on me, please. Don't even start."

"I wasn't starting. I was only going to say—"

"Yes you were. You were starting. I could tell." He reached back to pull on his seat belt, wincing as he raised his arm. "This has really pissed me off, Deb, and I have to think hard about what I did."

"Maybe first we could—"

"My life is about fixing cars, not wrecking them. So there's that on my conscience. Plus I am not a fan of being locked up with drunks and losers all afternoon. So I would really appreciate it if you would spare me the lecture and get me home so I can start figuring out how the hell I am going to get to work for the next three months."

I held still, counting to four. "No lecture, Michael. All I wanted to say—"

"Start the car, please. Would you please just start the car?"

So I did. And drove us home in silence. And never said the sentence I had wanted to say and wanted him to hear: Michael, I still love you.

IF THE CULTURAL FOUNDATION of Japan's mission off the Oregon coast in 1942 was the premise that surprise is valorous, the military situation was an equally vital consideration. Thus far the Pacific war had been hugely one-sided.

Pearl Harbor occurred in December of 1941. In the months following, Japan defeated Western armies almost as though there were no resistance. Land forces readily captured the island of Guam in mid-December. By Christmas, Japan had won Hong Kong, ending Britain's long rule. After a fierce two-day battle, Japan likewise forced U.S. troops to surrender on Wake Island.

When the Japanese stormed ashore in Luzon, General Douglas MacArthur had to retreat, pulling his troops down the Bataan Peninsula toward Manila. By New Year's Day, Manila no longer flew the American flag. The Malay Peninsula fell next. Singapore surrendered soon also.

Although Japan's tactics replicated the book published in 1925, the novel contained less brutality. For having supported the British, for example, some five thousand Chinese captured in Singapore were summarily executed.

The march of Japanese victories continued. The Battle of the Java Sea cost America three destroyers and two light cruisers. Japan gained technological advantage with new, long-range torpedoes. Capable of traveling more than five miles, their propulsion left no trail of bubbles to guide ships in evasive maneuvers.

Java fell soon after. Japan won victories in Corregidor, then three posts in Manila Bay known as Forts Hughes, Drum, and Frank, and ultimately all of the Philippine Islands. On April 9, the same date on which Robert E. Lee had surrendered to Ulysses Grant at Appomattox seventy-six years previously, the U.S. force at Bataan capitulated to its Japanese invaders.

Japan's army had planned for twenty-five thousand prisoners of war at Bataan. Instead, there were seventy-six thousand. The forced march these soldiers endured, later aptly named the "Death March," included assaults, starvation, and outright murders. By the time the captured men reached Camp O'Donnell for internment, between seven thousand and ten thousand had died.

Such atrocities inspired rage and retaliation, in time. But for much of 1942, the number and severity of defeats gave a pummeling to American morale. Japan was winning the war decisively.

The imperial high command next approved a surprise invasion of the island called Midway. Victory there could ensure the destruction of the remaining U.S. Pacific fleet. Japan would thereby establish the southern bulkhead of its empire. The northern end, meanwhile, would be the Aleutian Islands of Alaska. Battleships set sail for Midway on May 27, 1942. The Alaskan force launched the following day, with the I-25 submarine among the convoy.

However, the Admiralty had grown overconfident. This time the Americans were ready, thanks to 120 musicians from the sunken ship California. Reassigned as cryptanalysts, they had broken the Japanese military code. U.S. forces knew in advance that the Midway invasion was under way.

A flotilla sped out to meet the Japanese fleet. In an epic clash, four of Japan's twelve aircraft carriers went to the bottom, taking with them many captains, a vice admiral, an admiral, and thousands of men. On June 6, U.S. Admiral Chester Nimitz declared, "Pearl Harbor has now been partially avenged."

Midway marked a turning point in the war. Granted, years of hostilities remained ahead. Guadalcanal, Okinawa, and Iwo Jima would be purchased in blood. But Japan's expansion had nearly reached its zenith.

Yet not all of the drama would occur in the South Pacific. In fact, the day after Nimitz's report, the Japanese captured two American territories in Alaska's Bering Sea. Historians dispute the reasons for Japan's invasion of Attu and Kiska, tiny Alaskan islands offering scant resources. Perhaps they promised a firewall should Russia enter the Pacific war. They might provide an airbase for sorties against the United States.

Whatever the motive, the islands' capture established a vast swath of ocean under Japanese control. From Kiska's latitude of 51 degrees north, following roughly the longitude of 175 degrees east, the domain reached the Solomon Islands at 9 degrees south. That span, 4,100 miles, is greater than the distance from London to Zanzibar, and the domain stretched west all the way to China. Were this area land, Japan's rule would have eclipsed the Roman Empire's.

CHAPTER 4

I WOKE BEFORE IT WAS LIGHT. The new normal. Michael was not in bed. That was normal now too. At night when I switched off the lights he would lie beside me, fully dressed, until I fell asleep. In the morning he was always gone.

Restlessness is contagious, of course; I never slept through the night anymore either. I'd climb out of bed and navigate by the light of various digital clocks—on the bedside table, the TV. I might find him snoring on the couch, still dressed. Or drinking coffee in the kitchen with papers spread all around, and I'd pull out a chair and sit by him with no one talking. I wanted so badly just to hold his hand. Or I'd see his truck was gone, Michael out driving who knows where, and he wouldn't return home till after I'd left for work.

At least that option was nixed for ninety days. Pulling a quilt from the bed, I wrapped it around me and padded through the pre-dawn house. I checked the kitchen first because the little light over the stove was on. There was a coffee mug on the counter, but a sip told me it was cold.

On the table I saw his drawings again.

Now more of the faces were familiar: the sunglasses guy, the one with a scribble next to him, the one with mouse ears, and others whose significance I could only guess. Maybe someday he would clue me in. Thirty-one mysteries.

That morning the pencil beside the papers was broken in the middle.

Was Michael broken in the middle? Was I? What about those people he kept drawing?

Maybe it was all of us. The cop. The Vietnam vet. The Professor. Maybe every single person on earth was broken in the middle.

A blanket on the living room couch showed where Michael had tried to sleep, or had watched TV in the hope of getting bored enough to doze off. Instead, the blanket was wound in a knot.

Finally I found him in the guest room, sleeping on his back on the rug. No blanket, no pillow, beside him a plastic bag filled with water that earlier in the night had probably held ice for his shoulder.

My sister Robin said when her babies were newborns, she could spend hours staring at them. That's how I stood over Michael on that early morning in the gray light. He was large—sometimes I forgot—so much bigger than me. One arm was thrown out wide, but the hand on his stomach was thick and broad. His chest swelled and shrank like a bellows. Keep breathing, lover, just keep breathing.

The bend of his leg reminded me of a weekend trip up to Seattle, one rainy January years back, in a semi-fancy hotel room where we got a little wild. I wound up riding his thigh like a horse until the gallop took possession of me, and I came so hard he laughed afterward. The memory brought a wave of longing so strong my knees almost buckled.

Now his head had fallen to one side, and it appeared uncomfortable. I took a pillow from the guest bed and tucked it under his neck. It didn't wake him. Spreading the quilt over both of us, I nestled under his arm. Michael shifted, and I worried that he might roll on his side, with his back to me. He started that way, but his hurt shoulder made him turn back, and I moved with him so that we wound up spooning.

As Michael's arm circled my waist, his hand came up and cupped my breast, warm and still. No caress, he just held me, steady, and continued to sleep.

Dear God, what I felt to be touched by him. I lay there with eyes wide.

LATER, AFTER DAWN, I heard my alarm from the other room. Michael had returned to sleeping on his back, so I was able to slip away. While a pot of coffee brewed, I checked email from work. Central Office wanted to know if I was returning to the Professor's that day, and I replied yes. I was in for the duration if he was.

Before leaving for Lake Oswego, I checked on Michael. He was awake and putting down his cell phone. "Gary's coming by to bring me in today. I'll see at work about getting a ride back."

"I'd be happy to pick you up on my way home."

Wincing, he stretched his shoulder forward and back. "I'm the one who made this stupid mess. I should be the one to clean it up."

EIGHT YEARS HAD PASSED since I finished my social work degree, and somehow I had not returned to the Portland State University campus once. I'd expected to visit often, to attend lectures or audit conferences. But then I moved in with Michael, and work proved to be plenty educational.

Not to mention pouring all my time into patient care. I couldn't see myself informing some dying man or woman, "Hey, I'd love to stay and help you with your anguish, but I have to go hear a lecture on anguish."

Still, I pulled onto campus that morning feeling as though I had been missing something. Maybe I would try harder to follow department doings. Not long ago, those people had been my kin.

The parking lot I'd used was serving as a staging area for construction of a new building, so I had to hunt for a place to park. Then I hoofed it over to the library, a U-shaped building of glass with giant stone monoliths at either end. Everyone I passed on the sidewalk seemed incredibly young. Which probably meant that, to them, I looked incredibly old.

That early in the day, only a few people were working in the computer area. I sat at a terminal, and they did not even lift their heads. My old screen name and password were still valid—like access to the library, a little gift to local alumni.

When I searched nonfiction books in stock for the name Reed, the screen listed a biography of former U.S. House Speaker Thomas Reed, and a collector's guide to fine china by Alan Reed. That was all. I did another query under Reed, B., and the sole item was a textbook on quantum mechanics by B. Cameron Reed.

"Pardon me," I said to the young woman at the information desk.

She wore a Chinese-style military jacket, and below her ear she had a tattoo of a turtle. Such a tender place. I wondered how much the needle had hurt.

The young woman set aside a textbook she was reading; the cover said something about chemistry. "How can I help you?"

"I'm looking for books by Barclay Reed. The historian."

"One second." She slapped keys with the speed and punch of an airline attendant dealing with an overbooked flight. "I'm finding several Reeds. What did you say the first name was?"

"Barclay."

She ran her thumb down the right-hand side of the screen. "Barclay, Barclay. Nope. Sorry. No books here by that guy."

That was puzzling. "Why would the university library not have a former professor's books?"

She shrugged. "No idea. Let's try books in print."

The young woman pounded away on her keyboard. "Here we go, there's a bunch of them. Just none on our shelves, for some reason. Weird."

"Are they about World War II?"

"Titles look that way. I can try interlibrary loan, if you want. He'd probably be on the shelves at Lewis and Clark. It takes two days."

"No thanks." I backed away. "I'll figure something else out."

CHERYL WAS STANDING in the garden when I arrived that morning. I couldn't help giggling. "Did he evict you?"

"The Professor is having stomach discomfort. He does not like to pass gas with a woman in the house. Aren't these azaleas lovely?"

They really were, extravagant pink bushes along the house's side yard. The rest of the garden was mathematical, as if it had been mapped on paper before anything was planted. "Do you think he did this landscaping?"

"Once upon a time, perhaps. But I'm afraid his gardening days are ended."

"I suppose." And then I heard his voice, booming inside the house. Cheryl had left the front door open a few inches. "The call of duty," I said.

Cheryl gave my arm a squeeze. "Have an interesting day."

"SHE HAD THE TEMERITY TO RETURN," he said, snapping the newspaper to keep it upright between us. "Bravo for Nurse Birch. I wager at the office they all say, 'What a plucky gal she is.'"

I stood at the foot of his bed. "I have something to get off my chest."

"Don't we all?"

"I suppose. But my own conscience is enough for me to worry about. And I would appreciate the courtesy of face-to-face for one minute, please."

Ever so slowly he lowered the top half of the newspaper. His hair remained in its upright shock, his eyes glinting with mischief. He must have had a good night's sleep. "Proceed."

"I was not completely truthful yesterday about something."

"Let me guess. You're not actually a nurse. I could have determined that by the degree of competence you demonstrated."

This man was a skilled conversational swordsman, thrust and parry and hop out of range. Regardless, I fenced on. "I told you the truth when I said I didn't strike your gong yesterday. But I did touch it."

He dropped his arms, crumpling the newspaper in his lap. "Everyone touches it, Nurse Birch. That gong is irresistible."

"Maybe so. Anyway maybe that touch was what you heard."

"I didn't hear anything. I simply wished to reveal to you how predictable and common you are. How unspecial." He frowned at the newspaper. "I was being a . . . I believe your word is 'tester.' You failed."

And he snapped the pages up between us again.

LATER IN THE DAY, the Professor permitted me to bathe him.

By that time in their illness some people have lost modesty, the body a flagrant display of medical facts they no longer have the stamina to deny. But for most patients I've cared for, it's important to maintain every modicum of dignity possible. The ego relinquishes its powers with a reluctance that I do not judge, but rather admire.

I remember Tanya, a woman with ovarian cancer who insisted that I refresh her bright red lipstick every two hours. Easy enough. I met Tanya's need like clockwork. After she died, the first thing I did was apply a fresh layer.

There was Ted, a fireman with an inoperable stomach tumor. His wife made a poster of an old news photo that showed him carrying a limp boy from a building, the background all smoke and flames. The boy, Ted told me nearly every day, survived. The last time I saw that fireman, he was flattened with illness. But he still had the strength to hook a thumb at the poster and whisper one word to me: "Lived."

I love that. I love the times that people celebrate themselves for as long as they can. All dead people are the same. No two living people are.

BARCLAY REED WAS TOO FRAIL to lower himself into the tub, much less lift himself out. Assuming he would be of the modest kind, I managed to keep a dark blue hand towel draped over his privates the whole time. Likewise, I remained perfectly matter-of-fact while drying him off.

But after dressing the Professor, I did not take him directly back to bed. Instead I wheeled his chair around from the living room and sat him in it.

"Are we off to the rodeo, Nurse Birch?" he asked. "Giddyap."

I draped a blanket over his shoulders, which of course made me think of covering Michael a few hours earlier. I hoped my husband's day was going well. I had resolved not to check on him. He had made clear his wishes to reckon with yesterday's mishap on his own. Still, I was allowed to worry.

I rolled the Professor to the sliding doors and pushed one back. It was a cloudy day, the lake as still as a painting. I wheeled him out on the dock, then locked the brakes.

"Such adventures you take me on, Nurse Birch. I feel intrepid."

"Did you swim from here very often?"

He shook his head. "Swimming prunes the skin and makes a body clammy."

Well. So much for my fantasy of taking a dip from that deck. Lake Oswego would remain unsullied by the unwashed likes of me.

The Professor continued: "I live here because of the light."

"Off the water, you mean? I love that too."

"That is not in the least what I mean. Please do not speak for me. Save that for when I am dead."

I let the word hang there, not responding, letting him know that it did not frighten me, that I felt no awkwardness or hurry to fill the silence and thereby mute what he had said.

Sure enough, a moment later he spoke again. "The light I mean is the dawn. The eastward view is finest at the break of day. I have few regrets in this life. But had I known the extent to which the last phase would confine me, I would have installed a larger bedroom window to allow the early light."

"If you like, Professor, I can come earlier in the day, and bring you out here for the sunrise as long as your energy lasts."

"Nurse Birch, that idea . . ." Instead of finishing the sentence, he closed his eyes and breathed with it for a while. He opened his eyes again. "That may be the first genuinely intelligent suggestion you have made."

"Thank you. I think." And I let him see me smiling.

But he coughed into his fist. "At this juncture, I must content myself with memory. I have seen a great many sunrises here. They must suffice."

"If you change your mind, let me know. Because the offer stands."

He said nothing for a while. A motorboat trolled past, sleek and clean, making a small wake that slapped the dock but did not splash. The couple on board waved to us. I waited, not responding, hoping to see the Professor raise one hand. They had turned forward by the time he did, a tepid gesture but at least he had acknowledged them.

"A great many sunrises, you said. Have you lived here a long time?"

"That is the only way an academic can afford a palace such as this," Barclay Reed sniffed. "By purchasing his house decades before a glorified pond becomes a domain of luxury and wealth."

"That reminds me." I moved in front of him. "A strange thing happened today. I went to the university library to check out one of your books."

"That is indeed strange, Nurse Birch. My work is not the sort of popular pulp with which I suspect you normally amuse yourself."

I was learning to let the Professor's insults go. They were a habit of his, condescension by reflex, and had no sting. "Actually, the strange thing was that they didn't have your writing there. Not one copy of one book."

His eyebrows rose. "Is that so?"

"I'm all done fibbing with you, Professor."

"Blast it all." He was grinning. "How perfectly proper of them."

"You're not surprised?"

His smile vanished. "What if I told you that in August of 1945, after two mass murders by atomic detonation, the American military possessed two more bombs, ready for use? That, had the Japanese not surrendered, our nation was prepared to destroy two more cities and kill everyone in them?"

"Is that true?"

"You tell me, Nurse Birch."

"I don't know, Professor. I've never heard about two more bombs."

"But do you believe me? That is my primary concern."

"I guess. Why wouldn't I?"

"Why not, indeed." He rubbed his bony hands together. "Furthermore, what if I told you that the Allies dropped thousands of leaflets on Hiroshima and Nagasaki beforehand, urging people to run for their lives?"

"We warned them? How could I have spent a full year of high school history on World War II and never heard about that?"

"And yet you believe me?"

"Well, you're blowing my mind a bit. But sure, I believe you."

"Fair enough." The professor spun his wheelchair to face me. "In my view, both uses of atomic weapons were justified. More to my point, however, may we stipulate that there remain significant untold stories from the Pacific theater of World War II?"

I had no idea how these questions connected to his books not being in the library. But the Professor was more fervent than I'd seen him. This was energy far beyond his insults, and I would not interrupt. "All right."

"Might we also agree that there could be keen interest among the public in learning such things? Might a scholar expect that his research on this topic would be in high demand?"

"Which topic? I'm not quite following you."

But the Professor was not speaking to me any longer. He had wheeled his chair back and was orating to the lake. "Now to the heart of our argument. Let us take as given that human ambition is a vile, pernicious form of entropy." He was not lecturing. He was ranting, and at an increasing volume. "Let us imagine a doctoral student, bright and able and oh so ambitious, an acolyte whom a professor therefore entrusts with certain discoveries in confidence, in advance of their publication. Might that young scholar experience a temptation to appropriate the findings for himself?"

"Wait. Someone stole your ideas?"

His fists pounded the chair arms. "Yes, blast it, yes. He might have succeeded too, but for a fortuitous coincidence. A faculty member on his thesis panel also served as history editor of the university press. When the young man presented a dissertation abstract nearly identical to my new book proposal, the editor knew at once that someone had plagiarized. He confronted the student, who alleged that I had filched his work." Barclay Reed shook his head. "It was admirably brazen."

"You put up a fight, of course."

"Nurse Birch, try to understand." Barclay Reed held out both hands, weighing each side of the argument as if he were a scale. "The young man was my protégé, whereas I was one semester shy of retirement. He stood at the dawn of his career, while I hardly needed one more publication for my résumé." He lowered his hands. "I believed it would be gallant to step aside, a graybeard making room for the young novice. Moreover, I assumed that with my imminent move to emeritus status, the whole dispute would evaporate."

"So what happened?"

The Professor took a moment to regain himself, clearing his throat, making a little circle with the point of his chin. "I miscalculated."

"What does that mean?"

"Seniority and reputation cannot solve all problems. Instead, the young man was lionized, whereas I experienced academic exile. Forget thirty-eight years on the faculty. Colleagues snubbed me in the hallway and department meetings. They declined to return my calls. There were no fond farewells, no retirement dinners, no valedictories."

"What about your book?"

"At the university press, the proposal died of editorial neglect. I sought publication elsewhere, without success. One day I spotted Townsend, a former colleague, at a restaurant here by the lake. I confronted him, and he delivered the truth. No one believed my proposal was true. Oh, they could verify certain details to know it was not complete fabrication. But the rest was less easily confirmed, and my credibility too damaged." He chopped a hand down. "It was like a guillotine blow."

"That all sounds so unfair," I said. "But it only involves your last book. Why take your old ones off the shelf? It's not like they stopped being true."

The Professor was calming now, or tiring, and he only shrugged. "It was a scandal. Universities experience them routinely, yet never know what response will be appropriate. I suppose I didn't either, or my self-defense would not have been as much of a nolo contendere."

"I don't know what that means."

"Perhaps you will look it up, when next you visit the library." The Professor pulled his blanket tighter. "Bring me inside, please. I'm feeling chilled."

NORMALLY MICHAEL WOULD HAVE BEEN HOME by the time I arrived. Somehow I knew without going inside that the house was empty. But I did not panic. He'd had to work out a ride, and that probably meant waiting. I took out my phone, confirmed that there were no messages, and put it away without calling him. Pestering would not help, nor bring him home any sooner.

The day had turned humid, and our home was not air conditioned, so I went through all the rooms, opening windows. I started the fan in the kitchen.

That was when I noticed that Michael had forgotten to turn my computer off. I sat and slipped off my sandals while the screen saver paged between photos of a slideshow I'd assembled years back: Michael in uniform about to ship out, my grad-school commencement in cap and gown, the kite surfers soaring behind our wedding.

As a social work student you find yourself opening all kinds of websites, to observe all sorts of social ills. So I'd been taught to clear the history after every online session. Michael said I was fooling myself, the Internet was designed to be the opposite of privacy. But I'd continued the practice at home, maintaining the hope that my searches, emails, and purchases were somehow not subject to snooping and tracking. Michael might have been right, but it was what I preferred to believe.

At that moment, the screen saver photos showed only one thing to me: temptation. I could spy on Michael's searches, and he would never know. Or I could honor his privacy, and he would never know. He might be shopping for a truck, checking bus schedules, ogling breasts. None of it was my business, unless I chose to make it so.

No. I was not going to be that kind of wife. Michael deserved an uninvaded life. Besides, I didn't need to spy. In general terms, I already knew what his issues were. What my husband needed was the tincture of time. That phrase comes from the bereavement part of hospice work, based on a crude but accurate truth: Emotional pain, no matter how severe, does diminish after a while, because time is somehow merciful.

No. His dignity mattered more than my curiosity. I moved the mouse to shut the system down, only to find that he had not even closed the sites he'd visited. One by one they refreshed before me. I was about to see some revelations in spite of myself.

The first one was an update on Iraq, towns secured, offensives under way, who controlled which cities. To my eyes it was chaos, as if Michael and his fellow soldiers had never been there. I clicked to end his session.

But one of the blogs remained up, three screens of it, so I had to close each one separately. There was no way to avoid looking.

It was called "Coming Home." The first screen was called "Great Expectations" and it offered five steps for convincing friends, family members, and co-workers to lower their expectations of you. When I closed that one, the next was "Guilty Conscience." It opened by describing a unit that had received incorrect intelligence and killed an innocent family, and how the soldiers were struggling to re-enter home life. That one I wanted to read, because I knew Michael's conscience was what kept him awake.

The last one bore another headline that hooked me: "Eight Signs Your Mental Health Is in Trouble." The first sign, in bold: You contemplate acts of violence. I closed that one as fast as I could.

And then the screen was blank. By habit, I went to clear the history, and discovered that I could also review any site visited since the last clearing. I hovered the cursor over that command.

"Hey, Deb."

I wheeled in my chair, heart in my throat. "God, you startled me."

Michael leaned against the doorframe. "Sorry. Just got home."

I took him in, his forehead shiny with sweat, his shirt darkened on the chest and under his arms. "Did you walk the whole way from the shop?"

He took a long draw from the glass of water in his hand. "I guess I did."

"Aren't you roasting?"

"Times two. But I liked it. I liked moving slowly."

"Oh. That's good, honey." By then I had collected myself. "Welcome home. Be with you in one second."

I turned to finish shutting the computer down, then spun the chair back to stand and give him a kiss, but Michael had already put his glass in the sink. He stood at the kitchen door. "I'm going to walk some more, Deborah. It might be good for me."

"Want some company?" I reached to pull my sandals back on.

But he shook his head. "Don't hold dinner."

Just like that he was gone, out into the sweltering evening. The screen door slammed behind him. And I wondered: What are they? Those eight signs that your mental health is in trouble?

IN ADDITION TO JAPANESE CULTURE and military successes, one other ingredient was critical to the I-25 submarine's Oregon mission: anemic American morale.

The effectiveness of Japan's warring had given the United States an unprecedented sense of vulnerability. President Roosevelt articulated as much in one of his fireside chats: "The broad oceans which have been heralded in the past as our protection from attack have become endless battlefields on which we are constantly being challenged by our enemies."

Anxiety found nationwide expression. The day after Pearl Harbor, based on rumors that an attack was imminent, Oakland closed its schools and ordered a blackout. Lieutenant General John DeWitt of the Western Defense Command proclaimed: "Last night there were planes over this community. They were enemy planes. I mean Japanese planes."

Similar rumors struck the East Coast. Fighter planes scrambled from Mitchel Field on Long Island to intercept enemy aircraft less than two hours away. Schools closed. Stocks on Wall Street plummeted.

There were no planes over Oakland, no bombers approaching Manhattan.

In 1942, only months prior to the I-25 mission, Los Angeles also experienced a panic. Air raid sirens sounded throughout the county. Just after three A.M., the Thirty-seventh Coast Artillery Brigade began firing antiaircraft shells. The shooting lasted an hour, with more than 1,400 shells fired—approximately one every three seconds.

Afterward, no one in a position of command could state with clarity what the troops had been firing at. Secretary of the Navy Frank Knox declared the entire incident a false alarm. Knox's diagnosis: "war nerves." After the war ended, Japanese officials said they had no aircraft in the vicinity at the time.

If hearsay could generate panic on that scale, imagine the power of actual fires. Civilians would scatter like ants. Dousing the blaze would require massive resources. Americans, convinced of superior Japanese military organization and ferocity, would lose their stomach for fighting the sons of samurai. *Shouri.*

Or so went the reasoning within the Imperial Navy. Thus did the admirals dispatch the I-25 to Oregon. It was one of twenty submarines of a new design. At 2,600 tons, these ships were large by the standards of the day: 357 feet long and 30.5 feet across. They were powered by twin diesels, 12,400 horsepower each, plus two 2,000-horsepower electric motors for silent running.

This class of subs was fast. Submerged, they could make 8 knots (9 mph), but their surface top speed was 23.5 knots (27 mph). Thus they could cover some 600 miles in a day. Perhaps their greatest value, however, was range: 25,928 miles—three times the extent of Allied subs. These vessels could sail around the globe without refueling. They were therefore dangerously well suited to conducting offensives all the way across the world's largest ocean.

The I-25 carried several deck weapons, including a pair of 25-mm machine guns. The main gun fired 5.5-inch shells, the explosive portion of which measured nearly 18 inches and weighed 60 pounds. This gun had a range of nine miles and sat on the stern for two reasons. The first was to leave room for a catapult on the bow, more on which in a moment. The other was to enable the ship to be shelling as it escaped.

Lastly, the I-25 had six torpedo tubes. It had sunk the British Derrymore, as well the Fort Camosun, a Canadian freighter carrying war supplies for England.

Yet in September 1942 the submarine's primary weapon was its passenger. He sat below while the weather stormed. Imagine the atmosphere: diesel motors chugging, water leaking in one seam or another, sweaty sailors, food odors, smoke from Kinshi cigarettes, and under it all the sharp scent of human fear.

CHAPTER 5

WHEN I OPENED THE PROFESSOR'S FRONT DOOR, I saw that Cheryl had pulled one of the dining chairs into the entry. Rising from the seat, she held a finger to her lips.

"What's up?" I whispered.

"We had a rough night last night."

"Sorry to hear that."

She motioned me into the living room, where she recapped the previous eight hours. "He just got grouchier and grouchier."

I scanned her notes on his chart. "For this one, that sounds normal."

"Way worse. Shouting at the television, at me, at his own body. I came in and he was jabbing himself in the side with one of the remotes. Look—" She went to the kitchen counter, bringing back a remote controller. The plastic casing was split. "It was like he was trying to stab his own kidney."

"Ouch. How much pain medicine did you give him?"

"He declined everything. He said lucidity was his only strength. Also that he did not trust me."

"Cheryl, he doesn't trust any of us." I turned the cracked device over in my hand. Broken pencils, broken remotes, that kind of a morning. "Does he have any notion of what's ahead?"

Cheryl peered at me over her glasses. "Who would have told him?"

"Someone must have. I mean he has already given explicit orders against more diagnostic testing. He did that in writing when Timmy was here."

Cheryl took the remote and tapped it against her chin. "We don't need tests to know what the situation here is, do we?"

"Not really. So what did you do?"

"I tried to reason with him. It was clear he was in tremendous pain. About two hours ago, he finally gave in. Like he'd set a goal of sunrise? It was a miserable haul until then, poor guy. I gave him a good dose, and now he's getting a deep break. If lucidity is one of his values, though, that's far from ideal. If we could just convince him to let us get ahead of it . . ."

"I'm with you," I said. "And there's my goal for the day."

"I don't know." Cheryl smirked. "With what it took to get that pain under control, I hope you brought something to read. He'll be out for a while."

Barclay Reed snoozed till afternoon, waking with a bundle of needs. Because he'd slept with his mouth open, he was desperately thirsty. I refilled his jug and brought a fresh straw. He sucked and gulped, the whole time keeping his eyes trained on me. I suspect the Professor intended to appear intimidating; actually, he looked like a little boy. I offered to wipe his gums with glycerin too, to re-establish decent pH and moisture levels. But once I'd prepared the swab, he snatched it from me and did the job himself.

Although the task was less strenuous than brushing his teeth, it left him depleted. I took the stick from his lax fingers and tossed it in the trash.

The morphine had corked the Professor's digestion, too. I gave him a mild laxative and heated some apple-onion soup I'd brought earlier. Then I spoon-fed him, his arms flaccid on the bed while he gulped and swallowed and opened his mouth for more. When I set the bowl aside, perhaps to prove he had the strength, he lifted one hand to scratch his chin. Instantly he frowned at me, hard, with his whole face.

"What is it?" I said. "What do you need?"

"Someone here that I can trust."

I didn't blink. "To perform what task?"

"Nurse Birch, I am a highly credentialed scholar. I have a PhD, and thirty-one years with tenure. I've published nine books, each one recognized for its depth, substance, and historical import."

"Yes, I know. Very impressive."

"Yet look at me."

"I'd say your color is pretty good for the night you just had."

"Not my color, blast it." He bugged his eyes at me in disbelief. "My whiskers. I am not some pseudo-scholar, hiding his ignorance behind the costume sagacity of a beard. I am accustomed to impeccability. Today, between my fatigue and that contemptible dullard medicine your night witch forced upon me, I lack the stamina to maintain a proper appearance."

It was true. He had a white scruff on his neck and face, though to me it didn't look bad. "Would you like me to shave you?"

"Nurse Birch, would I like to swim in a river filled with crocodiles? Of course not. But if it is the only way to reach the other side?"

"You could wait till someone else comes, someone you place more confidence in."

"And risk a colleague or former student visiting and finding me like this? Unacceptable."

I was about to say that he did not seem to have guests of that kind, or visitors at all, when I realized how cruel it would sound. "Professor Reed, here's what I'd like to suggest. How about if I shave you, and you coach me all the way? Every step, and we'll do it just the way you like."

He narrowed his eyes at me.

I smiled. "I suspect you might even enjoy giving me instruction."

"Bah. You annoy me, Nurse Birch. But what alternative do I have?"

He was fussy, and I loved it. We spent easily five minutes getting the water in the sink to the proper temperature—which I thought was just shy of scalding but he praised as ideal. I locked his wheelchair in front of the mirror and watched him stretch to see his reflection, while I rolled up my sleeves and placed towels on his chest to shield him from the wet.

The Professor used an old-fashioned brush and a bar of bay-scented shaving soap. Fortunately, his razor was normal. He barked at me to shape his sideburns identically; they had to be perfect before I could move on to anywhere else. I did just as he commanded.

Over the next few minutes, though, the atmosphere changed. As I proceeded down his face, and across, he couldn't speak or I might cut him. And I was bent close, concentrating. Inch by inch down the length of his frame, Barclay Reed began to relax. Maybe it was the hot water, the humid room, or maybe the simple experience of allowing someone to care for him.

The feelings were mutual. For me, there was the gratification of providing an intimate service without compromising his dignity. It was not just a bit of hygienic care; it was also a meeting place. By the time he raised his chin so I could shave his throat, the Professor was calm and still.

When I had finished, I razored over everything again, drained the soapy water, and washed his whiskers from the sides of the sink. He remained quiet the whole time. I was in no mood to break the spell. I toweled his face dry and set his shaving kit exactly where it had been beforehand.

"Where did you learn to do that?" he said at last.

"I used to shave my husband. I did it for years."

"Every day?"

"If we weren't in a hurry."

"Your concentration revealed something, however." Barclay Reed assessed his reflection, turning his face this way and that. "You don't do it anymore."

I continued drying my hands. "How do you know that?"

He ignored my question. "What happened?"

I drew back one step. He wanted to walk on personal ground.

It seemed that the Professor had softened the slightest bit, his eyes one degree less pinched. Also he had shown concern for me, which I hadn't expected. I hesitated. I wanted the moment to last. Then I relaxed the professionalism an inch, almost the way he had lowered the newspaper a day before. "He had to go away for a while. When he came back, he didn't want me to shave him anymore."

"Nonsense. It is a great pleasure to be shaved. Where did he go to learn such foolishness?"

"To war," I said. "He went away to war."

The Professor moved his chin in a circle, stretching his neck as though he wore a too-tight tie. "A dark place to obtain an education. Nonetheless, I would imagine any husband who survived a war would want his wife to shave him more than ever."

Ouch. But I nodded. "So you would think."

"That change is quite articulate about your overall situation."

I didn't answer.

"Yes. Diminished intimacy. Reduced contact. Perhaps loneliness."

I sat there, thinking: See if I ever lower my guard with you again, mister.

The Professor cleared his throat. "Do something with me, Nurse Birch."

"Excuse me?"

"Anything. I have missed an entire morning and some of the afternoon, out of the frustratingly small supply remaining to me. I'm desperate to do something so the day is not an entire waste."

I roused myself. This patient had just caused me pain, speaking about Michael with such accuracy. But the situation in this house was not about me; providing hospice care was always about the patient. Also I happened to know exactly where we could go.

IT TOOK EFFORT TO PILOT HIS WHEELCHAIR through the garden without bogging down or harming the plants. He raised a hand to stop me when we reached the azaleas, which were at their peak: abundant, pink, and fragrant.

The Professor scowled. "Don't you find them shameful?"

"Should I?"

"They are so flagrant. So unapologetic."

"That's how they attract bees, though. They have to be showy to survive."

"If only there were an analogous opportunity for me," he said. "I would willingly perfume myself and wear pink if that would prolong my life."

I chuckled. "Actually, a few things could make a difference. In how long you live and how well you live. If you want, I can tell you about them."

"If I want." He folded his hands in his lap. I was standing behind him, holding the wheelchair handles, so I could not see his face. "What I want, Nurse Birch, is to know what will occur. Likely you know as much about death as I do about the Pacific Theater in 1942."

"I doubt that, Professor Reed."

"Don't patronize me. I am asking for something important." He pointed at a little wrought-iron bench in the garden. "Sit there, please, and tell me in plain language."

The bench was painted dark glossy green. I sat leaning forward, forearms on my thighs, putting our faces on the same level. "Ask away."

He cleared his throat. "My prognosis, please. The unvarnished truth."

Barclay Reed had gone to that place right away. I read it to mean that he was prepared to hear everything. "You have kidney cancer with multiple metastases. The five-year survival rate is five percent."

"I presume the process is irreversible?"

"Yes."

I expected a reaction, but the Professor only nodded. "Continue."

"Well. You may experience more pain, worse than last night, because there are bones involved." I slowed because I was nearing the crux. "Last night you declined help for your symptoms, which is your prerogative. But I urge you to reconsider." I stood, stepping toward him. "For many patients—"

"Halt right there. No drama, Nurse Birch. Just give me the prognosis."

"All right." I went back to the bench. The stones beneath were coated with moss. I looked at his profile, the large old man's nose, his stubborn jaw. "What else would you like to know?"

"A great deal." The Professor bent forward, his face inches from the pink blossoms. He took a noisy sniff. "For now, tell me this: What goes last?"

"What do you mean?"

He blew on the petals, which fluttered from his breath. I thought, what ideal circumstances for this conversation. When it is time to hear some of life's hardest news, who would not want his face surrounded by flowers?

"At present, I am enjoying a floral scent. My sense of smell and my appreciation of it prove that I remain a sentient being. At some point I will cease to be sentient. What will be the last part of Barclay Reed to go?"

"Oh, I see. The ears go last. Research indicates that hearing functions till the very end. Which creates an important opportunity, actually. If there is something you'd like to be hearing, a favorite piece of music, or—"

"Ha." He sat back. "I know precisely what I would like to hear at the end."

"What is it? I can make sure that happens for you."

He scoffed. "Impossible."

"It's not, though. I've done that many times. Especially with music."

"I said it is impossible."

I knew better than to push. Another day.

Meanwhile the Professor ran his hands up and down the chair arms. "How long will all of this take?"

I dug my thumbnail into the bench's metal scrollwork. "It's hard to predict."

"Nurse Birch, you are weakest when you are evasive."

"I'm not evading anything. Each person is different."

"Your best estimate, then."

"Anywhere from four weeks to ten."

"What? The oncologist told me six months at a minimum."

"Oncologists know lots of things that I don't," I said. "But they are notoriously over-optimistic. Maybe he wanted to give you hope."

"Hope?" The Professor sneered. "To a dying man, hope is a cruel lie."

"No sir," I said. "There are many kinds of hope. You can hope to live longer. You can hope to complete unfinished business, professional or financial. Or spiritual."

His frown was instantaneous. "Oh please."

"Well," I persisted. "You can hope to minimize your suffering."

"You keep bringing that up," he said, leaning into the azaleas again. "Why?"

"I want you to consider preemptive analgesia."

"Continue."

"If a nerve gets energized, it takes more medicine to quiet it. But if you act before the problem starts, it requires less dosage. You can still function."

Now his face was immersed, petals against his newly smooth cheeks. "At this point in my life, I do not desire to become addicted to anything."

"Addiction? I'm describing how to avoid suffering. Last night—"

"Enough, Nurse Birch." He sat back, fingers still holding a blossom. "Apart from evangelizing on doping me, this conversation has been illuminating."

"Is that how you would describe it?"

"Is any question more fundamental than what the extent of our existence will be? Now I know: four to ten weeks. If you are in error, we may stipulate that it is not a matter of four to ten years, or four to ten months."

"I would like to help you keep that time as fulfilling as possible."

"What makes you think my life was fulfilling before I became ill?"

I pointed. "The flowers in your hand."

The Professor jerked back as if the plant had stung him. He drew himself upright, wheelchair seat creaking. "Thank you for bringing me here. Now"—he waved a hand at the front door—"I don't want to miss the news."

BARCLAY REED DID FINE for most of the day, but at about four he started shivering. I turned off his AC, piled blankets on the bed, and brought him warm tea. But he shook in every limb. I placed a hand on his forehead and there was no fever. He had just taken a chill.

Melissa arrived, eager as ever. But when I went into his room to say good-bye, he looked miserable.

"Professor Reed," I said. "I don't want to leave you in this condition."

"Come, Nurse Birch. Worried about a bad grade on your job evaluation?"

"I hate to see a person suffer, especially when it is preventable."

A shudder passed through his whole frame, his jaw rattling. "Blast you."

"I am not the disease," I told him.

"Nor are you the cure."

"Why won't you let me help you?"

The Professor sniffed. "I have my reasons."

"You think this is stoicism but actually it is pride."

His eyes flashed. "You dare to lecture me about stoicism? Have you ever read the Stoics?"

"I don't even know who they are."

He threw his hands up, as if to say how could anyone converse with such a know-nothing.

"Forgive me then, Professor Reed." I stood and gathered my things. "I will go look up who the Stoics were. But I have no interest in standing by while you refuse to use your own powers of reason."

I suppose I knew just where to dig at him. I had just reached the door when he called out.

"Wait."

"Yes, Professor?"

He wrestled with himself, trying not to shiver. It lasted a few seconds, then his body was shaking again. "What did you call it? Preemptive?"

"Analgesia. Yes, sir."

He thrust his jaw forward as if he was furious with me. "This once."

I gave him a smaller dose than Cheryl had, in a time-release formulary so it would not knock him out. Then I sat in his kitchen and wrote a pain management plan for Melissa and whoever followed. By the time I left, the Professor was watching the BBC world report. All was calm.

"Have a good night," I called from the doorway.

He pointed a remote at me. "Don't you gloat."

ONE CHALLENGE HOSPICE WORKERS FACE is that our jobs are so intense, returning to the normal world can cause emotional whiplash. When you spend the day facing death, ordinary life can seem petty. Often, people who can't find a reliable re-entry routine just burn out.

I was lucky with Michael, and I remember the day I realized it. My patient at the time was a legitimately tough guy, Cleon, the longtime bus driver and all around strong-arm of a halfway house for troubled boys. A tall, dignified man, he had the nastiest case of Crohn's disease I'd ever seen: mouth sores, skin pustules, plus the usual digestive misery. Cleon quit his Marlboros when the illness put him to bed, but he still had a masterpiece hack of a cough. He was strong though, like a bulldozer, and so committed to his quiet wife and to helping those misdirected boys, he would not die.

Every day was worse, weight loss and complications, but Cleon refused to let go. I helped with symptoms the best I could, but there was little mercy for him, and the hours stretched long. The man was suffering.

One evening I stopped in the supermarket on the way home, and found myself waiting at the dairy case while a woman was choosing which eggs to buy. For some reason the shelves were not as full as usual. She opened carton after carton, finding a broken egg in each one. I stood there, not saying a thing, while the woman tried one after another.

"Can you believe it?" she said to me finally, holding the latest carton open so I could see that one egg was cracked. Her mouth was pursed as if she were preparing to spit. "Some idiot must have dropped the whole pallet of them. These people have the gall to charge two dollars and twenty-nine cents, but they don't have one decent dozen. This is a disgrace."

I turned and left the store at once. That's how badly I wanted to slap her.

The people in traffic had a similar effect, their hurry the utmost in triviality. I wanted to shout at them, "I have spent all day with a man who is suffering like a gladiator fighting lions, and you want to cut me off so you can sit at that red light one car sooner?"

When I reached home, I went in the back door. I leaned against the kitchen wall with my eyes closed. Michael came into the room. I opened my eyes and saw that he had halted in the middle of the kitchen. He was looking me over, and for a moment I was afraid he was in the mood for sex. Instead he took my hands and led me to the table. He pulled out a chair and waited till I sat.

"I drove an amazing car today," he said, moving to the refrigerator. "One of those new RS-Series Audis. Man, what a rig."

Michael didn't care that most of his customers were rich. The cars were what interested him and kept his mechanics motivated. He opened the fridge and reached in with both hands. "The guy's son banged into a curb and bent the control arm. For which I hope he gave the kid's neck a proper wringing, by the way."

In his right hand, Michael held up a jug of iced tea. In his left, a bottle of Pinot Gris from McMinnville, a vineyard we'd visited once, an hour's drive away. I pointed at his left.

"It's a simple fix," he continued. "Though Audi parts are pricey, times three. Afterward I took the thing out for a test rip."

He popped the cork and set the corkscrew aside. Taking a wine glass from the cabinet, he filled it generously. "I have never felt such compression before. Like the engine did not care what the load was."

He handed me the glass and pulled up his own chair. "You know that long hill, up to the campus of Lewis and Clark? Sixty miles an hour and the car never downshifted. Like the hill wasn't even there."

I held the glass to my nose and smelled peaches. I took a mouthful. Despite my eyes' best effort, a single tear spilled out. While I drank good cold wine, Cleon was still suffering.

Michael took my hand again. "Should I . . . um . . ." He kissed my knuckles. "Would you like to hear about the MG we had in today, too?"

I wiped my cheek and nodded.

"A beauty, Deb. Racing green with tan interior, chrome spoke wheels. A guy brought it in because of a wobble at high speeds, so I put it up on the lift. And man, the classic rack-and-pinion steering. Simple and tight."

He was holding my hand, running his thumb over my knuckles. I took a good gulp of wine. "Any others?"

"Late in the day there was a Jag XKE. A 1965 model, with the 3.8 engine. But a disaster. Came in on a flatbed." He bent toward me. "This college guy inherited it from his grandfather, who'd left it in a barn for thirty years, and he wants us to get it running again. Gary stood there, not saying a word while I went over the car, but I swear I could hear him calculating."

I leaned my head against my big man, melting, letting go. "Keep going, Michael. What else?"

There were times, too, when I needed to do all the talking. Details of what I'd experienced would only leave me in peace if I described them fully and put them out into the air. When that happened, Michael was reliable about listening, even if it took from the moment I arrived home to the second I fell asleep. He enabled me to work in hospice because every day I had a loving detox.

I remember his buddy Brian hosting a Super Bowl party one year, and I overheard him giving Michael a hard time.

"You are the worst snake I have ever seen, man," Brian said, bumping shoulders with him.

"What are you talking about?" Michael asked.

"Listening. I've seen you, giving Deb the Big Ear. I'm sure it gets you plenty of action. But man, don't you know that makes all us regular self-absorbed guys look really bad? You need to cut that shit out."

Michael laughed. "Go get me a beer."

But the next time I unloaded on him, standing at the sink and describing Charles—a forty-three-year-old guy with a brutally slow case of Lou Gehrig's disease, which was torturing his wife and breaking his daughters' hearts—Michael came up and hugged me from behind. "Sometimes I think you have the saddest job on earth."

"The opposite," I said, leaning back on him, "Actually hospice is the most enriching job on earth, because a person who is dying savors everything, takes nothing for granted, and that is contagious. When I've seen a man give what may be his last hug, the one you give me when

I get home is even better. When a woman can no longer taste her usual evening bourbon cocktail, I savor our wine that night more deeply. Sounds crazy, I know, but dying people have taught me how to live."

He squeezed my hand and sat back. "Unbelievable."

And I counted my blessings once again.

I HAD TO LET ALL OF THAT GO after the last deployment. As the blogger Michael was reading had advised, I needed to set lower expectations.

That proved hardest when he came home the third time. I thought after that tour of duty, which was also his longest, he would be desperate for me. Special meals. Nights with friends. Ardent lovemaking. I was game, though, if it would bring him back to himself and draw him close to me again.

We were now well into our sixth month of re-entry, and none of those expectations had come true. Touching Michael was like running my fingers along a plank, he was so unresponsive. One night I made the curry-cilantro chicken he'd always loved. He scraped the sauce off and picked at the bare meat before hiding it under his knife and fork.

As for friends, he'd been unable to conceal his impatience with their lives, the frivolity of their daily concerns. Sometimes I sympathized. I imagined he was probably feeling something like my recovery times from work: How could he enthuse genuinely over Brian's new grill when he was walking around with memories of being in battle? His school buddy would be carrying on about smoked chicken to a man whose memory probably included smoked villages.

As for lovemaking, which I thought he'd be craving? Not once, nor even close. I kissed him the way he used to like, on the edge of his mouth, but he barely tolerated it. I touched him during the night, and he rolled onto his stomach. I surprised him in the shower, and he turned the water cold. Nice metaphor, honey.

Some days I lived in a fog of longing. I could not see any way back to what we'd once enjoyed effortlessly. When I hugged Michael, his back stiffened. He'd push my hands away and say, "I know. I'm sorry. I know."

I talked it through on the phone with my sister Robin many times. She convinced me that passive silence was a mistake. Any reply was a good reply, if it started a dialogue.

The next time he pushed me away, we were in the bathroom. I stepped between him and the door. "If you are really sorry, Michael, quit saying that you know. You don't know." He glanced past me into the hallway, but I blocked his exit. "Promise me you will start seeing a counselor. So that you really do know. Promise me."

HER NAME WAS DR. DOREMUS. Her office was in a quiet neighborhood on the river. He'd found her through the Guard, which was enthusiastic about getting him help. She worked exclusively with former soldiers.

Right away she started him on prazosin, an anti-nightmare medicine I had some familiarity with, from two Vietnam vets I'd cared for. World War II soldiers, they march in bed like they're still following orders. But guys from Vietnam thrash and struggle all night. I hoped the prazosin would help Michael sleep, but after three weeks I found half a bottle of pills in the trash. He said he wanted to experience the horrible dreams. The fact that he was having them meant he still had a conscience.

Dr. Doremus also prescribed bupropion, an anti-anxiety medicine. An excellent call on her part. Michael didn't need every backfiring car or slamming door to scare him into battle mode.

But counseling came foremost, and the woman must have been good: Michael never missed a session. Any given day he might skip work, or drive to Bend for a change of scenery. He might forget my birthday, blow off social events, ignore Valentine's Day. But on

Wednesdays, Michael was responsible. Nineteen weeks and he was still punctual for Dr. Doremus.

During his sessions, I would call Robin for my own counseling. Every time she would steer the conversation to my well-being. "You take great care of your patients, you have incredible patience with Michael. But how are you taking care of yourself?"

I pictured her in her living room, with its view of Annapolis harbor. She and her husband both commuted to jobs outside D.C.

"What I guess I'm asking," she said, "and I know this is overstepping, is how long do you think you can live this way?"

The question set me to pacing the kitchen. "Michael was gone, on and off, for three years. He deserves my support for a lot more than six rough months. Truth is, I'm not sure I could ever leave him, not in this condition."

"I'm not saying you should go, Deb," she sighed. "Just that you could take care of yourself too."

But I was, I truly was. And those Wednesdays gave me hope. Michael never shared the content of his sessions with me, though of course I yearned to hear, and probe, and talk about all of it. As long as he was working on getting better, we were not standing still.

BECAUSE I HAD TAKEN THE TIME that afternoon to write Barclay Reed's pain-management plan, I was late to pick up Michael. He couldn't walk home from Dr. Doremus's office; it was miles farther than his car shop.

I preferred to arrive early because I loved that part of town, wandering the park between the Marquam and Burnside Bridges. Often there was an artists' market at the upper end. Though we rarely bought anything, it was a pleasure to stroll among the booths, surrounded by bohemians and the scent of patchouli.

I parked near the river-view hotel, hurrying around in the hope that I would catch Michael on the wharf walk. It was a bluebird afternoon and the city was out enjoying. I watched a stooped man in a long raincoat piloting a shopping cart full of cans and bottles. As he rattled past me, he touched the brim of his hat. Perhaps twenty Asians—all ages, all wearing white shirts and black pants—had spread a tidy picnic on the knoll. People strolled below, crowding the path along the river, but I could spot my husband among them two hundred yards off.

He was patrolling, head upright as always now, while he scanned every rooftop and window for the potential insurgents of Portland, Oregon. Beside him the water sparkled, but he paid it no mind. I could have been sparkling too, and he would not have noticed. What were your thoughts, lover, and how could I have helped you?

A sidewalk panhandler called to him. Michael dug out a coin and tossed it into his cup. Something about the way the man said thanks hooked him, though. Michael backed up two steps and replied. They conversed a moment, a few words apiece. But my husband did not leave.

It was not done for my benefit. Michael did not even know I was watching. After a few exchanges, the panhandler gave a longer answer, my husband nodding. When the speech was finished, Michael took out his wallet and placed a bill in the cup. The panhandler bowed his head low. Michael walked on, and for once he was not checking the rooftops.

By then the surges of love ought to have faded. There was so little coming back to me. Instead, having him home but damaged, I felt those swells in my heart more than ever. It took self-control not to run down to him.

He spotted me, and of all unexpected things, Michael smiled. It was like seeing the sun come out. I hurried down the grassy slope. By the time I reached him, though, the clouds had returned. When I reached to smooch him, I ended up kissing his neck.

"Hi, Deb," Michael said, and he kept right on walking.

Ouch. I felt my anger flare—it happened to be hiding right behind that surge of affection. I was no doormat. In the old days, he would have immediately heard a few words about not taking me for granted. But in the old days, he would have gladly kissed my lips.

I took a second to collect my temper, then hustled up beside him. "Any interesting cars today?"

Michael kept striding, north into the park. "Nothing special."

"Did you have to take a taxi over? Or could you time the trolleys right?"

"Taxi."

I'd had enough. I grabbed his arm. "How about a proper hello? You seemed friendly when we first saw each other. How about acknowledging me for two seconds? I am more than your ride home, you know."

Michael halted. "You had that look, when you ran down the hill. Now I'm waiting for you to ask. And you are doing the formalities before you ask."

"What are you talking about? Ask what?"

"How it went with the shrink today."

"I have said no such—"

"How am I doing. How did we process the truck incident." He slapped his chest with every sentence. "How was the session. How is the weather. How is every fucking thing."

"I didn't ask any of that."

"You were about to. Don't deny it."

"Well, I didn't have anything planned, Michael. But I am allowed to want to know how you are."

"See?" He put his hands on his hips. "Quit pretending, Deborah. The real inquisition was about twenty seconds away."

I gritted my teeth. "I was not asking."

"Every time I go to the shrink, you should see your face after. All eager and positive, so goddamn hopeful. Maybe he found the perfect insight this session, maybe now he'll start being his old self again. It is so impatient and optimistic. It is so fucking selfish."

"That's not fair—"

"How'd it go at the shrink today, how'd it go how'd it go how'd it go."

Two short-haired women were passing by, wearing tank tops that displayed their tattooed arms. The near one slowed. "Everybody OK here?"

"We're fine," Michael growled. It would not have reassured a deaf man.

"Thanks," I said more softly. "We're all right."

The woman had a silver ring pierced through a nostril. "You sure, sister?"

"Really," I told her. "Actually, this is good."

"OK," she said, as they rejoined hands and continued down the path. "Be kind, good people."

I turned back to Michael. He was staring at the sky as though counting the clouds. He appeared calmer now, so I waited for him to speak first.

He sighed. "I wish I had the answer you want, you know? Like I could march out of her office and say yup, we found the missing ingredient all right. Now I'm fine, life can go back to what it was."

"It's not going to be that simple."

"No."

I took his arm with both hands. For once, he did not clench at my touch. "You are not alone in this, Michael. And I am not afraid of what you are going through. I just wish you could let one little window open, so that instead of watching from outside, I could be a tiny bit inside this situation with you. I wish you could let me in."

"You want in?" Michael's face tensed, a deep crease in his forehead. I reached up to touch it, to smooth it, and he pulled away. I still had his arm, but he spoke with his back turned. "They are the people I killed."

"Who are?"

"The faces." He was whispering. "The ones I draw."

Of course. I should have thought of that.

"A sniper is not like regular soldiers, Deb. Other guys throw a grenade, and a whole building booms, someone else counts the bodies. They fire from a tank and an armored vehicle blows up, it's dramatic, all fireworks, but a hundred yards away. A sniper, he sees every person he kills. He watches as they step out of the shadows, away from their protection and into his domain. He sees their faces. And then he blows them away."

I put my hand on the broad of his back. "Oh, honey."

"In training they teach you about focus, having a stable pedestal, and controlling your breath. I practiced that for years. We aim, we shoot, we do the mission. But nobody said one fucking thing about the faces."

Michael was suffering. It was as simple and heartbreaking as that. I knew it, I had known it. But now there was a kind of simplicity. I pressed my forehead against his back, between his shoulder blades, and spoke at the ground. "So you draw them at night."

"That's when they come. And scare the living shit out of me. And rip at my conscience." He sighed, leaning back against my head. "And that, Deborah, is how it went at the shrink today."

FINALLY DURING THE NIGHT of September 8, the skies clear. Lieutenant Commander Tagami orders the mission to embark at dawn. Thus begin three forms of activity.

First, the I-25 surfaces. Ocean washes down the conning tower, the decks, and a strange steel catapult that runs backward from the bow. A half moon falls westward toward its setting. To the east, the lights of small-town Oregon glow against the last of the clouds. Sailors vie for topside tasks, to gulp lungfuls of fresh air or to glimpse the moon.

Second, the crew begins removing a metal shroud from the forward side of the conning tower. Behind that buttress stands an aircraft, disassembled.

Built for reconnaissance, the Yokosuka E14 has a wingspan of 36 feet, a length of 28 feet, a single engine with 340 horsepower, and a cabin with space for a pilot and rear-facing navigator. Nicknamed the "Geta" because the pontoons resemble a common Japanese shoe by that name, it carries only one weapon, a 7.7-mm rear-facing machine gun.

The plane's cruising speed is just over 100 miles per hour, sluggish even by 1940s standards. However, its range is nearly 550 miles, and it can fly as high as 17,780 feet. E14s have spied on fleets and harbors all across the Pacific, including preparations for the day of infamy.

On the deck of the I-25, the plane lies disassembled. Its frame-and-fabric wings lean against the conning tower, folded up like a hanging bat. The crew hurries into action. Some sailors pull the main fuselage forward. Others hoist the wings, bolting them into place. Still others attach floating pontoons. Additional trusses run from the body to the underside of the wings, enabling the aircraft to carry more weight.

Next a crew carries out two bombs, both 14 inches in diameter and weighing 170 pounds. Each contains hundreds of cubes of incendiary jelly. Whatever they do not set aflame upon impact, they will melt. As the crew attaches the first bomb, its weight tilts the small aircraft to that side until the crew latches the opposite bomb to its mount.

The E14 has become a hazard. Unlike the diesel that powers the sub, aircraft fuel can explode, as can the bombs. Either would sink the I-25 in minutes.

The third kind of activity is considerably more contemplative and is imbued with the power of ritual. It occurs belowdecks. To begin, Ichiro Soga has breakfast. But he does not eat with the rest of the crew. A traditionalist, his breakfast is the same meal that Japanese warriors have eaten before battle for centuries: soybean soup, rice, and chestnuts. The final ingredient is a bracing shot of sake. It warms the belly, fires the blood, and dulls any pain that might occur later.

Also in keeping with tradition, Soga has snipped a lock of his hair and clipped his fingernails, stowing these artifacts of his person in a small lacquered box. Should he not survive, this box will enable him to be buried on Japanese soil.

CHAPTER 6

"I WANT YOU TO INSTRUCT that whining gnat Cheryl not to come here anymore."

I halted in the Professor's doorway, carrying his breakfast tray. No patient had complained to me about Cheryl before. Families loved her for the support she gave them while still caring for the patient. She also routinely volunteered for hard-to-fill shifts—New Year's Eve, the Super Bowl night, Christmas morning—which made her a favorite among agency staff. I would no more call Cheryl off a case than I would disown my mother. "Professor, you can't be serious."

"How can a person with those hideous pointed glasses possess so rotund an intellect?"

I set the tray on his rolling table. "First of all, you seem better today."

"More credit to my hardy constitution than to the actions of any of you."

"Secondly, what are you talking about? Cheryl is a saint."

"This." He held up the day's Oregonian. "I asked her for a seven-letter word that ends in D. 'Where forbidden fruit grows.' She had the audacity to suggest Eden." He rattled the pages in my direction. "D at the end, not the middle. And seven letters, I said it clearly, yet she answered with 'Eden.' Bah. Spare me such mindless creatures."

"Orchard?"

"Of course it is orchard, Nurse Birch."

He prattled on while I adjusted his rolling table. "A woman like her should be kept miles away from the likes of me. A woman like her should be shot."

"I suppose."

He eyed me sideways. "You suppose she should be shot?"

I was distracted, arranging the plates. When I went to move the table over his lap, I discovered he was holding it. I stood back. "Something wrong?"

"I should be asking you that question, Nurse Birch."

"What do you mean?"

"Normally if I make a comment about someone being shot, I would expect a quip about it being a relief that I don't have a gun handy. Or an earnest lecture about not making jokes of that sort when the country is plagued by gun violence. Or a spirited defense of your colleague's Florence Nightingale ways despite her deplorable taste in eyewear."

"I don't know what you are talking about." I began setting out silverware, but he blocked my hand.

"Your pluck, Nurse Birch. Where has it vanished? Or do you have another misdeed you wish to confess?"

I straightened, one hand on my hip. "I have nothing to confess."

"Unburden yourself. Your concerns display as visibly as if they were tattooed on your forehead."

I glanced over at the bookshelf, all those titles bearing his name. When I looked back, he was watching me with complete calm.

"Would you consider yourself an expert on war?"

"Far from it. I know one region of one war. Granted, for four years it was a particularly horrific patch of Earth. On the scale of organized human violence through the centuries, however, the few million deaths under my scrutiny were a mere speck."

"Still."

He watched me for a moment, as if he were buying a melon not quite ripe, then made a come-hither gesture with one hand. "Out with it."

"Why don't men ever talk about war, Professor?"

He raised his eyebrows. "What you are asking is actually a large question, involving cultural norms of manhood and civilized behavior. Not to mention a society's capacity to lie to itself."

Putting his newspaper aside, the Professor counted down on his fingers. "The first lie is that they are being brave. That they have seen things mere mortal civilians could not stomach, and silence is self-control. Which is complete pap. The second lie is that they are being modest, downplaying their heroism so as not to appear boastful. Also nonsense."

He took the fork from my hand and rolled the table up to himself. "The truth is that they are carrying an enormous burden of shame and guilt over what the war compelled them to do. Not to mention the forbidden possibility that they enjoyed doing it."

He waved his fork like a conductor's baton. I noticed that the Professor was visibly at ease. It was like the afternoon out on the dock; lecturing calmed him.

"If you kill a man," he continued, "whatever the circumstances, he is on your conscience for life. Whether you used a tomahawk three centuries ago, a bayonet two centuries ago, a rifle one century ago, or a drone last Tuesday, his death was violent, premature, and by your hand. With the possible exception of the latest weapons, it's likely that you saw him die. I imagine that will shut anyone up as tight as a submarine door."

"OK," I said. "But let's say a man sincerely believed in the cause and followed orders. How does he recover from what he did? And how does his wife help him?"

"I have no answer for your last question. Wiving is not my area of expertise. As for how he recovers . . ." The Professor paused, his fork raised, fixing me with a long, penetrating stare. Merciless.

"I apologize." I opened his napkin, offering it to him. "I am here to care for you. Not the other way around."

Still he said nothing, only gazed off toward his desk while tucking the napkin under his chin. His face had gone blank. There was a distance to him, a remove like a plunge in cold water. I had never, in all my experience, felt more shut out by a patient. I busied myself with his chart, the blinds behind his bed.

Finally the Professor faced me, his expression pursed like a prune. "I want you to know, as a concrete fact, that I do not believe in coincidence."

"All right."

"I'm sure you do, Nurse Birch. I imagine you reading your daily horoscope, but I reject all notions of fate, destiny, or karma. Nonsense, all of it."

I did not follow his thinking, but I trusted that I would understand him soon enough. "That's your prerogative, Professor."

"I had no way of knowing when I dismissed all of those lesser do-gooders, Timmy and Sara and the ones from the other agencies. No conception that a person like you would exist. Much less that your husband might benefit." He tapped the tines of his fork on the plate, one, two. "Yes. Now that I do know, there is some clarity for me. It is not a coincidence. But I begin to understand what is supposed to happen here."

"And that is?"

"My, my," he mused. "Perhaps my last wish is not so impossible after all."

"Would you please explain, Professor? I don't understand."

He pointed at his desk. "Bring me the black binder."

I marched over. It sat on the back corner, a plain two-inch binder full of paper. I read the index card taped to the cover: "The Sword?"

He held out both hands. "Here, please."

"What is it?"

"The book I will not live to finish. The book no editor would publish because I was foolish enough to let my protégé's plagiarism accusation go unchallenged." He opened the binder and flipped through the pages. "And, as it turns out, a book that may answer precisely the question you posed to me a moment ago."

"What's it about?"

"I now know what needs to happen in my remaining time."

"I'm listening."

He laughed. "Brilliant. The most obvious thing."

I stood at his bedside. "Tell me. I'll do everything I can."

He weighed the binder in his hands. "You would not think so light an object could contain such a tonnage of importance."

"Do you want me to read it to you?"

His lifted his head, rediscovering that I was present. "You have no idea."

"Then I will do that."

The Professor pulled the binder to one side, as if I had tried to snatch it away. "There is a condition."

"I already said I would do my best."

"You must inform me, at the end, whether or not you believe it."

"Why wouldn't I? You're a historian."

"Who resigned from his university in a scandal and never published another word. Plenty of people will swear to you that this book is false—former colleagues, members of my own—" He stopped himself and cleared his throat. "I am not swearing to you that this book is true. I am making no such assertion. Perhaps all those editors were right, and my work is simply not credible. Perhaps this is a fabrication, a handful of facts ornamented with nonsense and invention."

He pointed a bony finger at me. "You must decide for yourself, without consulting any outside source, or expert, or superficial Internet nonsense. You agree to read this book to me, and at its conclusion declare whether it is a work of genius, a story that the world must be told, or the product of an old man's delusions. Whichever it is, I refuse to say in advance. But you must promise before we begin. You must swear that you will tell me whether or not you believe this narrative is true."

He had spoken with such intensity, there were flecks of white on his lips. I offered him his plastic water jug, and he sucked on the straw several times. It was not my practice to make promises to patients. Inevitably, some obstacle arose—in Central Office, at home, even something as minor as traffic—and not only could the promise get broken, but someone's critical life-concluding work might go unfinished.

The Professor's face was flushed with anticipation and doubt. I was mindful that he had implied his manuscript might contain something helpful for Michael. Forget coincidence; maybe life was just lining up. Maybe the questions and answers had somehow come to reside in the same room. So often the patients are our best teachers.

We regarded one another for a moment. Then I held out my hands. "I promise."

He released a huge breath. "Excellent." The Professor placed the manuscript in my hands. As I pulled a chair to his bedside, he worked the controls up and back, tilting the mattress to make his position comfortable.

I opened the binder in my lap and waited. At last the Professor laid his head back on a pillow and closed his eyes. The picture of contentment, he waved a hand at me, a conductor awakening the violins.

"To sailors in wartime," he prompted.

I flipped past the cover page and table of contents, turned to the first chapter, and began to read.

"To sailors in wartime, there is but one deity . . ."

AT LAST WORD COMES to the pilot's berth: His aircraft is ready. He dispatches his navigator, Petty Officer Shoji Okuda, before taking a few moments to collect himself. Soga knows that he was chosen for this mission, and not merely due to prowess as a reconnaissance pilot.

Dispatched to the attack on Pearl Harbor on a carrier, his plane was damaged on the way by rough seas. Thus he spent that infamous day as a spectator, imagining: If only an aircraft could be delivered by submarine, sparing it the grueling surface passage, and avoiding the reliance upon a carrier group.

Soga presented this idea to the ship's executive officer, Lieutenant Tsukodo, saying it would work for bombing the Panama Canal, aircraft factories, and naval bases. Tsukodo encouraged him to write a description for the Admiralty.

When Soga arrived in Yokosuka in July1942—eight months later—he received orders to report to his commander's office. At that meeting, in walked none other than Prince Takamatsu, the emperor's younger brother. An officer spread a map on the table, and the prince began to speak.

"The northwestern United States is full of forests. Once a blaze gets started in the deep woods, it is very difficult to stop. Sometimes whole towns are destroyed. If we were to bomb some of these forests, it would put the enemy to much trouble. It might even cause large-scale panic, once residents knew Japan could reach out and bomb their factories and homes from five thousand miles away."

Soga was ordered to perform a submarine-based firebombing mission. He was forbidden from telling his wife or young son anything about it. He knew the plane was small and slow. His creativity had brought both distinction and danger.

Now, on that September morning off the coast of Oregon, Soga has one other high qualification for the mission: his ancestry. He reaches behind his bunk for the object that symbolizes that history and reveals it in the submarine's dull interior light.

A sword. A samurai sword, which has been in his family for four hundred years. As the eldest son of the eldest son, Ichiro born of an Ichiro going back eighteen generations, he has a direct blood line to the warrior who bore that weapon in the fifteen hundreds. The handle is long enough to be wielded by two hands. The blade spans two and half feet, but Soga does not draw in the cramped space of his bunk. This weapon should remain sheathed unless it is to be used.

The sword will fly with him that day, as it does on every mission. He rests the weapon across his lap and contemplates his likelihood of success. Merely launching from a submarine, without the deck of an aircraft carrier or the length of an airstrip, requires consummate skill. The challenge will be intensified by the bombs' weight—which will slow acceleration, diminish lift, and eliminate margin for error. The waves will reach for his pontoons, eager to pull him down, and with him the glory of his nation and lineage.

He has managed a similar takeoff once before, off the coast of Australia. Launching successfully at 7:30 A.M., Soga performed reconnaissance of Sydney Harbor and a military base, landed near the sub, and watched the crew disassemble the plane. By noon the next day the I-25 was 460 miles away.

This new mission is vastly more challenging. He must fly over American soil, which no enemy pilot has ever done. He must release the bombs individually, maintaining nose control during the unbalanced miles, over targets he has seen only on maps. There can be no evasions or detours because he carries as little fuel as possible. He must land near the sub, the crew dismantling his plane at once. The I-25 must be submerged before a single American plane can spot them.

It is, in other words, a suicide mission. Nonetheless, Soga has made all foreseeable preparations. If it is possible for a man to survive, he hopes to do so.

At last orders arrive for the pilot to report to the deck. There is no more preamble. All that remains is the mission.

Soga climbs down the conning tower, walking to the aircraft with care. He does not want to get wet. Moisture at sea level spells misery aloft. Reconnaissance cockpits are notoriously cold, especially at altitude, which is why pilots wear leather jackets with fleece linings: not for fashion, but for warmth.

Soga steps onto the E14's pontoon, sword under one arm. Stretching his leg above the gunwale as if over a horse's saddle, he drops into the cockpit. The seat, worn from prior missions, conforms to his shape. He tucks the sword beneath his thigh, then clips into the five-point harness.

There are final instructions, last words before commencing a radio silence that will be broken only when he returns. Soga starts the E14's motor. It is like an animal under his seat, barking itself to life, then growling so roughly that the entire aircraft shudders. He runs down a checklist with navigator Okuda. Heat radiates back from the engine, warmth that will vanish upon takeoff. Soga reaches overhead, yanking the cockpit shield forward and locking it.

With the brakes on full, he nudges the throttle and feels the competing powers under his hands. It resembles the conflict within himself, between valor and apprehension, pride and fear. Okuda has gone silent, alone with his thoughts.

At that moment, the sun rises. Its light crests the trees of the coastline only miles away, fills the seaplane's cabin, indicates to Soga in which direction his target lies. East. His course is due east.

History, too, waits just over the horizon—but not only the history that will be made on this day. Today Soga is a warrior from a line of warriors, yet he will manifest something even greater in the years to come.

But not yet. September 9, 1942, has dawned. Soga releases the brake, then guns the throttle. The catapult flings the airplane forward, like a seal sliding on wet rocks to the sea. The E14 dips as it reaches the bow, quickly righting itself. Lift pulls the plane upward, gravity holds it back, sea splash yaws it to starboard. The engine strains. Water streaks up the windshield.

Then there is purchase, and momentum. The E14 skips across the tops of the waves. Soga pulls on the yoke, lifting the nose earlier than he would on an airstrip. But the speed proves sufficient. The aircraft clears the water. It rises free of the sub and all that held it back.

The E14 gains loft—fifty meters, one hundred, two hundred. As the nose levels, Soga permits himself a glance under the wings. On each side the fire bombs are tucked snugly beneath, as a man in a hurry would carry loaves of bread.

Okuda calls out coordinates and Soga pilots onto that heading. The ocean falls behind as he crosses the coastline, gaining ground, flying directly over American soil. Everyone below is asleep.

CHAPTER 7

WHEN I FINISHED READING, my mouth was dry. Of course the only drinking water in the room sat lukewarming in Barclay Reed's bedside jug. The straw, bent at its accordioned elbow, was not exactly tempting.

I closed the binder on my finger to mark the place and studied my patient. He had barely moved while I was reading, just the slow rise and fall of his chest. Generally the Professor was a quiet sleeper, so I wasn't sure exactly when he had drifted off.

But I was full of questions. Was any of this true? Why had I never heard about Soga before? Above all, how did the story of this bomber from seventy-plus years ago, as the Professor had implied, connect to the struggles Michael was having here and now?

It would all have to keep for another day. Hospitals have rhythms of vital-sign checks, chart reviews, and medication deliveries, which sometimes seem designed to prevent people from getting more than forty minutes of uninterrupted sleep. Hospice works the opposite way. Sleep is too restorative, too comforting. Interventions and conversations and general clinical bother do not justify waking a patient. The only time I will stir a person out of his snooze is in the final days, if a family member has arrived after traveling great distances. Even then, I often argue for delay. Dying can be an exhausting task.

People doing that hard work need all the rest we can give. That afternoon I knew: my curiosity would have to wait.

I checked my watch. Melissa would arrive any minute. Normally our agency doesn't provide round-the-clock care because there are spouses or children standing by to perform nonmedical duties. Someone like me drops by once or twice a day, seeing if everything is as serene as possible, providing moral support, medicines, or a refilled oxygen tank before heading to the next household. On a good day with smart route planning, I can help a dozen or more patients in a single shift.

But when there is no familial support system, no network of concerned neighbors, we do what we can to fill the void. When this happens, usually because the patient has outlived all of her friends, and sometimes because the patient has a difficult personality or lives in a remote place or presents emotional challenges to caregivers, we revert to a basic premise: No one dies alone. If every life has value, so does every death.

That's why one of the most important pieces of information in the Professor's profile was his lack of family members. For a time, we would be his family.

The agency definitely lost money on patients like him, but it was not my concern. Problems like that were for the fund-raising department to solve.

I found a blank appointment card in my pocket and tucked it into the pages. Rising noiselessly from my seat, I tiptoed back to his desk, setting the binder in the same corner.

"Not everyone is asleep."

I jumped. "You startled me, Professor."

"Soga miscalculated." Barclay Reed's hands were folded on his belly. His eyes were wide open. "But predictably. He believes the propaganda about Americans being lazy and overconfident. He has no way of knowing that they are not complete fools."

"How much of that story is true?"

"Precisely the question I intended to ask you, Nurse Birch."

"I studied history, I told you. I never heard anything about this."

"Thus may you rightly ask yourself: Why would a nation that prizes free speech and reveres its military prowess dismiss a tale so historic?"

"I don't know." I crossed the room to adjust his blankets. "Because Americans don't like stories that imply we might be weak?"

"A fair surmise. Indeed, in New York City Mayor Fiorello LaGuardia held a patriotic parade that included a skit with giant yellow rats being driven from the city."

"Oh, lovely."

"Yes. Some rats had the word 'Jap' painted on them. But as you'll see in later pages, there is more than bravado in question here, Nurse Birch. This pilot's conduct will challenge the American warrior ethos in ways our nation has historically shown itself reluctant to contemplate."

"What do you mean?"

He pointed at the binder. "It commences in only a few pages. Please don't say I won't live long enough for you to reach that far."

"I'm willing to keep reading to you, if that's what you mean."

The Professor sniffed. "Fine. Please note that you have evaded the central question, of whether or not you believe this narrative. Nonetheless, I find your answer temporarily satisfactory."

He reached for his water jug, glommed onto the straw, and took a long noisy draw. He half-closed his eyes at the pleasure of it, as if somehow he knew I was parched. I heard the straw slurp on the empty bottom, then he held the container toward me, rattling it side to side. "Refill, please. Also, in a few minutes I will need a bathroom trip."

I brought his jug into the kitchen but filled a glass for myself first. While I was drinking, I heard the front door open.

"Hiya, Deb." Melissa bounded in with her customary athletic glow. "How's everyone doing today?"

"Pretty good, actually," I said. "I read to him most of the afternoon."

"Read to him? Holy cow." Melissa dug plastic containers from her backpack. "You have the knack with this guy."

"Hardly. We're still getting acquainted."

"Ask Cheryl." Melissa arranged her dinner tubs inside the fridge. "She and I are lucky to get ten words out of him per shift. And those ten won't be exactly coated with honey. You, though, you get him."

"All right, Melissa." I leaned against the sink and crossed my arms. "What are you up to?"

She closed the fridge door. "He doesn't have an advance directive."

"What? How did that happen? The agency isn't supposed to start services without one."

"Timmy somehow missed it during intake." She placed her palms on the counter, angling one leg back to stretch her calf. "And if we are honest, out of his current care team, you are definitely the one to bring it up now."

"Probably." I put down my water glass. "Damn. I don't think this will be an easy one. Who knows what he wants?"

"Nurse Birch," the Professor bellowed from down the hall. "Where is my water? And I need to go to the john."

Melissa smiled. "I'd say he wants you."

"YOUR EVENING STAFFER JUST ARRIVED," I said, hurrying to his bedside. "I was catching her up on the day."

His face was furrowed like a walnut. "Thus our heroine makes her noble escape."

"I'll see you tomorrow," I said, handing him the jug. "You and I have some planning to do. Preparation."

"Of what kind?"

"Medical. I don't want us to encounter any surprises. So we'll be developing a plan for your treatment."

"What sort of a plan?"

"That's for us both to find out."

He interrupted his slurping on the straw. "You are being evasive."

"Not at all. I'm just being—"

"Evasive."

No question, the man was a prize. "We're just done for the day, that's all."

He set the water jug on his rolling table. "Thus have you instructed me to plan for some planning."

A terrier with a rag in his teeth. "None of this is urgent, Professor. And anyway, with Melissa here—"

"You will tell her nothing."

"Excuse me?"

"The Sword." He wagged a finger as though he were scolding me. "Strictly between us. No one else. And definitely not that sports-crazed girl. I hear her doing push-ups when I'm trying to sleep."

"I doubt that." I bent to arrange his pillows. And bless that curmudgeon, he leaned forward to make it easier. "But if you insist. Just us."

"I do. Especially in view of the fact that you haven't told me whether you believe my book thus far or not."

I straightened. "Didn't I?"

"Nurse Birch." He scowled at me as if I were a used-car salesman, trying to sell him a jalopy.

"Didn't you say you needed to go to the bathroom?"

"It passed. Now answer me."

"All right," I said. "I admit it. I'm not sure. Parts seem true."

"Such as?"

"The details. Size of the sub, the range of the folded-up plane, that sort of thing. But I can't sort out if you're just piling on those facts because it will make the other stuff more believable."

Rubbing his face, the Professor said nothing.

"Are you smiling at me, behind your hand there?"

He yanked it down and scowled. "Nothing of the kind. I was merely appreciating your skepticism. You mistrust my rhetoric."

"I'm not sure what you mean. But the writing reminds me of some doctors."

"In what manner? And would you please close those blasted blinds? Before the sun incapacitates me permanently?"

"Well, it's like this. Sometimes a baby doesn't start out right, won't latch on, doesn't nurse." I leaned to the window, taking the blinds' string in one hand. "The doctors perform all sorts of tests, and sometimes that works and they get the baby well. But there are cases when it doesn't. The infant worsens, so they double the testing, seeking trend lines, hoping to bend the curves. But all the data can't hide that they don't really know what's going on. And if the infant dies, which is one of the saddest things that happens in a hospital, the diagnosis on the chart will be 'failure to thrive.' As if it was the baby's fault."

I lowered the blinds. The room felt smaller, but not bleak. More private, protected. "Anyway, that's what your details do. They're supposed to convince me, but they might be camouflaging the part that's made up."

"Excellent syllogism, Nurse Birch. I can explain one thing, however, before you leave for the day—why those details matter very much."

I placed the string along the headboard so the Professor could open the blinds later if he chose. "I'm listening."

"Because they pertain to your husband. They demonstrate that, in order to understand a warrior, first you must understand his weapons."

"I don't know what that means."

"Whether the warrior is Ichiro Soga or your husband, regardless." The Professor shrugged. "First you must understand his weapons."

Then, peering into the little basket where I'd collected his remotes, he selected one, pointed it at the television, and turned away from me.

ONCE I CARED FOR AN ALCOHOLIC WOMAN with children in their early thirties, and in my view every person in that family needed a decade of counseling.

Mona lived in a railroad-style apartment, in a near-shanty, beside a road with constant traffic, and every time I arrived, her yard was full of cars. Sons, daughters, their girlfriends and boyfriends, plus the occasional drinking buddy. She had the deep voice and deeper wrinkles of a lifelong smoker. Mona also had inoperable bone cancer in her sacrum, and the tumor was causing constant pain.

With those situations, the options are lousy: sever the spinal cord, which causes paralysis for the patient's remaining life, or crank up the morphine, which puts the patient so soundly asleep she never eats again and dies of malnourishment. But Mona's enterprising doctor had devised an innovative treatment, using a local analgesic method originally designed for short-term recovery from surgeries like hernia repairs and C-sections. It was a sterile pouch, really, nothing more sophisticated than that, with a thin drip line inserted directly into the wound—or in her case, the tumor site. As the medicine oh-so-slowly oozed through, it muted the nerves locally, and Mona remained awake and alert. This little trick had probably bought her three months of life, pain-free.

The problem was the drip line. It was an invitation to infection. Any moisture, even an innocent drop of sweat, was perilous. My job was to make a house call at the beginning and end of each shift to sterilize the line and refill the pouch.

Medically, it was nothing. Ten minutes. Yet after four or five days I found myself dreading the stops at Mona's house. In the evening, there were always people out on the porch, drinking, often straight from the bottle. They would stop talking the moment I closed my car door. Although the men didn't bother to hide checking me out, no one greeted me, even if I said hello. Instead they made a cloud of cigarette smoke so thick I had to hold my breath as I passed through. I felt the heat of their stares and sometimes heard a muttered wisecrack and snickering after I had gone inside.

Morning visits weren't much better. There would be fresh trash on the lawn, cigarette butts in the sink, someone snoring on the couch under a threadbare blanket.

It wasn't the poverty. I have cared for plenty of people with no money. Some have been my favorite clients, in fact, because they showed appreciation and dignity despite severe material want—and it was humbling. I remember watching a woman eat cereal from a chipped and dirty bowl, for instance, and arriving home that night feeling pretty meek about the breakfast dishes I'd left in the sink.

And of course there was Ryan. On my first visit to his apartment, the man did not have a bed. Just blankets on the floor, a flattened pillow at one end. I arranged for the agency to provide a hospital bed and linens, then cut loose some cash so he could afford to heat his place to a reasonable temperature.

Ryan promised to give me something in return, though I insisted that he shouldn't. But who was I to know what a dying man's necessities are? He felt compelled to show gratitude.

Ryan is the man who carved me the hummingbird, which turned out to be a totem of my work, a permanent reminder that every patient is capable of enormous and unexpected gifts. My challenge is to remember that, and to see the person behind the problem.

At Mona's the problem was drink: hers, her children's, their friends'. While I was inside swabbing her med-line, I could hear the partiers through the screens. Their tone was bitter, caustic. One night the railing broke, and a man fell onto the lawn. It was the only time I ever heard laughter there. While he poured forth a recitation of filth to make a sailor blush, the rest of the crew roared and cackled. When he answered them by swearing with greater passion, their hilarity sounded like barking dogs.

Some days were not so bad, though I couldn't say why. They just went more smoothly, and I was less edgy. So I began keeping track: when was it easy, when was I uneasy. Eventually, I realized that my mood was established before I'd even gotten out of my car.

That's not unusual in medicine; the caregiver's experience can often be a useful diagnostic tool. A psychologist who is taking a patient's history and begins to feel depressed, for example, has received a clear indicator that the patient is depressed himself.

At Mona's house there was no obvious signal. It was something nuanced. I needed three full weeks to figure it out. One evening, when I was running a bit behind schedule, I noticed: There was a green Mustang on the front grass, its chrome back wheels jacked up but the rest of it in rusty condition. When that car was present, my mood was anxious. Yet I had no idea whose vehicle it was. How could I have subconsciously connected the car to the negative atmosphere at the house?

Before I could solve that riddle, the answer presented itself. On that night, I was late, and I hurried into Mona's room to check her line. Two men were sitting beside her bed. Her hair hung down into her face. The cigarette smoke was as thick as steam.

"It's a little close in here," I said, opening the one window that worked. No question, I would arrive home smelling of smoke. No one replied.

I turned to assess the situation. All three of them held large glasses of dark liquor. I asked Mona how her day was.

"Lousy," she slurred. "What else?"

"Sorry," I said, coming beside her bed. "But we can't mix these things."

I took her glass away. She glared at me, trying to focus. Meanwhile I carried the glass into the kitchen and poured its contents down the sink.

One of the men was at my elbow instantly, smelling of booze. He was much taller than me and stood too close. "What the hell you doing, little missy?"

"Giving alcohol to a person on pain medicines is a really bad idea."

"Well I'm her fuckin' son. And I say if she wants to hoist a few fuckin' drinks, it ain't gonna hurt nobody."

"Actually, it will. It will hurt your mom, perhaps seriously."

"Maybe you didn't even fuckin' notice, but she's already in a world of hurt, Miss Priss."

"Miss Priss? Is that the best you can do?" I stepped past him to finish filling Mona's pouch, but on the way I did something that I regret to this day. I laughed. One little snort, but it conveyed a long paragraph of contempt.

Now a man like that has little enough to shore up his ego, only a jacked-up car and a mouth full of bravado, and I had popped his tires. He glanced around to see who had heard. I looked too—just us. Then I went about my business, lines and pouch, while he stood in the doorway smoldering. I left without another word between us.

They fired me the following morning. I received the email from my boss before breakfast, so they must have called the agency mighty early.

Timmy Clamber was next, and he lasted one day. Not exactly a gay-friendly household, I'd say. Then heroic Grace Farnham stepped in, with her gospel voice and skillful diplomacy, and they kept her on. I felt relieved for the patient, the family, and myself.

I can't say that I forgot Mona, but she faded quickly because my next assignment was also a tough one. Allison was an elderly piano teacher, a devout Catholic, whose husband was a retired plumber and whose five grown sons either still lived in the house or were on the same block. She was in the final weeks of a valiant ovarian cancer fight. Allison had taken care of all of those men for so many years, she did not even know what her needs were, much less how to ask for them to be met.

For me it was a month of mind reading, guessing at signals, and biting my tongue while the fellas stood around with their hands in their pockets. At the end I was proud that she died pain-free, rosary in her fingers and a priest at her bedside in the final hour.

When I spotted Grace Farnham in the office a few weeks later, I went straight to her desk. Perhaps not the most organized worker in the office, she was searching for something among the piles of papers. I stood there a moment, liking the way she smelled—floral yet maternal, like a fourth-grade teacher. When she glanced up, I said I was glad Mona had finished life in her care because it guaranteed a happy ending.

"Lord, no," Grace said, pausing in her search. "That case was not pretty, Deborah dear. One sad household."

"But why? She had that great drip device."

"Well, it seemed like she was drawing pain meds through the tube faster, but I just gave her more. You know I'm not sharp on titrating dosages like you are. So it took me a bit to figure it out. Then I ran water on the tube and sure enough there were pinholes. That oldest boy of hers was diverting."

"What are you saying?"

"An addict, I guess. Or user, anyway. He was tapping her line to steal some injectable." Grace rubbed her forehead. "Oh, I wish you had kept on with that one, Deborah. It wouldn't have gone so badly."

"I'm afraid to ask."

"He messed up, of course, contaminated things, and gave his poor mama meningitis. As if her life weren't difficult enough." Grace shuffled the papers on her desk. "That Mona, she suffered hard."

Ouch. I had been on to that guy, I'd had his number. But I put my ego first and took the firing gladly. If I'd stayed, maybe I would have caught the diverting earlier. Maybe Mona would not have died in misery. And that is how one uncompassionate laugh can weigh a thousand pounds forever.

THERE WAS NO GREEN MUSTANG parked in front of the house when I reached home that night. There must have been some similar signal though, some subtle but accurate indicator, because anxiety surged in me the moment I pulled into the driveway. I'd been improving at that, diagnosing Michael's condition before setting foot in the house. Before I'd shut off the car that day, I could tell something was not right.

The news on the radio didn't help: a shooting at a mall in Ohio. After killing four people and wounding six, the gunman shot himself at the scene. A familiar story, sadly enough, and the randomness of its violence would make anyone nervous.

But even after I'd shut the engine off, I felt a tension in the quiet, as if I were a little kid caught at something and was about to get yelled at.

I climbed out of the car and peered around. There were no external indicators, no signs of trouble. Just Michael's shoes beside the front door, his socks tucked inside. That wasn't his routine, but the day was warm, and he'd walked home from work. So why would that put me on alert?

I have no idea. Nor can I say why the strange rhythmic sound from inside caused my stomach to flutter. But something made me turn the handle gently and open the screen door slowly so that it would not squeak. Something made me stealthy as I entered my own house.

Michael sat at the kitchen table, his back to me. My mouth went dry as I took it all in: Three racks of large brass bullets, polished to a yellowy shine, perhaps two hundred rounds per rack. His rifle, which we had agreed would always be kept locked in the hall cabinet because the big gun made me nervous, leaned against the counter. My husband wore camouflage pants, a tight white t-shirt, and one army boot. That rhythmic sound was Michael going back and forth with a brush, buffing the other boot so that it shined.

His neck was red with exertion, arm and back muscles flexed, head bent in concentration.

Nobody knew the statistics on returning soldiers better than me: Four hundred thousand men and women with PTSD. Twenty-two suicides a day. And here was my psychically wounded man gearing up as if he were about to invade the city of Portland. Of all the emotions I'd experienced since he came home, that was the first time I had known outright fear.

"Sweetheart?"

"Jesus," he said, wheeling in his chair. "Why are you sneaking up on me?"

"You didn't hear my car?"

"God almighty, Deb." He held the brush against his chest a moment, then pointed it at me. "Startling Michael Birch is not a good idea. Really not." He shook his head. "Understatement of the year."

He bent back to his boot, buff buff buff.

It felt like a hospice situation. The pressure, the heightened emotions, the vast difference in circumstances of people involved. And so I knew the rules for handling moments like that: Resist all urges to turn away, even though my insides were trembling. Find the courage to face directly into the wind.

"Any special reason you're suiting up today?"

Buff, buff. "Had a call from Gene."

"Gene?"

He paused, staring at the floor. "Jesus, Deb. Gene Cleaves? The guy who lost his leg in our IED attack?"

"I'm sorry. I forgot his name for a second."

Michael went back to boot polishing.

"How's Gene doing these days?"

"Finished PT and OT and now he wants to get his riflery chops back. Invited me down to the range next week."

"I see."

There was so much more I wanted to say. About lavishing affection on his gear when he could not spare one caress for me. About what shooting again might stir up in him. About how all of this was scaring me.

Then I remembered what the Professor had said earlier that day: First you must understand his weapon.

I crossed the kitchen and picked up the rifle. Heavier than I'd expected. Colder too. The gun seemed inert, just dull metal, but I knew it was capable of enormous things.

Michael was watching me intently, boot brush suspended midstroke. He rested his wrist on his knee. "What's up, Deb?"

I cradled the gun to my chest. Professor, I thought, I hope you are right.

Then I squatted, looking my husband full in the face. "Isn't it time you taught me how to shoot this thing?"

ICHIRO SOGA FLEW TWO SORTIES. He managed two take-offs, navigated two flights, and dropped four bombs.

Obviously his mission did not achieve its intended goals. Not even the mighty 1942 U.S. Department of War could have suppressed the news of a massive conflagration in the forests of southern Oregon.

Nonetheless, Soga punctured coastal complacency. He revealed weaknesses in American defenses. Eventually one of his bombs did inflict lethal damage.

His initial salvo passed over Brookings, a coastal logging town, then inland toward Mount Emily. The area is now known as Siskiyou National Forest; to Soga, the abundance of trees was staggering.

Understand the pilot's perspective: An island nation is perpetually starving. It is an inevitable consequence of geography. Some commodities are unavailable.

Thus do island nations possess few options. Those inhabited by peaceable peoples tend to suffer perpetual poverty. Think Haiti, think Zanzibar. Others entertain notions of empire. Think Great Britain in its imperial years.

Into this second category of ambition one might fairly add Japan in the early twentieth century, its islands tucked southeast of the Chinese trove of natural resources. Notions of empire in the Land of the Rising Sun were prompted by the imperatives of isolation. For Soga, therefore, what lay below him was a target too large to miss.

The first bomb fell and exploded. Both pilot and navigator saw it ignite.

With one wing 170 pounds lighter than the other, the plane yawed to the opposite side. But Soga kept the nose forward, maintaining steady rudder pressure with his feet. He flew six miles in that fashion, until they passed over an area known as Bear Wallow Lookout. There Okuda released the second bomb. There was no visible flame that time. This failure may have been the result of a lapse in Japanese incendiary technology, but the previous week's downpour might have been a likelier cause. The weather that kept Soga submerged had also drenched the region's trees.

Meanwhile, the first bomb's fire caught and grew.

If the U.S. coastal military forces proved insufficiently vigilant, the mainland was ready in other important ways. North of Soga's flight path, a series of catastrophic forest fires known as the Tillamook Burn had torched 355,000 acres in 1933. The flames had proved beyond human power to extinguish and only went out when the rains of the Pacific Northwest poured down. The blazes cost the timber industry $442.4 million in 1933 dollars, deepened the Depression in that region, and produced a plume of hot ash that reached ships 500 miles out to sea.

Since then, a system of fire towers known as the Advanced Warning System stood ready. The AWS was a civilian organization, loosely connected to the more militarized Civil Defense Corps. The AWS commander for southern Oregon down to the California line was one Donny Baker III, about whom more in a moment.

Howard Gardner of the U.S. Forest Service was first to observe the plane. A prospector, hunter, and woodsman, he was deeply familiar with the landscape. The bomb went down in a large, unlogged stand of timber. Later Gardner became the toast of the state, attending celebratory dinners in Portland and beyond—a tour that ceased only when he returned home upon the birth of his son.

While firefighters raced to the scene, it is worth noting that Soga's bomb revealed significant American weaknesses.

Foremost, the land he flew over in 1942 was the longest stretch of U.S. coastline without a radar installation. From Cape Perpetua in northern Oregon to Fort Bragg in southern California, a span exceeding 450 miles, the only tools for enemy observation were human eyes, either in ground patrols or in timber towers.

These facilities were rustic in more than construction. Most had communications systems so primitive, they verged on the comical. To reach the army command post in Brookings, for example, required calling the Driscoll Hotel. A person answering the phone would then run 500 yards to the command post, and the recipient would run 500 yards back to take the call. Also, the hotel closed daily from 8:30 P.M. till 8:00 A.M. During those hours, communication involved a thirty-eight-mile drive up the winding coast highway.

Dysfunctions in the chain of command exacerbated the problem. In the early daylight hours of September 9, Private Harold Moyer was foot-patrolling the Harris Park beach area when he heard a plane overhead. Limited visibility left him unable to identify the aircraft beyond noting that the tips of its wings were square. It beggars imagination how a soldier assigned shoreline duty would be unacquainted with makes and models of enemy aircraft. Moreover, under orders not to leave his position, Moyer obeyed. With no means of informing the command post, he therefore kept his observations to himself. Not until much later in the day, when an officer overheard him chatting in the barracks, did Moyer's superiors learn that he had seen the aircraft. Any opportunity for pursuit had passed hours earlier.

What explanation could there be for these lapses? Perhaps primarily, the officers in charge were woefully inexperienced. Responsibility for that portion of Oregon lay with the Army's 44th Division, 174th Infantry, Company G. The company commander was First Lieutenant Claude Waldrop, who had begun that assignment on August 8, 1942—thirty-one days before Soga's mission. Waldrop had the aid of Joseph Kane, who had become a second lieutenant in June and was assigned to Company G in late July. On this command, the paint had not yet dried.

When Kane learned about his soldiers' awareness of the bombing, inability to identify the aircraft, and failure to report their observations, he instructed them to remain silent in any interrogations by army investigators. That order shielded him from immediate repercussions. Later, it also earned him a court-martial.

In all, Soga's route flew him into the exact center of the least well-guarded part of the American coastline. In coming weeks, among U.S. military leadership, legitimate questions of espionage arose. How did the Japanese know precisely the most vulnerable place to attack?

MAINTAINING DISCIPLINED ADHERENCE to the mission plan, Soga flew back to sea on a heading the inverse of his inland approach. He spotted the I-25, landed, and observed as the deck crane hoisted his plane aboard. Once he went below, Soga informed his captain that he had spotted two freighters nearby.

Tagami ordered immediate pursuit. Simultaneously, a U.S. Army bomber on a routine patrol had spotted the Japanese vessel. The aircraft was captained by Jean Daugherty from the 390th Bomb Squadron, 42nd Bombardment Group, based at McChord Field in Washington. The I-25 was in the process of submerging, but its decks were just awash and the conning tower was plainly visible.

Immediately, Daugherty's bomber changed direction, bearing down on the sub. By then only its periscope remained above the surface. The plane dropped two 300-pound depth charges, set to explode at 50 feet under water.

After the bombs detonated, air bubbles and oil came to the ocean's surface. The bomber made another approach, dropping a third depth charge, but it did not elicit more bubbles or oil.

The army dispatched three other planes to the area. They too dropped 300-pound bombs, set to detonate either 45 seconds after release or when they reached the ocean floor. No evidence of the sub's presence remained.

Aboard the I-25, Captain Tagami determined that the damage was not extensive. He ordered the diesel engines shut off, electric motors started, and repairs made. The sub sat in silence. Soga returned to his berth, listening to the depth charges' detonations, then placing his sword back in a secure spot.

U.S. Army air patrols continued over the area, monitoring calm seas until night fell.

CHAPTER 8

THE PROFESSOR SLEPT THE MORNING AWAY. I opened my laptop and sat in the kitchen trying to reduce the backlog of paperwork. Between them, Medicare and Central Office never met a form they didn't like. Meanwhile, he dozed and murmured and barely moved.

It has always struck me as unfair: Just as a person nears death and wants to make the absolute most of every moment, his capacity to stay awake dwindles. The span of consciousness shrinks to fewer hours each day, then one hour, then minutes, then individual breaths, and then it is over.

And yet, that reduction also sharpens appreciation of each detail. I remember Horatio, a muscular Italian immigrant who worked most of his life in a coastal town marina pumping gas and selling supplies in the chandlery. In fact, he was the person who taught me what a chandlery was. Horatio had end-stage leukemia, beyond cure though he still went to the hospital once a week for platelet infusions. One bright October afternoon when the air smelled like nostalgia, I was helping him get settled at home after an infusion session. His wife pulled me aside to say the doctor had told them Horatio would not live till Christmas. But their daughter and only grandchild were flying up from San Diego for the holiday week. They had purchased nonrefundable tickets and were too broke to buy new ones.

I went to work, emailing Horatio's friends, contacting airlines, tapping the agency's wish budget. In two days we had tickets for the daughter and granddaughter to fly up for Thanksgiving instead.

Horatio thanked me with tears in his eyes. I told him I hadn't done anything but let people take care of him, and they'd been happy to do it.

"Don't you understand?" he said, fists pressed to his chest. "I will get to hug my beautiful Maddie one more time. Do you know how fantastic the hug of a six-year-old girl is? I may never let her go."

Life, Horatio taught me, life is the hug of a six-year-old girl: precious and sweet and all too fleeting.

WHEN I LIFTED MY HEAD from the online administrivia and saw that it was nearly noon, I went in to check on Barclay Reed once again.

He was lying in stillness. He blinked at me and did not speak. I came to the bedside and stood a moment, respecting his silence.

"Is there anything you need?" I asked him at last.

"Ten more years?"

"If I could, I would."

"Bah." The Professor took a deep, noisy breath. "They would be too tiring anyway. Might there be any fruit in the house?"

"I'll be right back."

In the fridge I found strawberries Melissa had left. They must have been the first of the season—large, unblemished, and, since it was June in Oregon, probably imported from the southern hemisphere. I washed and hulled them and left them in a colander. In the cabinet on a high shelf I spotted a stoneware bowl that I could tell was handmade. I reached up for it because sometimes bringing a household object out of obscurity is pleasing to a patient.

But then, a wonderful coincidence. On the bottom, the bowl's maker had painted a hummingbird. It was not detailed, like the carved one on my desk. This bird was an exercise in skillful restraint, a few deft brush strokes: wing, wing, body, beak.

I poured the berries in, and the contrast of red fruit and gritty stoneware made me want to take a photograph. Instead I brought the berries to the Professor, who raised the head of his bed as I set the fruit in his lap.

He recoiled, then lifted the bowl. "Where did you find this?"

"Top shelf in the cabinet."

"I have not seen it in years."

"I like it. The roughness of the pottery, you know?"

Barclay Reed scrutinized the bowl, turning it in a full circle before holding it back toward me. "Please use a different one."

"Really?"

"I'm asking you."

"All right." I hurried to the kitchen and returned with the berries in a plain white bowl. He took it without comment.

"Care to explain?"

The Professor picked up a berry and sighed. "The stoneware in this house was made by a member of my family who is no longer alive."

I left a pause for him to elaborate, but there was nothing more. "I have a plate in my kitchen," I said. "Fine blue china, handed down from my great-grandmother. I keep it on a high shelf where no one can bump it or break it. Is this bowl like that for you?"

He did not reply. Barclay Reed wore a strange expression though, possibly wistful, but it was hard to know for sure. Instead, he examined the berry with considerable care and put it in his mouth.

"Amazing," he said, chewing with his eyes half-closed. "Exquisite."

A little red juice ran out the corner of his mouth. He wiped it back with a finger, then reached down for another berry.

I lowered myself into the bedside chair and watched him work his way through the bowl. We remained in silence except for his chewing, Barclay Reed immersed in a tide of taste and sensations, while in my head I gave myself the lecture I eventually have to administer every time, no matter what my relationship with the patient is, or what the person's illness is, or what else is going on in my life. It happens with every patient, without fail.

The lecture goes like this: Accept. Accept. Do not deny that this person is weakening. Accept.

WHEN I RETURNED from putting the empty bowl in the sink, the Professor was rubbing his hands together.

"Nurse Birch," he harrumphed. "Are we still planning to plan? Or might we leap impetuously into the planning itself?"

"Yes." I reached into my briefcase. "I have some papers with me—"

"Let me guess." He placed a straight finger against his lips. "Trip to Paris? Escape to Rio? Or no. Are you more the Niagara Falls type?"

"This is called advance care planning." I flattened the pages on my knee. "It's a way of making sure—"

"I know what it does, Nurse Birch. It protects your agency from legal culpability if anything goes wrong in my dying."

"Of making sure that your wishes for your health care are memorialized—"

"An offensive choice of verb, I might interject."

"So your caregivers can obey those wishes, should you not be able to speak."

"But I—" He caught himself. "'Should I not be able to speak,' you say?"

I gave a small nod.

He made a tent with his fingertips. "And why must we 'memorialize' these instructions, pray tell?"

"To put you in charge, Professor."

He spoke in a voice dripping with condescension. "If there is one singular thing that I might clarify for you at this moment, Nurse Birch, so that we share a common understanding, it is that I am most decidedly not in charge. Indeed, having slept till nearly noon today, an achievement I last attained as an adolescent of seventeen, I submit that at present, cancer is driving this bus. Quite happily, you might say."

"I am not talking about today."

"You think I will have more control later? Are you that severely delusional?"

I folded my hands in my lap.

"What?" he said. "What could be upsetting our dear Florence Nightingale?"

"I would like to request, please, permission to speak five consecutive sentences without being interrupted, and without my premise being challenged, so I can explain this exercise."

"Oh ho, 'exercise' is it?" He began pumping his arms up and down as though lifting imaginary barbells. "One two, hup hup."

"Professor Reed, please."

He paused, his arms still raised. "Nurse Birch, are you not amused?"

"This is serious."

"I have known a lifetime of seriousness. Seventy-eight years of it."

"But all this banter—"

"Banter keeps the brain pink and fluffy." He lowered his hands. "Please don't spoil my fun. My pleasures are few enough now."

"Imagine if, instead of cancer, you had heart disease. And for some reason, down the road, your heart was to stop beating."

"There is simply no turning you aside today, is there?"

I held up an open hand. "Five sentences, Professor. Five."

He sighed, puffing his cheeks. "Fine." He waved a hand dismissively. "Do your worst."

"If that happened, the standard of care is for me to call 9-1-1, and the EMTs come. They might inject you with adrenaline, or shock you, or perform CPR so intensely your ribs break. By the way, it's not like on TV. Less than two percent of people with cardiac arrest who receive CPR ever recover. But an ambulance would rush you to a hospital, where the process would continue, and could include opening your chest and cracking wide your ribs for direct manual stimulation of the heart."

"I know more about that process than you might expect." He pulled his head back in revulsion. "Perfectly bestial. How many sentences was that?"

"I lost count. But there is a less automatic alternative. You can execute a document—"

"Once again with a morbid verb."

"You can sign a document that says you don't want that level of intervention, specifies what you do want, or puts someone in charge of making those decisions if you can't."

"Let us put a fine point on it, Nurse Birch, shall we? In the interests of my not falling back to sleep from sheer boredom? If I prevented the entire sequence, the 9-1-1 call, et cetera, what would occur?"

"Your heart would remain unbeating."

"I would die."

"If your heart has stopped, a person could reasonably argue that you are already dead."

"Touché." He digested this information. "Proceed."

"Medical professionals are trained to prolong life, often without regard to its quality. An advance directive lets you be as specific as you want: yes to chemotherapy, no to advanced life support, yes to donating your organs, no to cracking your chest. Or you can take a simpler route, a power of attorney, where you designate someone to make medical decisions on your behalf."

The Professor frowned. He stirred his basket of remotes but did not choose one. He surveyed the room, seeming to linger on the upper corners. "Would you please read to me from The Sword now? We've left the bomb fire burning, and I want to know what happens."

"Can we at least complete the power of attorney? And revisit the rest of this another day?"

"I'd rather not."

"I have a blank form right here." I raised the page in front of him. "Very simple. All it requires is for you to designate someone, and sign. Then I'll be the primary witness, and when Melissa—"

"Heretofore, Nurse Birch, I had not considered you a stupid person."

"What are you talking about?"

"Insensitive, yes, as you persist in this line of inquiry despite my obvious reluctance."

"For your own good, Professor. So that your preferences—"

"But stupid? I had not contemplated that possibility before now."

I put my hands on my hips. "Why do you have to insult me? I'm only trying to help you."

"Who do you see around here that I might designate?"

That shut me up.

But he continued, arms wide and voice rising. "Do you observe a long line of visitors? Children and grandchildren gathered from far and wide? Multitudes of former colleagues assembled to hear my valedictory? Wear marks on the rugs from the constant adoring traffic?"

"All I intended—"

"Nurse Birch." He was shouting now. "Do you honestly believe I would resort to concluding my life in the presence of a stranger if I possessed any other alternative?"

Ouch. The room had rung with his voice, and now it froze with his silence.

I bowed my head. "I am sorry."

"Stupid is an incorrect word. I amend myself. Cruel would be more accurate."

"I have no defense to make."

"Please leave me alone."

"I understand." I tried to look him in the eye, but he turned his face away.

"Leave the blasted document with me."

I placed it on the bed beside his hand. "I am sorry, Professor."

"Yes, well." He kept his gaze averted.

I left him, tail between my legs.

IN THE KITCHEN my hands needed some kind of task. I washed the two bowls and set them in the drying rack. The living room was next, but I paused beside the gong and admitted that nothing in there needed doing. I checked my watch. It was nearly a lost day. He had slept all morning, the afternoon was passing, and I had not even shaved and dressed him. We all have times when life intervenes and we get little done. But when our days are numbered, it feels like a kind of thievery. If there is ever a chapter of life with no time to waste, it is the last one.

I wiped the kitchen counters. I logged on to email. I ambled out onto the deck. It was full June, a glorious day, clusters of color in the gardens, rhododendrons rainbowing on the far shore. The lake was empty, no sailors or motorboats, perhaps too cool yet for swimmers. A breeze out in the middle stirred the surface and hurried away.

No. I would not let him lose a day completely. There were too few left.

His wheelchair sat collapsed in the hallway, and I unfolded it while rolling it into the room ahead of me.

The Professor raised his eyebrows but did not speak.

"We're way behind schedule for bathing and dressing today," I said. "But I'd like to get you outside before the afternoon is gone. It's a gorgeous day."

"Outside?"

"Right now." I pressed the button to raise the head of his bed. "Chop chop."

Within minutes he was settled in the chair, a blanket tucked under his legs. I wheeled him to the front door, jogging back to fetch his water bottle.

It sat on the rolling table, on top of the power of attorney document. I picked it up, seeing a wet ring in the middle of the page. But he had signed the paper after all. Barclay Reed had also written the name of the person who would be in charge of his final medical decision-making. Mine.

"WHAT DO YOU WANT ME TO DO?" I asked as we rolled up the driveway.

"Bear right toward the little bridge," he said.

"Fine." I followed his directions. "But that isn't what I meant. You signed the form. So tell me what I should do for you."

"Ah," he said, without elaborating. I felt a lecture coming, and waited.

We wheeled along the road, which smelled tarry from fresh repair patches. Though there wasn't much sidewalk space, there wasn't much traffic either. Just moms schlepping their kids home from school; it was that time of day.

Two boys on skateboards, eighth graders I'd guess, were already home, and had set up a ramp in a driveway. They were practicing stunts. I paused so the Professor could watch them.

I have no idea if they were talented or not, but their tricks struck me as impossible: spinning and flipping the board while they were not on it, causing it to leap with them when they jumped. The skate boards landed loudly, like planks clapped together, and the boys often missed. But they would hop up and try again right away. If one of them did something difficult, the other one would make loud crowd sounds of applause.

I wondered if the boys were aware that they had an audience. They never said anything, or glanced our way.

Then I remembered playing junior high basketball, how acutely we were conscious of our visibility, how exposed I felt whenever I made a mistake. At game's end, I could have named every boy, teacher, friend, or parent in the stands. So there was no way the skateboarders were unaware of the Professor and me. This was a show, put on entirely for us. One of the boys jumped over a pipe and landed on his board again.

"Ladies and gentlemen," the other boy cheered, arms in the air, "for the first time ever in the history of skateboarding . . ."

I aimed the chair and began strolling again. "That's pretty cool stuff, don't you think?"

Barclay Reed raised his thumb and pinkie. "Yo."

I laughed. "Did you really just say 'yo'?"

"Nurse Birch, what is the purpose of suffering?"

"Excuse me?"

"I'm weighing what instructions to give you. But the question concerns more than making sure I don't drool in public. There is the philosophical question of why we suffer, and whether it has any merit. Should I avoid misery without plumbing its potential value?"

"Entirely your call, Professor. It's your life."

"I've said it before, Nurse Birch: You are always weakest when you attempt to be evasive."

"I am not being—"

"You have witnessed how many deaths? Hundreds?"

"More than a thousand, by now."

"A thousand. And I have seen one. It was unforgettably horrible."

I leaned over so I could see his face. "Who was that?"

He turned away. "Not now, and probably not ever."

"Whose death did you witness, Professor?"

"Irrelevant." He waved a hand in a papal dismissal. "The point is that you have vast experience in this area. I am not ashamed of my ignorance, so I ask you not to indulge in modesty about your lack of ignorance."

I took a wheelchair handle in each hand. "You want to know what the purpose of suffering is."

"And whether it has merit."

I rolled him along, trying to organize my thoughts. Sunlight fell dappled through the trees. "Well. I can say that the suffering of my patients has been deeply educational to me."

"Educational?"

"It makes me appreciate this period of my life when I am in full health, knowing that my own days of dependency will surely come. It reminds me that most of my daily concerns are trivial. And it teaches me to pay attention so I can do a better job with future patients."

"All very well for you, Nurse Birch. But what purpose does suffering serve for the patient?"

I pulled his chair to a standstill. We had reached a little bridge, and a brook feeding Lake Oswego gurgled below. "You are not going to like my answer."

"Yours is not the only mind I will consult on this matter. Plato, for example, may have written something worth considering. But I am curious."

"What I have seen, in my work, is that suffering enlarges people." He opened his mouth but I pressed on. "I know, of course they'd rather not be in pain, or in fear. We all would. But there is a thing that I have seen." I moved around in front of him. "Many people, confronting their mortality, appreciate existence more. They realize that they are part of something greater than themselves. Spiritually, they enlarge."

"You are beginning to sound dangerously religious, Nurse Birch."

"I don't mean that, though there are plenty of times that religion is the way they enlarge. It's more like acts of generosity, or forgiveness, or humility, that people simply were not capable of making when they were well. It sounds corny, but suffering makes some people more loving."

Barclay Reed scowled. "While I was sleeping today, you must have had too much sun."

"I said you wouldn't like my answer."

A trio of girls on bikes came zooming past at that moment, the red-headed rear one calling to the curly-haired one at the front: "Amy. Amy, hold up."

They were around the corner and down the lane in five seconds.

The Professor watched after them. "To put a finer point on it, precisely who am I to shower with all of this eleventh-hour love? Melissa the sweaty nursemaid? Cheryl who cannot complete a crossword?"

"I didn't say it always happens."

He gripped the arms of his chair and cleared his throat. "Here is my instruction to you, for my advance directive."

"I am listening."

"No needless prolonging. And no suffering." He pointed his bony chin out at the lake. "None. Nada. Zilch."

"Earlier on, you were resistant to pain control."

"That was ages ago."

"One week?"

"Intellectually, that could be a century. Today I am better informed. I have experienced the benefit of medicinal assistance. Also I recall the death I did witness, how ugly the medical care was, how needlessly cruel, and above all, how indifferent to suffering."

"The death you don't want to talk about."

"Will not talk about. Moreover, I am not interested in suffering as a mechanism of character building. My character is already built."

"Fair enough. I understand."

"And will obey?"

"And will uphold your instructions completely."

"Good. Now what are your thoughts about . . ." Barclay Reed turned the wheelchair so that he was facing down the lane. The sun fell across his eyes, making him squint, and he tugged on a tuft of hair at his forehead.

"Yes?"

"What is the purpose of your husband's suffering? How has he been enlarged?"

Ouch. I had not expected the conversation to take that turn. My first impulse was defensive, protective as at the police station. But the Professor had signed his medical power of attorney to me, had just that moment given me instructions for the manner of his death. How could I withhold an honest answer?

Besides, the question had a weight all its own. What was the purpose of Michael's pain?

"I don't honestly know," I said.

"Are you shaving him yet?"

"Not even close."

The Professor ruminated, running one thumb back and forth on the rubber of one of his wheels. "Are you hopeful?"

"Almost."

He said nothing.

I stepped back behind the chair. "Time to head home?"

"One more thing." He stopped rubbing the wheel and lowered his hands to his lap. I noticed that he was staring out at the glimmering reach of lake.

Someone was hoisting the sail of a Sunfish, a triangle of red and white stripes. He narrowed his eyes, studying the little boat and its solitary sailor. "Inform me about what the need will be."

"I don't understand the question."

"You gain the powers of the advance directive when the need arises. I want to know when that moment will occur."

"There is really no sure way—"

"I have metastatic kidney cancer. That is a solid fact. Therefore I imagine an experienced medical expert can predict. I would like you to predict."

"Every person's prognosis is different."

He snorted. "The ever-evasive Nurse Birch."

"You always say that. But everyone has different appetites, different sleep needs, different immune systems. And different disease trajectories."

"For God's sake," he barked. "I am asking you how I will die." He pounded the armrest. "Please do me the courtesy of candor."

"Professor." I let the air settle around us. Holding his chair for balance, I squatted so our faces were level. I felt like a knight kneeling before the throne. "I can predict how, but not how fast."

"Be as honest as you dare."

I took a deep breath. "Your chart says you have cancer in many sites now. As the tumors grow, they will starve you, metabolically. You may have pain in your bones, which is a symptom we can suppress, but that's a distraction. The primary disease will only cause fatigue."

"Thus does a vigorous man sleep until noon."

"Actually, yes. Gradually you will begin wasting away as the cancer robs more of your nourishment. You will become weaker, and completing daily functions will be more difficult. Eventually, your digestive system will lose the competition for nutrients, and you will stop eating. At that point, life will be mostly about resting. One day you won't take fluids either."

I wanted to hold his hands, curled there on the blanket in his lap. They were so pale and vulnerable. But I had never felt invited to that level of contact with the Professor, and this was not the time to test his limits. So I continued to grip his chair.

"The final phase can pass quickly, or be frustratingly slow. But once fluid intake ends, it is a matter of days. The important thing for you to know is that almost one hundred percent of kidney cancer patients, very nearly all of them, die in their sleep."

The Professor was quiet a long time. "Thus not suffering is a possibility."

"And I will do my very best to make it a reality."

He nodded to himself while continuing to observe the lake. I turned to follow his gaze.

The little boat had pulled away from the dock, its red and white sail bright against the blue water. It worked at an angle close to the wind, beating steadily against the waves as it moved up the lake.

As we watched, the boat tacked back and forth across the mouth of the bay. Sometimes it struggled, heeling high so that the sailor had to lean out to balance the Sunfish. But finally the boat reached the point, breezing around the corner to find its way up the lake and out of sight.

Just as we both had known it would.

HIS GRANDFATHER WAS KNOWN AS BIG DON, his father as Mr. Donald. Thus was Donald Baker III instantly and ubiquitously called Donny. His diploma from Brookings Harbor High School in Curry County was issued to "Donny Baker III." In sum, under every circumstance, from infancy forward, the man was known by a diminutive.

Big Don had been a logger, rough-skinned and hard-knuckled. Mr. Donald, whose aptitude with numbers exceeded his skillfulness with an axe, operated a modest but successful accounting firm. Mr. Donald's wife was a homemaker whose pies won enough blue ribbons in local fairs to merit a brief profile, complete with apron-clad photo, in the Saturday "Home and Hearth" section of the Brookings-Harbor Pilot newspaper.

Donny's early years left a negligible mark on the public record. Born in 1924, he was of prime age for military service in 1942. Yet there is no evidence that he sought to enlist in any branch of the armed forces, nor that he suffered any malady that would have precluded enlistment. He served in Civil Defense but was mustered out of that organization after six months for reasons that remain undocumented.

When the state forestry department established a civilian safety program in the wake of the Tillamook Burn—the aforementioned Advance Warning System—Donny found his calling. In early 1942, a supervisor's letter supporting his promotion to "assistant area manager for fire prevention" asserted that Donny's "agility in the backcountry, as a result of hunting since childhood, befits him for modest personnel oversight responsibilities including on-the-ground involvement."

Which is to say that Donny Baker III patrolled the woods and hiked from tower to tower carrying not only binoculars, an axe, and a shovel, but also at all times a rifle. Brookings retailers recall that he was partial to Winchesters.

ON SEPTEMBER 9, 1942, Donny was not scheduled for duty until nine A.M. Informed of Soga's attack by his hunting buddy Howard Gardner, however, Donny dispatched a fire crew to the first bomb's landing site by 8:45.

Four miles from the nearest logging road, the fire struck a remote area with steep embankments. Donny must have been in his element, however, for he reached the scene by noon—and well before the army. His later report boasted that the blaze was extinguished by two P.M. Total acres consumed: three.

If the day's work had ended there, it would have been an unmitigated success for Donny Baker III. Instead, he nearly managed to get himself and his firemen killed.

An army patrol, approaching the scene that afternoon, heard shots in their direction. When they returned the volley, shouts from the fire team identified the source of the initial rounds as the sole crewman to carry a weapon. Army records indicate that Donny Baker III had thought Japanese troops were about to ambush his crew.

By the evening of September 9, Donny had returned to the Driscoll Hotel, where, still dressed in smoke-scented clothes, he held forth on the attack and his crew's backcountry firefighting prowess. Moreover, he displayed fragments of the bomb, announcing that in coming days they would be for sale to the highest bidder.

Instead, the following morning, Donny was detained for questioning by investigators with the 174th Infantry. The record does not contain the officers' names, but Donny later remarked that the two men were "tall and humorless."

While presumably aware that Donny owned other weapons, the

investigators deemed the rifle with which he had fired at the troops to be evidentiary, and confiscated it. They also directed that he be immediately discharged from the fire service for interfering with military evidence. As a final insult, they impounded his bomb fragments.

Following that intervention, Donny vanished from the public record of the 1940s. Civilian or otherwise, he would have no further role in World War II.

That December, a senior army staffer made the fragments into a pen holder, which he gave to a general as a Christmas gift.

CHAPTER 9

NINETY MINUTES FROM HOME, Michael spoke for the first time since our driveway: "Here." He pointed to a cattle gate held closed by a rusted chain. When I braked, a cloud of dust billowed around us.

He placed both palms on the dashboard. "You sure you want to do this?"

"Positive," I said. "It'll be fun."

"Fun," he said in a flat voice. He climbed out of the car and unhooked the chain. I watched his strong back flex as he lifted the gate and slid it back.

I'd driven us east up the Columbia River gorge, south into the forest, and every which way down increasingly rutted dirt roads. The whole trip, Michael sat as quiet as a tombstone. It was strange having him as a passenger. Before the road-rage arrest, he'd done all the driving. I was in charge of tunes, navigation, and snacks, and considered myself an expert. My motto was never late, never lost, never bored.

One rainy Saturday after his first deployment we drove hours east to Bend for an auction of car-repair equipment. He won the bidding on a hydraulic lift whose piston could hold twelve thousand pounds, and on the way home I read an entire book of erotica out loud to him. When he pulled up the driveway, we practically sprinted into the house.

Good times. Old times. Now my guts turned twists on themselves as he waved me through the open gate. I had never held a gun before, much less fired one. By trying to understand my husband this way, I was placing enormous trust in the wisdom of Barclay Reed, and the curmudgeon didn't even know it.

As I idled past the gate, Michael held out a hand to stop me. "One more thing," he said, holding the side mirror. "Joel."

"Joel?"

"This is his place, and he's got a mild case of scrambled eggs."

I felt my insides flutter. "Which means?"

"One time in Vietnam he called in a napalm strike and was a little off in his coordinates. Pretty much fried his sinuses. So he has some breathing habits that are distracting at first, but you'll get used to them."

"That doesn't sound like scrambled eggs."

"His brain might have gotten a bit cooked too." Michael scuffed a boot in the dirt. "Don't take him personally though. Basically Joel is harmless."

"Basically?"

"He does these rants. Like getting something off his chest? But there's always a grain of truth in there too. Also, Joel loves military history. If you want to get on his sweet side, ask about that."

He trotted back to close the gate while I drove a few yards ahead. After Michael flopped down into the passenger seat, I inched forward, dodging potholes. We passed one of those old factory safety signs: THIS SITE HAS GONE 1,000 DAYS WITHOUT AN ACCIDENT. But the zeros were actually bullet holes in the metal, each the size of a silver dollar. I could not imagine what weapon would punch a hole like that.

The house sat in a clearing: a pile of rough logs with 55-gallon drums beneath rain spouts on the corners. Two cars rusted in the side yard beside a refrigerator with no door. A port-a-potty listed at an angle by the shed. Half a dozen dogs lay flopped here and there in the dirt.

A tilted white pole flew, from top to bottom: the American flag, Oregon's blue state flag, the black POW/MIA banner, and a yellow one with a red snake that read DON'T TREAD ON ME.

Standing on top of a picnic table was a noodle of a man with a thin ponytail of white hair who peered into the distance with one hand over his brow. He may have been the skinniest person I'd ever seen upright, which from a hospice nurse is really saying something. Since he wore coveralls with no shirt, his arms were on display like those long balloons that clowns twist into animal shapes. The man also wore a cowboy-style holster, which held a chrome-bright pistol with a barrel as long as my forearm. If he had heard us drive up, he made no sign.

As we climbed out, the hounds mooned up at us with mournful faces. One drummed the ground with his tail, another snapped half-heartedly at a fly.

"Damn," Michael muttered.

I glanced over, and his face was blanched. "What is it, lover?"

"Dogs are out today. Can't stand them."

This was news to me. "Really?" I said. "Since when?"

"Since Iraq." He veered to give the animals a wide berth.

Still the man on the picnic table had not turned. Motioning for me to wait, Michael approached the string bean in overalls. I almost called him back. I didn't like the idea of him creeping up on an armed man.

When he reached the picnic table, Michael leaned over. "Hey Joel."

"God almighty," Joel said, right hand instantly on his holster. With his left he tugged a pair of ear buds down, and even across the dirt yard I could hear the tinny music playing. "Shouldn't sneak up like that, Milk." He held a finger over one nostril. "Knuh. Knuh."

I winced. The sound was half cough, half sneeze, with a rawness like the respiratory version of the sore where a scab has been picked away.

"You might turn the headphones down enough to hear a car coming in," Michael said blandly. "Or should I honk next time?"

Joel reached into a pocket to silence the music, then shuddered the length of his body. "Just waiting to hear from fat Leo. He's been getting lazy, not walking all the way out to Pistol Park. But I don't want him down range of you even one degree. Not with the big iron you bring."

"It's my wife who'll be doing the shooting today."

"Wife?" Joel turned and squinted at me. "No shit."

I gave a meek wave. "Hi."

Joel laid a look on me that was, to be plain, a flat-out ogle—shameless, thorough, top to bottom. "Hello, Betty," he sang, tipping an imaginary hat.

A bang came from somewhere to our left, and I jumped. By the time I realized what the sound was—the report of a gun—its echo barked from the right. I retreated toward the car.

Coming here was clearly a mistake. I could sit calmly with a person dying of the worst disease imaginable, but this place pushed every anxiety button I possessed. My nursing training had included two ER rotations, and some of those Saturday nights had convinced me that guns were the most unforgiving of tools. One mistake, however minor, and you were maimed for life, or you had maimed someone else, or somebody was dead.

"There's Leo now." Joel clambered off the table. "Knuh. Probably cursing me for making him walk that far. Not that the exercise would hurt him any."

Michael placed his hand on Joel's shoulder, and somehow it calmed him. I liked seeing how the older man respected my husband, no words said but the message in their gestures.

"So," Michael said. "What's new in that busy brain of yours?"

"Well now, Milk." Joel ducked his head.

"Go ahead. It's been awhile."

Joel tugged on his pony tail, then squared himself to Michael. "I've been thinking they ought to do away with the D in it."

"The D." Michael put his hands in his pockets. "Go ahead."

"Well now, why would they call it disorder, when it is the correct response to repeated periods of intense and violent and traumatic stress? Knuh. A perfectly healthy person would be freaked out by war, right? To my thinking, that makes the freak-out healthy. Oh yeah. I think they should call it PTSN, the N meaning normal. Or PTSA, for appropriate."

Michael nodded. "I hear you. Drop the D."

"What about you?" Joel said, turning my way. "What do you think?"

"Me?"

"Not asking the dogs," he said.

"Well," I hedged, trying to forget how his eyes had undressed me. "There are many kinds of unusual behavior that we ought to consider normal."

"There you go," Joel said.

"But you can put ten people in the same warfare situation, and only one or two will develop post-traumatic stress symptoms. It's true in plane crashes too, and in the area I know best, when people face terminal illness. Only a fraction of them have the recurring frights, jump at loud noises, or develop suicidal ideation. So we use the phrase 'disorder' because when most people experience trauma, eventually they are OK."

Joel stared at me as if I were covered with bugs.

"I've even read theories about PTSG, where the G is actually for growth, because some survivors of trauma experience huge personal growth as a result. New jobs, new directions, deeper faith."

He turned to Michael. "Is she bagging on me?"

"They're only labels anyway," I said. "I believe the important thing is how we take care of individuals, regardless of label."

Michael released Joel's shoulder and smiled. "This is Deborah. Ask her opinion, and you'll probably get it."

Without speaking, Joel extended his skinny hand.

I shook it, and it felt like grabbing a bunch of twigs. "Nice to meet you."

"Yeah, yeah. So, Milk." He turned to Michael. "What's your sport today?"

"The .50 at a hundred and fifty yards. With that scope I told you about."

"German optics cost too much. Set your own targets?"

Michael kicked the back of one boot with the toe of the other. "Always happy to save an old guy some steps."

Joel made a jangly laugh. "I can still out-mule you with a pack on, Milk, any day you like."

"I'm not dumb enough to take that challenge." As Michael went back to the car, I noticed he took the long way, keeping the shed between him and the hounds. Dog avoidance was a change.

Not that we'd had a pet of our own. But whenever we went to his school buddy Brian's for dinner, Michael used to spend a good half hour throwing a slobbery tennis ball for Elvis—Brian's square-headed black lab, a galoot as devoted as he was dumb.

Sometimes, too, when the agency provided a comfort companion for a patient, if the visit ran long, I would keep the animal overnight. Wrestling with the dog on the back lawn, sneaking it bits of supper when he thought I wasn't looking, Michael used to love those nights.

But I caught myself. I needed to remove the phrase "Michael used to" from my vocabulary. My task—including the reason I was standing at that shooting range at that very moment—was to understand the new Michael, to know the man he had become. Today's lesson, so far: No more dogs.

Joel and I watched Michael stride out into the high-mown grass. Another pistol report echoed from both sides. Then it was just us, not speaking, and a blue jay that screamed from the edge of the trees.

I looked down, and the ground around me was littered with shells, some brown and thinner than a cigarette butt, some brass and the size of my pinkie. Out in the field the mess was worse. There were dirt piles every fifty yards, with a hodgepodge of objects hung on posts or set on top: cardboard boxes, archery targets, bicycle helmets, furniture with the stuffing sprung. Every one of those objects was ragged with bullet holes.

A huge hill stretched across the back of the range, perhaps a mile away. I imagined it worked like a backstop for any bullets that went wild. Beyond that, it was Oregon timber country, giant trees for miles.

Joel stood beside me, and I could hear him wheezing. I imagined the thousands of scorched alveoli deep in his chest. With an injury like that, it was possible that every inhale hurt. I wondered how I would care for a patient like that. Pain can occupy a huge portion of a person's brain. He took a deep breath and covered one nostril again. "Knuh."

"Why do you call my husband Milk?"

Joel shrugged his bird-boned shoulders. "It's his fighting name. Sometimes guys are called by how they act when everything is at stake."

"Michael was milky?"

"If his face went all white, that was when he was most fierce." Joel coughed, and it sounded as if his lungs had been scoured with steel wool. "So I've been told, anyways. Course I never served with him."

An idea came to me then, not as a lightning bolt but like a window opening. "Michael says you know military history."

"No more'n any other fool who's served a hitch or two. I know textbooks ignore the Italian front of World War II, though it was some of the toughest fighting. I know the Armenian genocide really happened, a million and a half people slaughtered by the Turks in 1915. I know when I came back from Vietnam, nobody was stupid enough to spit on me, or any other soldier I knew, else they'd be dead and we'd be in jail. That spitting stuff was a bit exaggerated, maybe."

He rested a hand on the butt of his pistol. "Or are you going to prove me wrong about that too?"

I glanced over and he was smiling. Joel might be scrambled eggs, but he still knew what teasing was.

"What about the Japanese dropping bombs on the American Pacific Coast?" I asked. "Early in World War II?"

"Where'd you learn such a thing? I've never read one word about it."

"Not necessarily from a book. But maybe somebody told you, or you remembered—"

"Do I really look all that ancient?" He laughed, slapping his concave belly. "How to hurt a guy."

"I didn't mean that you were alive that long ago. I just heard something about a Japanese pilot in 1942. I don't know. He might have flown over the southern part of the state maybe."

"Somebody's selling you a bridge." Joel hooked one thumb in his holster belt. "I'll tell you what, Deborah. This whole country was a hair trigger after Pearl Harbor. If anyone foreign entered U.S. air space, they would have been blasted from the sky, oh yeah. Along with any birds in the vicinity, for good measure."

"I suppose you're right."

Joel gave me some serious elevator eyes again, just shy of leering. I suspected not many women visited his range. "Now you be sure to keep safety glasses and headphones on when shooting time comes." He tapped the side of his head. "Gotta protect those cute little ears of yours."

"Easy, tiger," said Michael, emerging from the tall grass. "Let's leave her cute ears out of this."

"No worries, Milk." Joel held up both open palms. "No mischief meant. She was just making me feel old a second ago, that's all."

"Well, I hate to break it to you—"

"Don't you start too." Joel squinted across the field. Michael had pounded stakes into the ground a football field and a half away, leaned a square of particle board against them, and pinned sheets of paper on the front for targets. "Knuh. You're shooting silhouettes today."

"All I ever use now," Michael said.

"Why does that matter?" I asked.

Michael kept his eyes on the field. "Until recent years, the military did not train people by having them fire at human forms."

"Then some genius decided silhouettes would desensitize us," Joel said. "Since people aren't shaped like circle targets. Oh yeah, better to practice on something closer to the real thing."

"It was pretty much the same when they taught us to bayonet mannequins," Michael added.

"Yeah, that really worked," Joel said. "Bayoneting a living human body is nothing now."

And they both laughed.

Michael dragged over a platform that provided a rest for the rifle barrel, to help my aim and spare me the gun's kick. When he opened a box of bullets, Joel tapped the first row on their tips. "Not around here you don't."

"I wouldn't waste them on a range anyway," Michael said.

"What's the problem?" I said.

"This kind, with the little hole at the top?" Joel held one up. "Fans open when it hits the target. Tears up everything in its path."

"But this kind"—Michael took one that appeared identical, except for the lack of an indentation in the tip, and placed it in my hand— "these are Geneva convention rounds, approved for use in war."

"Oh yeah," Joel said. "We only use nice bullets when we kill you to death."

I weighed the round. It was as long as my middle finger, shiny brass. The tip reminded me of the pen my father used when he was grading papers years ago—a strange association that felt totally out of place.

"Be right back," Michael said, and he jogged to the port-a-potty. The dogs watched him, and he kept an eye on them too.

Joel stood next to me, breathing loudly. We heard a clatter of distant pistol shots.

"So what branch of the military are you in?" Joel asked.

"No part. Just a former guardsman's wife."

"Honey." Joel looked at me as if I were a toddler fibbing to get another cookie. "This is America. Everybody's in the military."

"Sorry, but I'm a hospice nurse. That's about as nonmilitary as you can get."

He scratched his cheek with a thumbnail. "I'm sure it makes you feel good to think that way."

"It's not a matter of thinking. It's true."

Joel held his arms wide. "Oh beautiful for spacious skies. Another believer in the innocence of noncombatants."

"Excuse me?"

"Oh yeah. Knuh, knuh. You have no complicity in warfare at all. You are sweet and clean and would never hurt a flea."

"What are you trying to—"

"But us soldiers and sailors and airmen and Marines, we must be the Other, the stranger, the odd thing that people maybe thank or maybe hate, but either way we are something different and weird and scary and not at all like you good, nice civilized folk."

"I'd say that's a little bit—"

"That way," he charged on, "that way you don't have to recognize that you were the ones who recruited us, you and millions of people just like you. Oh yeah. You picked us out as too poor for college, too undisciplined for work, too patriotic for self-preservation, easy targets, easy marks. Then you trained us, you invented our equipment, you elected the commander in chief who sent us to war, you hired the Congress that drafted us, you paid taxes to support a military bigger than the next fifteen countries combined."

Joel was counting off the injustices on his skinny fingers. The moment felt identical to listening to a patient trying to reason with his mortality, protesting against something inevitable. My job wasn't to make sense of it, or even respond. This was about a poison he needed to get out of himself. It was, quite literally, a stage of grief.

"You bought the planes, oh yeah, big fancy fast planes, and the fuel for the planes that flew us to the foreign land. You made the trucks and the fuel for the trucks, and the seat and windshield and steering wheels and the tires, man, knuh, the fucking tires that brought us to the battlefield. Then you put guns in our hands and ordered us to pull the triggers, do it or we go to jail, do it or we die. And when we did what we were told you washed your hands and said killers, you fucking monsters and heroes and murderers. Then you watched TV and ate and shat and bought stuff, all the time telling yourselves over and over that your hands were clean, your conscience, you sleep fine at night, oh yeah, you got no complicity whatsoever."

"What's up, Joel?" Michael stood at my side. I could feel him bristling. "Did I miss something?"

Joel faced the ground. He swallowed hard. "Windy weather, my man. Knuh. Getting mighty windy on your old lady out here."

"That's what it sounded like."

"I'm OK now, I'm cool. She's cool too. Cool lady."

Michael remained between the old man and me. He ran his hands back through his hair, as though he were stroking down his hackles. "You off your meds or something?"

Joel shook his head, laughing. "Brother, I am never off my meds."

AFTER THAT, Joel stepped back by the shed, and everything went faster. Michael unzipped the gun case and affixed his rifle to the platform, its carrying strap folded aside. He handed me the orange headphones and plastic protective goggles. He focused the scope, showed me how to adjust the platform height, pointed to where I'd release the safety, and demonstrated how to load the gun.

I couldn't do it. My hands kept shaking. I reminded myself: I was the tough one, the expert in pain. I could do it.

But I dropped the round in the dirt. Michael brushed it off and handed it back to me. It was an odd thing, to receive a bullet from my husband. I thumbed the shell into the chamber. It slid in at an angle and stuck there. He had to take the gun off the platform and bang it against his palm to get the round out.

After that there were no more preliminaries. I clamped on the eye and ear protectors. He told me to lean down to the scope to find my target. Somehow the target had become mine. But the lens was hard to see through, its focused part a bright circle surrounded by darkness that kept moving around.

"You have to hold still to see squarely," Michael bellowed. I knew he was only raising his voice so I could hear him through the headphones. "Get close on it."

He leaned down and scooped his arms around, cradling me in against the gun. Oh, I felt the man in him just then, the strength of his arms, the way his gender masked vulnerability with certainty. I curved my back against him, as if to increase the surface area where we were touching. Michael pressed me into the weapon while my eye settled against the scope, and with arresting clarity the target came into view: a human torso with concentric rings around a yellow bull's eye on its chest.

"Fire when ready," Michael called, rising away.

For a moment I thought I might vomit. My mouth tasted as if I'd eaten something foul. But there was no way I would ruin this moment, squander this opportunity to understand my warrior by knowing his weapon, and I swallowed everything back.

I thumbed off the safety and touched my forefinger to the trigger. So this was what he did. Over and over, under the most intense time pressure imaginable. Take too long and the enemy spots you. Shoot too soon and you miss. Take too long and you die. I curled my finger and held my breath. I pulled a fraction, nothing happened. Then there was a burst and I'd blinked, and the bullet went wild to the right.

Joel was clapping his bony hands. "Woo-eee. Good banging, rookie."

"Yow," I said, rubbing my shoulder. "That really kicked me."

"You have to hug it tighter," Michael said, loading another round. "Love it right up close." He pressed me into the gun again, warm and alive on my back. I would have stopped everything to prolong that contact, but he was gone and upright and I was holding the weapon.

Love it up close. Right. I pulled the stock tight to my shoulder, suppressing a wince. I pressed my eye to the scope. Wrapping my finger around the trigger, slowly I squeezed, and again the burst came from under my arm. That time I had no idea in which direction the bullet had veered.

"OK, OK, headphones off."

"What is it?" I asked. The kick hurt less that time, but already I could tell my shoulder would be sore later.

Michael bent like a football coach inspiring his huddle. "You're throwing the bullet. You're pushing it out there. Just let the gun surprise you. It has all the power it needs, believe me. Just aim, and let the rifle do its work."

Let it surprise me? What did that mean? I put the headphones back on and wrapped myself around the weapon without his help. And squeezed the trigger like I meant it. This time I did not blink, and the gun stayed steady. Through the scope I could see a little dot I'd made on the target, a black puncture up in one corner. Damn if I can deny it: I felt a dirty little thrill.

We spent another hour, Michael instructing in a measured voice, though also pacing behind me before I shot. Joel crept forward to add a word or two. Breathe out all the way, he said, then a little more, and then fire. The air smelled of gunpowder, metallic and sour. I shot perhaps twenty times. Most rounds went wide of center. But each time I managed to nip the merest piece of that target, I felt a rush of pride.

"Enough?" Michael said eventually.

I nodded, gulping despite a dry mouth. "Enough. Thank you."

"No thanking." He started out into the field. "Let's see how you did."

But it struck me that there was one way I could take this day further, and I spoke without thinking. "Aren't you going to have a turn?"

He pulled up, arching his back as though he had taken an arrow between the shoulder blades. Michael stood that way fully half a minute, then shuffled a half circle back to me.

In a blur he snatched the rifle, loaded it, and hooked the strap with his elbow to pin the gun against him. It was scary, how quickly he brought one eye to the scope, leaned forward as if he were planting a spear in his enemy's chest. And held that way, frozen.

The moment sustained itself like a violin's high clear note. The summer meadow held its breath. Joel watched him with unmoving eyes.

Then the pistol rang out from the range's other side. Michael released a massive exhale. He opened the chamber to remove the round and held it in one palm.

"No," he said, thrusting the rifle into my hands. "Not in front of you."

I stood there wondering what I'd just done. As he strode off into the tall grass, Michael called back over his shoulder. "Feel free to shoot me anytime."

While my husband took things down, Joel came coughing up beside me. I turned to him, trying to rub my shoulder without drawing too much attention. "In the war, how do you decide who to aim at?"

He sniffed. "Depends on the mission. With a caravan, you take the lead driver. One shot and they pour out of the other vehicles like ants."

I imagined those ants, each one a human being, rushing into an ambush.

"In your nonengaged situation, though," Joel continued, "you pick the highest ranking officer."

"How do you know who that is? Do you learn their uniforms?"

"You can't count on that. Clothes in a battlefield get torn, passed around, generally trashed. One time I remember, though." He chuckled, leaning against the shooting bench. "These two VC standing side by side in my scope. Course, I know I'll only get one, on account of one shot gives your location away, it's pop and run and don't look back."

Joel raised an imaginary gun to his shoulder, sighting down its barrel, moving right and left, right and left. "So which one, you know? Who's the lucky guy? Then one of them pulls out a map and starts reading it while the other one's standing by. Dead giveaway, so to speak. Oh yeah. Hello, Officer Map, and good night."

He lowers his pretend gun. "Even today, you'll never catch me looking at a map. I'd rather stay lost than get popped."

Michael emerged from the field, holding up the target. "Check this out."

There were five punctures on the outermost rings, which I now realized meant they were nearly a foot off the mark, and one just above and to the left of the yellow center.

"Look-ee there." Joel took the sheet, cackling his approval. "Bang bang."

"Decent pattern." Michael began picking up brass casings from my shots. "Six on paper on the first day."

"Just lucky," I said. "With a good instructor."

"Don't be modest," Joel said. "Around here it's OK to admit it. You're a natural born killer."

"No." Michael paused in his clean-up and spoke at the ground. "One in the family is enough."

Joel wandered away while Michael packed up, but he ambled back with a gallon jug that had a bright orange top. "You mind if I do the OJ bit?"

Michael made a sour face. "Not a good idea, buddy."

Joel shuffled his feet. "If she wants to know what it's really like . . ."

"What are you talking about?" I asked.

"It's a nasty thing Joel does to teach people," Michael answered. "An exercise in perspective."

"Sometimes the truth is nasty, knuh."

"Actually," I said, "a little perspective would be helpful right now."

"See?" Joel leaned down into Michael's face. "Part of the story, Milk. You know it is."

Michael's shoulders slumped.

"Life ain't like Hollywood," Joel persisted.

"This is my wife—"

"Makes it even more important that she sees."

The Professor's instruction came to mind: To understand a warrior, understand his weapon. My shoulder hurt, but not enough to quell my curiosity. "I don't know what this exercise is about," I said, "but if it helps me understand . . ."

"There you go," Joel said. "C'mon, Milk. Explain the jug lesson."

Michael sighed and stood up. "Deb, what is the human body like ninety percent made of?"

"Water. Though it's closer to sixty percent."

"So here's this," Joel said, shaking the jug. It was full of water. Then he held it toward Michael. "Do the honors? Maybe fifty yards. Whatever you think for a definite hit."

Michael took the jug with a defeated air. While he strode back into the field, Joel skittered over beside me.

"In the movies, you know, a guy gets popped in the noggin, there's a little black dot in the center of his forehead, right?"

"Sure."

"And the hero, he always gets shot in the arm, right? Maybe a red blotch on his shirt, but he keeps on going."

"Pretty much every time."

"Well, I'm here to give you the news, which is that all that stuff is one hundred percent Grade A bullshit. As you are about to see."

"I've worked in emergency rooms, you know," I felt compelled to say.

"Maybe so." Joel eyed me. "But I'm betting you saw handgun wounds. Nobody, knuh, nobody came in after getting hit by a banger like this here."

"Is that kind of gun so rare?"

"Naw. But if anybody got shot by this, they went straight to the morgue."

Michael had returned, and he loaded the rifle without looking at me. "She can hit this one with her eyes closed," he said. The jug sat on a little rise of dirt, strangely homey among the tattered targets and cardboard boxes.

"You take your time there, Deborah, and just pop that puppy." Joel sighted down his pointing finger. "If you can, don't blink. Oh yeah. You need to see what happens."

I imagined it would make a little hole in front, a bigger hole in back. I'd read such things. Still, I was uneasy. Joel's energy—and Michael's reluctance—made me feel as if I was being played with somehow. Both men stood there, not saying anything more. Michael had agreed that this exercise would give me perspective. What would I accomplish by saying no?

Sliding eye and ear protectors back into place, I sat again at the platform table, lowered myself to the scope, and saw how much easier a shot was at that range. I could read the lettering on the jug's label. I aimed for the O in Orange, breathed out as Joel had told me, and squeezed the trigger.

There was a splash, of course, water spraying in all directions. But that was nothing beside the fact of the jug vanishing. It wasn't broken, or split into pieces. The container had disappeared completely.

I panned the scope over and around the dirt pile. There was nothing, not even the orange cap.

"I don't understand," I said, sliding off my ear covers.

"Look here," Joel answered. He drew a hand across his chest at sternum height. "You hit a human being anywhere above this line, there's no neat bullet hole or little old bleeding. You hit a guy anywhere here on up, you pop his fucking balloon."

It was as if he had punched me in the stomach. I staggered back, my arms dropping. This was what they saw. This was what they remembered.

I turned to Michael, who stood with his shoulders still stooped. I came before him, wilted. "Thirty-one times?"

His lips pressed hard against one another.

"Oh, lover." Forgetting the boundaries I had promised to respect, the reserve and fragility of my husband, I fell into him, just pressed myself against his chest. All those people, no wonder he drew their faces night after night. I burrowed into him.

After a while Michael raised his hands and placed them on my back. They were as stiff as boards, nowhere near the caress or comfort that I needed. But I thought: I'll take it for now. I'll take it, and take it, and take it.

FOE BOMBS OREGON!!! So read the 72-point headline in the September 10, 1942, edition of the *Oregon Journal* of Portland. Beneath, smaller headlines declared that the sub might have been sunk. Also that Japan was preparing a major attack on the U.S. coast. Also that the submarine had returned to Tokyo.

The initial headline was correct, the smaller three not so.

Two days later, hubris had overcome alarm. An editorial cartoonist drew a giant boot stomping out a fire. The boot was marked "US Forest Service," while the tiny whiff of remaining smoke was labeled, "Jap incendiary raid."

By September 14, the *Times* of Coos Bay carried an advertisement for "war risk property insurance." The attack had disrupted local capitalists not a whit.

Meanwhile the I-25 carried four more bombs. Although sailors biding their time on the ocean floor had no way of knowing how severe a fire might be scorching the Oregon woods, by every other measure the mission had been a success. The catapult worked, the plane took off and landed, and at least one fire was burning. Moreover, Soga was still alive.

Lieutenant Commander Tagami ordered the sub to draw westward, away from shore. Some days would need to pass before another mission could constitute a surprise. Furthermore, instead of attacking at dawn, Soga would fly when a bomber was least expected, at night.

On September 29, 1942, twenty days after the first bombing, the I-25 surfaced sixty miles north of Brookings. This time, the bomber flew over a blacked-out coast. For navigation, Soga therefore relied on the Cape Blanco Lighthouse, which sat on a promontory above dramatic cliffs.

Documentation of this flight was less thorough than that of the first, except to note the difficulties Soga experienced. The mission began after midnight, and taking off was vastly more challenging in the dark. Nonetheless, Soga flew successfully toward Mount Emily, Okuda released both bombs, and the E14 turned back to sea. However, on his return Soga could not find the submarine.

Without the I-25, death was certain. Only weeks before, a Japanese ship had sailed out of a bomber's range, and the aircraft's pilot and crew were never heard from again. Now low on fuel, Soga circled back past the lighthouse, then reversed course again. In the predawn light, he finally spotted the submarine's wake.

This time the plane dismantling and storage took place without American discovery. The I-25 cruised to the bottom unattended by depth charges.

Nonetheless, Soga's extra flight time bore consequences. Two lookout towers, fully manned this time, reported sighting (and identifying) the aircraft at about 5:20 A.M. Nine people confirmed hearing an explosion. By 7:15 a U.S. Forest Service supervisor near Grassy Knob, Oregon, had spotted rising smoke. Before a fire crew reached the site, wet weather spoke again, and the blaze sputtered out.

The second bomb remained unaccounted for. Search teams from the 174th Infantry, the Forest Service, Civil Defense, and the Advance Warning System all spent the full day scouring the approximate target area. They returned at dark without success. The unexploded device lay somewhere in the undergrowth.

The I-25 waited through another week of bad weather before Tagami ordered his crew to sail for Japan. On the way he damaged one Allied oil tanker, sank another, and torpedoed a Russian submarine so expertly it sank in seconds. The men returned to the port of Yokosuka with legs swollen by beriberi, an affliction of submariners who receive insufficient vitamins.

Soga's second mission experienced a media blackout, as the U.S. Department of War sought to suppress news of incidents that could spark a panic. So began the process of this unprecedented invasion falling out of public memory.

In Tokyo, however, Soga's mission led to headlines, crowing that Japan had struck the American mainland. When the submarine reached home port, Soga was whisked away on a victory tour intended less for celebration than for propaganda.

The firebombing team would never serve together again. A few weeks later the I-25, refueled and re-provisioned, set out toward Australia. However, the USS *Patterson*, a destroyer, encountered the sub near the New Hebrides Islands and sank it. All hands perished.

Navigator Okuda had already been reassigned to a special team of attack pilots known as the "divine wind." The term derived from the thirteenth century, when it was used to describe typhoons that drove away the invading fleets of Kublai Khan. Okuda's team would go on to sink 47 ships, damage 368 others, kill 4,900 sailors, and wound as many more. The Japanese translation of divine wind: kamikaze.

By New Year's Day 1943, America had begun achieving greater military success, which shifted Japan's naval strategy. There would be no more salvos conducted on the U.S. coast. Furthermore, the Allied victory at Guadalcanal in February drew the Japanese fleet into a defensive posture, which the Admiralty was forced to maintain for the duration of the war. Despite their capacity for stealth and destruction, submarines became primarily supply tools. Japanese expansion had reached its zenith, and the long bloody decline had begun.

Hailed as a national hero, Ichiro Soga was also the Oregon mission's sole survivor.

HIS STORY DID NOT END with two small fires, however, and one man alive to tell the tale. The attacks of 1942 constituted only the first chapter.

Nearly three years later, on May 5, 1945, the Reverend Archie Mitchell of Bookings went on a fateful picnic. He was leading a group of thirteen- and fourteen-year-olds on an afternoon outing near Klamath Falls. They were joined by his wife, Elise, a Sunday school teacher who was six months pregnant. The end of the school year was nearing, and with it the conclusion of that spring's Bible group.

By then Japan stood on the precipice of defeat. The thirty-five-day battle of Iwo Jima in March, for example, brought 26,000 American casualties, including 6,800 deaths before the Allied victory. But Japanese losses were nearly triple that number. Of the 22,000 soldiers stationed on the island at the battle's start, only 216 were taken as prisoners of war. The rest died, committed suicide, or starved in the tunnels beneath Iwo Jima's rocky soil. While the image of Marines raising an American flag on the island's summit became iconic, some military tacticians questioned whether the territory was worth such a high cost.

The answer came in two forms: First, Iwo Jima prepared the Allied forces for the clash at Okinawa, at eighty-two days the longest battle of the war. While sacrificing 14,009 American lives, that clash cost Japan more than 77,000 soldiers and provided the Allies with a base of operations only 340 miles from the Japanese mainland.

Second, the island footholds were military prizes because they provided staging support for B-29 bombers. These aircraft, which could fly 3,200 miles without refueling, also cruised at 30,000 feet—above the reach of all Japanese defenses. Thus did the Allies bomb at will, including the firebombing of Tokyo in March. Almost sixteen square miles of the city burned, with an estimated 100,000 fatalities.

On the May afternoon that Rev. Mitchell embarked on his picnic, Okinawa remained at full rage, outcome unknown. However, ninety-one days later American planes would drop thousands of leaflets on Hiroshima, urging people to flee. Two days later, an atomic bomb would level the city. (The Enola Gay took off, incidentally, from that previously debatable staging ground at Iwo Jima.)

Three days further down the calendar, Nagasaki was next to experience mighty atomic fire. Two additional atomic bombs, hidden on a classified navy ship, would never be loaded onto a bomber. Instead, on August 15 the emperor surrendered.

Thus in Oregon that May, the war was charging toward its conclusion. For a man of the cloth, years of prayers were on the verge of being answered. Yet the reach of warfare is often longer than anyone anticipates.

On the winding uphill drive toward their picnic site, the pregnant Elise Mitchell felt carsick. Her husband pulled over, encouraging everyone to take a walk to clear their heads. They wandered in various directions, Archie ambling over to a road construction crew with whom he chatted about fishing. His wife and the students headed the opposite way.

When they were some hundred yards apart, Elise called to her husband: "Look what I found."

There was an explosion. Branches flew in the air. By the time the minister and road crew reached the scene, a cloud of dirt had risen. Inside the dust, they found Jay Gifford, Edward Engen, Sherman Shoemaker, and Dick Patzke, all dead. Elise Mitchell was dead as well, her dress on fire until the men put it out. The group's one girl, Joan Patzke, lived a few minutes more.

These unfortunate people proved to be the only mainland casualties in all of World War II: civilians, innocents, a teenage Bible study group and a pregnant preacher's wife. Almost three years after his aircraft dropped firebombs on American soil, Soga's mission had claimed its victims.

CHAPTER 10

I WOKE THE NEXT MORNING to a clanking in the house. Dawn
was still hours away, and I lay there listening. Had I dreamed it? But
then the sound came again: Michael's weights, from the basement.
Changing the circular plates of iron on the bar, that was the source
of the clanking. He was lifting again.

Michael had never felt weak to me, even the skinny version of him
that came home from the war. But I had fallen in love with a big man,
burly and strong. As I imagined him down there beside the furnace and
water heater, red-faced under the bench press, or squinting his whole face
during a slow bicep curl, I felt supremely glad for him. Maybe exercise
would teach his brain how to make endorphins, the pleasure chemi-
cals, once again. Maybe lifting would wring out some of his anguish.

Perhaps his arms would become mighty again too. I rolled onto
my back and played an old movie for myself. We were making love
on our wedding night, I will never forget, and Michael stood from
the bed, his arms hooked under my legs, and he held me in the air
while we continued moving together. I was splayed and powerless,
hanging against him with my arms around his neck, while he was
tireless, as if I weighed nothing. But he did not use my vulnerability
to hurt me. He used it to bring me joy. He held me in the air and
kissed my throat. I surrendered to him with all that I had.

Thus I did the most unexpected thing, that morning, while he strained and sweated, and the weights clanked from below like the plumbing of an old house: I fell back to sleep.

And woke hours later to a silent home. By then Michael had left on his long march to work. I stood in the kitchen waiting for the coffee to brew, thumbing absently through the newspaper. Flipping it aside, I found one of his paper piles beneath. I leaned over, studying the drawings once again. Who were these people, and what had happened to make them unforgettable? The man in sunglasses, the one with the squiggle beside him, the one with mouse ears. Something was different. I couldn't see what, but these pages were not like those of the previous days.

I poured a steaming mug, checked emails from Central Office, but kept returning to the table. What had changed? I spread the three sheets of paper out beside each other. I took a sip.

And then I realized. Usually his drawings required four pages. I went to the recycling bin and fished out a fistful of papers. Sure enough, each day: four.

So I counted the faces on the previous night's sheets. Twenty-nine.

Regardless of what happened for me at the shooting range, something had shifted in Michael too. He spent the early hours lifting weights. He had two fewer ghosts haunting him.

I knew it was a milestone, but there was no one I could celebrate with. Except perhaps Barclay Reed. I wanted, and with urgency, to inform him that he had been right. My going onto Michael's turf, my willingness to learn a warrior's weapon, had helped to heal one of his wounds. Or no: two.

I wanted to know what else the Professor would suggest.

First, however, I had to confess that I had been unfaithful.

"He wasn't an expert," I explained. "Just a Vietnam veteran who knew military history. So I asked him."

"Nurse Birch, you disappoint me beyond words." Barclay Reed furrowed his brow. "Did you not consider this conduct a violation of your promise? Not to consult outside sources before deciding whether The Sword was true?"

"I don't think I broke any promise, Professor. I was making conversation. Besides, he didn't know anything."

He folded his arms. "Well, I am sure. Furthermore—"

But his eyes bugged before he could continue; he leaned onto his side and threw up. The Professor's startled expression revealed that he was every bit as surprised as me. It was like a beard of nasty on his chest.

"That's too bad," I said. "Let's get you cleaned up."

He blinked at me slowly, like an owl, and vomited again.

It was a long morning. Barclay Reed's body had involuntary work to do. I did what I could to help him, providing a basin, fresh clothes and bedding, a bath at noon. But even after his stomach was empty, it continued to heave so hard that he broke out in a sweat. He was in misery. We could do things to prevent an episode like this from happening again. But for now, the contractions would cease only when his body had finished what it needed to do.

"Should I go to a hospital?" he asked late in the morning.

"You could. That's a choice you could make."

"Isn't my treatment your decision? You are the expert."

"As you would say, let's consider." I wiped his forehead with a damp cloth. "One possible explanation for what you're doing today could be an obstruction. If you go to the hospital, a doctor will thread a nasogastric tube up your nose and down into your stomach, where it will remain for up to four days. If there actually is an obstruction, you'll undergo surgery to resect your bowel—basically cutting out the blocked area and sewing everything back together. Plus whatever recovery time that requires."

The Professor's face went blank, all emotion suppressed. "I presume there is an 'or' coming?"

"Well, yes. Or you can stay here, and wait, and see if the discomfort passes, and you are spared the whole ordeal. Obstructions are usually painful, and you seem to have more nausea than pain. So you have a choice."

He stared past me. "I accept your recommendation, Nurse Birch."

"But I didn't—"

"I accept, I said."

And he continued to be ill.

Toward evening a gentle misting rain began, easing the humidity and bringing a feeling of calm. I bundled the Professor in a blanket and wheeled him to the sliding doors. As I opened both of them wide, he took a huge slow breath.

The rain made a washing sound against the lake's surface, which splashed from the raindrops like a million eyes winking. Even so, perhaps because there was no wind, someone was out waterskiing by the point.

"Blasted fools," the Professor muttered.

"I imagine the rain would sting," I said.

"And I imagine they think they will live forever."

We stayed there, me standing behind his chair like a knight's vassal, while the storm dwindled and grew quiet. He fidgeted with the blanket, tugged on the tuft of hair at the crown of his head, shifted in the chair.

"Yes, Professor?"

"That stomach distress today. I gather there is no obstruction."

"Apparently not."

He sighed. "The descent commences. I am going to die."

A perfectly healthy person would want to die, I thought, after the morning you just put in. But I didn't say it, or speak at all. I used the pause to think. What door was he opening with this conversation? How could I help?

"Professor Reed," I said, "has anyone ever told you about the Four Questions exercise?"

"What would give you the idea that I am up to any form of exercise?"

I chuckled. "This isn't a physical workout. It's an emotional checklist."

"Explain."

"Sometimes people have unfinished work in their lives, in their relationships. The Four Questions clarify what work remains, to help get it done productively."

"Has today not been uncomfortable enough for your patient? Must we embark on self-actualization as well?"

"We don't have to, of course." I studied the back of his head, the white bristling hair. But his posture remained as erect as a soldier at attention, so I ventured one step further. "I'll just say that often people find that physical symptoms are alleviated by greater emotional calm."

"If this exercise of yours prevents future days like today, I am willing."

"I can't guarantee anything, Professor."

He gave a papal wave. "Proceed."

I tucked the blankets snug against him. "Be right back."

From the kitchen I fetched a clipboard. On the way I remembered the first time I'd seen a patient answer the Four Questions.

Her name was Alaina, she'd been a dancer, then founded a dance school for children. She was eighty-four and suffering. Her breath came in bursts, shallow and pinched, though the chart at the nursing station said her metastatic ovarian cancer had no respiratory involvement. Try telling that to the woman struggling for breath.

This happened early in my clinicals, during a rotation at an inpatient hospice house. The facility served people who were dying, and whose family could not care for them at home: hundred-pound granny can't turn three-hundred-pound grandpa in bed, spouse of a dementia patient is exhausted, or, as in Alaina's case, devoted husband injures his knee from too many trips up and down the stairs while caring for bedridden wife.

On that day I was shadowing a seasoned social worker who

turned to me in the doorway. "I think she is ready for something beautiful to happen."

I could not imagine what that might be, considering the skeletal woman in the room whose breath came in gulps. While I lagged with misgivings, the counselor strode in with a cheery hello. Sitting in Alaina's bedside chair, she took out a pen, raised her clipboard, and asked four questions:

"Is there anyone you need to say 'I'm sorry' to?"

"Is there anyone you need to say 'I forgive you' to?"

"Is there anyone you need to say 'thank you' to?"

"Is there anyone you need to say 'I love you' to?"

"Yes," Alaina wheezed, giving one or two names for each question.

"Six people in all," the counselor said, flipping to a fresh page. "Who would you like to dictate a letter to first?"

"A letter?" Alaina's face looked confused. Her eyes searched the room, coming to rest on me. I smiled at her nervously, and she turned to the counselor.

"Lydia. I would like to forgive my daughter."

The volunteer spoke as she wrote: "Dear . . . Lydia . . ."

And Alaina, there in her dying bed, stopped panting. It was immediate, and not at all subtle. Her breath eased. Her shoulders relaxed.

"Dear Lydia," she began. "I have loved you from the moment I knew I was carrying you."

BARCLAY REED HAD ROLLED his wheelchair closer to the doors. He was leaning forward, elbows on his thighs. I slowed, not wanting to interrupt, but he must have heard me. "Nurse Birch, do you have favorite smells?"

"I think you are enjoying one of them right now."

He nodded. "It's fascinating. Although I'm unschooled in neurology, I know that scent and memory are connected in some fashion. Yet while I am seated here, I cannot remember when I last smelled anything consciously."

"We visited your azaleas not too long ago."

"True. That was sublime." The Professor sat back in his chair. "So is this. Rain on a lake. A pity you can't bottle it."

"If we could smell this all the time, it might become less special."

He half-turned his head, eyeing me. "What is this exercise you've been plotting? Not another legal form I must sign?"

"Not at all. I just ask you four questions, and you answer them. Maybe there'll be more for you to say, if you want, but that's it."

He tugged on the tuft of his hair. "Do your worst."

"Is there anyone you want to say 'thank you' to?"

His hand came down at once. "I beg your pardon?"

"Is there anyone you would like to say 'thank you' to?"

"What is this game, Nurse Birch?"

"This exercise investigates whether you have unfinished business in your emotional life, and maybe it will spark some communication."

"You wish to know if I have anyone to thank."

"If you said someone's name, I would write it down. And after all four questions, you might dictate a letter to me for that person, saying whatever you wanted to express. In some cases I've seen—"

"You imagine there is someone to whom I owe a debt of gratitude that has gone somehow unexpressed?"

"I don't imagine anything," I said. "I'm just asking a few simple—"

"What the hell else?"

"I'm sorry?"

"I mean, the audacity of this inquisition."

"It's not an inquisition. And if you really don't want to—"

"Don't you dare try backing out." He wheeled to face me. "You had some purpose in ruining my reverie."

"Yes, I did: to help you."

"By reminding me that every stick of furniture in this house, every page I've published, every credential or accolade I've ever received was attained despite competition, politics, professional jealousy, and spite? And you want to know if I am grateful? You want to know who I would thank?"

"Well, some people do find—"

"I spit on everyone." His eyes were wild. "I did it alone."

"OK, OK. I didn't mean to—"

"What are the other questions? You said there were four."

I stared at the clipboard, though of course I'd written nothing there. "It's obvious I've made a mistake here."

"Don't weasel. You are accountable for this so-called exercise. I want to know the other three. Ask me, Nurse Birch."

"Professor." I set the clipboard on a side table. "I intended to do something peaceful, and instead I've made you angry. I apologize."

"Ask me."

I closed my eyes. How could I have misread him so completely? I opened them, and he was glaring at me like a bull about to charge.

"Can I just say first that you were right, and Michael has made real progress, thanks to your suggestion that I learn the warrior's weapons?"

"Ask me."

I felt bullied. But what options did I have? I stared at the gong, hanging on its stand by the wall, but it provided no alternatives. Finally I gave in. "Is there anyone you want to say 'I forgive you' to? Is there anyone you want to say 'I'm sorry' to?" I sighed. "Is there anyone you want to say 'I love you' to?"

At that last one, the Professor's jaw drew back. His face went soft.

"What is it?"

"Nothing," he said. "Nothing. That is all of them?"

"Just the four. Gratitude, forgiveness, apology, and love."

"Yes, well." He ran a thumb around the upper arc of one of his chair tires. "Nurse Birch, there is a possibility that I may have over-reacted. These questions are simplistic. And reductive. But I understand the intention of them now and conclude that it is benign."

"Thank you, I think."

"Moreover, a direct answer would be that there is no one."

"I'm sorry?"

"You are often evasive, Nurse Birch, to the point of my frustration. But you are not a devotee of denial. For example, when I said that I was going to die just now, you did not offer diversionary platitudes or false hope. It may be the one thing I respect about you. Nevertheless . . ."

I waited, leaving him plenty of room. He studied his thumb on the wheel, pondering. "Nevertheless, you cannot suppress your optimism. It is a character flaw. Therefore, as with the advance directive conversation not days ago, today you again ignore the degree of my solitude."

"Professor, I'm only making sure we don't miss something important, just because I was afraid to ask."

"Perhaps you imagine I have a secret daughter, lurking out in the world somewhere, waiting to appear at the perfect heroic moment—but there is no such daughter."

"What in the world are you—"

"My life's 'emotional work,' as you put it so tidily, was completed long ago. Between my intellectual domain, and my kingdom of one in this house, it has been years since there was anyone to whom I needed to say anything."

"There's not one person you have unfinished business with?"

He snorted. "Unless you count yourself, and this gambit is all a pathetic bid for me to excuse you for breaking your promise about The Sword."

"That has nothing to do with—"

"The one lesson I have learned so far from dying is that it is the most alone thing a person can do." The Professor raised his voice again, rousing himself as though he needed to persuade a crowded lecture hall. "No one else feels the pain. No one shares the dwindling energy. No one else spends a day vomiting, enduring both the physical discomfort and the humiliation of doing so in front of another person. Therefore no—" he pounded the chair arm with his fist. "Blast it. I say there is not one person of any kind with whom I need to do one more emotional thing of any kind."

He turned his chair away from me. "Have I satisfied your prurient interests now, Nurse Birch? There is no one."

"Well." I picked up the clipboard and held it against my chest. "I think that is incredibly sad."

THE 22ND ANNUAL AZALEA FESTIVAL of Brookings, Oregon, was not the event the boosters had planned. In fact, some declared the 1961 festival a bust.

Yet its success mattered economically to the people in that region. The craggy Oregon coast remained undiscovered as a tourist destination. Therefore, each May the chamber of commerce hosted the Azalea Festival: a parade, complete with high school marching band and crowning of the year's Azalea Queen, followed by a cookout at Azalea Park—where footpaths snaked among plantings and sculptures, and flowering trees numbered nearly one thousand.

In June, just weeks after the disappointing festival, three Jaycees met over beers to discuss ideas for generating greater tourist interest the following year. The Jaycees are a junior chamber of commerce, which admits no person over the age of forty. Thus few Jaycees of that era had served in World War II.

However, one of the men, Doyle Rausch, remembered a fall morning when he was a child and heard an aircraft later identified as a Japanese bomber. Over the course of the evening's suds, he suggested to the other Jaycees—Bill McChesney and Doug Peterson—that they find the pilot and invite him to the 1962 festival.

Though McChesney and Peterson had lived in the area for years, neither knew about the bombing. The greater catastrophes of World War II, and the nation's efforts to regain prosperity, had relegated this assault into obscurity.

Peterson embraced the idea as a potential boon to tourism; he promptly wrote to the Japanese Consulate in Portland seeking information about the pilot. In August, Vice Consul T. Nishimaki mailed a response that contained two critical pieces of information: the name Ichiro Soga and an address.

The Jaycees wrote to Soga, tendering an invitation. They also sent a missive to the U.S. State Department, inquiring whether the visit was permissible. The federal government answered favorably, adding however that the travel cost must be borne locally. Soga also replied, saying that he would be glad to visit, but his wife, son, and daughter must accompany him. Airfare would cost $3,000 in 1961 dollars.

Letters and news reports from the time offer a contradictory chronology, but the gist of all accounts was this: Over the winter, Soga and the Jaycees developed a plan for the visit. The Oregon group sent a letter to President Kennedy, asking for his endorsement. The idea of inviting this special guest to the 1962 Azalea Festival appeared in the *Brookings-Harbor Pilot*.

Public objection was immediate. It first saw expression in letters to the editor. Mrs. Otis Gadberry's epistle typifies the tone: "We think the Japs should stay over there, and we here."

Mrs. Chester Davis likewise penned, "If they want to make a celebrity of someone, a lot of boys around here have been in the war and should be far more recognized than some Jap who tried to burn Mount Emily."

"I don't think much of it," wrote S. E. Albin. "The pilot could have killed us."

Bar fights began, occurring with sufficient frequency that the local chief of police approached the Jaycees in concern. The group responded by de-emphasizing the tourism potential of Soga's visit, in favor of the higher principles of peace and mutual understanding between people and nations.

News of the conflicts reached Soga. He sent a letter questioning whether his visit would improve relations after all. The Jaycees dispatched a telegram reassuring him that the opposition was a loud group, but small.

In March, the Jaycees began fund-raising: $300 from their treasury, $500 from the Chamber of Commerce, then smaller gifts from around the region and California.

Days later, a full-page advertisement appeared in the *Brookings-Harbor Pilot*. The text was a broadside against rekindling old animosities and causing veterans undue pain. It contained language offensive to contemporary ears, but reflecting some portion of postwar public opinion.

> It seems that this fellow, who missed killing a lot of innocent people, should now be honored by us for his mistake. This whole procedure makes as much sense as giving a man a gold medal for not robbing a bank when he walks past the door.
> Soga's sole claim to fame is that he was the sole Nip pilot who bombed the mainland of the United States by air plane. . . . Why stop with him? Why not assemble the ashes of Judas Iscariot, the corpse of Attila the Hun, a shovel full of dirt from the spot where Hitler died? . . .
> We the undersigned residents of the Brookings-Harbor area are absolutely opposed to such kind of publicity.

Below the text stood 141 names in black and white: four bold rows of thirty-five, plus one more atop the left-most column, befitting the leader of this unapologetic declaration of xenophobia: Donny Baker III.

DOUG PETERSON, THE JAYCEE who had first suggested inviting Soga, owned and operated a drugstore. In the spring of 1962 the local school board came to his pharmacy, asking if he sincerely intended to bring Soga to Brookings. When Peterson answered yes, the board members told him they would no longer patronize his store. A few days later, a picket line formed outside. WE DON'T WANT SOGA, the protestors' signs read. WE WANT EICHMANN.

Bill McChesney likewise reported losing customers at his dental practice. He had greater concerns, however. A late-night caller announced that he was aiming a high-powered rifle at McChesney.

Not all the apprehensions existed on one side of the Pacific. Soga worried that the visit could be a trap, and that he could be prosecuted for war crimes.

It was not an unwise imagining. No former member of the Japanese military would have been unaware of the work of the International Military Tribunal for the Far East. This judicial body, its twelve members personally selected in 1946 by U.S. General Douglas MacArthur, weighed charges of severe war crimes committed by twenty-eight senior military and political leaders (instigating war, crimes against humanity), as well as lesser offenses alleged against another 5,700 Japanese people (primarily prisoner abuse).

Modeled after the trial of Germans at Nuremburg, the Tribunal received criticism for exonerating the emperor and his family of responsibility for the war. Critics also argued that the panel was biased by design; one of the judges was a survivor of the Bataan Death March.

Nonetheless, the case proceeded. Prosecutors took more than six months to make their case, calling 419 witnesses and admitting 4,336 pieces of evidence. The defense required nearly eight months to present its rebuttals. With many judges issuing dissents, the final opinion ran 1,781 pages. Of the twenty-eight senior officials, one was found mentally unfit, two died during the proceedings, two were sentenced to long prison terms, and sixteen received life without parole (although the thirteen of them still alive a decade later were indeed paroled).

The remaining seven—war ministers, prime ministers, chiefs of intelligence or branches of the armed forces—were sentenced to death by hanging. The executions took place at Japan's Sugamo Prison in a single day, December 23, 1948.

China conducted its own trials, resulting in 504 convictions and 149 executions. Therefore the sole pilot ever to bomb the mainland in U.S. history could hardly be faulted for his concern. In a letter to his daughter, Soga revealed a suspicion that, were he not arrested outright, he might be publicly humiliated. In particular, he remarked that he was afraid of being "pelted with eggs."

Coming from a land in which honor is more valuable than wealth or power, and a nation still staggered by the blow of unconditional surrender, Soga could not rescind his acceptance of the Americans' invitation without a loss of standing. Therefore he developed a strategy. He would bring his family's ancient samurai sword. If circumstances turned disrespectful, if his wartime duties were mocked or marred, he would restore the Soga name by committing seppuku.

This form of ritual suicide by a blade was traditionally reserved for samurai. However, upon their surrender, many generals and senior ministers had performed self-disembowelment to avoid the dishonors of capture, torture, or imprisonment.

The pilot prepared a similar plan. If the Americans sought to shame Ichiro Soga, the sword would have the last word.

CHAPTER 11

THE BASEMENT SMELLED OF SWEAT, and I could not have been happier. I stood at the head of the stairs, listening, enjoying, imagining what the sounds told me. There were clanks with pauses between them—that would be when Michael was arranging the weights for the next set of lifting. A series of faster clinks would follow—the lifts, Michael's breath measured at the start but increasingly strained as he reached number eight or nine. And when the bar clattered back into its frame, my husband would pant like a bellows.

When we first lived together, I used to watch him work out. I'd pretend to read the paper, but I wasn't fooling anyone. "Don't mind me," I told Michael while he grunted and strained. "I'm just objectifying you."

He locked eyes with me. "Feeling's mutual." And he returned to lifting.

I learned to leave him alone, though, because it was all too animalistic for me, and my excitement was distracting to him. Still, it was all I could do to wait upstairs till he finished, and not pounce when he came into the kitchen for a glass of water.

There would be none of that now. Becoming comfortable enough to lust openly for each other again, when we were not even kissing or holding hands, felt as distant as alpha centauri. Still, if he was working out in that dusty cellar, it did my heart good too. When there were no sounds, I assumed he was taking a break and trotted down.

Michael had pulled his equipment out from under the tarps that had covered it for the past two years: rusty iron weights, gleaming chrome bars, gray plastic dumbbells. And of course the bench, on which Michael lay red-faced, his chest heaving.

"Hi, sweetheart." I leaned down to kiss his forehead. "How was your day at the shop?"

He jerked back. "What do you mean?"

I kissed him anyway. "I don't mean anything. How was your day?"

"That's not the way you put it. You said, 'How was your day at the shop'?"

"OK. And?"

"So you're checking up on me now? What, did you go by and ask Gary where I was or something?"

"Honey, I don't know what you're talking about. I just had a rough day with my patient so I was just asking—"

"This has nothing to do with any stupid patient."

I took two steps backward. "Please don't disparage the people I care for."

"Why are you keeping track of me?"

"Michael." I leaned back against the stairway, body language as neutral as I could make it. The chest of his shirt was dark with sweat. "All I was doing was greeting you, making conversation. Why are you annoyed?"

"Like you don't know."

"Honestly I don't. I thought it was an innocent question."

"All right, look." He stood abruptly, almost popping upright. "I don't know what you're up to. But I do not need anyone's permission to take a day off from work and go to Joel's range with Gene."

He strode to the far side of the bar and began removing rings of weight. There was a speed to the way he did it, a fury. I let everything boil for a minute, while he came to the near side and slid rings from there too.

"Sweetheart," I said eventually. "You don't need my permission to do anything."

He put one hand on his hip. "Then why did you ask about the shop? Unless you knew I wasn't there, which means you were checking up on me."

"Sorry not to validate your paranoia, Michael, but I was fully occupied with my patient. All day today, believe it or not, my life was not about you. I don't know why I mentioned the shop. You could decide never to go back there again, and I would support that as I support everything you do."

He narrowed his eyes at me, then turned to slide a new weight on the near side of the bar.

I continued leaning on the stairway, wanting to leave, wanting to stay. "How was Joel's?"

Michael wiped his face on an upper arm. "At least he put the dogs in the shed this time."

"How about Gene? How's he doing?"

"It's brutal, to tell you the truth." He continued changing the weights. "A piece of his prosthetic leg isn't right, gives him a terrible limp. It's hard to watch. Still, when we got down to shooting, he kicked my ass."

Michael shuffled around the bench to add a weight on the bar's far side. "It was good times, for a while. Then he and Joel mixed in it about Nagasaki, and whether we were right to drop a second bomb after Hiroshima, and there was no shutting either of them up."

"I can't imagine any argument today would make a difference to the people who died back then."

"Times three." He shrugged. "Or didn't die, if you take Joel's side. But some of these guys, they smell a little burned gunpowder, it amps them up and there's no coming down."

That was when I made my mistake. I thought that because

Michael was talking, because the conversation had shifted to his friends, his temper had cooled. Maybe if I hadn't had a hard day with Barclay Reed, I might have been more patient, and waited to bring up the drawings.

But no, I'm not allowed to blame personal woes on work. I chose my profession. No one forced it on me. I spoke too soon because I was eager. I wanted my husband healed. So I ignored the impatience I had seen in him just seconds before, and forged ahead. "I saw that you had two fewer faces."

"What's that?" Michael was settling on the bench again.

"Your papers this morning. There were twenty-nine."

He shook his head. "Will you ever leave me alone?"

I should have listened and let it go. But I couldn't help myself. "Who were they, Michael? How did you get rid of them?"

"Look, I go to the shrink every goddam Wednesday. Isn't that enough?"

"Do you talk to her about the faces?"

Michael closed his hands into fists, then stretched his fingers wide. "Not individual ones, no."

"But the group of them? The thirty-one?"

"Look, what is this? First I can't leave work. Now do I have to report to you what happens with my goddamn shrink?"

With that I realized that Michael was not the only one suppressing some rage. "You don't, do you?" I raised my voice. "Dr. Doremus doesn't even know about them. You're up all hours drawing, night after night, and she doesn't even know."

"You think it's so important, you go to the appointment this week." He threw up his hands. "You take over, Deb. I could give a shit."

"This isn't about her, Michael." I advanced on him. "It's about you. It's about getting rid of all the things that are haunting you."

"Those two stopped haunting me because I realized yesterday that I was glad I'd killed them, all right?" He twisted his neck side to side. "They would have wasted as many of my buddies as they could, not to mention their neighbors and families and anyone else. So I blew them away, they never even saw me coming. Now I have to live with the fact that I liked killing them, that I'm proud of it, that part of me digs being a murderer."

I held the railing for balance. "Michael, all I want is to help you get out of all this pain."

He lay back, speaking to the ceiling. "You know nothing about my pain."

"Maybe not. But I know a lot about pain in general. You have twenty-nine horrors inside you. Tell me about one of them."

Michael spoke through clenched teeth. "Not a chance."

"Just one. You pick. Which would be the easiest to talk about? The squiggle guy? The one with mouse ears?"

"You think any of them are easy?"

"Some must be easier than others. After all, you just made two go away."

He fell back on the bench, grabbing the bar with both hands. "Right this second I would like to make you go away."

Ouch. I fell back against the stairs. Michael gripped the bar, popped it off the safety frame, and began banging it up and down. His motions were so abrupt, so jerky, I worried that he might injure himself. So, as they say in my line of work, I removed the impediment to calm. I went upstairs, closing the door behind me.

WHY HAD I HANDLED THAT SO BADLY? Why did I press on about who those two absent faces were, when what really mattered was that they were gone? Most of all, how had I become one of Michael's problems?

I picked up my cell phone and hit the speed dial for my sister Robin. But when the call went straight to voice mail, I hung up.

The last time Michael barked at me, it was that afternoon in the park after Dr. Doremus. He'd been furious with my impatience for him to make progress. And here I'd done it again. Too eager to crow about the two gone ones, too excited that we could somehow magically tick down the rest of the faces and they would vanish one by one.

It would not be that easy. I had to quit being so hopeful. Some of those faces were never going away. All of them were going to put up a fight.

The weights clanked from below, every sound reminding me of past strengths and past intimacy. If we could have made love once, just one damn time, it would have healed so much between us. I knew that with certainty, but I was powerless to make it happen.

I went outside and sat on the stoop by the kitchen door, staying there for hours.

There was plenty to distract me. Late commuters hurrying home, a pickup with a loud muffler, swallows darting after mosquitos. Some teens cranked pop music as they passed in a minivan, every window open.

As the light dwindled, I saw two kids on bikes with noisy training wheels pedaling up the road, their parents ambling behind. The Franklins: both pediatricians, their home five houses up the street, probably moving out of our neighborhood the moment their med-school loans were paid off. Michael had let them borrow his truck a few times, a load of garden mulch, that sort of thing. We waved at one another but did not strike up a conversation, which at the moment was a relief.

The air was humid despite the afternoon's shower. Maybe it had rained only at Lake Oswego. Lights came on in houses here and there. Heat lightning flickered over the city. Hard day with patient, hard day with husband.

Before the war, the remedy for a tough work day was to unburden myself to Michael. He would not know Barclay Reed's name, but he'd hear plenty about his personality, and prognosis, and any moments of grace along the way. Not anymore. Since the third deployment, Michael had not asked one question about a patient. It was almost like I didn't have a job.

Sometimes life was difficult, that's all. A down day. Nothing sleep and a fresh start couldn't fix. But I wanted to cry.

Instead, I remembered my first patient at the agency. I'd lost people during training, but this was my introduction to the death of someone who was totally my responsibility. And it was a rough one: a plucky fourteen-year-old named Sally who had leukemia. When she lost all her hair, Sally looked like an adorable baby chick.

Sally died on a Thursday morning, a beloved stuffed hippo tucked under her arm. Back at Central Office that afternoon to finish the case's paperwork, I sat at my desk and lost it. Just lowered my face into my hands and bawled.

In a place like that, you can't cry long without feeling a reassuring hand on your shoulder. I raised my head. It was Timmy Clamber.

He leaned against my desk and folded his arms. "OK, darling. Spill."

I told him about Sally, choking up again as I did so.

Timmy wagged a finger at me. "No more sobbing, Deb. Not ever."

"There's nothing wrong with crying," I sniffed.

"In your personal life, no. But for this job? First of all, you'll run out of tears. It's a sorrow a day around here." He bobbed his head, which jiggled his dangling crucifix earring. "Yes, it's hard to see patients hurt, but remember, darling: You're not the one doing the suffering. They are."

He moved behind my chair and began massaging my neck and shoulders. Timmy had powerful hands and I leaned into them.

"You have to be strong for them," he continued. "You have to be steady. That way they can fall apart and you will still be there, solid like a tree. My goodness. The reason you're holding back tears is not because you don't have a heart, but because you do."

There on the little concrete step outside my screen door, I knew that Barclay Reed was about a month from dying of cancer. And

Michael had just passed the six-month mark at home. In different ways, they were both suffering. Meanwhile I was healthy, and I wasn't carrying memories of shooting anyone. I had to be solid like a tree for both of them.

Eventually the mosquitos drove me in. The basement door was closed. Either Michael was still down there, sweating out his rage, or he'd gone out the front door to walk it off. I wandered through the dark house, undressed by letting the clothes puddle on the floor, and crawled into my solitary bed.

AS THE TIME OF SOGA'S VISIT APPROACHED, American officialdom began to lay the contentious issues to rest. The Kennedy administration responded favorably to the Jaycees' inquiry. Temple Wanamaker from the State Department wrote, "On behalf of the president I congratulate the Brookings-Harbor Jaycees for their efforts to promote international friendship and goodwill." Mark Hatfield, Oregon governor and a World War II veteran, also wrote in support of Soga's visit.

Then Claude Waldrop granted an interview to the *Portland Oregonian*. Recall that Waldrop was commander of the 174th Infantry at the time of the bombing. The incident had occurred on his watch. Waldrop's junior officer, Second Lieutenant Joseph Kane—who memorably had ordered soldiers to keep quiet about seeing Soga's first flight and failing to report it—was court martialed for deceiving investigators. Yet for Waldrop, time had healed this wound.

"I have no animosity," he told the newspaper. "He was doing a job and we were doing a job."

Although the momentum of these sentiments quelled some of the dissent, it did little to bolster the fund-raising.

Eugene Reiling, a World War I veteran and commander of VFW Post 966, wrote in the *Pilot* that he "can't see why we should pay for someone's way here who was trying to bring disaster to us."

By mid-April, the Jaycees had collected less than half the money. Several made personal loans to cover the difference. Later donations rewarded their risk.

On May 3, 1962, the Jaycees formally invited Soga and his family. That step prompted another round of letters to the *Pilot*.

World War I veteran R. C. Baugh wrote, "To us, an invitation to Fidel Castro, or erecting a monument to John Wilkes Booth, would be just as sensible a project."

Marion McElroy added, "The point in question should not be whether Soga is still an enemy or a person worthy of tribute. The main issue is how the $3,000 should be spent." She suggested library books.

Jean Willard proposed that Brookings invite the astronaut John Glenn and his wife instead.

A few voices joined the debate with another point of view. "We are forgetting the most important factor," wrote Helen Lucas, "the art of forgiving."

Bill Krieger declared that opponents to Soga's visit "thrive on hatred. We have looked with considerable distaste on (prejudice in Little Rock) and anti-Semitism in Germany and elsewhere. The war is long over, and Japan and the United States are joined in a firm effort to fight the threat of Communism."

The ministers of seven area churches issued a joint statement of support for the visit. Once the pulpits had spoken, dissent quieted—though it did not cease.

In the days counting down to Soga's arrival, security plans became increasingly thorough. Deputies drove to more than a dozen area homes, inviting certain people to skip the Azalea Festival that year. There is no record of which houses police visited, nor whether the list of dis-invitees included Donny Baker III.

By then he had appeared in the public record six times: on a marriage license, on the birth certificate of his daughter Heather, on a pilot's license that certified him as equipped to fly a single-engine aircraft, and on a filing to create a corporation for a nursery business he and his wife had opened south of Brookings. The sixth occasion was a brief notice that he had won a regional shooting competition in the pistol division. Aside from his name on the newspaper ad, the first of his appearances, Donny was not evidently a leading spokesman among the opponents to Soga's visit. Primarily those voices belonged to battle veterans, whose animus to all things Japanese was explicable.

By then, events had too great a momentum to change direction. On May 24, the Soga family disembarked in Portland. They walked down the airplane's steps onto American soil. Ichiro was a small man in a gray suit, fifty-one years old, his hair combed neatly back, wearing square black glasses. His wife, Ayako, wore a yellow blazer, her head in every photo tilted to one side, an expression of listening with great interest. Son Yoshi stood stiff-backed at his father's elbow. Daughter Yoriko hovered demurely two steps behind, her eyes on the ground.

Dignitaries greeted them warmly, even effusively. The Japanese pilot bowed to each person who addressed him but spoke only to his son, who translated the reply. When volunteers met them inside the airport to help with the baggage, Ichiro Soga insisted on carrying his own suitcase. There was a brief awkward moment when a zealous volunteer insisted on helping, until Yoshi stepped forward.

"Please pardon," he said. "My father wishes to manage for himself."

At that the volunteer stepped aside, and the delegation proceeded to the cars. In a photograph from that moment Soga held the suitcase not by its handle, but under his arm, against his ribs. He alone knew that within, wrapped in fine fabric, a 400-year-old relic of pride and honor lay tucked among the clothes, a stealthy weapon secreted like a pilot in a submarine.

CHAPTER 12

THE THUNDERSTORM HIT AT AROUND TWO. Or that was when the noise woke me. I lay diagonally on the bed, so I knew without moving that Michael was not there.

It was a good summer ripsnorter: flashes of lightning every few seconds, thunder distant at first, but approaching steadily till it struck right above our neighborhood. It was like standing beside the tracks as a freight train came barreling through, a big noise but complete safety. I remembered the August storms of my childhood in upstate New York, how scary they were, yet reassuring as the front moved over our town and on to the next.

Finally one crash hit directly overhead, rumbling away across the sky like a chair thrown down the stairs, and I gave up on sleep. The bedside clock read 3:18. I pulled on a shirt and shuffled to the kitchen for a glass of milk.

The room was pitch black. I only noticed because I was usually annoyed at how every appliance came with a little clock that had to be changed forward at daylight savings and set back in the fall each year, not to mention putting out a steady and unnecessary nocturnal glow.

I stood in the doorway, letting my eyes adjust. Had we lost power in the minute it took me to walk from the bedroom? Or perhaps the kitchen circuit breaker had blown? If so, the reset switch was in the basement, but the flashlight lived in the kitchen junk drawer.

I took a step toward it and banged into a chair. Now I was confused. The breakfast table normally sat against the wall, but in the dark my eyes could make out that it was against the back door for some reason. I slid a hand along the oven and there was tape over the clock.

I slid the chair aside; it made a trumpeting sound against the floor.

"Jesus, Deb, would you shush?"

Lightning flashed, and I saw Michael. The image was brief, but it told me so much.

He was crouched under the table in full combat gear: a military helmet, flak vest, and desert camouflage fatigues. A bandoleer of ammunition hung over his shoulder. He was clutching his rifle.

"Michael honey, what is going—"

"Shhhh, I said."

The storm thundered above us, the rain poured down. I knelt and crawled toward him. The gun smelled of oil. "Sweetheart, what is it?"

"Mortars," he whispered. "Two hundred yards."

I knelt beside him. "Michael, you are home now. There are no mortars."

"The Franklins. They're using them."

"Lover, you are in Oregon now."

He clutched his rifle closer. "You think I don't know that? This is the last thing I expected."

I could have said the same. My strong man, hiding under the kitchen table with a weapon in his hands. I had no doubt that it was loaded. Every instinct told me to run, get safety, find shelter—everything but my heart. "Michael, I want to be near you right now. I am going to touch you, so don't freak out."

I placed my hand on his upper arm. The muscle trembled. "OK?" I said. "Can I get closer?"

His nod was like a little boy's, wordless and tentative. Michael's bent legs had pinned him against the door, so I could not exactly snuggle up. But I wrapped my arms around his shoulders as far as I could reach, and whispered, "Michael, what do the Franklins do for a living?"

"They're doctors. For kids."

"Do you think they are the kind of people who would have mortars?"

He ran his hand up and down the stock of his gun.

"Besides," I continued, "who would they be firing at?"

He faced me, blinking several times, pondering. His chin trembled.

After his second tour, Michael wept all the time. At movies, TV commercials, the closing minutes of professional sports games. When he said good-bye to that slobbery dog Elvis after one barbecue, Brian laughed.

"Pretty sure you guys will see each other again," he joked, but Michael's face was creased at the brow.

After the third deployment, not one tear. No more room for sadness. Now, after six months at home, he buried his head in my shoulder and took several huffy breaths. I squeezed him closer, ready for the downpour. Release it, lover.

Instead, he calmed. Michael shifted his legs, and the gun was awkward between us. Closing my hand on the barrel, I aimed it at the living room and slid it away on the floor. He did not resist, only burrowed closer against me. Something about removing the gun shifted his energy, his mood.

Another peal of thunder smashed the air above us, and Michael flinched. Every muscle went rigid. The nightmare of a man wide awake.

Oddly enough, I remembered a time we drove to Idaho on vacation and went to a zip-line playground in the forest. I was nervous, insisting Michael go first. After he went whirring down ahead of me, I reached out and touched the wire. It was alive with tension, the strength of the cable versus gravity's pull on my husband, the metallic intensity.

That is what Michael's body felt like, under the table on our kitchen floor. He was not going to cry, no, because he was not sad. It was something else.

I pulled back and his eyes were wide, like a horse about to bolt. And finally I realized the thing I had missed from the day he came home. Somehow I had overlooked it completely. He was not bitter, he was not confused, he was not resentful. This man was terrified.

PERHAPS THE MOST ASTONISHING THING is that no recording survives. Ichiro Soga visited factories, schools, and city hall. There are photographs at each place: grainy 1962 newspaper quality. There are news reports, stories, and letters to the editor. Yet not one inch of motion pictures remains, nor one minute of audiotape.

Thus is the warrior's voice lost for all time. Eyewitnesses, interviewed later, speculate that it would not have mattered. Soga did not speak to people directly during his visit. Whenever someone addressed him, his son Yoshi would translate into Japanese, Soga would lean close to whisper a reply, which Yoshi would then deliver in a strong, clear voice.

"Factory is most industrious." Or "Coastal landscape is most beautiful." Or even, "Hot dog is most delicious."

This latter pearl of diplomacy occurred during the Azalea Parade, which, as the organizers had hoped, enjoyed record attendance that year. To appease critics of Soga's invitation, festival boosters did not invite him to march in the parade, give a speech, or sit behind the red-white-and-blue bunting on the reviewing stand.

Instead Soga joined the local audience, standing among loggers, fishermen, and their families, and, while a reporter stood near, accepting one teenage boy's offer of a classic boiled American hot dog, striped with yellow mustard.

Elaine Howell was crowned 1962 Azalea Queen. Her court included not only the runner-up princesses, but also five former queens. They rode in open convertibles.

One woman came forward to address Soga in Japanese. The *Pilot* reported that he listened closely to Lizzie Hinks of Mount Emily, who had learned some phrases during her college years in New York City. Soga bowed to her, but as ever, did not answer directly. Instead he whispered to Yoshi, who replied in English.

Later Soga toured a plywood plant. He attempted to play the bagpipes and laughed at his lack of musicality. He strolled the beach, still wearing black wingtips but exclaiming through his son at the beauty of the dramatic rock formations offshore. He spent an afternoon in Azalea Park, where he praised the abundant flowering rhododendrons. To the great amusement of a gathered crowd, he struggled to understand the purpose and operation of a parking meter.

On Sunday he and his wife attended Christian services. While Ayako knelt during prayers, head bowed, Soga stood at the back, tape recording the hymns.

If the critics of his visit confronted him at any time, there is no record. The *Pilot* makes no mention of any incidents. In one photograph of the parade, Donny Baker III lurks in the background. A blur of black and white, his arms-akimbo body language nonetheless conveys scorn and disapproval. Apparently he minded both his manners and the sheriff's warning, and kept to himself.

There was one misunderstanding, however, in the parking lot after the religious services. Apparently Yoshi, translating for his father, described the house of worship using the word "shrine," which prompted a passing member of the congregation to speak up.

"This is a church, not a shrine. If you want to see a shrine, go to the woods where your lousy bomb went off."

The speaker of those words went unidentified, but their effect was immediate. Soga asked many questions about what the man meant. Jaycees and churchgoers attempted to change the subject, but Yoshi persisted on his father's behalf. Yes, there was a monument where his last bomb fell. Yes, it was a memorial.

Within the hour, Soga and his family rode in a black Ford at the rear of a six-car motorcade, vehicles inching along a rutted road, their destination a small clearing at the edge of the woods. As people disembarked the mood was somber, lacking the bemused chitchat that had characterized the rest of Soga's visit.

A trail led into the woods. There was some confusion about who should go first, what protocol to observe, until several Jaycees led the way. Soga insisted upon going last.

When they reached the monument, a pillar of mortared river rock with a bronze plaque on its face, Soga whispered to his son. Yoshi read the words aloud.

"In memory of Elise Mitchell, Age 26, Dick Patzke, Age 14, Jay Gifford, Age 13, Edward Engen, Age 13, Joan Patzke, Age 13, Sherman Shoemaker, Age 11, who died here May 5, 1945 by Japanese Bomb Explosion."

And below that: "Only Place on American Continent Where Death Resulted from Enemy Action in WWII."

Soga spoke to his son, who asked the assembly: "Who were these people?"

"A Bible study group," one of the Jaycees said. "And the minister's pregnant wife."

Yoshi murmured to his father, who stiffened. After a moment he bowed at the waist till his head was even with his belt buckle. He remained in that position, facing the ground, for several full minutes. The Jaycees shifted from foot to foot, but no one spoke.

At last Soga straightened, his face flushed, and he directed a speech to the monument. He went on for several sentences, bursts of words between long pauses, after which he bowed as deeply again. Yoshi waited till his father had returned to an upright stance before speaking.

"My father says, 'I had not known anyone died. I was ignorant of this fact. It was war. Terrible things happened on both sides. But this woman, these children, a religious group? It is a shame on my conscience. It is a stain on my honor.'"

By the time Yoshi finished translating, Soga had already marched back down the trail. When the group hiked to the trailhead, they found their guest inside the black car, all of its doors and windows closed.

THAT NIGHT, THE LAST OF SOGA'S VISIT, the chamber of commerce hosted a farewell dinner. This time he was the guest of honor, his place card at the head table with Jaycees president Mike Moran, the group's public information officer Rev. Del Roth, and at the far end, the mayor of Brookings, C. F. Campbell.

Soga did not leave a written record of his thoughts during the U.S. trip. Nor had he confided to family members, at least as they recalled in later interviews. Therefore, there is no way of knowing what his plans were on that evening. Photographs from the event confirm, however, that he arrived at the reception carrying a suitcase, which he subsequently handed to his son.

Did the boy know he was playing the role of Okuda, wingman to his father? Did the former bomber pilot intend a dramatic, unexpected blow? The 1962 Jaycee equivalent of an attack at dawn? A sudden self-sacrifice in the name of ancient honor? History leaves only speculation.

During the cocktail hour, while the Americans downed drinks and enjoyed raucous laughter, Soga moved from person to person in the crowd, bowing wordlessly. His wife remained near, Yoshi hovering on the other side, but whenever people spoke to Soga, at all times he caused his son to reply. It seemed he would go the entire trip without addressing a single American directly.

There was a hubbub in one corner. Soga happened to be nearby, among local clergy. Someone was angry. A photo from the moment shows Soga turning in the direction of Donny Baker, whose nose is inches from that of a uniformed sheriff's deputy, and whose finger is pointed at the Japanese visitor. Donny's shout brought the rest of the room's conversations to a halt:

"Are you saying this Nip bastard has more of a right to be here than I do?"

Soga crossed the distance between them so quickly, his son had to bump past two people to remain close. Bowing, Soga spoke and Yoshi translated. "Is this a local citizen I have not yet had the pleasure of meeting?"

Thus did they stand face-to-face. Donny reached for something inside his jacket, but then he scowled at the deputy and jammed his hands in his pants pockets. Scrutinizing the members of the Soga family from head to foot, he pointed with his chin. "What's with the suitcase? Gonna fill it with silverware?"

Yoshi did not reply. Meanwhile the deputy made his decision. "You can stay, Donny, but you'd best behave yourself."

"Or what?" he replied, though he was backing away. "Or you'll do what?"

The mayor's wife appeared, informing the Soga family it was time for everyone to take their seats. The murmur of conversation recommenced.

There were speeches and jokes, an exchange of gifts. Yoshi stood at the podium and read into the microphone from notecards filled with Japanese characters. He said he spoke for his whole family, then thanked the community for its welcome and generosity. In the middle of his remarks, Soga rose from his chair.

Yoshi turned to his father, the speech trailing off. Fortuitously, a reporter for the *Pilot* sat just below the head table, a photographer stood near, and thus was the sequence of events memorialized.

Photos show the pilot not bowing in the least, as he had during the entirety of his trip, innumerable times daily. To the contrary, he stood ramrod straight. He spoke to his son, quietly as ever, and Yoshi translated for all.

"On this day my foremost wish is to express gratitude. You good people of America have been most generous. Let us agree that we have made progress toward peace. This is our task on earth, and to teach these things to our children."

The crowd applauded politely. Yoshi straightened, at attention for his father.

"That is not all." Soga maintained his rigid posture. "I visited the shrine today. I learned the human consequences of my mission. Children, and a pregnant woman, died in a circumstance of worship. Thus do I also feel sadness and shame."

The room had gone utterly silent. Donny Baker leaned against the back wall, scowling, shaking his head at every word.

"War does ugly things," Soga continued, through Yoshi. "Its necessities turn good people into ugly creatures. In all nations this is true. All creeds, all races. Once fighting ends, both victor and defeated must choose: to deny what took place and resume life as before, or to acknowledge the moral consequence of what war required them to do. I belong to the second group."

Moving a water glass aside, Soga placed the suitcase on the tablecloth. He pushed the brass clips, popping the spring latches open. He turned, facing not the assemblage, but his son—who continued to translate but in a wavering voice.

"In our culture, if we behave with honor, we bestow honor on our name, and family, and nation. If we cause dishonor, we must take responsibility, on behalf of our ancestors and for the sake of our children, to restore that pride and legacy. This I intend to do. Here. Now."

He raised the top of the suitcase and brought out a bundle of cloth. Unwrapping the colorful silk, with a flourish he revealed the sword. People made noises of surprise. He lifted it above his head, displaying it to one side of the room, then the other: The handle had been restored, newly wound with fine thin rope that ended in decorative tassels. The scabbard had been polished until it shone.

Soga continued speaking to, and through, his son. "I am a direct descendant of samurai, most honored of Japanese peoples. This weapon has been in my family for nineteen generations. Four hundred years, more than twice as old as your good country. Today it has one more use to serve."

Yoshi leaned toward his father with his mouth open. But the pilot silenced him with a raised hand and continued speaking. His son translated in stutters.

"This sword has shed blood many times. It could do so again tonight, and thereby return honor to the Soga name."

He drew the blade, long and bright and slightly curved. Someone gasped. Soga held the sword in front of his face, tip pointed at the ceiling.

"But as I said, we must learn from wars. We must make our choice, to deny or to acknowledge. So it is that today my honored lineage will serve another purpose. Would the honorable Mayor Campbell please come forward?"

The mayor hoisted himself from his seat and worked his way behind the chairs. Soga's posture was so straight, a photo from that moment makes him appear to be bending backward. The mayor seems to not want to stand too close.

Soga sheathed the blade and held the weapon out horizontally. "May this sword become a lasting sign of peace between people and nations."

The mayor looked around, then back at Soga. "I don't understand."

Yoshi's face was pinched with emotion. He leaned forward to explain. "It is a gift. This treasure of our family. He is giving it to you."

The mayor rubbed a finger under his nose, glancing around.

"Thank him," his wife called from down the table.

A nervous titter passed through the crowd. At last Mayor Campbell accepted the sword from Soga's hands. He gripped it in one fist, turning to the microphone. "On behalf of the good people of Brookings, and Oregon, and the United States of America, I thank you for this unforgettable gift."

The people begin to clap. Mayor Campbell held the sword high, and the crowd rose to its feet. Soga stood erect amid the applause. He glanced at his wife, who was weeping. He touched his son on the elbow, and the boy bowed.

Donny Baker rolled his eyes. "Give me a goddam break."

Once the noise began dying down, Soga ushered his son aside. At last he stood at the podium himself. He cast his gaze over all of them, waiting until the room was quiet. Their faces were raised toward him. He bowed once more, as formally as ever. Then, lifting himself on tiptoe to bring his mouth to the microphone, he uttered a single word:

Shouri.

CHAPTER 13

"SO WAIT." I closed the black binder on my finger. "You set that up, right?"

"In what regard, Nurse Birch?" Barclay Reed folded his hands in his lap. "What are you implying?"

I sat in the kitchen chair I'd moved to his room for reading. "When you used the word *shouri* earlier, repeating it. You were preparing me." I laughed. "No way is this historical."

"You've made your decision then? This book is a falsehood?"

"How can it possibly be true? You describe events that happened right down the coast from here, but I've never heard about them. You have the only mainland deaths in all of World War II, but somehow everyone forgot about it? And then this guy just gives away a sword that had been in his family for four hundred years? As a symbol of peace?" I set the binder on his bedside table. "Right."

"The decision to surrender one's weapon hardly originated with Ichiro Soga." He sighed expansively. "There is a long and venerable tradition."

That tone was familiar, how he stretched the word "long" as if it had three syllables. The Professor was hinting that he would gladly deliver a lecture on the topic. Those little talks lifted his spirits immeasurably, so I encouraged them whenever I could. "Teach me about it, please."

"Cincinnatus, for example. George Washington."

"I've heard of one of them, anyway."

He raised an eyebrow at me. "Lucius Quinctius Cincinnatus—after whom, inexplicably, the city in Ohio is named—was a Roman aristocrat of the fifth century B.C. When the Sabines and Aequi battled Rome and had captured the consul, the Senate declared Cincinnatus dictator. This decision granted him enormous military and political power, plus societal authority akin to that of a deity. He appointed a second in command, they mustered two armies, and in an attack on dual fronts that military strategists study to this day, they defeated the invaders and captured their leader."

"Hooray for the home team."

"Whereupon," the Professor harrumphed. "Whereupon Cincinnatus abdicated, rejecting all power and glory, and rowed back across the Tiber River to his farm. Nineteen years later, when a senior official attempted a revolt, Cincinnatus came out of retirement to defeat the traitor, again promptly surrendering power afterward. You have not heard of him? More's the pity, since it confirms that our culture has the attention span of a flea. But I'll have you know, the Romans considered Cincinnatus a model of civic virtue for fully five hundred years."

It was all I could do not to sit back and put my feet up. Nothing pleased this man more than displaying his learning. "You said something about George Washington too."

"Please tell me you know about his return to peacetime life."

I shrugged. "Not much."

"What manner of education do the schools provide these days? Establishing the first modern military that is constitutionally subject to elected civilian control represents unprecedented—"

"What about Washington?"

He frowned. "My digressions have been known on rare occasions to have instructive value, Nurse Birch."

"I'm sure they do. But I also know your supper is almost ready, and I want to hear about Washington."

"Supper." Barclay Reed shook his head. "It is a fetish with you. Must a meal forever be thusly worshiped?"

It was no idle question. In the past few days the Professor had entered the wasting phase, his appetite waning just as cancer began consuming him more aggressively. Already under the blanket his hip bones were plainly visible, and his legs looked as thin as crutches. His face was drawn, sagging under the cheekbones as though some of his skin had melted.

Yet he'd skipped breakfast and barely picked at lunch. Now I had a tarragon chicken and pasta casserole baking in the oven. When I'd made it before, he'd gobbled two strapping helpings.

But dinner had a larger purpose than appealing to a patient's taste buds. The more the Professor received sufficient calories, the longer he would live. In the wasting phase, the math was simple: Food equaled time. "Every ounce of nutrition we can pack into you today—"

"How appetizingly you put it."

"—is that much more strength and stamina tomorrow."

He tugged that tuft of hair again. It was becoming like a tic with him, his thumb and forefinger pulling on the widow's peak. "Boring," he sang.

"Please, then. About the first president."

"This incident occurred before he was any such thing." Barclay Reed moved his chin in a circle, seeming to recollect himself. He cleared his throat. "The Continental Congress debated at length and without success over what form of government the new nation should take. Finally, they sought advice from the general of the armies that had won their liberation from Great Britain. After prolonged evasion and delay, in December of 1783 Washington rode to them on horseback from Virginia. He was arguably the most respected and powerful man in the New World. Some people feared that he would declare himself king. Others hoped that he would."

Barclay Reed paused, sipping water from a straw.

"Go on," I said. "Please."

"Appalling that you are ignorant of this basic history. Washington arrived not in military uniform, as everyone expected, but in a plain brown suit. He gave a brief speech on the importance of the nation's soldiers returning to lives of peace and productivity. He declared that he intended to do precisely that, at his beloved farm Mount Vernon. And in conclusion, he gave the Continental Congress his sword."

"Just like Soga."

"Had our pilot been emperor of Japan, yes. But the point remains."

"Which is?"

"Soga believed in his own sincerity. He was no longer dropping bombs, or training pilots. The I-25 submarine lay in rusting pieces on the ocean floor. But you see . . ." The Professor raised one finger. "There was a degree of self-delusion. Soga had convinced himself outwardly, in the name of honor. But it was untrue, or he would not have brought the sword, just in case. It took the shrine to show him his hypocrisy. Only when he had relinquished his weapon did he end the war within. Only an unarmed man can say he has truly ceased fighting."

The connection for me was instantaneous: "But how can you lead a man to that realization? How do you help him to see?"

"Ah." The Professor studied me sidelong. "Your husband."

The kitchen timer began ringing. It surprised us both, our eyes meeting as though we had been caught at something.

Barclay Reed recovered first. "Nurse Birch, is he a warrior still?"

The oven timer chimed again. I stood, smoothing down my slacks. "I'll be right back."

HE WOULD NOT EAT. I watched, pretending to look elsewhere while the Professor moved things around with his fork. While the BBC blared on the large screen, he would dig absently at his plate, but the food never quite made it to his mouth.

I tidied his room, calculating. If he ceased getting nutrition, Barclay Reed would live two weeks, perhaps less. He sipped from his straw, and I made a mental note to monitor how much he drank in the course of my shift. Without hydration, it would be over in days.

I returned the black binder to its place of honor on the desk. By now we were reading from it every day. Yet Cheryl did not even know the book existed. I'd learned that with subtle fishing expeditions. She thought all the Professor read was the newspaper, dwelling to an unhealthy degree on the crossword puzzle. Once at the shift change I asked Melissa if she had noticed *The Sword*.

"I did. I was cleaning his room and asked about it. Making conversation, you know? Since he doesn't open up to me much. He said it was an old abandoned project. I offered to throw it out and he said sure. But then he changed his mind, in case anyone ever studied his papers. Fickle old fella."

I suppressed a smile. "Scholars like to hold on to their old research, I guess."

Another forkful left the plate. If anything went in, it was barely a morsel.

"Professor, I think we need to talk about your diet."

Instead he switched off the TV. "How did you choose this line of work?"

"I'm sorry?"

"How does any sentient person decide that hospice is a satisfying profession? I cannot imagine anything bleaker."

"You want to know my story?"

He pushed the rolling tray away. "The brief version."

Always a dig with this guy. But it was the one tale I never tired of telling.

"I grew up in a college town in upstate New York. Both my parents worked at the school. Mom was in admissions. She was tough, hard-handed, farm-raised. Early one January morning, she was driving to work when a guy still drunk from the night before veered across the road and hit her head-on."

I paused to see how this affected him. His reaction would determine whether I continued.

"Blast." The Professor tugged on his white tuft of hair. "Proceed."

"She spent six weeks in an ICU, machines and tubes and no role for us but to wring our hands. Five surgeries. We spared no medical extravagance. When her kidneys shut down, dialysis. When that lowered her blood pressure, dopamine by the bucket to raise it. Which increased the need for more dialysis. Round and round, till one day in the hallway my sister Robin asked a resident when he thought Mom might regain consciousness. He said, 'At no time has anyone here considered that a possibility.' She gave him holy hell until his boss sauntered up to declare that everything they had done had been at our request. Worse, he was right. Our ignorance had tortured the poor woman."

I slid the reading chair closer to his bed, but stood behind it. "We met with the hospital's ethics committee, brought in a minister Mom loved, and the next day removed the machines. She lingered an hour. She was sixty-two."

Barclay Reed nodded, unable to face me, for once reluctant to speak.

I lowered myself into the chair.

"Six Januaries later, Dad found out he had pancreatic cancer. Inoperable, unresponsive to chemo. He lived seven months. But you know what? Not one night in the hospital. The local hospice provided medical care, and the rest was up to us. Robin's husband stepped in with the kids, and she took a leave from work. She said she could make up the lost income anytime, but her father was only going to die once. I was teaching high school English by then and had the summer free."

I stared at my hands. This was the hard part. "For some reason, Dad had always wanted to learn to play the bassoon, but never did. We rented an instrument and found a teacher, this nerdy guy with a tiny mustache who came twice a week. Dad took lessons in the living room, then in bed when he grew weaker. The cancer spread to his bones, so we gave Dad lots of pain medicine. The teacher would assemble Dad's instrument, lay it across him to hold, and play at the bedside. Without our asking, he started coming every day."

I used to consider the bassoon silly, droning and nasal. In those weeks, I realized it was actually like a cello: introspective, melancholy.

"Hospice kept my father pain-free and made all the other medical parts work smoothly. That meant we could do everything nonmedical, the stuff that really mattered. Though most of it was actually little things."

Memories flooded back to me, that long summer with the house as quiet as if a newborn baby were napping. Robin and I had never been closer.

"We had a blue china plate," I continued. "Handed down from my great-grandmother. My father loved using it on special occasions. Our birthday dinners, when we graduated from high school. We served him every meal on that blue plate until he stopped eating, and he loved it. Little things."

The Professor held perfectly still. I suppose I was the one giving a lecture this time.

"When he died, Robin was holding one of his hands, and I held the other one. And of all things, our nerdy bassoon guy was standing at the foot of the bed, playing Bach."

The Professor darted a tongue across his lips. I slid his cup closer, and he gulped down some water, nodding slowly. "Excellent."

I stood, tugging a corner of his blanket snug. "That winter I took a hospice volunteer training course. To give back, you know? But after three patients, I knew I'd found my calling. I quit teaching to start school out here."

"Explain this to me." The Professor took a moment to organize his thoughts. "A surgeon sees his patients heal and go home. A primary-care physician prevents illness. You never receive those forms of gratification. In the end, all of your patients are gone. Doesn't that depress you?"

I smiled. "Actually, I'm like that musician, playing in a stranger's bedroom, making his life pleasing for as long as possible. Besides, caring for someone during the most vulnerable time in their lives, what could be more gratifying?"

"Are you suggesting, Nurse Birch, that Barclay Reed is at the most vulnerable time in his life?"

"What do you think, Professor?"

He fussed at the casserole with his fork. He pushed the basket of remotes away on the bed. He stared into space, blinking.

"At first I suspected it was appendicitis," he said.

"What was?"

"The soreness in my lower abdomen, the fever and weakness." He spread a palm on his belly. "One Sunday afternoon the pain intensified, till I swear I saw stars. With what in retrospect may not have been my wisest judgment, I drove myself to the emergency room. The doctor was cast for his job, handsomely gray at the temples and bright-eyed despite obvious fatigue. He did tests, white blood cells and I don't recall what else, only to conclude that they were inconclusive. He had been reluctant to incur the expense of a scan, but at that point he felt there was a choice. I could go home and risk a rupture, with potentially fatal internal bleeding, or undergo a scan. Some people fear those machines, I've heard, because they're noisy and close. Nonsense. It's just a machine. Later he brought his laptop to my room, if that is what you can call one of those emergency spaces defined by a curtain yanked round you on a shower rod. He pulled up the results, exclaiming 'Now isn't this interesting?' But any medical layman could see what the scan had discovered. My appendix was inflamed, oh yes, but more importantly—as he showed me, as I could not fail to see—it pointed like a hot finger directly at my kidney. At the tumor on my kidney."

"Uh-oh."

"He said it was operable, in which case my troubled appendix had just saved my life. The following day a surgeon opened me to excise the tumor, but the growth was not as firm as they'd expected. The thing burst, sowing progeny throughout my innards. He performed suction, I was told, meanwhile observing that the entire lining had white dots of metastasis. He took the offending appendix, then sewed me up without having removed any of the cancer."

The Professor pointed one rigid finger at the ceiling. "I will never forget that scan image, and the inflammation sticking upward. *J'accuse.*"

With that, his hand flopped in his lap like a dove taken down by a hunter.

I leaned forward and placed an arm on his bed. I was still wary of touching the Professor, but I wanted to be closer, for both our sakes. "Thank you for sharing that story."

"Yes, well."

"As you would say, Professor: Blast."

He sniffed. "As you would say, Nurse Birch: Ouch."

And there it was: The fact of his mortality. I felt a swell of compassion for this strange, brilliant, difficult man.

When Barclay Reed had asked me a few weeks back what the purpose of suffering was, I should have answered by saying that it had the potential to create this very moment. Because this was the place where my work always arrived, every patient, every time.

If you think of a person, anyone, even someone you dislike, if you imagine for a moment how one day they will lose everything— family and home and pleasures and work—and people will weep and wail when they die, you cannot help it: You feel compassion for them. Your heart softens. What's more, every single human being is going to experience this same thing, without exception: Every person you love, everyone you hate, your own frivolous struggling self. It is the central lesson of hospice: Mortality is life's way of teaching us how to love.

The path before the Professor would not be a long one. My job was to make the journey as good as possible for as long as possible. How to do that would unfold one moment at a time.

I pointed at his dinner. "You're not going to eat any of that, are you?"

He studied his fork before laying it down. "Apparently not."

"Let me get it out of your way then." I scooped the plate from his tray. "Is there anything else I can get you? Anything you think you could eat?"

Barclay Reed grinned at me, his head tilted forward like a boy asking for seconds on ice cream. It was as playful as I had ever seen him. And we had just reached such a trusting place.

"What?" I asked. "What is it?"

He raised his hands as if in prayer, then drummed the fingertips on one another. "Might there be any more strawberries?"

MICHAEL WAS CURLING DUMBBELLS in the driveway when I came home. The weights looked cartoonishly large, like balloons connected by pencils. He wore a sleeveless T-shirt, his arms engorged by effort, his face radiant.

What I felt, plain and simple, was lust. He was so strong. There in the car I remembered a time when I climbed away from Michael in the middle of lovemaking and stood at the bedside just to ogle him there.

He smiled. "What's up, Deb?"

"Oh lover, I'm just admiring you."

He held out his hands. "Do it closer."

As I climbed out of the car, he finished his curls without turning my way. Yet it made him sexier. He was concentrating. At a previous time, I would have pawed him shamelessly, pulling him into the house, hiking myself up on the kitchen counter. Instead I watched him finish. He put the weights down and wagged his hands as if to dry them.

"Hi, lover," I said. "How was your day?"

"Not great," Michael answered. "Frustrating."

Well, good-bye lust. Once upon a time, arriving home meant I could recover from my day by spilling about it. Now whatever happened at work was obliterated by whatever I found in the driveway. I suppose I was learning to live in the present, but sometimes it felt mighty tiring.

I gave him a kiss on the neck, tasting salt. "What was frustrating?"

"Gene. Or his plastic leg, anyway. I decided to help him out, you know? Getting the replacement screw. But it's classic Defense Department contracting. The prosthetic uses a rare gauge. We drive all over town, finally find one the right size, and then the slot turns out to be reverse-threaded."

"What does that mean?"

"Normal screws tighten when you turn them clockwise. His leg's slot is designed for a screw that tightens counterclockwise, don't ask me why in hell." He picked up the dumbbells again. "We spent the whole day, literally nine to five, chasing one screw, and we totally struck out. I came out here to lift so I wouldn't go smashing things in the basement."

Michael began pumping again, alternating arms in sets: three with the right, three with the left. His chin pointed forward on each curl, as if his jaw could pull the weight upward. And his breath came loudly in the rhythm of each lift and drop.

"You know, sweetheart," I began.

"Yeah?"

I leaned back on my car. The thought was: Assume a casual pose, and perhaps the message will arrive more lightly. "That's something I've been meaning to talk to you about."

"Smashing things?" Michael continued lifting as he grunted his reply. "Cause I haven't broken anything, Deb. Not a toothpick."

"Well, sweetheart, you broke that guy's car—"

"He had it coming."

"—and almost every morning there's a few pencils."

"Look." Michael paused, both arms down, the weights pulling his shoulders into a curve. "If it is now a problem when I break a freaking pencil—"

"I'm not saying that. I'm just thinking about the other night."

The right arm started again, a slow upward grind. "Which night?"

"The thunderstorm."

He switched to his left, eyes fixed ahead, but I knew that was not about lifting anymore. Michael did not want to look at me.

"You were upset," I continued. "Which is fine, of course. Except that you took out your gun."

"And did nothing." Lift, drop. Lift, drop. "Not even load it."

"How was I to know that? Sweetheart, it scared me."

"In the hands of a responsible person, a gun is nothing to be afraid of."

He was making me do this, forcing me to reason with him about something that should have required no argument. "Would you say you were a responsible person that night?"

Michael dropped both weights on the lawn. "You can't give me one second's peace, can you?"

"Actually, peace is exactly what I want to give you."

"After I already said I was frustrated." He pointed a stiff finger at me. "Nagging is not peaceable."

I let that one go. Michael regretted saying it, too. I sensed it in the way he strode away across the lawn, swinging his arms out and back like a giant bird. I stood there on that lovely July night, still in work clothes, just wanting to step out of my clogs and drink an iced tea, maybe sit a moment before making a dinner I would probably eat alone.

In a minute he had flapped his way back. "Tell me," Michael said. "Tell you?"

"Come on." He waved his hands in invitation, though it seemed more like a boxer taunting his opponent from across the ring. "You've got a bone to pick, I should hear you out. Dr. Doremus says that all the time, that people who care about me are worth paying attention to. You go ahead."

"Really?"

He held his arms wide. "I'm not lifting."

"Well."

I tried to picture it then, the meeting room or restaurant where Soga gave away his sword all those years ago. What it must have taken for him to decide, to make a personal surrender, to give up a defining part of his past. But this time the idea would not come from the warrior himself. Would Soga have offered his sword if his wife had suggested it?

"I think you should get rid of your gun."

He staggered backward as if taking a blow. "You think what?"

"It's time to quit being ready for a fight. Give up your gun."

"Jesus, Deb. Talk about left field." He pressed both palms against the sides of his head. "You are even more out of touch than I thought."

"I think that weapon is a danger. I think you will not rest until it is gone."

"Do you know what it takes to do that? Find a buyer for a firearm as powerful and expensive as the .50, background checks, the works?"

"I didn't say it would happen easily. But as a first step—"

"Stop it. Just stop." Michael grabbed his weights and headed for the house, pausing by the screen door. "You are completely fucking clueless."

I stared at where he had been standing. The door hissed closed. A robin darted out of the trees and across the yard. I heard kids calling to one another down the street. But then I remembered that moment under the kitchen table, and something inside me turned into heat.

"I am not the clueless one, damn it," I said, yanking the door open. "I am the one keeping this household—"

Michael stood in the kitchen, a weight in each hand. He seemed gigantic. I sympathized with the guy whose car he had crushed. What it must have been like to see that big pickup bearing down on him.

But then I noticed something worse: He had gone white, his face and chest and arms, so ruddy red a minute before, appeared almost bloodless. Milk.

"Say it again," Michael growled.

"Lover, please calm down."

"Tell me to get rid of the gun again."

"All I am saying it that I do not believe a person who owns a military assault rifle is making himself an instrument of peace. The war is over."

"War is never over in the minds of the people who fought it."

I paused at that. "Probably you're right. Which makes me very sad for you. Sad for our country, too, if you think about all the veterans out there. But carrying a gun in the mind is very different from carrying one in your hands."

He shook his head. "Do you honestly think we would be safer if I got rid of that world-class weapon?"

"With all my heart."

"You are wrong, Deborah. Dead fucking wrong." And as he said the last word, Michael drove the weight in his right hand into the wall.

The drywall gave, of course, a pair of round holes each about the size of a compact disc. He was lucky not to have punched a post, or the night would have involved an ER trip and a month with his hand in a cast.

The blow must have stung anyway, given how Michael fluttered his fingers and sucked on a knuckle. Almost immediately, though, he grabbed the dumbbell's handle and pulled, but it was stuck in the wall.

"Michael, wait—"

He set his feet to try again, yanking hard, which shook the wall, and—yank, yank—likewise the shelf above it, where I kept my reliable old mixing bowl, a yard-sale soup tureen I used twice a year, and on a little wooden stand, my great-grandmother's blue china plate.

When the weight came free of the wall, Michael staggering backward, it was like slow motion how the plate wobbled off its perch, tipped forward, did one complete somersault, and fell on the table with a clear, high shattering note.

"Oh perfect," Michael said, gesturing with the dumbbell at the scatter of broken china. "Perfect."

"Ouch," I said. "Ouch."

"Now I am the true shit," he said. "Asshole of the century. You know, I have been really trying, Deb. Really truly."

I had nothing to say in reply.

"I stifle myself all day long, I stuff it all down, and still I break something precious to you. I could say I'm sorry till a month from now, but we both know no apology will put that thing back together." He looked back and forth between the dumbbells in each hand. "Swear to God, Deb, sometimes I think I ought to just fucking die."

Then he was past me, storming out the door, heaving the weights onto the lawn where they landed with brute thuds. Through the screen I saw Michael stomp away up the street while his body twisted and turned as if he were wrestling his way free from a nest of vines.

I stood there in the kitchen, taking it in. With shards on the table, chairs, and floor, the plate clearly was miles beyond repair. I felt as if all I had ever been was tired.

Even so, I wanted to yank back the door and shout at Michael—no words, no argument, just one great blasting scream—to yell out all the anger and frustration and impatience that I swallowed like poison day after day.

But he was gone, and I was not the screaming kind anyway. There was nothing else to do but get a wastebasket and, one more time, try to pick up the pieces.

ICHIRO SOGA DID NOT RETURN to the United States of America for ten years. During that interval he opened a hardware store in Tsuchiura, a town eighty miles north of Tokyo. Business grew slowly, paralleling Japan's glacially incremental economic recovery. Soga invested his entire savings, precluding the expense of further foreign adventures.

He did, however, maintain a correspondence with town leaders in Brookings. Indeed, after his visit in 1962, three hundred and fourteen people received personal thank-you notes, their tone formal but appreciative, and written in English thanks to the translation and penmanship of Soga's son.

The debate about his visit, although quieter, did not entirely fall silent. Letters to the *Pilot* continued with passion unabated.

When word of Soga's visit reached Beth Issacs of West Palm Beach, Florida, for example, she mailed an epistle to enlighten her fellow Americans in the opposite corner of the country: "I feel compelled to condemn you for your complete lack of integrity and charity."

There were no full-page advertisements, however, or contentious selectboard meetings with signs carried and voices raised. Mayor Campbell continued to serve, the Azalea Festival crowned a new queen each May, and World War II blurred further in the soft focus of memory.

If Donny Baker III maintained any ill will toward Soga and those who had championed his visit, his opinions remained out of the public record. He too suffered the preoccupation of business necessity, though in his case the circumstances were of success beyond any expectation.

The explosion of 1960s suburbia in California's Bay Area sent ripples far up the coast, as residents of the Golden State spilled into southernmost Oregon. Erecting houses by the score, they needed trees, shrubs, plants, topsoil, reflecting globes, trellises, bird baths, bulbs, shovels, rakes, hoes, seeds—all supplied by the prodigious inventory of Baker's Nursery and Garden Supply, two miles south of Brookings. Around this enterprise lay the quiet fields and rich soils of the nation's largest source of Easter lilies. While the nation raged over civil rights and Vietnam, their white blooms opened dependably, silent trumpets through the tumultuous springs of the late 1960s.

Donny prospered, joining the local Chamber of Commerce, and—despite his disdain for the group's invitation to Soga—the Jaycees. Donny also became a philanthropist, albeit on an extremely modest scale. A bench in Azalea Park bore a brass plaque honoring Mrs. Donny Baker III on the occasion of her tenth wedding anniversary.

His priorities were best illustrated, moreover, by Donny's single appearance in the *Pilot*—after his daughter's performance in an elementary school Christmas pageant. He stands awkwardly beside Heather, a beaming youngster who holds a clutch of carnations. The news item quotes an unnamed parent declaring that Heather has "the voice of an angel."

Donny's other marks in the public record came in 1969, after he purchased a used single-engine aircraft and began filing flight logs. Cruising at low altitudes, he flew as far up the rugged coastline as Tacoma, as far south as Santa Rosa.

Donny rarely ventured inland, with one exception that subsequently merited an inch of news space. When the Brookings-Harbor High School football team made the regional playoffs in 1970, Donny flew over the game, towing a banner that read GO BRUINS GO.

In sum, these were hardly the behaviors of a man engaged in, much less passionate about, geopolitics. Nevertheless, it took only one thing to heat his ardor back to a boil: an item in the *Pilot* in November of 1971 announcing that the following spring, Ichiro Soga would be visiting America again.

A decade after his first visit, Soga arrived attired precisely as before: a pressed suit, wing tips, and black glasses, albeit with appreciably thicker lenses. The welcome assembly contained fewer dignitaries, but if Soga had emotions about that diminution he made no comment to the *Pilot*—which apparently assigned one Piper Abbott to chronicle the visit, since every story of his trip bore her byline.

What differed from Soga's first visit? First, his daughter, Yoriko, served as translator. Attired in modest dresses, she stood at his elbow like an acolyte. The softness of Yoriko's voice had a diplomatic effect; people in conversation with Soga had to lean forward in order to hear her. From the photographs it appears as though his daughter's modesty caused others to bow.

Second, on the initial visit Soga's expression had been uniformly stern, whereas Piper Abbott's photographs from 1972 portray a man wearing a nearly constant smile—on the beach, outside a movie theater, in the foyer of the public library where he made a donation toward the purchase of new children's books.

Inside, in a private moment apart from his retinue, Soga stood before the sword. It hung in a glass display case, beside a scale model of the I-25 submarine. He bowed low and long. When he returned to the assemblage outside, Piper Abbott photographed him smiling once again.

One other image is emblematic: At an evening gathering, someone handed him a copy of the *Oregon Journal* of Portland from September 10, 1942, with its giant headline: "FOE BOMBS OREGON!!"

In the 1972 photo, Soga holds the newspaper high. It is a moment the equal of "Dewey Defeats Truman" from 1948—although Soga's smile is possibly even more toothsome than that of the man who won the presidency despite the *Chicago Tribune's* erroneous headline.

Third, Soga no longer played the role of silent warrior, a mask of inscrutable Asian reserve. Through his daughter, he spoke. He conversed. Above all, he asked questions.

Banking in particular received close attention. Piper Abbott filed numerous photos and articles about his willingness to try American convenience foods like potato chips and ice cream on a stick, and his visit to the giant redwoods ninety miles south in California's Humboldt County. Yet fully half of the pictures of Soga's second visit show him standing outside a bank, asking questions at a breakfast with bankers, or peering into the opening of a vault, the foot-thick iron door swung back to display whatever fascinations lay within.

Although Brookings' bankers embraced their fellow capitalist, not everyone responded as warmly. Soga was scheduled to give an address in the school gymnasium, with posters thumbtacked around town advertising the date and time. Some enterprising booster had placed topmost on the posters a large 1941 photo of the bomber pilot in battle gear: a fur-lined leather jacket, the thick leather hat with flaps over his ears, the goggles. On the morning of Soga's speech, Brookings awoke to discover that all the posters had been decapitated.

Recall that thirty years had passed since his Oregon mission. In 1972 Toyota sold its one-millionth vehicle in America. In 1972 Honda introduced the first tiny Civic automobile, which likewise subsequently sold in the millions. America and Japan were now allies, if only because of the imperatives of commerce.

Moreover, geopolitics had turned the nation's attention elsewhere. An arms race with the Soviet Union shaped American defense policy. Oil shortages orchestrated by a Middle Eastern cartel created a growing economic dirge.

Nevertheless, some people continued to fight the battles of yesteryear. Once an enemy, always an enemy. A sheriff visiting the local rifle range found several missing poster heads stapled to targets. They were riddled with bullet holes.

School officials canceled Soga's speech. An armed deputy attended all of his remaining events.

But here a fourth difference appeared in the pilot's conduct. He was sixty-one now, father of grown children, a man of business. When Piper Abbott asked his response to the vandalized posters, the answer that Yoriko translated was immediate:

"I cannot fault a person for maintaining anger. War leaves deep scars. In my small view, however, the world has learned since then. Now we see that we can coexist. More: We can prosper. This, if I may say, is preferable to enmity."

Then Soga issued a spontaneous invitation. "I would welcome conversation with anyone who sympathizes with defacing the posters. I would like to learn whether there may be some means by which we could understand one another."

"Soga Answers Vandalism with Invitation," read the headline in the next morning's *Pilot*. Two days later, a local citizen replied in a letter to the editor.

"Challenge accepted," the letter said. "If the Jap pilot shows up at my place of business, I'm willing to stop work for a couple minutes. But this will be no formal tea ceremony. Soga can expect an earful. You don't bomb my town, then win my friendship with a few polite bows and a fancy suit."

The signatory of that letter to the editor? Donny Baker III.

THE CARAVAN ARRIVED at Baker's Nursery and Garden Supply at 7:45 A.M., shortly before it would open for business. Piper Abbott rode in Soga's car, beside his daughter. Soga was silent for the whole ride.

As the group disembarked, Donny emerged from behind a stack of wheelbarrows. He wore blue work pants, a gray t-shirt, and a battered tractor cap. While Soga tugged his jacket sleeves snug, Donny stood with fists on his hips.

"Good morning, sir," Soga said through Yoriko.

"Morning," Donny replied.

"Might we tour your company?"

He shrugged. "Suit yourself."

Compared with other places Soga had visited—the factories, restaurants and banks eager to display every detail with pride—this presentation was perfunctory. Donny waved an arm at the shrub display, stood briefly in the doorway of the tool shed, marched through the greenhouses without pausing for questions. The group was back by the cars in fifteen minutes.

Soga clasped his hands behind his back, then murmured to his daughter. "Honored sir, my father says it is his impression that you are unhappy with him, and his visit to your town."

Donny bristled. "Tell your dad I am unhappy with the Japs who bombed Pearl Harbor, and their war, which killed something like a hundred and ten thousand American soldiers and sailors, and wounded another quarter million."

Many of the Jaycees shifted uncomfortably. Piper Abbott memorialized the conversation in her reporter's notebook. Yoriko translated, her mouth to her father's ear while he nodded gravely. She delivered his reply in so quiet a voice, Donny was compelled to step closer in order to hear.

"My father says, these are terrible numbers. Terrible. Likewise the Japanese suffered. More than two million military deaths and three hundred thousand civilian deaths. Also terrible."

"Yeah, but they brought it on themselves, by attacking us." Donny poked at the air in Soga's direction. "Without even declaring war first."

Soga listened to Yoriko, then bowed to Donny deeply. She leaned near, waiting while her father pondered. Then she translated his reply.

"My father says, with the battles over, now we must choose whether to continue to fight in our hearts, or recognize the dangers of all war—"

"Kinda late for that, don't you think?"

She continued without translating Donny's interruption. "My father says, would you rather I remain across the ocean, your adversary forever?"

"I guess I'd like it if your whole damn country stayed out of our business. Selling cheapo cars that otherwise would have been bought from American companies, and coming around here so everyone can suck up to you."

"My father says, I am too insignificant to speak for my nation. I represent only myself, one small Ichiro Soga." When she said his name, he bowed. "I did not choose to fight in war. I was conscripted. Also I believed it was virtue to serve the emperor, and honorable to uphold the Soga name. Today, I believe it is beneficial to make reparations between people. That is the only reason I have come."

Donny scratched his neck. "Last time, you know, they spent three thousand dollars to bring you here."

"I am most grateful."

"Ask me, it sounds like the list of things you need to repay is getting longer, not shorter."

As his daughter translated, Soga stiffened. She scrutinized his face, then murmured something further. He shook his head no, but at that moment Piper Abbott stepped out of her role as reportorial witness.

"Yesterday he gave that exact amount of money to the public library," she said. "For children's books."

"Well, I don't know," Donny said. "Seems fishy."

For a moment, the two men regarded one another: Donny a full head taller, rounder, scruffy, his eyes squinted, Soga impeccable and reserved. He scanned the nursery, peering down aisles as if it were an inspection, then whispered to Yoriko.

"What is your pride?" she translated.

Donny drew back. "What in hell does that mean?"

Father and daughter conferred before she answered. "What is the one thing you make or sell, of which you are most proud?"

"I don't know." Donny turned, regarding his business: the greenhouse, the sheds, the day's first customers arriving. "I guess it's my trees. I sell damn good trees."

Soga and Yoriko exchanged words. "Which is your proudest tree?"

"Most folks get excited about myrtlewood," Donny said, " 'cause we grow them great around here. But I say there's only one king tree in this part of the country." He pointed to the furthest row in his place. "The redwood."

Soga smiled his widest grin. He murmured a reply, gazing at Donny's face while Yoriko translated. "My father requests if he may purchase a redwood tree."

Donny shrugged. "Long as he uses good American dollars."

She spoke again. "After purchase, my father invites you to join him."

"In what?" Donny put his hands on his hips. "This some kind of joke?"

"My father wishes you to help him plant this proud king tree at the shrine for the people who were killed by his bomb."

IN THE PHOTO, taken that afternoon and published in the *Pilot* the following day, an all-male group stands arrayed beside the monument. The exception, Yoriko, remains behind her father, face turned as if she would prefer to be invisible. Soga, because the digging caused him to perspire, persuaded Piper Abbott not to photograph him in his shirtsleeves. He has just put his suit coat back on. He holds a shovel, its blade resting in the soil. He is shaking hands with the mayor, the tree beside them as slender as a fawn.

The other shovel lies on the ground at the feet of Donny, who stands on the photo's periphery, fully an arm's length away from the nearest person. His position indicates either a photographer too shy to instruct him to join the line, or a man unwilling to move one inch nearer to the events at hand. His face is as pinched as if he has just eaten a lime. His arms are crossed, hands fisted, eyes narrowed. The body language is unambiguously articulate: Donny Baker III is furious.

CHAPTER 14

SPACKLE, TAPE, AND PAINT—those we had in the garage already. But on the way home from the Professor's, I drove to a construction supply store for drywall. I had not enjoyed eating breakfast in a kitchen with two circular holes in the wall, and I was not looking forward to dinner there either.

There was a line, all builders and carpenters collecting material for the next day's work. I stood waiting, acutely aware of my yellow skirt, while men in work boots ordered plywood or pipe, shingles or nails.

"How you doing today, ma'am?" The guy had sidled up without my noticing: tall, lanky, tan as leather with bright green eyes. He wore a red t-shirt like all the store's employees and a name tag that said "Andy."

"Hi," I said. "Hello, I mean."

He tongued a matchstick from one side of his mouth to the other. "Help you find something?"

"Drywall. But just a small piece, for a wall repair."

"Hate it when that happens, don't you?" Andy ambled off. "Lean your chair back too far, or carry a ladder without paying attention, and suddenly you need a quarter sheet and not an inch more."

"Yes," I said, following him. "Or swing your tennis racket in the kitchen."

"Right," he turned to grin at me. "That'll do ya."

What a ridiculous moment. Why did I lie to him? Something about his rolling gait, his long-limbed ease. It was the opposite of Michael. Plus he looked about twenty-five years old. What would he know of post-traumatic husbands?

"We might have something in scrap." He led me past a display of ceiling fans, through corridors of windows and doors, until we reached the rear of the building. I stayed a few steps back, watching the tape measure sway in his tool belt, spotting the gap on one side between his t-shirt and loose jeans, a glimpse of skinny flesh.

"Hey now." Andy pulled up short. "This here looks promising."

A broken drywall board leaned against the wall, four feet by eight, with a bend about two thirds of the way down. "Let's see how we do." He squatted, running the tape measure out each way. "You got a clean twenty-six inch piece on this end, and maybe forty, forty-one going the other way. Either of those do it for ya?"

I leaned toward him. I mean, what was the harm? He turned, and his face was inches from mine. He smelled like sunburn. I smiled. "The smaller part would be perfect."

"Lucky day." Andy pulled out a box cutter and sliced away. Straightening, he held the shorter segment out like a platter. "Always glad to make something useful out of something broken."

"You're so right," I said. As I took the segment we made eye contact, and he smiled, in no rush to break away. It was a little thrill, I admit it. A sensation I hadn't experienced since before Michael's third deployment. Not that I needed the flirting of a stranger to make my days worthwhile. Only that this Andy made me feel like a desirable female again. And I liked it. "What do I owe you?"

"On the house," he said. "It would have gone in tomorrow's trash anyhow."

"Well, thank you. I owe you one."

Andy smirked, moving that matchstick again. "You come back anytime."

As I placed the drywall on the passenger seat, I enjoyed a little daydream, the first of its kind in a long, long time. In my imagination, Andy asked me oh so casually out to the back lot behind the sheds, all weeds and privacy and shade, or to some empty office upstairs in the store. Maybe it was a weak moment. Maybe my marriage was in greater trouble than I had allowed myself to realize. But in the fantasy, I said yes.

Then I started the car and steered for home. And I admit it: Instead of feeling guilt, everything was lightness and the windows were open. I turned the radio up loud.

"WHAT IN THE HELL ARE YOU DOING?"

Michael came into the kitchen with sweat rings under his arms. His face was red too, whether from exertion or emotion I did not know.

I was kneeling by the wall, the pair of holes from his barbell punch now cut to a single neat square, repair tools on the floor, a spackle scraper in my hand. "I'm patching things up from yesterday."

He put his hands on his hips. "I should be doing that."

"I'm happy to."

Michael shook his head. "You should have left it for me to fix."

"I don't mind, lover."

He barked: "Stop calling me that."

"Why?" I stammered. "Why wouldn't I call you lover, Michael?"

"Because it's a fucking lie." He began pacing by the kitchen table. "And you know it. I haven't been your lover in almost a year."

Ouch. It was as if he had drained me dry. And I did not pause to fill myself with kindness. "What am I supposed to call you then? Milk?"

He spun on his heel. "Who told you about Milk?"

"Joel did."

"Fucking Joel."

"You need to understand something, Michael," I said, looking down at the scraper. How I wished I was not on my knees just then. "There is a ceiling, you know. A limit to what I can withstand."

"Are you kidding?" Michael sneered. "I knew that before our wheels touched down on U.S. soil." He paced again. "Hell, I knew it when I was still in Iraq, watching wives ditch my buddies by the week. We all knew. It's not like on TV, one video after another of joyous family reunions at some football game, or sitting in Santa's lap, and surprise, Daddy's home. For every one of those, there are five hundred like us."

"Well, I only realized it this afternoon. And I am not ditching anyone. I am just admitting that there is a limit."

"That's what you say now."

"Why are you so hard on me, Michael?"

"Cause life is hard on me. Times ten. Got a nice call at the shop today. Another guy from my unit ended himself. Troy, from Ashland."

"Oh honey, I am so sorry."

"Running the car in his garage," Michael scoffed. "Total lack of originality."

It was troubling to consider that my husband had developed a hierarchy for methods of suicide, apparently with points for creativity. Before I could say anything, though, he had yanked open the screen door.

"Why are you always leaving?" I asked him. "Where are you going?"

"Same as ever: Back on patrol."

The air pump eased the door closed behind him. The kitchen was painfully quiet. I looked at my repair job, all of the prep done, and decided to pack up the tools. I would leave the hole there for now. It was closer to the truth.

TO WIPE BARCLAY REED'S FACE AFTER SHAVING, I used the softest terrycloth hand towel in the house. He poked his jaw forward to give me better access. When I returned from throwing the towel in the laundry, I evaluated the man watching television from a wheelchair.

He had lost ground during the night. His skin had taken on the waxy appearance of a body not getting enough nourishment. His skull seemed to stick out from his neck. The Professor was in rapid decline. If there had been a family, this is the day I would have told them to gather distant relatives and begin making farewells, because it would not be long.

"You're staring," he said.

"Making sure I didn't miss any spots."

"Is that so, Nurse Birch? Or are you trying to see through my poker face and decide whether or not you believe my book?"

"Does it always come back to that? To belief?"

"To a historian, no other question matters. To a discredited scholar, all the more. Where do you stand today?"

"Honestly?"

"That is the only way I wish you ever to speak to me."

I picked up the black binder and flipped through the pages. "Well, I'm skeptical. No offense, Professor, but this guy is acting like some kind of Gandhi. The world would not forget such a person. Everyone in Oregon, at least, would know his story. There'd be a Soga High School, or Soga Park, or Soga Boulevard. Right?"

"One would hope." He picked at the tuft of hair on his forehead. "Or, conversely, the lack of such places would evidence the need for a book such as *The Sword*."

I heard the front door open and close. Melissa must have arrived early for her shift.

"So what's the point of this section, then? The pilot has already given up his sword. Why plant a tree?"

"He has begun to empathize with his adversary. He is engaged in a dialogue that reveals his former opponent's inner thoughts, and thereby gives him the tools to persuade that enemy to join him in peace."

"Isn't it usually the victor who determines everything when a war ends? Isn't that who shapes the peace?"

"You are confused, Nurse Birch." Barclay Reed closed his eyes, keeping them that way long enough that I thought he might have fallen asleep. Then he blinked back into our conversation. "Formal policies between nations bear little connection to the actual attitudes of their people. Soga is three decades past the days he released four bombs, during a conflict in which all sides dropped bombs by the tens of thousands. The Japanese surrender ended the fighting, but it did not give him peace within himself."

I heard Melissa in the kitchen, fussing at something, which meant that my shift was over. But it barely registered. "So why plant a tree?"

"Only through genuine empathy with the former enemy can soldiers of both sides become humans again." He waved a TV remote at me. "Consider your husband. Is he at peace?"

"Hardly," I said, feeling uncomfortable with the direction the conversation had taken. But my mouth opened, and I revealed all kinds of private things. "Michael didn't go to make war on anyone. His mission was reconstruction. Maintaining equipment and vehicles for building water systems, schools, roads. The insurgents? Their mission was chaos. All they wanted was to see the place burn. I mean, who shoots at guardsmen who are trying to build a sewer system?"

"It may be extremely difficult to find rapport with enemies whose primary goal was disorder."

"And who are still at it today, busy as ever. So it's not like he can buy a plane ticket to Baghdad, quick make some Iraqi friends, buy them a beer, and it's all over."

The Professor stewed for a minute. "Perhaps," he said, then paused.

"Perhaps what?" I asked. "I'm listening. I am really listening right now."

He turned to me with the strangest expression, as if our conversation had been abstract until that moment, and now he realized that my husband was an actual person, with actual pain from an actual war.

"Perhaps there is some way he may yet empathize with his adversary."

"Professor, I just explained. How can he possibly do that with insurgents?"

He looked me over again. It was like a mirror, how his stern gaze caused me to consider. "Perhaps they are not his adversary anymore."

"Who else could it possibly be?"

The Professor switched on his television, foreign news filling the screen, the volume too loud for my taste. I could not press him at a moment like that, but I sure wanted to. He had cut the conversation off in the middle, and I realized that a person refusing to speak is every bit as frustrating as one refusing to listen.

Damn this job sometimes. I put the binder on the desk and left the room to brief Melissa on his pain and anti-nausea meds, as well as the night ahead.

When I came out of the bedroom, I found a woman standing by the gong with her back to me, hands on her hips. Dressed all in black, her short hair teased into a dark spiky thatch, it was definitely not Melissa. She was staring out at the glimmering lake, tapping one foot as though the view bored her.

I drew up short. "Hello?"

The woman took her time turning. She had an Asian appearance and was working her jaw as though something was stuck to her lower lip. It made her look more than a little scary. If Melissa was ill or had to cancel, I could not believe the agency would send this person to fill in. "Excuse me, who are you?"

"I'm D," she said.

"Yes? Can I help you?"

"D Reed, dammit." She crossed her arms. "His daughter. Now who the hell are you?"

THE NEXT HOUR WAS what the Professor would call an inquisition. Every decision questioned, every plan challenged. D was not the first family member in my experience to confuse medical intervention with love—sometimes they are opposites—or to equate the badgering of caregivers with providing care herself. Yet every time I suggested she go say hello to her father, her response was to fire a new barrage of questions.

When she started asking about pain-medicine dosages, I explained that health care privacy laws did not permit me to answer.

"How convenient," she glowered, storming away into the living room.

Melissa arrived and I briefed her in the entryway. She had an unpleasant night ahead of her. On my way down the driveway I switched on my phone, intending to call the agency and let them know that—surprise—our patient record was incorrect. Barclay Reed did indeed have surviving family, which could raise all sorts of questions. Also, I wanted to warn them about D's attitude, and the likelihood that she would have complaints.

Before I could dial, my phone pinged with half a dozen voice mails. Three were from Michael's number, three from a number I didn't know. Please, not the police again. They had made it clear they would not give him another chance. Before I had listened to the first message, my phone rang.

The woman said she was calling from the office of a United States congressman. "Your husband gave us this number," she explained.

I stopped short. "Is Michael all right?"

"Fine." The woman said. "We're having an incident with him, though."

"What sort of incident?"

"Your husband wanted to bring a Veterans Affairs complaint to our attention. Which he did, persuasively. We now have a grievance on file, a docket number, and it is in our caseload mix."

I swallowed hard, waiting for the bad news. "Why are you calling me?"

"He won't leave."

"I'm sorry?"

"Your husband refuses to leave. He's blocking one of the building's doorways. We could call the police, but we don't want press involved."

"What is your address?" I began trotting down the road.

She told me, and I marveled. It was completely across town from Michael's auto shop. Walking there must have taken half the day.

"I'll get there as soon as I can." By then I was standing beside my car. Fully in the shade when I parked that morning, now it basked in afternoon sun. I opened the door and a roasting hot breath blasted out at me.

THE CONGRESSMAN'S OFFICE was in a building with metal detectors and two guards in the lobby. I strode across the marble courtyard, past the fountain, feeling the sun reflect off the tall stories of glass.

Michael was lying across the right-hand set of double doors, making them impossible to open. But it was silly: There was another set on the left, not thirty feet away, through which people came and went at will. In the foyer, a group of people watched him while mostly chatting among themselves. I would have expected a crowd on the square too, but it was near the end of the workday. Michael was dressed in desert fatigues. He looked large and awkward and, quite frankly, a little pathetic.

But when he heard footsteps approaching, he raised his head, recognized me, and did the most unexpected thing. He smiled.

There was no irony in it, no sarcasm. It was the real thing. And I had not seen him since he stormed off the night before. I was completely disarmed. Michael's smile. It was all I could do not to burst into tears.

I squatted in one side of the doorway. "Hey there."

"Hi, Deb. How was your day?"

It could have been a conversation in our backyard, he was so easy and offhand. As though he blocked buildings' doorways several times a week. "Full of surprises," I answered. "But I'm glad to see you."

"Same here." Michael was still smiling.

"So." The last thing I wanted to do was change the mood. If we were going to have a moment of connection, that doorway was as good a place as any. But I glanced inside, and the guards were standing beside their desk, watching us. One rested his hand on a nightstick. I waved at the building, the fountain, the doorway. "What's going on?"

"You know . . ." he began, rubbing a thumb against the palm of his other hand. "You know the other day, when I went to Joel's?"

"Sure. You said he and Gene had an argument."

"Times two. But before they got into it, Joel had one of his rants."

"I'm familiar with them."

"Yeah, he feels terrible about that."

I put a hand on Michael's leg, and he did not withdraw. "Not to worry."

"The whole noncombatant thing gets him revved. But this recent one, the new rant, it's a big part of why I'm here."

Guard inside be damned, I was not going to rush this moment for one second. "What was it about?"

"Treatment of returning soldiers throughout history. Did you know one-third of the Union dead in the Civil War were buried before the bodies had been identified? Or that black soldiers in the South, coming home from World War I, were beaten for wearing uniforms in public? And now there are tens of thousands of guys like me just waiting, you know, standing in line for help? We trusted our country, we fought for it, and now it is blowing us off. It happens in every war, is the point. Soldiers are mistreated when they come home. Joel said everyone complains about people spitting on Vietnam vets, but who knows? Maybe that was more honest."

I kept my hand on his thigh, in no hurry to lose contact. "I thought we had your benefits all set, sweetheart. Have you been waiting for something?"

"Not me. Gene. You should see how he walks because of that prosthetic leg. Hunchback of Notre Dame. Frankenstein."

"That doesn't seem fair."

"Times fifty." Michael began wringing his hands. "When he took me to Joel's, it's his right leg he hurt, OK? So not only does he have to drive with his left foot, but also he has to lay his hurt leg across the passenger seat. Basically, Deb, Gene has to drive with his stump in my lap."

"Ouch."

"All because they can't get him one damn screw. It's a strange one, I admit, but really? This guy served three deployments, and they can't get him a simple screw?"

"It sounds ridiculous. But the woman who called from the office here sounded responsive. She said they were working on it."

"Come on, Deb. That's total bullshit."

"What do you mean?"

"Do you know how long Gene has been gimping around that way, can't walk without pain, can't even stand at the stove and make dinner, while they fritter and dither and don't do a goddam thing?"

"I'm afraid to ask."

"Seven months." He was barking now, poking a rigid finger into his palm. "This guy sacrificed his leg, and they've stalled him for seven months."

"That can't be true."

"He came home before I did, right? Didn't finish the tour because of his wounds, obviously. He had surgery, recovery, PT, all decent enough. Then the leg they gave him came with a faulty part. He's been waiting on this screw since December ninth. And here we are mid-July." He poked that same finger in my direction. "Deb, it is unjust."

"Well, honey." I sat back, hands to myself. "It's not like they have a bin full of spare screws in some back room here—"

"Of course not. But I keep all sorts of strange things in my shop's inventory, stuff I may never need, because it costs almost nothing and it's worth having handy for emergencies. Do you have any idea how undignified it is for this guy, this goddam hero, to have to put his stump in my lap?"

I don't know why I couldn't just agree with my husband. Something about needing to defend our society, about explaining that we were imperfect but had good intentions. Maybe, too, I felt a tinge of guilt over my little fantasy at the lumberyard. Maybe I was compensating by being overly rational.

I sat back on my haunches. "I'm not saying that making Gene wait is OK, Michael. Just that maybe you should be reasonable. Now that you're in their file, I can't imagine it would take much longer."

"Reasonable?" Michael pounded his thigh, right where my hand had been. "He has been reasonable, Deb. And calm. And patient. And where's it gotten him? To a place where it is somehow acceptable for them to jerk off all day, while he hobbles around like fucking Quasimodo."

Michael ran his hands up and down his legs, calming himself. A breeze strummed the fountain, sending light spray harmlessly across the plaza.

"Look, Deb," he continued, his voice low. "I didn't need you here. I could have made this little fuss just fine on my own. I had them call because I trusted you. I thought you were on my side."

Right then, I understood what Barclay Reed had meant. Iraqi insurgents were not the only adversaries Michael needed a truce with. It was me, too.

Here I had thought all along that we were at peace—or at least coexisting in some temporary place, in which he had his difficulties and I was helping him back to sanity. When actually, I'd been preventing peace the whole time: overeager after the Dr. Doremus sessions, pushing too hard about the face drawings, coming on too strong as a voice of reason right then.

Once upon a time, loving Michael had been the simplest thing, as natural as breathing. But now here I was, doing it in the worst possible way.

And there in my thinking, like some bizarre role model, was Ichiro Soga. He had made the decision to empathize with his adversary. He had more than earned forgiveness, but still never asked Donny Baker to give up his stubborn views. Instead, he managed to bend toward his adversary. Whether Soga's story was real or a fabrication did not really matter. The idea that it might be true was good enough.

The hell with being reasonable. The hell with respecting a governmental process. I would choose Soga's path. I would bend.

I stood up, and held out a hand.

"What?" Michael scowled. "I'm not leaving."

"Come on. We're going to go get some answers."

He stared at me a long while, considering. I just kept my hand out there, as steady as . . . well, as a tree planted beside a monument.

At last my husband stood, brushed off the seat of his pants, and took my hand. I loved it, his large strong paw, warm from his afternoon of sitting in that doorway in the sun. That may sound like high school romance, like silly infatuation, but for one crucial fact: It was our most intimate touch since the day Michael came home.

And we walked inside that building holding hands. Together.

TWELVE ADDITIONAL YEARS ELAPSED before Ichiro Soga flew to Oregon for the third time.

By 1985, U.S. relations with Japan had normalized, propelled by commerce, and in particular the soaring demand for consumer products. Millions of Americans drove Japanese cars, listened to music on Sony Walkmans, and squandered vast fortunes of time playing video games made in Japan. Brookings itself had a sushi restaurant, on Pacific Avenue near the wharf.

Forty-three years had elapsed since Soga's two missions over Mount Emily. Brookings had grown prosperous, new houses sprouting on the ridges with breathtaking views, the formerly gritty harbor now boasting hotels and restaurants.

Xenophobia dies slowly, however. When news of the impending visit spread, letters to the *Pilot* criticized not only Soga, but those who welcomed him.

The Japanese guest stayed only briefly. He had a specific purpose. Now seventy-three, he had sold the hardware store in Tsuchiura and retired. Although he continued to wear the pressed suit and black shoes, his glasses were thicker than ever, his walk noticeably slower.

At a breakfast in a hotel conference room with the chamber of commerce, in English sufficiently broken that the reporter for the *Pilot* paraphrased rather than quoting directly, Soga revealed his intention: With a portion of the proceeds from his store, he wished to establish an exchange program.

He had come to Brookings to invite four high school students, to be selected by the community for their intelligence, deportment, and interest in mathematics, to travel to Tokyo for the famed Tsubaka Science Exposition later that year.

There would be scientific exhibits from around the globe, Soga explained, a true world's fair. The students would have opportunities for meetings, meals, and cultural enrichment. Above all, he said, the trip would foster greater warmth and understanding between the peoples of two great nations.

At that point in Soga's remarks, one chamber member pushed back from his table and left the room. Now sixty-one years old, Donny Baker III was notoriously impatient, dismissed small talk, and would tell anyone who asked that he would rather be hunting or flying his plane. Not known for social niceties, he let the conference room door slam behind him.

His departure apparently represented a minority view. According to the next day's *Pilot*, when Soga finished his speech, the rest of the chamber members "roared their approval."

The following autumn, the school board held a news conference to announce the four young ladies selected for the trip: Lisa Phelps, Sara Cortell, Robyn Soiseth, and—interestingly, inexplicably—the angel-voiced cherub now a twelfth grader, Heather Baker.

One can only imagine the discussions that ensued in the Baker household following the announcement. There is no public record, no letter to the school board or the *Pilot*. But the names had been declared publicly, with media present. For Heather's family to decline her selection would insult the board, Soga, and the other girls. So she packed her bags.

Donny did not join his wife in driving Heather six hours up the coast highway and inland to the airport in Portland. The girls flew to Japan accompanied by several chaperones, including one local grandmother who had traveled extensively in the Orient in the 1950s.

Soga was waiting at the Tokyo airport to greet the entourage. In a first-person account she wrote afterward for the *Pilot*, Heather Baker described the former bomber pilot's welcome as "tearful."

He had arranged host families for each of the girls. They enjoyed a week of sightseeing and courtesy tours, as well as full days at the science expo. The visitors received bouquets and necklaces. They visited a temple and the Imperial Gardens. They saw a performance of dancers in traditional kimonos.

At the final dinner the four girls gave Soga gifts made of redwood and myrtlewood—bowls, salad tongs, and a clock—all products of Brookings. Again he cried, one hand over his brow to conceal his embarrassment. The fearsome warrior had become a weepy old man.

When Heather landed in Portland, she was greeted by her mother alone.

CHAPTER 15

WITH CERTAIN PATIENTS the fading comes almost as a surprise, weeks of minuscule changes, then arriving all at once, and that was my experience with Barclay Reed. In the days immediately after his daughter appeared, he seemed to vanish into himself. The hollows under his cheekbones deepened. His eyes seemed larger.

But when I offered the Professor anything to eat, he would turn away from the plate, tugging at that tuft of white hair at the top of his forehead as if that small nervous gesture could sustain him somehow. As his appetite declined, the cancer devoured him.

I was carrying another untouched meal from his room to the kitchen, while D sat at the table eating yogurt with fruit on top. Blueberries and peaches, lush midsummer peaches, and they looked lovely. Seated facing away so she could enjoy the view, she was using the stoneware bowl the Professor had asked me to put away. The one with the hummingbird on the bottom.

"That is a lovely bowl," I said.

"It will suffice," she answered, taking another spoonful.

"Did you make it?"

"God no." She tossed her head as though a fly had tried to land on her nose. "My doormat of a mother made it."

"Your mother." I went to the sink, rinsing off Barclay Reed's plate. "What became of her?"

"She died."

"I'm sorry. I didn't know."

"Decades ago. But I wouldn't expect old Barclay to volunteer that information, given that he murdered her."

I shut off the water. "What did you say?"

"Ask him. He'll tell you without apology. Look—" She pointed her spoon at the wall of photographs. I remembered that when I first came to the house, I noticed several frames had been removed. "There's your evidence."

"I'm sorry, I don't understand."

"He's savvy enough to get away with it, evidently. But the grieving widower in public could not bear to see her face in private. Guilt will do that."

I scanned the remaining pictures. This time I saw the little Asian girl with her hands on her hips, and recognized her. "I see he left your photo up."

"Against my specific request." D bent over her bowl and took a big bite.

ONE OF THE FUNDAMENTAL IDEAS of hospice is that the patient is not the only person who needs care. The family does too. So may neighbors, co-workers, even the nurse and volunteers if a case requires heroic effort. I know of an inpatient hospice facility that keeps a room unoccupied for forty-eight hours after the patient has died. Family members can come to grieve and celebrate as they remove grandchildren's art on the walls or flowers from the windowsill. Staff can visit too, remembering the patient and honoring the privilege of providing that person with care. Only then is the room considered ready for the next human life to fill the place with decorations, gather loved ones, and walk the final road.

By that thinking, D was my patient now, too. And she was suffering, whether she would admit it or not. This absurd murder accusation was a troubling symptom. My job was to favor neither her nor the Professor, but to care properly for them both. I stood at the sink watching her eat, wondering what would be a good point of entry.

"What line of work are you in, D?"

She remained angled toward the lake. "I am an academic."

"Like your father."

"In no way whatsoever," she scoffed. "He is a discredited scholar of a discredited discipline, his whole field now recognized as an exercise in subjectivity, sexism, and nationalism."

Her attitude might be different from Barclay Reed's, but her aggressive manner of speaking was similar enough that I smiled. "What is your field?"

"Gender studies. My focus is the link between patriarchy and violence." At last she half-turned in her seat, though still not far enough to face me. "And what are you, some kind of glorified candy-striper?"

I let the insult stand without a reply. That felt better than defending myself, stronger. It was as though a little chemical reaction hung in the air between us, the electrons of her aggression attempting to interact with the neutrality of my decision not to engage.

"Excuse me a moment, please," I said.

And I went to check on her father.

HE LAY IN THE BED LIKE A LUMPY RUG, visibly flattened by fatigue. But he was awake, and I leaned in over him. "How are you doing today, Professor?"

He gazed directly at me, his eyes the dark brown of tree bark. It felt like the first time our eyes had actually met. "Has she come to watch me die?"

"More likely she has business with you that she needs to finish."

"Our business, such as it was, ended years ago."

"Well, you and I have business to discuss, anyway."

He shrugged. "Do your worst."

This was not the manner of a killer, no defensiveness or paranoia. D's claim was ridiculous. Besides, we had a more immediate issue. "In your initial patient workup, and repeatedly since then, why have you said you had no surviving family members?"

With what seemed like great effort, Barclay Reed thumbed the button that lifted the upper half of his hospital bed. "You may feel misled, Nurse Birch, but the situation is not as it seems."

"Maybe so, but there are implications for your care."

"Can it wait, please? I am bone tired."

"Yes. But we'll need to discuss it later."

"Agreed." He set the bed controller aside. "The woman is strategic, I'll grant her that. I sent word of my illness in March. She deliberately waited till I was too tired to match wits with her."

I checked the water level in his bedside cup. There was no visible difference from two hours earlier. I set it on the rolling table, which I swung over his lap. "Maybe we can figure out a way for you to give D what she needs without sacrificing too much of yourself."

"Maybe piglets will flap their little wings and lift off the ground."

"Just in case they do, let's try to get some breakfast in you. It may boost your energy. I'd like you stronger right now, if possible."

He sighed. "I hereby temporarily submit to your culinary dictatorship."

"I'll alert the media." I countered, starting for the door. But he took in a breath as if to speak, and I turned. "You need something first, Professor?"

"Blast it all."

"What's the matter?"

He tugged at his tuft of hair. "I have come to a realization that I am reluctant to admit."

"I'm listening."

Barclay Reed focused away across the room and spoke in a low voice. "I am glad that you are here."

D WAS NOT THE WORST OFFSPRING I had encountered. Adult children can be astonishingly selfish when a parent is nearing the end.

I have seen families demand that clinical teams do more to prolong their loved one's life when the poor patient is so battered by interventions, anything more would be cruelty. I wait for the right moment, then suggest that sometimes the most loving thing we can do is to stop trying to cure what cannot be cured.

I have seen people tell patients to keep fighting—typically sons speaking to fathers—when clearly all the exhausted patriarch wants to do is rest. I bide my time, then point out how hard the patient has fought already, and ask them to consider giving him permission to go.

Sometimes the people listen, and the patient dies at peace. Sometimes they don't listen, and the patient dies anyway. Nature will have her way.

But the winner of tough family members would have to be Kevin. His mother Dana was a lovely retired attorney who'd had a series of heart attacks. I met Dana during inpatient training, when the illness was well advanced and she had already told everyone, "Enough." She seemed at peace. Under her orders, a surgeon switched off her pacemaker, I arranged for clergy to visit; family members made the trek and said their good-byes.

But not Kevin. He refused to come. He lived only ten miles away, but days passed and he did not show. Dana asked me to call him.

"I can't get there," he said. "Business is crazy right now."

Dana's daughter Felicia, who lived two hours south, came every night after work, missed her daughter's school play, and told her husband she would make it up to him when it was all over. She called Kevin too, but he evaded her.

When Felicia finally reached him, one night when I happened to be standing with her in the ICU waiting room, she put him on speaker.

"Don't worry," Kevin said. "I might not be able to make it to the hospital, but everything else is taken care of. It's all set."

Felicia bugged her eyes at me, as if to say, can you believe this? "I'm right here with Mom. What else on earth is there to take care of?"

"The logistics," Kevin said. "I'm on top of all of it."

And then, unexpectedly, Dana rallied. I've seen it happen once or twice with congestive heart failure—if the situation involves excess body fluid due to low urine output from failing kidneys. The patient stops eating and drinking, preparing to die, but that brings the fluids gradually into balance, and three days later she's better. A week after everyone told Dana good-bye, we rode a medical transport to take her home. It was my first transition of that kind, which is why I didn't know better about checking the apartment beforehand.

When we opened the door, we learned what logistics Kevin had been talking about. The apartment was empty. Not a stick of furniture, no art on the walls, no rugs underfoot. Felicia checked, and the fridge was cleaned out. In fact, the whole place smelled of fresh paint.

I found Dana standing at the bedroom door, arms limp at her sides, and over her shoulder I saw the only thing Kevin had overlooked: one wire hanger on the closet floor.

D was prickly, no question. The murder accusation made her a contender. But she would have to get far nastier before she outdid Kevin. A woman that bitter would have minimal openness to a support group, I suspected, or bereavement services. But would she turn down a therapeutic massage?

"NOT INTERESTED," D said that afternoon, back at the kitchen table, eyes on a book. "I am extremely particular about who I permit to touch me."

"A sensible policy," I said. Barclay Reed was asleep again, which meant I had some time. My next move, because this work is so often about courage, was to pull back the chair beside her and sit.

D did not raise her head, the book in front of her like a little fortification. Sighing, she slipped a bit of paper in to hold her place. "Has he told you about losing his post at the university?"

"On my third day here."

"Whatever his explanation was, don't believe it. He is the most expert liar that ever lived."

"I believe he has been generally honest with me."

She snorted. "Has he read to you from his so-called unfinished book?"

"Actually, I have been reading it to him."

"Perfect," D said, throwing her hands up as if to say it was all just too incredible. "Classic Barclay. Vanity right to the end. All for a pack of lies."

I could not resist asking. "*The Sword* is not true?"

"It's complete nonsense, which is why no publisher would touch it."

"Your father thought that was due to the scandal."

As she spoke, D addressed the book on the table rather than me. It reminded me of the Professor's impromptu lectures.

"My father has hobbled together a mishmash of unrelated facts and speculation," D said, "presented in a context that never existed except in his imagination. The heartwarming story of an apologetic warrior? It is a concoction to salve American guilt about the ruthless obliteration of two Japanese cities. A fabrication to sugarcoat the extermination of hundreds of thousands of innocent civilians. It is a fairy tale."

"Wow." I had nothing else to say.

"And while we're chatting," she was talking louder now, and faster, "the reason he didn't fight the plagiarism charges—I'm certain he has propagandized about that fiasco too—is that he was caught red-handed. Richard Blount, that brilliant young scholar?

Now he's a department chair at Columbia, a serious and respected intellect, but that scandal nearly killed his career in the cradle. Barclay pretends that he chose not to defend himself out of nobility and restraint. Actually, he was guilty as hell. His conduct was indefensible."

With the s in her last word, a fleck of spittle flew out and vanished on the rug. It was a giveaway. D's excess passion made her argument weaker.

So, just like when she'd insulted me earlier, I let her assertions breathe. Maybe there was some kernel of truth in them, too. Portland State would not remove the Professor's books from the library if everything were as he'd described.

But *The Sword*? I wanted that to be true. I wanted it for Barclay Reed's sake because he needed so badly to be believed. I wanted it for Michael's sake as well: If Ichiro Soga could change from a warrior into a man of peace, it might be possible for my husband too.

D was staring at me, and I realized she was waiting for an answer of some kind. "I promised your father I would read the whole thing before I decided whether or not it was true."

She picked up her book again, using that slip of paper to open to the page she'd left. "I just saved you the time."

"Thank you." I stood. "But I keep my promises."

I left her there to read on undisturbed.

MICHAEL WAS SITTING on the back stoop when I pulled in the driveway. Before reaching a standstill I had already taken the data in: sneakers and socks on the step beside him, a glass in his hand with lots of ice.

I climbed out of the car to the fragrance of phlox, which bloomed flagrantly in our neighbor's garden. Michael basked in the afternoon sun, eyes closed. Barefoot Michael. It was another one of those moments when I just reenlisted, when it didn't matter how hard life was right then, or how tired I was feeling, because I felt the irresist-ible pull of love.

I called to him over the roof of the car. "Hiya, handsome. How's your day?"

"I am the greatest walker that ever lived."

"Is that so?"

He nodded. "Well, you've got your Gandhi, your Lewis and Clark—"

"Don't forget Johnny Appleseed."

"A piker. Guy didn't have to deal with one minute of Portland traffic."

I came around to kiss his cheek. "Which I gather you did today?"

Michael opened his eyes. "Am I allowed to brag?"

"I think you just were."

"Then can I brag some more?"

I pushed his sneakers aside and sat. "I'm listening."

"OK, I had just reached the shop this morning when the con-gressman's office called to say the screw had arrived."

"You did that, Michael. You made that happen."

"So I walked there to pick it up."

"That must have taken forever."

"Two hours. Then I swung by here—"

"Oh, honey."

"Then walked to Gene's to drop it off."

"Johnny Appleseed falls three notches. And Gene must have been so appreciative."

"Actually, he got all awkward on me. But I made him put the screw in, and strap his leg on." Michael laughed. "Of course he insisted we go for a walk."

"Wait, though. Doesn't Gene live on the north side?"

Michael jiggled his glass to tip an ice cube into his mouth. "Uh-huh."

"Then why'd you come by here? That must have added an hour at least."

"Yeah." He crunched the ice, swallowed it, stared into his cup.

"Sweetheart?"

"To get my gun."

"I don't understand."

"I brought him the .50, Deb. The big one. Four hundred rounds, too."

"You walked halfway across this city carrying a high-powered rifle?"

"I didn't figure any taxi would want me for a passenger. But it was in the zip-case, so everything was all legal." He chuckled. "Never in my life saw drivers more ready to let a pedestrian cross the street."

"Oh, Michael. Congratulations. And thank you." I threw my arms around him, but he did not respond. I hugged him closer, but he still held solid so I let go. Then he rattled himself another piece of ice to chew.

"Was Gene pleased, at least?"

"Like I said, awkward. He didn't want the gun, even though it's way better than his. But then he seized on it, you know? And started talking about how this was a great gift, because now he could really sharpen his shooting, and that would help him start the process of getting shipped back over."

"What? He wants to be deployed again? That's crazy."

"Times five. I get it, though. The guy was a janitor before the war, no power, no respect. Join up and you get training, responsibility, rank. But there's no way anyone wants a one-legged soldier."

"Did you try to talk him out of it?"

"Well, I wasn't going to lay down the whole disability thing. So I told Gene the most spectacular pile of horse shit about the explosion day, because he has no memory of it. About him being a hero. The lives he saved, including mine. Duty done, mission accomplished, that kind of thing. You should've seen him, standing straighter. Literally, his body changed." Michael held the icy glass to his forehead. "Today I learned the power of a loving lie."

"A what?"

"The truth didn't matter, Deb. I would have told Gene anything to help him. My conscience doesn't feel so great about filling him with bullshit. But I got the gun out of the house for you, and now he has a functioning leg."

Again the Professor had been right. Or was it Soga? "I am proud of you."

He shrugged. "Crazy fuss over one little screw. Madness."

"Still," I said. I wrapped my arms around my knees, since he was uninterested, and hugged myself for a while instead.

THE 51ST ANNUAL BROOKINGS AZALEA FESTIVAL featured a special guest who had not visited in years. In 1990, Ichiro Soga was seventy-eight years old. Nearly forty-eight years had passed since his American mission. Yet the controversy in anticipation of his arrival remained virulent and visible.

Jack Eggiman, a Pearl Harbor survivor, wrote the *Pilot* to castigate a man "who dropped a little bomb in the weeds. There are not enough words to put on paper the contempt I feel for the Brookings Harbor Chamber of Commerce and the people of this town who are trying to make this individual a hero."

Yet when the festival arrived in May, and with it the visitation of a stooped and elderly man, the community's embrace appeared devoid of controversy. At the welcome banquet, Leanna McCurley showed him a giant sandwich she had made in the shape of a submarine and plane. A photo in the *Pilot* shows a presentation so detailed, half an olive serves as Soga's flight helmet.

The Japanese visitor presented another check for the library's programs for children. He gave giant carp wind socks to the mayor, Chamber of Commerce president, and library director. When they appeared perplexed by the gift, he swung one in the air so they could see: It was like a giant fish-kite, but secured in one place on the ground instead of flying high on a string. In turn, the welcome committee presented Soga with a walking stick made of myrtlewood, the tree of local pride.

Controversy surfaced at the festival parade because Soga wore a hat decorated with a small American flag on the brim. Several veterans declared that they were insulted. Staff Sergeant Shirley Laird, who drove the lead Jeep in the military portion of the parade, gave his explanation to the *Pilot*: "He's still a Jap."

Otherwise Soga's visit resembled the others: touring the port of Brookings, inspecting local fisheries. He stayed at the home of local banker Henry Kerr.

In general there was less bowing this time, not due to any diminution of manners, but rather because the guest showed fatigue in the afternoon and therefore participated in fewer activities than in past years. Toward the end of each day, he appeared to lean more heavily on the myrtlewood cane.

The next-to-last evening, seven local churches sponsored a dinner that caused an unexpected reunion. Heather Baker—now twenty-three years old, a college graduate working in Portland and engaged to the owner of a small hotel—hailed Soga from the moment she entered the room.

Heather was taller than Soga now, full haired and buxom. Soga was diminutive and frail. When he made a deep bow to her, she responded by giving him a bear hug. The moment was sufficiently moving that the crowd applauded. It was also immortalized by the lens of the indefatigable Piper Abbott.

All the while, Donny Baker kept his own counsel in matters concerning Ichiro Soga. There were indicators, however: Although he now served as treasurer of the Chamber of Commerce, he remained at his business rather than attend any festivities during the visit. He did not appear at the event where his daughter behaved so photogenically. Donny was mum about Soga, yet somehow managed to be universally considered on that topic to be as rough as sandpaper.

By contrast, his conduct upon seeing the *Pilot* the following morning was revelatory. Under a headline that in 1990 could only be read as tongue-in-cheek—"World War II Officially Over"—the newspaper devoted nearly half of the front page to a photo of his daughter embracing the Japanese man.

The subsequent sequence of events can be reconstructed by Heather's interview with the *Pilot*.

Donny saw the photograph and swore. "Damn it to hell."

He stood, throwing the paper down. He paced a moment, refilling his coffee cup and glaring at the front page again. "That Jap bastard," he said, storming from the room. He returned strapping on his holster, a pistol clipped in its slot.

"Where are you going with that?" Heather asked.

"Just you keep shut," he said, wagging a finger at her. "You've already done enough."

As he pulled on a windbreaker, Donny's wife wandered into the kitchen. "What's going on?"

"Back later," he said, and with a slam of the door, he roared off in his truck.

IT WAS 7:00 A.M. Donny was expected at 7:30 for the daily pre-opening tasks at the nursery: unlocking the safe, turning on computers, and activating the watering system. He was due at a meeting of the Chamber's finance committee at nine o'clock. Lunch was with the builder of a new subdivision, to negotiate a landscaping contract.

Instead, Donny drove east of town, to the Kerr home. The household was barely stirring. However Soga, perhaps due to the eight-hour time difference between Japan and Oregon, was awake, dressed in his suit, and strolling in the garden. Piper Abbott sat parked in the driveway waiting for eight o'clock, when the Japanese guest was scheduled for a breakfast meeting with the school board.

Donny pulled into the driveway and called out his truck window. "Hey, Soga."

The pilot paused in his meandering, smiling as if by reflex.

"C'mon," Donny said. "Let's go for a ride."

Ichiro Soga raised an eyebrow but did not say a word. Leaning on his myrtlewood cane, he hobbled to the truck. Donny opened the passenger door, and Soga climbed aboard.

CHAPTER 16

CHERYL MET ME at the door the next morning. She blocked the doorway and looked at me over the tops of her purple cat's-eye glasses. "Chat a sec?"

"Oh no. Has he begun dying?"

"No," she said, gesturing down the driveway. When I stepped back, Cheryl pulled the front door closed behind her. She had her things already packed, the bag's strap over her shoulder.

We ambled out onto the road. The pavement was dark from rain, but the skies were clearing, and it felt as if the humidity might burn off.

"What's up?"

"I just wanted to check in with you about the daughter."

"A charmer, isn't she?"

"I thought it might be just me. Last night we had a fair dose of 'What are you doing to him?' and 'Why isn't my father in a hospital?'"

"So there's a need for education about hospice?"

"It may take a little more than that," she chuckled. "I also heard 'Are you completely incompetent?' and 'Are you trying to kill him?'"

"Oh, Cheryl." I put my hand on her arm. "I'm sorry."

We had nearly reached her car, and she laughed. "I would like to make some clever observation about apples falling near trees. But

Professor Reed actually has some charm, way down deep. While this peach of a gal . . ."

"I haven't found the sunny side of her either," I said. "Are there any immediate issues we need to deal with?"

"The problem is solving itself. She's leaving today."

That stopped me cold. "She's not going to see him through?"

"Apparently not. She asked if I would referee their last conversation. That was her word, referee. I told her my shift was ending and you could help with that."

"Lucky me."

"Sorry." Cheryl slid the key into her car door. "Like I said, a real peach."

BARCLAY REED'S SKIN looked loose and thin, translucent like an onion, which I recognized as dehydration. I checked his chart and the level in his water cup. Two ounces since ten P.M.

"I know," he said, blinking open his eyes. "I know."

"I can swab you with glycerin," I offered.

"Thank you, no." Pressing the button to lift his bed's upper half, he took several deep and noisy breaths. "Let me see if I can manage a few swallows now. I have a feeling I'm going to need a bit of fortification."

As I brought the straw to his lips, he glanced past me. I turned to see his daughter in the doorway.

The Professor sucked hard, draining the cup with a noisy slurp. Pulling away from the straw, he forced a smile. "Good morning, Deirdre."

I moved back by the desk, getting out of the way, less a referee than a guard. I hoped they would not hurt one another needlessly. But I suspected their needs were beyond my understanding.

"It's D," she said.

"D is not a name," he replied. "It is an initial. An abbreviation to signify a bad grade." He turned his face to me. "Why call yourself by a nomenclature that sounds like the verge of failure?"

Oh, you are not finished yet, I thought. She came when you are weak, but you are far from defeated.

D rolled up one sleeve of her sweater. "Am I a failure, Barclay?"

"Why ask a question whose answer is foregone? We both know you have risen admirably. Perhaps meteorically."

"Anger is a formidable motivator."

The Professor sniffed. "Anger is a snake that eats its own tail."

D tilted her head back, watching him down her nose. "It is such a shame that your aphorisms are so far superior to your intellectual integrity."

He crossed his arms. "You do not know what you are talking about."

"I know the truth."

"You believe you do. Which is arguably worse."

She rolled up her other sleeve. "Your claims of innocence exist in outright denial of university arbitration, severance without pension, and academic disgrace. Not to mention other matters of guilt we could discuss."

"Deirdre, you fatigue me."

"Reality fatigues you."

He mused a moment, eyes unfocused. "You are utterly without mercy."

D stood straighter, shoulders back. I realized she was taking it as a compliment. "About that much, you are correct."

"Yes, well." He picked at a thread on the blanket. "At least we know where you learned it."

"Ah—" She opened her mouth to speak, but nothing came out.

He had bested her. She could not deny her parentage. It was his trump card.

"I think," I said, returning from my corner by the desk. "I think the Professor could use a bit of rest now."

"Don't call him that in my presence. He is not a professor anymore. He is a nothing."

And she left the room. But I knew D was not done yet. It felt more like a boxer, going to her corner between rounds. I brought the Professor his basket of remotes, taking the water cup to refill.

He raised his eyebrows. "Ah, a father's pride and joy."

"I don't know," I said, shedding my neutrality in family matters. "Looked to me like a snake eating its own tail."

For once he did not bother to hide his smirk.

D DROVE OFF SOMEWHERE to do errands. I cleaned the house, washed the few dishes, and gazed at the lake for a while before returning to the Professor's bedside. Late that afternoon, he awoke with a start.

"I'm right here," I said, rising from my chair. "What do you need?"

"Has she left yet?"

"No."

He relaxed, sighing.

"Do you want to speak with her again?"

He closed his eyes, pondering. "One more salvo, don't you think?"

"I think you should do what's best for you."

The Professor opened his eyes. "Nurse Birch, is there a recipe for the ideal last parental conversation? Some script you might supply?"

"Not that I know of. But you can decide in advance what you'd like to accomplish. It may not happen, but it's still worth a try."

I raised the water cup. He put the straw to his lips by reflex but did not take any that I could see.

This was all a huge exertion for a man in his last days. Any moment now, Barclay Reed would begin actively dying. It would require all of his time, demand all of his energy. A man not eating and barely drinking will soon sleep the last of his existence away. I was determined to make it peaceful.

Which meant finishing business with Deirdre, however unpleasant, as soon as possible. "Shall I call your daughter in?"

"Yes. But then please do not leave the room."

"I wouldn't think of it."

D STOOD AT THE DOOR with her hands on her hips. It may have been a power pose, but the fact that she hesitated at the room's threshold revealed her true emotions. I knew her suitcase sat by the front door. I knew she'd charged her phone and computer for the trip. Her escape was almost complete.

Yet in some ways, I felt worse for her. D's father was dying, and she had no inkling of how to make peace with him. When he was gone, D would have to figure it out all by herself.

When she finally strode in, it was as purposeful as if she were coming to receive a diploma. As she halted at the foot of his bed, the Professor bowed ever so slightly. "Yes?"

"It's time I recommenced my life," D said. "I have a conference in San Francisco, then I'm going home." She placed two fingers on the bed frame, but jerked them back as though the wood were hot. "I am saying good-bye."

Barclay Reed gazed at her, his fondness unconcealed. "We both are."

"I do not forgive you."

He harrumphed. "Perhaps one day—"

"Not likely."

"Please know," he persisted in a quiet voice, "should the kindness arrive to you some years hence, that I accepted your forgiveness today."

"How can you accept what I have not given?"

"I am the one doing the giving, Deirdre. Should the time come that you find the character and self-esteem to forgive me, please remember that today I absolved you from any guilt about how long it took to arrive."

"It's not Deirdre," she said to the floor, her voice choked. "It's D."

And she was gone.

We heard the door close, the rental car start up and drive away. We listened while a breeze stirred the tree outside his bedroom window. There was a scent of newly mown grass. The Professor let out one long sigh.

"I'm sorry," I said to him. "But I also think that was a pretty spectacular and wise gift you just gave her. Years from now, she will thank you."

"Yes, well." He adjusted his bed angle an inch. "Some time ago you told me that suffering was educational."

"I believe that." I expected him to say something about his daughter next, about what his hurt at her hands was teaching him about the long patience of parental love. But he surprised me.

"Instruct me then, Nurse Birch. What are you learning from your husband's suffering?"

I all but gulped. "Excuse me?"

"Your Michael. What is the latest thing his pain has taught you? Perhaps it will prove instructive."

So I told him about Gene, and the screw, and the gun. This time the professor did not interrupt once, until I explained about the loving lie.

"Clarify," he said. "Your husband knowingly fabricated heroism by his friend in order to convince him to take the rifle?"

"Not just that. Also to make him feel better about himself, in a way that only a fellow soldier could do."

"Hold right there, please." Barclay Reed silenced me with a raised hand. "I've just made an interesting connection."

"I'm listening."

He shifted in bed. "Here I am up to my neck in disease, we both know I'm in real trouble. Yet my mind just this moment acquired a new idea." The Professor pursed his lips. "I may keep learning right to the very end."

I thought: People generally die as they have lived. For a scholar, learning might be as habitual as breathing. But all I said was, "Would you like to share what you learned?"

"You'll see momentarily," he said. "First I need you to refresh my memory. What was that exercise called, the four inquiries?"

"The Four Questions, yes. I'm sorry you found it so annoying."

"Do I recall accurately that one of them concerns apology?"

"Yes: 'Is there anyone you wish to say "I'm sorry" to?'"

The Professor rubbed his hands together. It was the most animated I'd seen him all day. "Could you please fetch some paper?"

"DEAR DEIRDRE."

I sat at the bedside, taking dictation. Fingers interlaced in his lap, he continued in his best lecturing voice.

"Or as you would have it: Dear D. You are correct, as ever. Blount's research was impeccable. Mine was the sloppy work of a tired mind."

I paused with the pen, but the Professor continued his oratory.

"He had made all the true finds, a sailor in uncharted waters, while I circled below like a shark, hoping something edible would fall from the stern. I justified it to myself by reasoning that his career was so green, it could easily withstand pruning by a senior historian. I was motivated by selfishness, greed, and ego."

It was hard for me to write those things, because I did not believe them. If the Professor had impressed me with anything over the months, it had been the integrity of his intellect. But he persisted.

"Therefore I admit to you, now, today, and for all time: After decades of admonishing students for cheating, I committed precisely that academic crime. It was the wrong thing to do. I was wrong."

He waited for my writing to catch up. I ached to interrupt, but before my hand stilled he spoke again.

"Obviously I paid a high professional price, but it was a pittance compared with the loss of your esteem. Therefore today I wish to apologize—not in a vain hope of changing your opinion of me at this late hour, but for the sake of my own conscience. I am sorry, genuinely sorry. I congratulate you on your immense career achievements despite my misdeeds. I wish you all continued success."

At that he held out one hand. "There. May I sign it?"

I swallowed. Incredible. But his arm was outstretched for the clipboard.

"Here you are," I said, handing it over with the pen. He wrote his name in a fierce burst and shoved the clipboard back at me. I scanned the letter. There was a space between my writing and his signature, where I imagined he would write if not exactly "your ever-loving poppa," then at least "fondly" or maybe even "love." But it was blank, a space of missed opportunity.

"Nurse Birch, would you please mail this epistle immediately? I relish the idea of it greeting her when she arrives home from the conference."

"I'm not supposed to leave you alone."

"Might we agree that, personality idiosyncrasies aside, I have been generally undemanding in the final wishes department? I wish to call that trump right now."

"I don't know, Professor." I was tempted to add that I did not want to mail a letter that said what this one did.

He raised his right hand. "I, Barclay Reed, do solemnly swear not to die while you drive to the post office and back, so help me God."

What could I say?

The drive along Lake Oswego to the post office was lovely, dappled light through the trees. Sometimes there is a guilty pleasure in taking a break from the bedside. Meanwhile, in the gaps between houses, I could see the water flashing, beautiful and untouchable. I remembered that in May I had hoped to swim in that lake, had meant to ask the Professor for permission to use his dock.

Of course I would make no such request now. We were weeks past anything like that. Merely asking would amplify how my life was healthy and his was waning. I hurried down the winding shore road. The time for pleasures like swimming had long passed.

HE WAS YELLING the moment I opened the front door.

"Nurse Birch. Nurse Birch."

I came running.

The Professor had raised his bed's upper half as far as it would go. His face was as white as a fish's belly. "Did you mail it? Is the letter gone?"

"Are you all right? What's the matter?"

"I'm fine, if you did as I asked."

"Yes, of course." I pressed a hand flat on my chest. "You scared me."

"Don't be a weakling. I'm fine." He coughed, just once, but hard. "You did indeed mail the letter?"

"I just said yes."

He looked at me sideways, eyes narrowed.

"Don't you believe me?"

"I do, Nurse Birch. To a point."

"Professor." Collecting my wits, I stepped up beside the bed. "You don't have to trust me. It's OK because I know that despite mistakes I've made here, I have behaved in a consistent and trustworthy manner. So if you have doubts, they are about you, and I'm not taking them on."

"Blast it all, I didn't mean to imply—"

"The letter to your daughter went in the blue collection box outside the Lake Oswego post office. A sign said the box is emptied at 4:30, so I was in time for today's mail. That is the truth, whether you trust me or not."

Barclay Reed bowed his head like a child being scolded. After a moment he raised his eyes and read my face. "You have something you wish to add."

"I do. That letter wasn't true, was it?"

He took the controller and leaned his bed back a few degrees. He tugged at the white tuft of hair on his brow. He sniffed and sighed.

"Righteousness is my daughter's power," he said. "She needed it, growing up with an overbearing father, and a mother so subservient it drove everyone to frustration."

I could feel a lecture beginning. They'd become rarer, so I was ready to pay attention and have my question answered later. Of all the patients in my experience, Barclay Reed was the one for whom listening mattered most.

He raised his eyes, staring at the blank of the switched-off TV. "Shinju was Japanese. We met during my Fulbright. Her name means 'pearl.' She was extremely intelligent, attractive in a modest fashion, and regrettably lacking in confidence. It was winsome, in the quiet way of humility. I reasoned that moving to America would diminish her disposition toward female servitude. I miscalculated—as does anyone who expects marriage to solve a relationship problem rather than exacerbate it. Shinju could not choose which movie to watch, what to eat, where to vacation, anything. She elected not to have a will, not to express personhood at all, despite the increasingly vocal urgings of her husband."

He picked at the blanket. "When she developed heart disease, it was the same. Concealed for fear of inconveniencing me. Did you know that heart disease affects more women than men?"

"Actually, I do."

"Yes, you would. At any rate, a heart attack took her. At a supermarket on Boone's Ferry Road. She was juggling grocery bags, but in adherence to her beliefs, she stepped aside for some man in a hurry, and the weight was too much for her. She was young. Only forty-one."

"I'm sorry for your loss," I said. "But D told me . . ."

He raised his eyebrows. "Yes?"

"D called you her mother's murderer."

"Did she indeed?" Barclay Reed sucked in a huge breath. He rubbed his face with both hands, then kept them over his eyes as though he were a hiding toddler. Finally he let his arms fall. "Perhaps I oversimplified."

"If there's something you need to get off your conscience, Professor, now might be an excellent time."

"Oh, it's not even approximately as you suppose. I only meant that I implied her life ended there in the parking lot. Dramatic license, et cetera." With one finger, he began making figure eights on the blanket beside his leg. "In point of fact, an ambulance arrived in minutes, and emergency workers revived her. The police notified me, I collected Deirdre from school, and we rushed ourselves to Providence Portland Medical Center. A nurse led us into Shinju's ICU room. I feel it no weakness to confess that the array of machinery was intimidating."

I nodded. "Naturally."

"Moments after the nurse departed, various devices began beeping, an alert sounded on the intercom, and a team of men and women charged in as we backed out of their way." His finger stopped doodling and he closed his eyes. "There are few things I would wish to unsee from my life. But those next moments left images that will never heal."

"The team coded her."

"Precisely." He opened his eyes. "They pumped her chest brutally. They shocked her heart with those paddles. They lifted the hospital gown and spread her legs wide, modesty be damned." He poked the air with an imaginary syringe. "They jabbed needles repeatedly into her thighs."

I had heard countless stories like this. I had even experienced a few during my training. Coding teams had a sincere desire to save the patient, but I knew how gruesome it could be for the family.

"The needles I can explain," I said. "They wanted to give her adrenaline. When the heart's not pumping, there's no blood pressure, so veins and arteries lie flat. They were trying to hit one that would take the injection."

The Professor swallowed noisily. "Someone might have informed us. Instead we witnessed this ongoing violence, stupefied, until one of the men in scrubs glanced over his shoulder, realized Deirdre's presence and mine, and bellowed, 'What the hell are they doing in here? Get them out.'"

"Ouch."

"Indeed. Though the hallway was little better."

"You could still hear?"

"Everything. Particularly their tone when they had succeeded. One might expect a note of triumph once Shinju's heart beat again, whereas I discerned a clear disappointment. Someone asked how long she had been arrested, and when the answer of six minutes came back, someone else told a Dr. Bronsky it was time to have 'the talk.'"

"What in the world is 'the talk'?"

"You're the medical professional. I assumed that you would know."

"I have no idea. It sounds like telling a kid about sex."

He waved me off. "I learned soon enough as a young man strode up to us, looking as earnest and bright as a new penny. I asked if he was the physician in charge. He allowed that he was a mere resident. Nonetheless, it was his duty to report that Shinju's heart was failing. Compromised blood flow, diminished electrical self-control, without doubt it would continue to arrest. They could restart her heart as many times as we wished, but each episode incurred brain damage, and brought no greater likelihood of recovery. 'Plus,' he felt compelled to add, 'it is not a gentle intervention.'"

I couldn't help butting in. "At least they didn't crack her chest and perform manual massage."

"They might have, given the opportunity. In fact Shinju's heart arrested again as we were speaking. Alarm alarm, everyone rushes back in, and Deirdre and I listen while the whole process completes another iteration."

"Why didn't someone move you away? You shouldn't have had to endure—"

"Nurse Birch." Barclay Reed frowned. "Need I remind you that we are discussing intensive care? In such units, the patient's family does not exist."

"Someone in there sent Bronsky to talk to you."

"True. He returned as well, after another six-minute success. He asked whether we wished for them to continue to respond, or would we rather let nature take its course. I must say, I found that expression artfully put. Nature in command, rather than the Grim Reaper."

"What did you decide?"

"There was no decision. Why continue to torture her body, knowing my pearl would never recover? Deirdre cried that I was giving up, I must not love her, how could I, et cetera. They sat us in an adjacent waiting room that resembled the inside of a mausoleum. Some minutes later, Shinju's heart stopped once more. Dr. Bronsky entered her room and read the time aloud to a nurse taking notes, 6:46 in the evening. Meanwhile I held Deirdre, who thrashed and flailed, screaming that I had killed her mother." He turned his face away. "She was only thirteen."

"That certainly explains why you've insisted on hospice. And how you became a murderer in D's eyes. But what about the kitchen photos? She called them evidence."

"A touchy subject." The Professor glanced at me, as if to confirm that I was listening, and then away. He tucked the blanket snugly around himself. "I am at peace with my actions at the hospital. My guilt feelings, though copious, had other causes. Marrying Shinju removed her from a culture in which her notions about gender and power may have been accepted, appreciated, perhaps even admired. Under the weight of that culpability, I could not bear my wife staring down at me during meals. Nor, I might add, eat out of bowls she had made. When I removed the photographs, my daughter saw only additional betrayal. She asked to go away to preparatory school in New England. I granted her wish. Aside from briefly at holidays, she never truly returned."

"Your intake papers explicitly said you had no surviving family."

"Not because I was disowning Deirdre. She had disowned me. Regardless, the information I provided your intake nurse was indeed falsehood."

"It makes a difference," I said. "Legally."

"Ah." For a fraction of a second, his eyes met mine. "I apologize."

Who was I to sit in judgment? I who would be alive next month? "Accepted, Professor. Of course."

"What a day. First my daughter, then you. Two apologies in one afternoon. A tragedy." He shook his head. "I must really be on my way out."

The Professor's eyes were glistening, but I saw the slightest hint of a grin. He motioned to the reading chair. I sat, taking the black binder, but not opening it yet. "What about that letter?"

"Yes, well." He chose one of his remotes, turning on a television but muting the sound. "Blount was ambitious, with legitimate scholarly potential. But compare: He spent two semesters in Japan, whereas I lived in Kyoto for three years. He had read about Japanese culture, while I was married to a Japanese woman. He was twenty-seven years old, but I had been publishing on the Pacific war for thirty-six years. What findings could he possibly possess that I would stoop to stealing?"

"So your last words to your daughter are words of deceit?"

"I told Deirdre a tale to make it easier for her to forgive." The Professor fixed me with his gaze. "What your husband would call a loving lie."

He had me, the old coot. Yet even as I stood there, admiring his calculating ways, the man deflated before my eyes. The battle of wits with Deirdre, the letter, the story of Shinju, all of it had required his last drop of stamina. Barclay Reed's shoulders drooped, and his face went slack.

"Professor," I said. "Did you just surrender your sword?"

He ran a tongue over dry lips. He needed a swab, but I waited till he finished what he had to say. Finally he lifted his head and gave a wan smile. "*Shouri.*"

WE SAT IN SILENCE FOR HOURS. From time to time he would tweak his tuft of hair. When he dozed, I stretched my legs. I was exhausted too. Yet the day was not dull. It felt meditative. Respectful. For once, we were enough.

Late in the afternoon I realized that he had been scratching his chin. I came to his side. "Would you like me to shave you today?"

"Nurse Birch." He swallowed audibly. "I am afraid I do not have the energy to leave this bed."

"You don't need to. Just wait there."

By now I knew the man's face. His cheekbones were not quite symmetrical. His chin was difficult to get completely smooth. The rest of it—warm water, soft cream, the quiet scratch of the razor—felt so familiar it was intimate.

The Professor was quiet this time, no banter, simply allowing his senses to experience what it is to be shaved by someone, the close attention, the care not to cause hurt. I didn't clutter the air with words, and I was careful not to spill one drop of water on his sheets. He stretched his jaw forward, making it easier to shave his neck.

Afterward I used a fresh towel to wipe and dry his face. There was no way to do that without its becoming a caress, but neither of us objected.

Barclay Reed lay there blinking at me. It was a companionable silence. I had been sitting on the bed, but now I straightened and collected the shaving things. Everything felt wonderfully tender.

"Wasn't I a handsome man?" he said at last.

I snapped the towel in his direction. "You devil."

He ran a palm over his face. "Wasn't I, though?"

DRIVING DOWN THE ROAD TO OUR HOUSE, I spied Michael digging in the trash. There's no other way to describe it, given how he jumped at the sight of me, slammed the lid on the garbage can, and hurried back by the screen door.

"Sweetheart, how are you?" I called, getting out of the car.

Michael shook his head as if to clear it. "Hey, Deb. How was your day?"

"Everything OK?"

"Fine," he said. "Splendid."

Splendid? I had never heard him use that word before. Michael crossed his arms and grinned at me. It seemed almost as if he was acting.

I could not help it. I started toward the trash can. "Looking for something?"

"Nope." Michael hurried to get there before I did. "Just bringing some stuff up from the basement. You know, cleaning around where I work out."

"Was there trash down there? I didn't know that."

"Lots. Look." He took the lid off. The top third of the can was filled with papers, his pages of drawings, the faces.

I picked up a handful. "Why didn't you put these in the recycling?"

"Don't know." He shrugged his big shoulders. "I guess I didn't want anyone to see them."

"Oh."

"But you're right. About the recycling, I mean." He snatched the pages from my hand, and tossed them in the bin behind the trash.

He was behaving so oddly. "Michael, is there anything you want to share with me about those people?"

"What do you mean?"

"You just seem so cagey right now. I want you to know that I am willing to listen to anything you want to say. Maybe I could help. Like with Gene."

His shoulders lowered. The exuberance vanished. "Or the thunderstorm night," he muttered.

"Exactly."

Michael started away across the backyard, then turned. "It's hard for me."

"Perhaps if you just shared about one of the faces."

"You really don't know."

"So tell me." I followed him across the lawn, the sheets in my hand. "I recognize some of them now. The one with the squiggle next to him, the one in sunglasses. Yes, and here's that dude with the mouse ears."

"Ha." One great peal came out from Michael, but it was icy cold. "Mouse ears? Honestly, Deb, you have no clue."

"Then give me a clue. Who was he?"

He shook his head. "Nobody. No one."

"Tell me, sweetheart."

"You want to know?" he shouted. "You want to know?"

"Of course I do. And I want you to be free of it."

"Fuuuuck." Michael breathed hard several times through his nose, like a rhino deliberating when to charge. Then he slapped the papers in my hand. "OK. All right. Request granted."

He fumed to the end of the lawn and back. He took another lap, glaring at me. I just stood there, arms crossed, waiting.

Eventually he came to the back stoop, where he pointed for me to sit. I went there, pressed against the screen door while Michael paced in front of me. I realized I was about to have my first real taste of his war. Seven months after he came home, and this would be the first.

"We were half a dozen miles southeast of Sadr City, heading to a planning session, not even on patrol. The nasties were using EFPs, a kind of homemade shell but instead of having a bullet shape after being fired, it goes flat. When it hits a Humvee, the hole is two feet wide."

Michael wiped his forehead, drying his hand on a pant leg. "They nailed us from the right, on the passenger side but low. I sat back row on the left. Somehow no one was killed, but everyone had injuries, cuts and scrapes. Count that as one time an armored Humvee did its damn job. Gene, though, he was riding shotgun. His lower right leg was torn clear off, boot and all. We all piled out, dizzy from the blast and temporarily deaf, but mad as hornets. There was no one to shoot back at. We attended to Gene right away. I knotted the tourniquet myself. Everyone else either set a perimeter or loaded up in the caravan's other vehicles."

Michael glanced at me then, still pacing, his face pinched and pained.

"You don't have to—"

"Don't stop me Deb, now that you've started it."

There are moments with every patient when you know, no matter how much you want to offer medical knowledge or personal comfort, that your task is to close your mouth. It's not easy. Your ego asserts itself, your desire to help. But they need you to shut up.

I squatted forward, closer. "I'm listening, sweetheart."

"I hate Iraq. The heat, the smell, the boredom. But the thing I hate most is the dogs. They're everywhere, like pigeons in any U.S. city. Lurking, barking, sometimes you hear them fighting in an alley. Anyway, Gene's loaded on the chopper and gone. Later a squad will come for the Humvee, drag it back to base for parts and demolition. Last thing before pulling out, I go back to make sure we aren't leaving any gear behind. Ammo or whatever. The vehicle's all bent doors and flat tires. Behind it there's a dog though, some mutt of a street-thing, lapping away at a puddle. But this is Iraq, Deb, the giant sandbox. There are no puddles. I take a step closer, and sure enough, he's drinking Gene's blood."

"Oh my God."

"Just a dog, right? Doing its nasty doggy business. But I blasted that fucker, the impulse arrived and I obeyed it, no hesitation, no processing, just gave it the 30.06 at point-blank range."

Michael took a huge inhale, but it came out in broken huffing. "The round just about cut the dog in two. Somehow, though, he didn't die. Not right away. He yowled and tried to move. But his back was broken, along with a bunch of other stuff. His guts were out. I know I should have finished him. I didn't, though. I left him there, writhing, because I knew. Any minute, another dog would be along to make supper out of him."

Michael stopped pacing. He stepped past me to open the back door. "That's 'the dude with mouse ears.' You can see why he'd be with me forever. Just a dog, but my conscience will carry him around till I'm dead."

He shuffled into the house, moving like he was a hundred years old, pausing to speak through the screen. "Then again, Deb, when I left him to suffer like that, knowing he would get eaten any minute, I also learned a valuable lesson. Maybe the fundamental lesson of war."

I stared at the pages between my feet, those scribbled faces. "And what is that?"

"There will always be another dog."

BROOKINGS AIRPORT LIES ONE MILE from the town center, north on highway 101. At an altitude of 459 feet above sea level, it offers two paved runways, each 2,900 feet long. The airport provides fuel service, military-grade lighting, and a beacon from sundown to sunrise.

Nineteen single-engine planes stand parked in tie-downs, plus four two-engine aircraft and one helicopter. The FAA call name for the airport is BOK.

For take-off limitations, one runway has redwoods 125 feet tall, located 2,900 feet beyond the tarmac's end, therefore requiring an elevation slope ratio of 19:1. The other has 15-foot pines at a distance of 380 feet, for a lift ratio of 12:1. To the east lie the heavily treed mountains of the Siskiyou National Forest. To the west, the flat expanse of the Pacific Ocean.

According to his manifest filed for that day in May 1992, "Donny Baker III and passenger" arrived at BOK at 8:10 A.M. Why did it take forty-five minutes to travel three miles from the Kerr home? No record accounts for that interval.

Piper Abbott had followed Donny's truck. Thus she was equipped to report her observations and fill gaps in the narrative with interviews later that day.

The truck parked beside a single-engine plane, immaculate white with blue stripes down the sides. The wings spread above the cockpit, supported by struts down to the lower fuselage.

"This is a Cessna," Donny explained to his passenger, who had eased himself down from the truck with the assistance of his myrtlewood cane.

"These others are Pipers," Donny waved down the row of aircraft. "Which is fine if that's what you learned on."

"Low wing," Soga observed.

"Exactly," Donny said. "They land easy as pie, but airborne you can't see jack below you. The Cessna's overhead wings let you take in the view."

"Most excellent aircraft."

"This one's a 182. No big deal in the world of 747s, but around here a 182 means something."

As Donny spoke, they circled the plane, Soga alternating between leaning on his walking stick and using it to point as though he were touring another bank.

"See," Donny continued, pausing to pick a speck of something off the fuselage, "everybody from here to the Atlantic learned on a 172, it's the classic trainer. But when you get your own, if you can afford that one step up, and buy the 182, it says something. You've arrived."

The aircraft stood 29 feet long with a 36-foot wingspan—nearly identical to the E14 that Soga flew in 1942. It offered a top cruising speed of 145 miles per hour and, with a fuel tank in each wing, a range of 900 nautical miles. Donny's habit was to refuel both tanks after every flight. That day, therefore, he could have comfortably flown to San Diego.

Soga was nodding as he listened. "Most excellent," he repeated.

Donny hitched up his pants and took in the surrounding scene. Low morning light angled in over the trees, casting their shadows far down the tarmac. At that moment Piper Abbott photographed them—an unremarkable picture, two men beside an airplane, significant only in context and the length of their shadows.

Donny unlocked the passenger door. Soga stiffened, but Donny indicated a step on the strut that had a small traction strip. "Just put your foot there."

Soga extended the arm holding his cane, like a wing, and Donny supported his elbow. It was the first time the two men had touched. The Japanese guest stepped on the footplate, rose even with the door, and plopped backward into the seat. He laughed, settling the cane in beside his leg. One wonders: Did it feel like a sword? Or like the passage of time?

"You are one plucky S.O.B., Soga," Donny marveled. "I'll give you that."

He secured the passenger door, circled the plane to release the tie-downs, and climbed into the pilot seat. But instead of sitting back, Donny fidgeted. The door was pressing the holster into his side. He adjusted the seat back, shifted himself, wrestled with the strap inside his windbreaker. No luck—the grip dug just below his ribs. He tried sliding the holster forward, but the pistol wound up pointed straight at his crotch.

Finally he capitulated: "Aw, what the hell." Reaching in, he undid the holster altogether and tugged it out. The pistol clunked against the cockpit floor. Donny squinted at Soga, who took a long appraisal of the gun, then returned to scanning the switches and dials.

"What do you make of that?" Donny asked.

"In my flight years, I too carried a weapon always. Against my left leg."

Donny dropped the pistol in the cubby behind his fuel selector valve, on top of some pencils and a little notebook. As they each buckled in, he flicked switches, and the engine growled to life. Soga's grin was visible from outside the aircraft.

"That's right," Donny said, putting on aviator sunglasses. "Ain't a man alive doesn't love that sound. Two hundred and thirty horses, climb rate better than nine hundred feet a minute."

He slid on headphones and motioned for Soga to do the same. They idled while Donny reviewed his preflight checklist. "What do you think?" he asked.

Soga surveyed the cockpit, the instruments and indicators, and held his hands wide. "No stick."

"This yoke here does the same thing." He moved the wheel forward and back. "Elevators, yaw control. Pedals are the same too."

As Soga nodded in understanding, Donny raised the idle and the plane began to roll. "There's my six-pack," he said, tapping a cluster of indicators. "But I bet you have no clue what that means. Do they even have them in Japan?"

"Six-packs?"

"It's an indicator array, Soga. Look." He tapped each of the dials with his fingertip, two rows of three. "Air speed, attitude, altimeter on top, then vertical speed, turn coordinator, and gyro—that's like a super compass."

Soga nodded. "Most excellent." However, he stretched upward in his seat. Donny noticed with a scowl. "Can you even see anything?"

Soga shook his head. "Six-pack is most excellent."

"Hang on a damn second." Donny applied the brakes and reached over between Soga's legs. "Should have done this before you got in, but I didn't figure you'd be shorter than my wife. Now hoist yourself up, if you can." He pulled forward the seat crank. "Up, up, let's go. I can't lift you all by myself."

Soga pulled on the overhead handle, straightening his legs till his bottom rose off the seat, while Donny turned the crank as high as it would go. "How's that? Can you see over the dashboard now?"

"Excellent view," Soga said, lowering himself. "Many trees."

"You are high maintenance, buster," Donny said, shaking his head.

They taxied to the runway with redwoods to clear. But that choice presented no difficulties: Donny goosed the throttles, the engine roared, and by the time they passed over the trees, the aircraft was well aloft and headed out to sea.

Donny Baker III kept meticulous flight logs. Papers he later filed indicate that initially they flew west. Then he chose a course of north-northwest, into the prevailing wind, following the coast.

That shoreline provides dramatic views as huge monoliths of stone rise from the sea. Soga leaned forward to peer out the window. From time to time he commented on some landmark, but Donny made no reply. Eventually they reached a stretch of shoreline where there were no houses, no settlements.

Without warning, Donny pulled the yoke to the left. At the same time, he stepped hard on the right rudder—not unlike deliberately making a car fishtail. The plane skidded in the air, loose items in back tumbling across the cabin.

With identical controls right in front of him, Soga knew precisely what was happening. The aircraft was in an intentional yaw, one set of controls making a left turn while another set banked to the right. But he did not protest, nor speak at all. He simply reached up and, to keep from falling out of his seat, he clasped the overhand handle with both hands.

Donny saw this reaction and reversed direction, the yoke pulled right and the left rudder pedal lowered. The Cessna shuddered and leaned, things sliding in back again. Soga held on as he was pinned against his door.

"Hell with it," Donny growled, levelling off. "Never mind."

At Gold Beach, Donny arced the 182 southward, putting Soga on the ocean side of the view. With a tailwind they made quick mileage. Donny increased their altitude, the altimeter dial slowly turning clockwise as they navigated eastward toward the Cape Blanco Lighthouse.

"They say you used that as a landmark."

"Towns were all blackout. It was navigation beacon."

Donny snorted. "Kind of defeats the blackout, right?"

"Mission was never about city or people. Was about forest."

"I helped put your goddam fire out, you know."

"Truly? Did not know that, sir."

"Yeah," Donny groused. "I led the team that found the site, put it out fast, showed the army who was boss of the woods, and got repaid with a friggin' demotion. Plus they took my gun—and the bomb fragments I found."

He maintained an eastward heading, continuing to climb. Soon they reached four thousand feet, pointing straight at Mount Emily. The timberlands provided a view entirely of green. Suddenly Donny shoved the wheel away, and the nose dropped. Both men rose against their seatbelts as the aircraft plummeted. Pencils flew out of the cubby. The pistol rattled in its place.

"Vertical speed?" Soga asked, tapping one indicator.

"Yup." The needle had rushed from white into yellow, and was now pinned at the outer extreme of red—a loss of 1,500 feet per minute. A start at four thousand feet meant two minutes and forty seconds till impact.

As if in confirmation, the altimeter spun down counterclockwise. The attitude indicator showed a 30-degree rate of fall, and its bobbing globe, normally half white for sky, was all brown. In fact the view out the windshield revealed all forest and no sky. The Cessna plunged like a stone.

"What if we bought it right here?" Donny said. "Huh? What if I just augured us right the hell into Mount Emily?"

Thirty-three hundred feet. Three thousand. The plane was tilting over onto its right wing. The engine whined.

Soga placed a finger on the altimeter. Twenty-seven hundred. "Your daughter would feel the loss of you, sir, for many years."

"Yeah, maybe. But what about you, mister bomber pilot? What if I just spread you all over this forest right now?"

Twenty-two hundred feet. Eighteen hundred. The dive was accelerating.

Soga bowed. "With respect, sir, I thought to die here fifty years ago."

"Should I pull us out?"

Twelve hundred feet. The engine began overspeeding, revving on nothing as air rushed past the fuselage with a high shrill note. Both men's ears began to ache.

"Maybe this was where everything was supposed to wind up," Donny said. "Maybe we both got on this flight fifty years ago."

Soga gripped his overhead handle again. "You have a great deal more to lose today than do I."

"You mean Heather."

Nine hundred feet.

"Also your wife and home. Also respectful community and prosperous life."

Six hundred feet.

"Much loss in order to kill an old man who will not live long anyway."

Four hundred. The Cessna was shaking from nose to tail.

"You clever bastard," Donny said. "Check this out."

He balanced the wings with his feet, then pulled the yoke hard against his belly. The nose began to curve away from the ground, and Donny jammed the throttle forward, the engine pulling them horizontal. The air speed indicator zoomed into red as they roared through the curve, passing two hundred miles an hour as the aircraft curved, and strained, and leveled off at four hundred feet.

The G forces of arresting the fall pinned both men hard in their seats. Outside, the sky came back into view. Soga pinched his nose and swallowed to ease the pressure in his ears.

"Yee-haw," Donny yelled, slamming the dashboard with his hand. "What the hell do you make of that?"

"From thirty degrees of slope to level? At that speed? I have never flown an aircraft that could recover from such a dive."

"What?" Donny laughed. "You thought we'd already bought it?"

Soga adjusted his eyeglasses. "Most excellent aircraft."

"I should say the hell so," Donny continued laughing. "But if you thought we were going to crash, why didn't you grab the gun? You could have shot me and saved yourself. Or pointed the pistol and forced me to pull up."

Soga shook his head. "Force is no longer my way."

Donny pondered that as he navigated south, easing the throttle back, starting a fresh climb. For several miles, neither man spoke. Soga relaxed his grip on the handle. Soon they were droning down the coast again. Off the left wing, the northern edge of Brookings came into view. Donny banked eastward, inland. The ocean fell away behind them. The world below lay all in green.

"You know my daughter admires you," he said at last.

Soga bowed his head. "As I admire her."

"You and me, we're old guys. From a different time."

"With respect, sir, you are still young man."

"Naw," Donny said. "But look here." He pointed. "That's where you dropped those goddam bombs of yours."

Soga leaned toward the window again. "Appears most different."

"The trees are fifty years taller. But I want you to listen a second."

Soga sat back. Donny stared ahead, into the sun's glare.

"Yes?" Soga said.

Donny chewed his upper lip. "Aw, hell."

"There is a problem, sir?"

Donny removed his sunglasses. "It's Heather giving you that damn hug."

"Most excellent young woman."

"Hell, I know that," Donny said. "You think I don't know that?"

"No, sir. Of course."

"It's just that if you can become a peacenik, you of all people, after we whipped your country's ass to China and back, not to mention burning Tokyo and blasting the shit out of two other cities, and yet you come here all these times, and then my daughter can hug you like that, do you get it? Goddamn it, do you get it?"

"So sorry," Soga replied. "I do not understand."

"Do you think you're better than me, somehow?"

Soga shook his head. "Never."

"Well, that's my point exactly. If you can do it, and she can do it, what in the hell does it mean if I can't do it?" He banged his fist on the armrest. "Goddamn it."

Soga made no reply.

Donny glared at him, then put his sunglasses back on. He faced forward, wringing the steering handles. All at once he laughed loudly. "Fine. Fine." He lifted his hands from the controls. "Your aircraft, mister."

"I do not understand, sir."

"We're over your old route. We'll pass the memorial any second. Fly it again now."

"Truly?"

"Before I change my mind."

"Has been many years."

Donny folded his hands in his lap. "We ain't on autopilot, bub."

Soga straightened in his seat and took the wheel, checking the air speed and altitude. He squeezed the handles, testing their feel. Then he eased to starboard, heading southeast, leveling off as they passed deeper over the forest.

"Hah," Ichiro Soga said. "Most excellent."

"Yeah." Donny Baker III interlaced his hands behind his head. "Yeah."

CHAPTER 17

MOSTLY HE SLEPT. But that was good news, because it meant the cancer was gentle. No need to stupefy him with pain meds, just maintain the anti-nausea drugs—which were working well. He did not toss in bed, and never objected when two hours had passed and I needed to turn him again. As a result he had no sores, zero. Clinically, his case was one of the better ones.

The hard part for me—and of course I had the easier job by far—was experiencing the decline of the Professor's mind. During a long doze, he would mutter strange phrases and random thoughts. "Tenure review. . . . De Gaulle Airport . . . cumulo-nimbus."

But then something recognizable would emerge that told me he was doing some kind of mind-work, some processing task, and his intellect was still functioning. "Elevation above sea level. . . . No stick."

Yes, I was still reading *The Sword* to him. He seemed to find pleasure in it, even when asleep. His breathing eased. He spent less time tugging on that tuft of hair.

Now and then he would come fully awake, launching into a discussion midway as if we had been talking for hours. Those conversations were jewels.

"Nurse Birch, you said it enlarges people and I disagreed. I have now changed my opinion."

It was noon on a Friday in high summer, and those were his first words of the day. "What does?"

"Suffering. You asserted it on the bridge. You used the word 'enlarge.'"

"Oh. I probably did. What changed your mind?"

"Contemplating Deirdre."

I drew my chair closer to his bed. "I'm listening."

"What did you think of her?"

"Well, what you think is more important right now."

He threw up his hands. "Will you ever desist from being evasive?"

"All right. I was surprised at how you signed your letter."

"Barclay instead of Dad or Father?"

"No. That you didn't say love. As in: love, Barclay."

"We are not a family that expresses affection overtly. But that is exactly the point I want to make about suffering, and how it is enlarging me: I have realized that Deirdre will experience her father's love for many years."

"Through an untrue letter?"

"Through inheritance." He sniffed. "My daughter will receive this house and all its contents. Oswego Lake has grown so posh, the proceeds will make her relatively rich. Thus I will have provided for her, in spite of her spite."

"Sounds less like generosity and more like revenge."

"Not one bit," he said. "As I allow myself to imagine, her benefits will be free of any fatherly vindictiveness."

The Professor had begun using his lecture voice, and I sat back, pleased to hear it once again. "Help me understand."

"Consider the effect, when she's living in a nicer house. Or driving a nicer car. I imagine her sipping a cappuccino by a fountain in Rome. Or no. Strolling a side street in Paris—with a lover, for her sake I hope so. Finding a petit parfumerie, and she enters with a little tinkle of the *clochette*."

He shook two fingers as if to ring an imaginary bell.

"Deirdre will not be thinking of me in the least," he continued. "But I can sit here with you today, and know that I will be giving her that moment in the future, and feel keen pleasure in it. Money is not love, quite possibly the opposite. But if my years of mortgage payments provide her with middle-aged comfort, I confess to a wry kind of contentment."

I waited a moment before replying. "Isn't healing amazing?"

"You find my reasoning to be healing in nature?"

"I do."

"Then yes, Nurse Birch. It is."

We fell into a long silence. Even in his awake spells, the silences were getting longer every time. We were preparing ourselves.

"At any rate," he said at last, "as I am disposing of my estate, one item remains in question."

"I'm listening."

"As well you should, given that it concerns you." He pushed the rolling tray toward me. The black binder lay on top.

"I don't understand."

"*The Sword*. I want you to have it."

"Professor, I can't possibly accept—"

"Editors are not going to change their minds about my credibility. It will never see print. But to me the book signifies this whole ordeal we have undertaken together."

"Thank you very much, but I can't."

He thumbed the binder forward, inching it off the table. "If you refuse to catch it, my book will fall to the floor."

"I am serious, Professor."

But he kept pushing. When the binder tipped off, I grabbed it in one hand. "Too many people at the end of their lives show excessive generosity to their caregivers. I am here because it is my job."

He sneered. "You mean to suggest that your experience in my home has at no time transcended the professional?"

"Of course not, Professor. I just—"

"Here is a concrete manifestation of that truth. And it is something no other person on earth would comprehend. Only we understand."

He was right. Deirdre insisted the book was a fiction. I hadn't made up my mind yet, and the Professor wasn't helping. About two things, though, there were no questions: *The Sword* was helping me with Michael. And reading it with Barclay Reed was establishing a relationship unique in my experience.

I sat back. "How about if I keep this here until you don't need it anymore? Then I would love to have it."

"That would please me."

I held the binder to my chest. "In that case, thank you."

"On the contrary," he said, relaxing back into the pillow. "I should be thanking you. I have labored whole days working up the courage to offer it to you. I imagined you would refuse it. Thus I am immensely gratified that you accepted."

What a notion. The main thing that giving a big gift required was courage.

Did I have the nerve to give Michael what he needed? And if I managed to figure out what that was, could I have faith that he would accept it? Was I capable of behaving as boldly as the Professor? In that instant, an idea occurred to me—the smartest, riskiest idea of my entire married life.

MICHAEL WAS WEIGHT LIFTING OUTSIDE AGAIN, this time with his shirt off. People who flaunted their fitness annoyed him—runners in short-shorts, Zumba ladies with tassels on their bum. But that day the temperature was in the 90s. He was working out in the shade.

I indulged in watching his back muscles shift and clench as he alternated curls with each arm. I knew every sinew of that back. Two days before the end of his first deployment, Michael hoisted a generator onto a truck and came home with torn muscles and daily pain.

It was January, Oregon's wet season. After dinner, I would turn up the heat in our bedroom. I'd microwave a damp towel till it was so hot I could barely carry it, then smooth it across his back while he moaned with relief. I worked massage oil all over his shoulders, thick neck, and especially that clenched lower back. The room smelled wonderfully of sandalwood. I was determined not to stop till my hands ached.

Each time I promised beforehand that the goal was relaxation, not foreplay. But it rarely worked out that way. Michael would reach a certain degree of relief, his back would unknot just enough, and he would roll over.

By then I was in a state myself, and off we'd go. The rain could fall, the wind howl, and we were safe. Michael began to call the bed our tropical island, because we went there for vacation so often.

Now those memories were my vacation. Meanwhile, he dropped the dumbbells on the grass and shook his arms loose. The muscles flexed and relaxed. No question, my husband was getting his physical strength back. Between his workouts and all that walking, the man was in formidable shape again.

"Michael?" I called from the edge of the lawn.

When he turned, I expected to see the weight-lifter expression. Instead he appeared sheepish. Maybe even intimidated.

And no wonder. My schedule with the Professor meant that we no longer saw one another in the morning. So we hadn't spoken since he told me about shooting the dog.

"How was your day?"

"Cars." He wiped his face with his upper arm. "Broken, then fixed."

I slipped off my sandals and barefooted it across the lawn to kiss that sweaty arm. "How about Michael? Broken, and then fixed?"

"Still in the shop, Deb."

"Well, one of the parts you've been waiting for has come in."

"Is that right?"

He bent to pick up a weight, but I pulled him upright. "It is. I hate to interrupt, but I brought you something."

Michael sighed. "Can I just finish here, please? I'm really not in the best mood right now."

I was beginning to think I had made a mistake. But I persisted. "Right now? How about all the time, sweetheart?"

"This year." Michael gripped the handle. "I'm in a bad mood this year."

"So hold on a minute. I think I have the cure."

His shoulders dropped, and his expression was pained. He did not even bother to hide it.

Maybe my idea wasn't so brilliant after all. Maybe I should have mulled it over for a couple of days. Maybe I was too much in the thrall of the Professor and his well-reasoned notions.

"If I see what you have now, can I please go back to my workout?"

"Wait one second," I said, sidling back to my car. "Just wait right there."

All my earlier certainty had abandoned me. I felt like a bomber, who might bring peace and reconciliation or who might set a forest on fire.

"When I say three, you have to clap your hands."

Michael swayed with impatience. "Damn it, Deb. I'm really not—"

"One." I grabbed the rear handle. "Two." I opened it an inch. "Three." And I swung the door wide. Michael, bless him and his indulgence of his wife, clapped his hands rapidly. From the backseat, the dog burst out with a bound. She ran directly to the noisy man, who was squatting by the time she reached him. She barreled into him, knocking him back on his butt and licking his face.

"Oh my God," Michael said, his voice quaking. "Oh my God."

The dog, a black Labradorish galoot I'd found at the Humane

Society that afternoon, was shameless: sniffing Michael everywhere, snouting his crotch. Michael's head hung as though he were stunned. The dog leapt side to side over his legs, smacking him with her wagging tail. I inched across the lawn, hoping.

When at last Michael raised his face, he was smiling. "I think he likes the salt from my sweat."

"She. It's a she."

"OK," he said. "She." And then his face dissolved in tears.

I knelt and wrapped my arms around him. Michael burrowed against me and bawled like a calf.

I could not help weeping with him. Finally we had arrived at the truth. Not the angry man who barked at me, or punched a wall, or smashed his truck in road rage. Not the frightened man, armed and cowering in his kitchen. But this man, here in my arms, this wounded, grieving man.

I felt wetness from his tears through my shirt, and had one fleeting thought that I had missed something by never nursing a child. But Michael sniffled and brought me back to the present, to his warm and sweaty presence against me. It would not last, it was only for now. So I said nothing, did not move, and was supremely grateful.

Then the dog poked her nose under his arm, and between us, wagging and wiggling till she was inside the embrace as well.

Michael ran a hand down her flank. She was sleek like a seal.

I leaned to his ear and whispered. "Is she OK?"

"She's fantastic. What's her name?"

At the shelter they called her Stella, fine enough but not a name to keep. I was about to say we should name her together, when a better idea arrived.

"Shouri," I said. "Her name is Shouri."

Michael cradled the dog's face in his hands. They regarded one another. "What is that?"

"A Japanese word. A patient taught it to me."

"What's it mean?"

"Shouri means . . ." I paused, feeling my throat close with emotion. Victory, surprises at dawn, something about a sudden blow. But then I offered my own made-up translation. "It means good things will happen."

Michael rubbed the dog's ear and she leaned into his touch. "Hello, Shouri."

ICHIRO SOGA CLIMBED DOWN from his seat in the Cessna 182 as cautiously as if the ground were molten, then stood on the tarmac clapping his hands in glee. Donny Baker III hurried beneath the wings, attaching the tie-down straps before handing Soga his cane.

For once, Donny did not refuel upon landing. Instead, he helped Soga into the pickup truck, and they drove off to their various appointments. Piper Abbott, ever diligent, tailed them once again. Her interview with Soga that night brought her the tale of what had happened on the flight.

The following morning Donny provided the Japanese pilot with a penultimate tour of Brookings—with Heather sandwiched between them in the truck. They visited the harbor, Azalea Park, the upland avenues away from the sea. Donny also chauffeured through some less-known sites: the vast lily farm, a high view down on the broad Chetco River, the county's tallest redwood.

Afterward Soga and Heather embraced in the Kerrs' driveway. Soga bowed deeply to his fellow pilot. "Aw, cut that crap out," Donny replied, shaking the foreigner's hand.

There were other good-byes: Jaycee leaders, the mayor. Then the city's rented limousine transported Soga to Portland, where he boarded a plane to San Francisco, connecting to Tokyo.

Four years later, the Brookings roads department announced plans to erect a highway marker that would direct people to the memorial shrine. A sign at the site would acknowledge Soga's gift of the tree, and the date of its planting. The sponsor of this plan was none other than Donny Baker III.

Public reaction revealed that controversy over Soga, even in 1994, had not ceased. "We feel it is a slap in the face," Elmer Hitchcock wrote in the *Pilot*.

City officials invited Soga to attend the dedication of the highway marker. When the question of the travel expense arose at a Chamber of Commerce breakfast, Donny suggested that the business group pay Soga's airfare. Many of the members present responded by laughing.

"Look," Donny said. "I'm late to the party on this, I know. But I got my reasons for wanting to talk to him again. Besides, whatever the guy did all those years ago, he has made our town a pile of cash since then." He pointed at two brothers sitting together, who between them owned half of Brookings' restaurants and nearly all of the hotels. "You guys alone ought to shell out for Soga's plane tickets. You've made a killing because of him."

The motion carried. The town's invitation went out with an offer of free travel.

Donny began preparations for a different kind of tour: This time Soga would take a ride on a seagoing commercial fishing vessel, spend a day at a working logging site, maybe kill a night strolling among the hippies in Portland.

"Enough of this banking bullshit," he told Heather. "I've got ground to cover with this guy. Let's show him the real Oregon."

A reply to the invitation came from Soga's son in a handwritten note marked by reserve and formality.

"It is with deep regret that I must inform the honorable people of Brookings that Ichiro Soga cannot accept their kind invitation. My father is not at present strong enough to make the journey. He has lung cancer."

CHAPTER 18

IN THE MORNING I WOKE EARLY, but Michael was not in the house. I pulled on clothes and went searching. He was not in the guest room, no clanking rose from downstairs, there was no one in the kitchen. I put on coffee and went into the living room. In the middle of the rug lay one of Michael's military boots, and it was ruined.

The top had been chewed, the sole gnawed up by the toes, and the tongue ripped from the boot entirely. I snatched the pieces up, rushing them to my closet while calculating how I could find a replacement boot before Michael discovered what Shouri had done. Otherwise there would be a hurricane. This was not any old shoe the dog had destroyed.

I put the pieces in a plastic shopping bag, stuffed a t-shirt in on top of it, and hurried it all out to my car.

They were out on the back lawn, Michael and the dog. He was kneeling in the grass and throwing a tennis ball. Where had he found such a thing in our house? The dog was chasing the ball at full speed and snagging it with her mouth.

She dashed back to him faster than I thought she could run, plowing into him headlong. He fell over on his side, grabbing the ball for a tug of war.

"Shouri, huh?" Michael said. "Maybe instead we should call you Spaz."

But he was laughing. Laughing.

THAT DAY, THE PROFESSOR AND I had three brief conversations. I wanted more. I longed to share with him how his gift had inspired me and helped my husband. But those three snippets were all he had the energy for. Otherwise he was quiet, doing his work, making his path. When he did awaken, his agenda mattered infinitely more than mine.

"How old am I, again?"

"You are seventy-eight, Professor."

He wagged his head. "How in the hell did that happen?"

"That you've lived so many years?"

"That they passed so quickly. As brief as lightning."

IN LATE MORNING I took Barclay Reed's pulse, and his hand was cold. His feet, too. It was a chilly premonition. The circulatory system had begun prioritizing essential organs. But a dying person feels cold every bit as much as a healthy one, so I added a blanket for his feet and gave his hands a vigorous rub.

The Professor opened his eyes. "Thank you."

"It's nothing," I said.

"Have you decided whether or not you believe?"

"*The Sword*, you mean?"

He nodded, swallowing noisily.

"What I can say is that the book is bringing up things that are helping Michael. Knowing his weapon, giving a courageous gift. So to me, it doesn't matter whether or not it's true."

"It is the only thing that matters now." The Professor grimaced as though he had a terrible sore throat. "The only thing."

LATER I FOUND HIM SLEEPING with his mouth open. I could see it drying out. I opened a fresh glycerin swab, and wiped around his gums. Those are tender tissues, so it can be an extremely intimate form of care.

Barclay Reed appeared to like it. After I had swabbed the near side of his mouth, he turned his head and opened wider so I could reach the far side.

"Professor, is there anything you might want to eat or drink?"

He frowned. "It's all shut down now."

"If you're comfortable here for a moment, I'd like to go get you something."

"I doubt I have the strength to chew."

"Trust me."

Quickly I hulled three strawberries, and rinsed them in the sink. I reached for the ordinary bowl, but then decided to take a risk—and used the one his wife had made instead.

"Not fair," he said.

"What's not fair, Professor?"

"As I grow weaker, you become more stubborn." He made a feeble cough. "You are an inferior listener, as well. Didn't I just say that I can't eat? And I certainly don't want that bowl."

"I always listen," I said. "But not everything is said out loud."

I picked a berry, the reddest, ripest one. I reached across the bed and held it directly under his nose. After a perplexed moment, Barclay Reed understood what I was doing. He took a long, deep sniff.

"Ah. Heaven."

The way he was positioned, I had to put the bowl on his bed so I could stretch my hand to keep the berry beneath his nose. But he hooked the bowl closer with the crook of his arm, snug against his ribs, and something in the room relaxed. Under the sheets, the Professor uncrossed his legs. The hummingbird bowl was permitted again. Some old knot had untied itself. Then he smelled the berry under his nose deeply once more. "Yessss." He nodded. "Absolute heaven."

Though eventually my arm grew sore from its own weight, I kept that berry in place till Barclay Reed was sound asleep again.

TWO MORNINGS LATER, Sunday, when Michael took Shouri for a walk, I decided to visit the weight room. I told myself I intended to finish the cleaning he'd begun with the papers a few days before. But if that were the whole truth, I would not have waited till my husband was out.

By then I felt tired all the time. Like a little bird, endlessly zipping from one needy man to the other, trying to ferry a little nectar back and forth between them, flying as fast as I could. It was exhausting. I hadn't gone to yoga in months, hadn't participated in the book group since Michael came home. Forget those activities, though. A nap would have made more sense.

But on that morning I wanted to be in his space without him there. I was curious how it would feel now, in this different phase of our marriage. There was none of the base temptation I'd felt earlier, when I considered snooping in his computer's history. This time I had higher aims: learning, and maybe understanding.

Immediately I marveled that he could exercise in such an unpleasant place. The light came from bare overhead bulbs. The floor was gray cement. The air smelled musty and stale. Tools lay scattered here and there, stacks of neglected books, moving boxes we'd never unpacked. Against the wall leaned posters we'd owned before living together—his red Ferraris, my Springsteen in concert—which each of us had vetoed for the walls of our mutual household.

At least Michael's gear was tidy. The weights were organized, dumbbells on the floor in order of size. But over some of my parents' old furniture, the tarps we'd thrown years ago had visibly mildewed. I suspected they were the cause of the basement's poor air quality.

Obviously Michael didn't mind, but it would be no great task to clear them out. Not remembering even vaguely what was beneath, I lifted the nearest tarp with care. That was when I made my discovery.

On my father's old desk, the one he had used for grading papers, three bottles of ceramic glue made a little tent over a work space. And there, in the middle, sat two-thirds of a reassembled blue china dinner plate.

At first it did not register. I had grown too accustomed to receiving bad news, to absorbing emotional blows and the whole downward spiral. I did not recognize good news when I saw it. I had no idea what to do.

I sat on the weights bench with the partial plate in my lap. So that's what he had been doing in the trash the other night: digging for remnants. There were lots of shards on the desk, some as large as a dime, some as small as a sliver. I ran my fingertip over the repaired portion and it was surprisingly smooth. Michael was not a man with fine motor skills. I could not imagine how painstaking this project must have been.

"Oh, lover," I said out loud, since he was not there to object to the word.

What did I know about Michael's interior life? At one time I had known it nearly as well as my own. But this was a total surprise.

The man was trying. I had to give him that. He was sincerely trying to repair what had been broken.

The fact that he had concealed it was part of the sweetness. He hoped someday to surprise me with a finished plate. Incredible. After all he had been through, enough to crush the kindness out of anyone, somehow this man had a reservoir of it left. I felt his marital commitment more in that moment than I ever had before. It wasn't noisy or passionate. It was quiet, and patient, and slowly piecing itself back together.

Maybe sometimes love shows its true self, and reveals how much deeper it can be than anyone would have imagined.

I stood renewed, ready for the day. Then, hoping to remember how the pieces had been situated before I lifted the tarp, I tried to put everything back just the way I had found it.

By the time man and dog returned, I had packed a picnic. A blanket lay folded in the trunk of my car, under an umbrella just in case.

Michael saw me finishing in the kitchen. "What's up, Deb?"

"We're getting away. Time for a day at Cannon Beach."

MICHAEL AND I WENT THERE a few times in our dating days, but I had forgotten the scale of the place. Waves crashed against giant rock formations, seagulls circling the crowns. When we stepped out of the car, I was stunned all over again.

The coast was foggy, clouds clinging to the shoreline trees. A few hardy souls walked the low-tide edge, but the iffy weather had kept most people away. The air was damp, with a sour salty taste. We leashed Shouri and began the trail to the beach. Michael alternated between scanning the cliffs and parked cars for potential attackers, a soldier's attention and worry, and paying attention to the dog, who wanted to run ahead.

I yearned to confess what I'd found in the basement, and how it reaffirmed my optimism. But I knew that if I did, it would be annoying at best and undermining at worst. Another opportunity to keep my mouth closed.

When we reached the sand, Michael unclipped the leash and Shouri went sprinting. She dodged side to side, as if evading some invisible predator, then dashed away up the beach.

"I hope she comes back," I said.

"She'll never leave us," Michael answered. As if to prove his point, he picked up a branch as wide as his arm and twice as long. Having turned back to look at us, Shouri halted her escape, pink tongue hanging. Michael jogged to the water's edge and flung the branch way out. The dog bolted down the beach and dove in after it.

The water remained shallow, a long tidal flat under the surface, and she porpoised back with the branch in her teeth.

So this was what it would be like now. No matter what our moods were, there would be this exuberant presence as well. Packing the picnic had prevented me from checking Michael's drawings that morning, but I was willing to bet there was no face with mouse ears.

We ate pork sandwiches and drank lemon tea. I shucked off my shoes and lounged on the blanket. Shouri ran away and back, rested with us a while, then made another circuit. I poured water into Michael's cupped palms, and she licked it up greedily. Panting, she settled beside us at last.

"Dessert?" I asked.

Michael lay beside me, raised on one elbow. "What do you have?"

I reached into the canvas bag and pulled out a strawberry. Kneeling, I brought it within an inch of his nose. Michael opened his mouth but I drew back. "How does it smell?" I asked.

He shrugged. "Like a strawberry." And opened his mouth again.

"I mean, how good does it smell?"

He gave in, and took a whiff. "Smells great, actually."

"You can have it, you know . . ."

"Uh huh. If I do what?"

"Take another dose first," I said. "Enjoy."

He did, eyes closed that time as he took a long, deep sniff. "How did I forget about strawberries? We haven't had them once since I've been back."

"I brought a whole fresh pint."

He lay back on the blanket. Shouri curled up against him, paws working the sand. "OK, what do I have to do?"

"Tell me another."

He stroked the dog's ears. "Another what?"

"From the faces."

"Damn, Deb. You will not quit."

"Apparently not."

"Killing the dog wasn't terrible enough?"

"It was terrible. I won't argue with that."

"Then why?"

I shifted closer to him. "Because we went shooting and you drew two fewer faces. Because you explained about Gene's screw, and together we made it better. Because you told me about mouse ears, and—"

"Deb, you need to know something."

"I'm listening."

"Some of them will never go away. Never."

I nodded. "I know. They're part of you."

He patted Shouri's head, and her tail thumped the sand. "I mean, I would sure as hell like them to."

"So pick one of those. The worst one."

He shook his head. "Impossible."

"Yes," I said. "The man with the hat. Or sunglasses guy."

"Sunglasses, oh. I will be grossed out by him for the rest of my life."

"What about the one with the extra scribble? What happened with him?"

"God, Deb." He turned away. "It's not a scribble."

We sat in silence, waves chanting against the beach. A gull cruised over us, wings motionless, before floating away inland. I handed him another strawberry.

Michael considered it, then pinched off the green crown and popped the fruit into his mouth. I listened to my husband chewing, swallowing. It made my mouth water. But I had eaten plenty at the Professor's house.

I dug in the bag for another berry. "That's the worst one? The scribble?"

Michael took the fruit without a word. He smelled it deeply, then ate it just like the one before. Shouri sniffed, and he offered her the leaves from both crowns. She horsed them down.

"It was only by accident that I saw him." Michael sat up, wiping sand from his leg. "We were transporting a backhoe that afternoon, to fix a water line, and that's a slow job. So I was on advance, securing the route."

He was cross-legged, elbows holding his knees, his eyes trained out to sea. "The guy was not expecting me. I spotted him with the scope placing an IED where the crew would pass later. I watched his caution, his whole method. It was a triggered device, so he would decide when to blow it. He would time it to kill a lot of us."

I put a hand on Michael's arm, and he did not pull away.

"I was toting a .308, heavy barreled, a bitch to carry. The range was nothing special, just over five hundred yards. But he was sideways to me, which made him a smaller target, with rubble in the way. Just like they trained me to do, I waited. He kept checking over his shoulder, up and down the street, but never once at the rooftops, where I lay on my belly. After he finished planting the bomb, he started back toward a building. A white building, baking there in the hot Iraq sun."

I could picture it: the intensity of the moment, the power of his gun, the desert heat as different from foggy Oregon as possible.

"No one was in danger anymore because I had seen him. The water line crew would take another route and a squad would disarm the device. But the guy? He was about to get away, free to blow off my buddies' arms and legs another day."

"It was your job to prevent that. It was war. You were saving lives."

Michael shrugged my rationalization off like a horse shakes away flies. "It was early, with the sun still low, so he cast a shadow on the building's white wall."

"Was that the scribble?"

"Let me tell it."

Michael squinted into the distance, as if seeing the Iraq street again. "I held fire till he had almost reached the building, hoping he'd look back because it would make him a bigger target. And bingo, he did it, as if I'd written a script. Only it wasn't to scout his escape route. It was to admire the job he'd done, the cocky fool. That little show of pride turned him full-body to me, gave me a perfect line."

Michael stared down between his knees. "It was a clean hit, just below the collar bone. Like Joel's OJ jug. Lungs and guts spraying everywhere. They spattered on the building like . . . well, actually, like a giant comma."

"So the mess on the wall," I said. "That was the scribble?"

Michael stiffened. "Let me tell it."

"Sorry."

"First thing afterward I have a routine, reloading and check-ing my perimeter, because when you've been focused on a shot, you pay no attention to the world around you. Then I radioed in the kill and IED location. I was panning the scene through the scope, in case he had accomplices. That was when this person stepped out of the shadow of the building, dumbest move imaginable, and I leaned down to pop him too."

Michael rubbed his face with one hand. I offered him another berry. He dangled it by the stem so it looked like a little heart.

"It was a boy. Maybe eight years old? Nine? He had seen the whole thing, Deb. The IED planting. The spray. The remains on the ground, all of it."

"That is truly horrific."

"I don't know if he was the guy's son, or nephew, or what. Maybe a total stranger who for some random reason happened to be stand-ing there. Whichever, he witnessed everything. And you know, you just know he will never forget. Put that one on me forever. I didn't only blow away an insurgent bomber. I also planted the seed for the next war in this kid in a way he'll remember when he's ninety years old."

And then I realized. "The scribble is a person."

"Yes, Deb, and the worst kind: a person whose innocence you have obliterated, so the chain of violence continues." Michael poked the strawberry at the air. "Here comes your next soldier, in your next war, and the next one, and the next one, forever and ever amen." He tossed the berry to Shouri, the whole thing, and she gobbled it. "The thing I don't get, though? How does a man do these things, and go on living? How?"

"You're doing it right now."

"Except that it's not working. It's not even close to working."

Slowly Michael folded onto his side, inching down in the sand, almost burrowing. I spooned him, wrapped an arm over his shoulder, snaking a leg between his. We pretzeled on the blanket, my chest against his huge back.

All at once exhaustion poured over me, flowed through every inch of my veins. And I did not resist. I let myself sink into the sand too.

"I love you, Michael," I murmured into his shoulder blade.

He did not answer. I felt with a pang the inadequacy of my words. To a man with Michael's conscience, mere wifely love would be small comfort.

Yet he pulled my arm tighter, bringing my hand in against his chest. I could feel how fast his heart was beating. A gust of wind threw sand so we closed our eyes and lay still. I was nearly asleep, that quickly. Passing strangers would have taken us for lovers, but I knew better.

THE DOG WOKE ME. She was shaking water off, her license and ID medals jingling. But when she kept doing it, I opened my eyes and saw that her sides were heaving. I sat up.

Michael was not on the beach in either direction. Instantly I knew something was wrong. I stood, scanning the trails along the cliff. It was late in the day, and all the other people had gone home. I jogged down the beach. Nothing. I doubled back, running the other way, my heart racing the longer I went without finding him. And then there: His clothes were piled at the foot of the bluffs. I spun and spotted him, way out on the flats, just where the water's depth made him change from walking to swimming.

Michael was strong, but not a strong swimmer. And I could see his head, among the giant rocks, bobbing in the waves.

Before I had realized anything, or wakened all the way, I stood ankle deep in the water, shouting. "Don't you dare, Michael Birch."

His head swiveled toward me like a periscope. I had never seen his face whiter. Chalk. Talc. A ghost.

"Don't you dare." I yelled so hard my voice cracked. "Don't you do that."

Michael leaned his head aside with every stroke of his arms, awkwardly gaining distance. His kick sent up little plumes. It felt as if the whole world stood poised, about to roll down some enormous hill to destruction, and all it would take was the least nudge. But not if I could help it.

I tugged off my sneakers and started to shuck my jeans, then gave up and waded in fully dressed. The water was cold. Strong too, sucking me outward. Michael had heard me, and he paused, treading water, looking outward, then back toward shore. I ran in the shallows till it was too tiring, then flopped forward and began to swim— keeping my direction parallel to shore so the riptide would not yank me out too fast.

My husband kept turning, toward land and then away, trying to decide.

"Michael," I yelled. "Don't you—" But the water swamped me and I went under. It was hard to swim with wet clothes on. When I sputtered up to daylight again, the surf was rough enough that I could not see Michael. It frightened me. I surrendered, pointing myself straight out to sea, and let the undertow do the work.

By the time I was sixty yards out, I spotted him again. Michael had begun moving toward me. I breast-stroked in his direction. When the water was neck-deep on him, he began striding. I stretched my toes downward, but they did not touch. I finally reached him almost a hundred yards out, at a depth where he could stand but I had to keep treading water.

His skin was still white, and he was shouting. "All I want to know is if I will be OK someday. Tell me I will be OK."

His face wore such anguish, hollowed and raw. I answered honestly. "I don't know."

A wave slammed his back. "Then lie to me."

He had a point. What would it cost me to give the man hope? Where was my loving lie?

My jeans were sodden and heavy, fatigue weighing me down too. How much longer could I keep treading water?

Then a wave broke over me, a huge salty gulp that left me sputtering. Without thinking, I grabbed Michael's bare shoulders. Of course I was weightless to him, but holding him also meant I could quit working so hard. I held on with both hands. We were face-to-face in the swirling water.

I moved deliberately, but slowly, so he would know what I was doing before I did it—though I was not about to be stopped.

I kissed him.

It should have been nothing. He was my husband, for God's sake. We had been together for twelve years.

Instead, it was everything. I kissed his cheekbones, I kissed his eyebrows, I kissed the hinge of his jaw. And then I held his face in my hands and kissed his lips, his lovely Michael lips that even with all of his body's stony muscularity he could not keep from being soft.

The dog had followed me, and a wave walloped her into us. But Michael held me hard, staring as though he was drilling into my core. It felt like one of those moments with a patient when you know that what you say next will be indelible. So you try to find the courage to say the truest, rightest thing, and then you hope.

"You are going to be OK," I told Michael, clinging to him. "You will not be the same, but you will be OK. You will even be happy again, someday. When that day comes, I will still be here. Right here."

God bless that man: He placed one strong hand between my shoulder blades, pulling my body against him, and he kissed me back.

The ocean gulped and whirled. And Shouri swam circles around us as though she were in orbit.

SOMETHING HAPPENED on the way up the beach. Maybe it's simply that I was freezing, and needed more from Michael than silence. But my mood turned more sour with every step. By the time we reached his clothes, I was livid. This suicide gesture on his part might have scored well on Michael's originality scale, but he had genuinely scared me and put us both in danger. I watched him start to dress, threading a leg into his underwear, but I was seething and shivering, so I started for the car.

My soaked clothes slowed me, and Michael caught up at the parking lot. He took my hand, but I shook him off and bustled ahead.

I'd left my phone behind to be free of it for the day, but as soon as we'd opened the doors I checked my messages, playing them on the speaker. There was just one, from Cheryl. I listened while sitting sideways and wiping sand off my feet.

"Hi Deborah. I know it's Sunday and your first day off in forever, but Professor Reed is in active decline. I'm happy to do my shift but thought you'd want to know just in case. The old guy is on his way out."

Ouch. And there it was. I sat there with my foot in my hand. Nothing to do but accept.

Michael flopped soggily into the passenger seat, his color back to normal. If anything, he looked a bit ruddy. A chilly swim will do that to a man. "Sorry, lover," he said. "Is this professor one of yours?"

Oh, it was a point of entry, wasn't it? An overture to show that now, finally, he remembered I had a job, a life, a heart. But the answer that came out of me was salty with spite.

"Lover?" I said, starting the car. "Isn't it a little late for that?"

"DID YOU HAVE ANY DINNER?" Cheryl asked.

I was sitting at Barclay Reed's bedside in wet clothes, listening to his breath. It was uneven, deep then shallow then deep. "I'm fine, thanks."

"When did you last eat?"

"Lunch. A picnic. But really, I'm all set."

"All right then. Call me if you need anything."

I waved without taking my eyes from the bed and its skeletal occupant. "Thanks for letting me know."

Twenty minutes later Cheryl was back with takeout Chinese. When I protested, she wouldn't listen. "You need your fuel," she said. "It's going to be a long night."

I put the bag of food aside. "It will be too short for me."

IN AUGUST OF 1997, the selectboard of Brookings, Oregon, entertained an unprecedented motion.

"Whereas in view of his international efforts at peacemaking," the proposed resolution read, "his courage demonstrated in times of peace as strongly as in war, his generosity, his humility, his disinterest in seeking fame or gain from his actions, his repeated financial support on behalf of children at the county library, and his many gifts and gestures to demonstrate affection for the people of this city and region, therefore do the people of Brookings, Oregon, hereby declare, decree, and ordain that Ichiro Soga is an honorary citizen, now, from this date forward and for the rest of his life."

The proclamation's language came from Tom Hacker, an attorney in town also known as a skilled banjo player. The original idea, however, and the motion introducing the proposal for formal consideration, both came from a senior selectman, the white-haired man at the end of the table: Donny Baker III.

Retired from business by then, prohibited by his wife from flying more than fifty miles away from BOK, occupied with his two grandchildren during their monthly visits from Portland, Donny had turned to public service not out of political ambition, but to fill his now ample free time. According to an election interview in the *Pilot*, Donny's goal was "to give back to this community that has been so kind to my family over the years."

In response to Donny's motion, the usual vituperative letters appeared.

His phone rang often late at night, but when he answered, the callers hung up. Had he still owned the nursery, a boycott might have ensued. For some, the passage of more than five decades was immaterial. Soga's wartime actions would never be erased by his peacetime conduct.

Over the summer the debate proceeded, but in a decidedly even fashion. Every letter to the editor received a response from Donny. When a VFW post announced its opposition to Soga's honorary citizenship, although Donny was not a member and lacked the military credentials to become one, he marched into the clubhouse on three consecutive nights to debate any and all present.

"If free airfare a couple years ago didn't get him here," Donny told Piper Abbott, who now served as editor in chief of the *Pilot*, "this honorary citizen thing ought to do the job right quick."

At a selectboard meeting in August, following discussion of bonding for water-line improvements, Donny hijacked the agenda. He snapped his fingers at board chair, Amy Burgoyne, until she formally recognized him.

Donny stood. "We have argued about this guy long enough," he said. "We need to make a plan before it's too late. Passing this resolution would be the town of Brookings finally being as generous as Soga." He glanced at his attorney friend Hacker, in the back row of the public seats, who gave him a slow nod. "So now I move to call the question."

Perhaps the lawyer had educated Donny in Roberts' Rules of Order. Calling the question requires the chair to end debate and bring the issue to a vote—provided the call is seconded. Ben Rosen, one of the three younger men who had purchased Donny's nursery business, promptly raised his hand. "I second the motion."

A bank president with an MBA from the University of Portland, Amy Burgoyne was no fool when it came to anticipating political consequences. Therefore, to protect everyone from the exposure of a roll call, she conducted a voice vote. Although there were several nays, the proclamation carried by a decisive margin.

After the meeting, Donny Baker picked up his wife and they drove down the coast to the shrine's highway marker. They hiked to the site with the slow gait of people in their seventies. Upon arrival, they sat with their backs against the stone monument, looking out at the forest and Soga's tree. There they remained until the sun passed noon and their stomachs were grumbling. As they ambled back down the path, Donny's wife wiped leaves and pine needles off his backside. All that remained was ceremony. On September 22, 1997—fifty-five years and thirteen days after Soga's first mission over the Siskiyou Forest—Mayor Nancy Brendlinger signed the proclamation naming him an honorary citizen.

Soga received the news of his new citizenship in bed. There is no record of his reaction. He died eight days later.

When Donny Baker III learned of Soga's death, he drove out to BOK, climbed aboard his plane without starting the engine, and sat there till long past dark.

IN OCTOBER OF 1998, Yoriko Soga traveled to Brookings on her own initiative, without the benefit of free airfare or an invitation from anyone. She arrived without fanfare. She had a task to perform, one last errand at her father's request.

The owner of a transportation software business that employed seventy people, Yoriko was unquestionably an accomplished woman. Her husband was a physician, their two daughters were in college, and the family divided its time between a fine if snug apartment in Tokyo and a quarter-year share of a beach house on Kanucha Bay in Nago. She was fifty-three and wore gold earrings and bracelets, plus a necklace of black pearls.

The only person aware of her arrival was Donny Baker III, because he had developed a correspondence with Soga family. He met Yoriko at the airport and drove her directly to the memorial shrine parking area. Once they had parked, she changed out of low-heeled business shoes into running shoes and embarked up the trail. Wheezing a few steps behind, Donny followed her gamely to the site where those innocents had died.

The stone marker was unchanged but for the slow spread of copper-colored lichen. By contrast, Ichiro Soga's redwood now stood twenty-six years taller, its lowest limb extending well over her head.

"Did you know my father?" Yoriko asked, gazing up through the branches.

Donny leaned against the redwood's trunk. "Not as much as I'd hoped to."

"Yes?"

"Most of my life I had certain ideas." He fiddled a fingernail in the bark. "Your father made me think. . . . I guess that some of them might have been wrong."

"He made many people think," she said.

"Yeah, well. Now that I figured the guy out, I could have used another conversation or two."

Yoriko bowed. "He lived eighty-six years, sir."

"I had things I needed to say to him."

"It is a good full age, sir."

"I know." Donny spat behind himself. "So why do I feel ripped off?"

"Yes sir," Yoriko said. "That is one of the things death does expertly."

With that, she knelt before the stone shrine, and from her shoulder bag produced a black lacquered box the size of a brick. It resembled the small one into which her father had placed his fingernails and hair all those years previously, so that should the mission fail he might still be buried in Japanese soil. Now, obeying her father's instructions, she opened the box. She reached her hand in and scooped. There, at the foot of the monument and in the shade of the tree, she spread Ichiro Soga's ashes in the dirt.

The *Pilot* was on hand, a reporter and photographer standing at a respectful remove. Rather than a long story and large photos, however, for once the coverage was characterized by restraint. A photo of a woman kneeling, a few lines of text beneath. Otherwise, her visit went without further mention.

Improbably, Yoriko spent the night at the Baker house, in Heather's childhood room. The following morning Donny listed his airplane for sale. In fact, he never flew again. When his term on the selectboard ended, he did not seek reelection. He has not appeared in the public record since, even to this day.

That afternoon he drove his guest to the airport. There were no witnesses to their parting. She returned to Japan, and the Soga family's sojourns to Brookings came to an end.

While Yoriko's trip was the last gesture, however, it was not the last word. The full, unapologetic, and unfortunate spectrum of human nature appeared in a letter to the editor of the *Pilot* on October 21, a few days after her departure.

"I wonder," wrote Tom Vanderlinden. "Why do we honor someone who tries to set fire with a bomb?"

CHAPTER 19

I CLOSED THE BLACK BINDER and placed it quietly on the table. My patient was now breathing as deeply as a bellows, seemingly unaware that I had been reading to him. I stood and went for a walk through the house.

Evidence supporting the Professor was everywhere. The shelves of Japanese books. The gong, of all things.

Still I felt a nagging suspicion. It was too neat. Writing the letter to his daughter, then admitting its falsehood to me, meant he could have it both ways. The fact that in all my years of living in Oregon I had never heard one mention about this series of incidents—the pilot, the apology, the sword—none of it. Could the world forget a story such as this?

The books and gong could have been his wife's. He had admitted that she made the pottery. All the Japanese he had spoken was rudimentary. A beginning judo student could say as much.

Meanwhile, from a scholarly standpoint, the university's actions discredited Barclay Reed completely. They didn't just fire him. They removed his books from the shelves. I could not imagine a more thorough repudiation.

What about his daughter? He had never directly contradicted her accusations. Prickly people can still be right.

Oh, it was a mess. Was I being manipulated by a falsehood, to elevate a narcissist's dying vanity, or entrusted with a tale that should not disappear? I wanted to believe, and I felt inclined not to believe.

What is the purpose of skepticism? To assert our independence of mind? Or to put ourselves in a position of superiority to the person we suspect?

If I used only my hospice attitude, a different question took precedence: Why withhold the thing the patient most wants? Give him that thing, for the little time he has left. And if it is a lie, then it is a noble one, a fib that means forgiveness, a falsehood that brings a man peace.

I returned to the bedroom. Barclay Reed's respiration had changed, entering the Cheyne-Stokes phase: a series of increasingly dramatic huffs, followed by long apnea with no breathing at all. For families, that stage can be hard to hear. But I knew it meant that his body was trying to find the right carbon dioxide level, and the normal respiratory feedback system was breaking down. The Professor was not in distress, he was dying.

Somehow that decided it. This story's truth was necessary for me, and for Michael, and for the Professor. That outweighed the importance of whether the historical record was accurate.

I leaned over the bed rail, bringing my mouth down beside his ear. "Professor. Barclay Reed. If you can hear me, guess what? I just finished your book. I finished *The Sword*."

He did not move. His raggedy breath continued, like a metronome with a broken spring.

"I want you to know." I looked into the whorl of his ear, the tiny white hairs, his powerful calm. "I think the story is true. Every word."

The instant I'd spoken it, I felt relief. "I didn't look it up, or ask anyone," I continued. "I just read it. Right here with you, and my mind is made up. I believe it. I believe you."

There was nothing. No response, not even a hitch in his breathing.

Well. I sat back. Apparently my indecision had come at a price.

I'd always believed that hearing was the last to go. But I had waited too long.

I checked my watch to time his respiration cycle, so I knew it was two full minutes before he spoke.

"Good."

One dart of his tongue around the lips, and silence again.

That was the Professor's last word. The final lecture.

Later he started a repeating motion, raising his left hand a few inches, rubbing his thumb and forefinger against one another, only to drop his arm with fatigue. Oh, when the weight of your own hand is too much to bear. I studied the Professor, wondering what it was he needed, not understanding his agitation.

Then I recognized the thumb-and-finger motion: It was just like the way he teased that tuft of hair on his forehead.

I pulled my chair against the bedside, reached over, and stroked his brow. His left hand fell to the sheet, and I felt his whole body relax. He liked it. Two fingers, that's all it took to provide that little bit of care, to mimic and repeat the tugging motion I'd seen him do so many times.

I imagined Barclay Reed as a little boy, upset by something and performing this little gesture of self-comfort, this fidget, and it was an action so small and vulnerable, it filled my heart with pity: for the patient lying there in bed before me, for D who deserved relief from her internal torments, for Michael who I wanted to love so much and so well his demons would disappear, even for myself on what I hoped would be some far distant day.

Must we die? Must everyone at last die? Yes, everyone.

I held the Professor's hand as he dwindled, his breaths growing longer and slower by the minutest degrees. The night dawdled along. At one point I thought he had ceased. But experience told me what would happen next. After an interval so long I would have thought no person could survive, he took a huge inhale, and continued breathing for hours more. I stayed with him, nothing greater than that, but essential because I stood between Barclay Reed and his being alone. Outside, the night may have wheeled across the sky, but here was the universe's one still place.

We live our lives on a whole planet, seeing and learning and going from place to place. But eventually there arrives a time for each of us, when our world becomes smaller: one house, one floor of that house, and near the end, one room, one little room to which our whole gigantic life has been reduced.

And when that happens—this is a thing I have witnessed, this is a thing I know—that room becomes sacred. It is the holy, modest place in which we will perform perhaps the hardest task of our life: letting it go.

I whispered a bit to the Professor about the importance of historians, about the valor of a vigorous mind, about how much I had enjoyed intellectually jousting with him, even though I had landed one blow to his twenty.

But when it began to feel like chatter, I quieted. Enough words had been said.

I took his hand in both of mine, unafraid of touch now, confident in its power, lowered my temple to the inside of his wrist, pulse on pulse, and held him like that until the breathing stopped. And the drum beneath his skin went still.

BARCLAY REED MADE A HANDSOME CORPSE. His eyes closed, hair sticking straight up, mouth slightly open. He had a forward set to his jaw, as if he had entered death on his own terms. I could ask no more for any patient. I would want no more for myself.

I went to my briefcase in the kitchen and drew out a blank death certificate. Sitting at his bedside, I filled it out: name and cause. I wrote the date, the fifteenth of August, a Monday, this man's last day on earth. I checked my watch. Four-eighteen A.M.

Then I sat back. There was no hurry, of course. It is not an emergency when a man is dead. For a while, nothing needs to be done.

After a time of feeling his death, accepting it, I positioned the Professor in bed. No one would see him in this comfortable pose, but I would know, and that was enough. It was something I did every time, out of respect. His mouth hung open. I tucked the black binder, of all things, under his jaw to hold it closed. I cried a little. That made wet darknesses on his white shirt, so I stepped away from the bed.

"Barclay Reed, the world is a lesser place without you."

I called Central Office, which would retrieve the message at six and relay it promptly to a funeral director. When I put the Professor's shaving kit away, the bathroom cabinet's glass shelf made what felt like excessive noise.

That gave me an idea. I went into the living room, no one to worry about offending now. I stood wide-legged before the gong. Lifting the cloth-headed hammer from its little leather sling, I drew back and gave the thing a good hard whack.

The sound was so loud it obliterated thought. A great harsh clanging crash. After that, a long steady drone, the gong wobbling back and forth on its straps, the edges blurring with vibration. Fully half a minute later when I slid the hammer into its sling, still the metal hummed. I had to respect its determination to keep ringing.

All at once I realized that my clothes were still damp. No wonder I felt clammy. I'd been sitting in wet jeans for eleven hours.

The laundry room felt unduly bright. I switched off the overhead, and, undressing in the light from the Professor's bedroom, I tossed all my things in the dryer. While they tumbled, I wrapped myself in a towel and returned to the living room.

Day was approaching. Dim light crept down the skin of the lake. Another idea came to me.

I slid open the glass door and tiptoed out. No other houses had lights on inside yet. I tossed the towel over a chaise and stood naked at the dock's edge. It felt as if some kind of ritual were under way, and my nudity was solemn. But when my skin grew goosebumps, I knew I could not linger.

Feet together, I took a deep breath and dove into forbidden Lake Oswego.

The water was fantastic, clean, and warmer than the air. I stroked out fifty yards or so, feeling the ocean's salt rinse from my hair, beach sand fall from my skin. I took a big gulp of the lake and it was delicious.

The light was growing, so I swam hard back to the dock. Draping the towel over me, I lay on the chaise and shivered while the sun came up. It was modest at first, peach tones on the clouds highest overhead. But then it grew, until the whole eastern sky was a chaos of reds and pinks. At last the sun broke the horizon, a streak of yellow beaming down the lake, and I understood what Barclay Reed had said. His dock truly was a magnificent place for a sunrise. I felt grateful to him.

After dressing I checked on the Professor, who now was pale and cool. I slid the binder out from under his chin, and his mouth remained closed. I leaned over him. "Good-bye, smart man."

Collecting unused medicines and the last of the paperwork, I piled it on the black binder and brought everything out to my car. Standing there, though, I had a moment of doubt. Did I really believe the story of Ichiro Soga? Had I been overly persuaded by the needs of a dying man? Was there any real way of knowing?

A query on my phone told me that the public library in Brookings opened at nine. A search for directions said it was a solid five-hour drive. If I left first thing after the crew arrived, I could be home by dinner.

Which made me think of food. Back inside, I reheated a plate of Cheryl's untouched Chinese. By the time I'd eaten and cleaned up, it was six-thirty. I picked up my phone again. I could have texted Michael and told him my plan, but no. It was time to call Deirdre.

I USED THE INTERSTATE AS FAR AS EUGENE, then turned for the coast. Normally my road trips went inland, up the Columbia River gorge: foodie towns, jock towns, with giant windmills spinning on the ridge. Now I saw the other Oregon, rural and rugged. Trees grew beside the road so densely, I felt like I was driving through a tunnel. I reached some logged-out lands, stumps across the hillside looking like an old man's crew cut. The traffic crawled, logging trucks and tourists. Eventually I reached a glimmering place, the roadsides opened, and I saw the source of all that light: the Pacific, endless and green.

As I continued south, stone monoliths began rising from the sea—like Cannon Beach, but bigger and wilder. A sign warned that I had entered a tsunami zone. I reached for the phone to text Michael about it, but there was no service and I hurried on.

All along the way there were signs counting down the distance to Brookings. Still the place took me by surprise. Not its existence, but its era. My imagination had frozen the town in 1962. Now the fast-food chains, traffic lights, and contemporary cars seemed out of place. Then I spotted businesses named Azalea: a real estate office, a bowling alley. And then Azalea Park, whose pull I could not resist. I climbed out of the car and trotted through the place: Redwoods overhead like great mothers with broad skirts, a chapel facing the ocean, and beyond the baseball diamond, a fantastic vista of the Chetco River far below.

The view had a calming effect on me, and what I found waiting there was Michael. Healthy or ill, he lived in my still place, in my quiet heart.

I could have called him, but it was time to go. Time to find out.

One turn off the coast highway brought me to the Chetco Community Public Library—handsome yellow clapboard and gray stone. For a minute I sat in the car, preparing myself. I wanted to believe the Professor. I wanted my hopes for Michael to be based on more than a loving lie.

The foyer featured an elaborate carving of a whale. A metal bin on wheels sat below the overnight return box. I took a deep breath and went in.

The woman at the main counter was tall and gray haired. Bent to a computer without sitting down, she had the tense motions of a person under stress. She gave me a half-second glance. "Yes?"

"Hi," I said. "I'm here to research something."

"Reference." She pointed with a pen.

I followed her gesture to a desk where an enormous man sat sorting some papers. He wore the cleanest, whitest shirt I'd ever seen. An elastic band circled each of his arms, holding golden plastic wings onto his back.

"Good morning." He greeted me with a thousand-watt smile. "Is there any way I may be of help to you today?"

"Nice wings."

"Thank you." He leaned forward. "Our children's program begins in five minutes. Would you care to join us?"

"Thank you, but not right now. I'm not sure how to say this. But I was told a story about a Japanese bomber pilot . . ."

"Ichiro Soga, yes."

"You know about him?"

"Naturally. He was proclaimed a citizen of this town."

"So he is real?"

"Real?" The enormous man flashed his stunning smile again. "You'll find everything right over there."

Like a game-show host revealing to a contestant what she's won, the man raised a hand toward the long wall on his left, where there hung a large glass display case.

I saw the sword first, of course. It drew me across the room. The handle was more ornate than I'd expected, while the scabbard was polished but plain. Considering that the weapon was now nearly five hundred years old, it appeared to be in excellent condition.

But that glass case held more. The resolution granting honorary citizenship, signed and framed. Plastic models of the I-25 submarine and Soga's pontoon airplane. A photo of a square-faced Japanese man in a bomber jacket and fleece-lined cap.

Beneath the glass case, a large green folder leaned against the wall. When I opened it and saw it was full of news clips, I brought the folder to the nearest work table. My hands trembling, I opened it wide, and read.

Everything from *The Sword* bore out: names, dates, those nasty letters to the editor, countless stories with Piper Abbott's byline. I felt euphoric, not sure whether to laugh or cry.

As I read, I realized: Barclay Reed had sacrificed his reputation to save the career of a young scholar. This man for whom pride mattered so much had chosen to suffer indignity on another person's behalf.

The folder revealed a few things Professor Reed had not known. Three years after Soga's death, the state legislature named his redwood an "Oregon Heritage Tree." Letters denouncing that decision showed that for some people, peace would never come.

To me, it mattered more that the Professor's story was true. It was all true.

When I'd read enough—it took perhaps two hours—I put the folder back by the display. With my phone I took a photo of the sword. I was no longer tired. In fact I felt exhilarated, full of energy for the drive home and whatever lay ahead.

I knew that the following morning I would receive my next assignment: a new patient, my next experience in learning from mortality how to love the one and only life that we are given. Last thing before leaving the office, I would stroke the back of the hummingbird again, to remind me that every patient brings unexpected gifts. And if Barclay Reed's stubborn wisdom led to the healing of my husband, then he might have given me the greatest hummingbird of my life.

I also knew that on some future day, Michael would present me with the old blue plate, as repaired as it could be, and I would respond with genuine delight. I would feign surprise, however, because he had taught me the power of the loving lie.

I stepped outside into a bath of sunshine so bright it left me blinking. As my eyes adjusted, I noticed the enormous man eating lunch at a picnic table, his white shirt wrinkled where the wings had been attached. I waved. "Hi."

"Oh hello," he said, giving me a beatific grin. "Did you find everything you were looking for?"

"Yes, thanks." I said it out of politeness, but as I heard myself, the answer weighed more than that. I had found some things, oh yes. Between the black binder and the photo of the sword, between the Professor and Ichiro Soga, I could prove to Michael possibly the most necessary truth of our violent time: It is possible for a warrior to become a man of peace.

The sun kept up wonderfully, a dazzling energy to my left as I drove to Salem and north. It set as I approached the outskirts of Portland, August evening coming on gently, and I marveled at the possible span a single day could contain: from the Professor's deathbed and a stolen swim to dusky arrival at my driveway.

Michael was sitting on the back stoop, Shouri snuggled in his lap. He stood, still holding the dog. He wore a desert camo shirt, but it was sleeveless and I admired his powerful arms. This was a beautiful man.

By the time I'd organized my things, Michael was standing by my door. As I climbed out, he stepped back. He held the dog like a shield.

"What is it?" I said. "Did something happen?"

"I thought you were gone." He shifted his hands under Shouri. "I thought you'd left me."

"Oh Michael," I said, "only for the day."

"I called Central Office, your sister. No one knew where you were."

"Why didn't you call me?"

"Because, Deb." He squinted as though the sun was still up and he was staring at it. "You're the one who always calls me."

"Put the dog down for a second." I said.

He lowered Shouri to the ground, then squared off as if to start a wrestling match. I took both of his hands. "You know you could have killed us both."

"That was why I swam back. I couldn't have you on my conscience too." He let go, jamming his hands into his pockets, retreating two more steps. "And then I thought you'd left me for swimming out like that."

"Look," I said. "Do you know why hospice works, Michael? It's simple. The patients let us help. Even though we have no idea what they are going through, even if they are suffering incredibly, they accept our good intentions. They trust in how desperately we want to help. So they allow it."

I closed the gap between us again, not letting him get away. "What if you did that, Michael? Would it be so terrible if you accepted how deeply I love you, and how much I want to help? What if you just allowed it?"

Michael stared at the ground. I had put everything before him. There was nothing for me to do but wait.

After a while, I can't say how long, he began bending forward, hands still stuffed in his pockets but his chest inclining, ever so gradually, inch by inch, until his forehead came to rest on my chest. The dog nuzzled between our legs but it was Michael I felt, the full, strong, damaged weight of him. I wrapped both arms around his head.

In less than a whisper, he breathed it against my breast: "I surrender."

AUTHOR'S NOTE

The story of Ichiro Soga is based on actual events.

In September 1942, reconnaissance pilot Nabuo Fujita flew two missions over the Oregon coast, dropping four incendiary bombs. In 1962, on the first of many visits, Fujita gave his family's ancient sword to the town.

Three parts of Barclay Reed's manuscript are fictional: First, the character of Soga is invented because there was an insufficient record to recreate Fujita's personality. Second, other characters—Donny Baker and his family, Piper Abbott—are composites of several people. Third, the bomb that killed the Bible study group almost certainly was not one of Fujita's. More likely, it resulted from a separate Japanese campaign that attached incendiaries to small balloons and floated them in the jet stream over to the United States.

Virtually all the rest of Barclay's book is historically accurate: military details from the 1940s, the text of the full-page ad opposing Fujita's first visit, the monument where the bombing victims died (Fujita's tree towering beside it to this day), and the certificate of honorary citizenship. There truly was a 1925 novel that foretold the attack on Pearl Harbor. Names and statements are real too: U.S. military officers and politicians, the mayors of Brookings, the 1962 Azalea Queen, the bombing victims, the girls who visited Japan, even the woman who made a cake shaped like a submarine.

The Brookings *Pilot* newspaper truly exists, and every letter to the editor was written by the actual person identified. Regrettably, all of the letters are quoted verbatim.

SOURCES AND ACKNOWLEDGMENTS

In 2010, I read an essay by Barry Lopez in *The Georgia Review* that mentioned a Japanese pilot planting a tree where Americans had died in World War II—in Oregon. I thought, *What?* An online search brought me exactly one newspaper article, about the pilot's death, written in 1997 by a young *New York Times* reporter, Nicholas Kristof. That obituary was the seedling from which this novel grew.

First, though, I needed to learn. Foremost, I am indebted to my colleagues and teachers in the hospice movement: Sharon Keegan; Angel Means; Zail Berry, MD; Don Schumacher; and my dear friend Dianne Gray. My thanks to the exemplary Ira Byock, MD, for introducing me to the Four Questions (and ninety-nine other important ideas), and to many clinicians, ethicists, health policy experts, volunteers, and above all people from all walks of life who shared the stories of their loved ones' end-of-life experiences.

My agent, the mighty Ellen Levine, believed in this novel when it was only one-third written. Jennifer Brehl, my editor at Morrow, improved the story from the very start—suggesting a way to weave Soga's story through the rest of the narrative and reducing many flaws along the way. It is an incredible gift to have these two smart women guiding and supporting my work. Thanks also to Tavia Kowalchuk and Andy Dodds, for their effort and creativity in helping my words find readers.

I want to salute former U.S. Marine Corps Force Reconnaissance Captain Russ Ayer, who taught me about the veteran's life and showed me how to shoot a big gun. Bonnie Ayer generously shared her experience as the wife of a returning combat veteran. Former Vermont National Guard Staff Sergeant Jim Gosselin was kind enough to tell his war and homecoming stories as well. Carolyn Edwards, PhD, former director of mental health services for the Vermont National Guard, gave me a sobering education on the psychological condition of returning soldiers and airmen.

For additional information on guns, I relied on the expertise of Justin Cronin, who can make choosing a holster an act of autobiography. Eyes and ears, Dr. J. David Halsey, MD, deepened my understanding of aviation, from the g-forces at the bottom of a dive to where the cup holders are located in a Cessna 182. His flight simulator may be the coolest thing I have ever seen on a computer.

For World War II history, I read many books, none more helpful than *The Rising Sun: The Decline and Fall of the Japanese Empire, 1936–1945* by John Toland—as rich a portrayal of the Pacific theater as you can find. To learn more about the Iraq War, the best of many books I read was *The Good Soldiers* by David Finkel. Steven Ericson of Dartmouth College instructed me on samurai culture and directed me to additional sources. Details about Fujita's bombing runs came from *Bombs over Brookings* by William McCash, plus *Silent Siege: Japanese Attacks Against North America in World War II* and *Panic! at Fort Stevens: Japanese Navy Shells Fort Stevens, Oregon in World War-II*, both by Bert Webber. In addition, the staff and documents at the Chetco Community Public Library could not have been more helpful. If you're ever in Brookings, Oregon, stop in and see the sword.

I entrusted a few people with early drafts and benefited enormously from their feedback: Josie Leavitt; Susan Huling; Nancy and Andrew Milliken; Josh Hanagarne; Candy Page; Mike Dee; Geoff Gevalt; and above all my brother in fiction and biking, Chris Bohjalian. My actual brother, Mike Kiernan, MD, did wonders to improve the medical accuracy and provided the story of an inflamed appendix pointing at a kidney tumor. Most of all, I'm grateful to the person who convinced me to abandon a stalled project in order to write this one, then gave the incalculably valuable gift of listening to the entire first draft read aloud—the incomparable Kate Seaver.

Finally, a tip of the hat to my buddy Doug Rich, who made it possible for me to swim in Lake Oswego.

ABOUT THE AUTHOR

Stephen P. Kiernan has published nearly four million words over several decades as a journalist, winning more than forty awards, including the George Polk Award and the Scripps Howard Award for Distinguished Service to the First Amendment. Author of the novel *The Curiosity*, Kiernan has also written two nonfiction books, *Last Rights* and *Authentic Patriotism*. He lives in Vermont with his two sons.